this book belongs to Janet
read ... yonn

“Ah, Hetty,” he ... you, hasn't it? The lovin... He worked one hand free and delicately looped a heavy lock of hair behind her ear. “Do you have any idea what a rare and precious blessing that is?”

“I know.” She leaned closer. “Because I know what a blessing loving you is.”

It was more than that, Hetty realized. It was torment and temptation. The muscles of her arms and shoulders trembled, taut with urgency, and there was a hot, tight wetness between her legs that refused to be ignored.

It frightened her, this sudden, aching need, and yet it set her free in ways she could not begin to comprehend.

Pressed tightly against her she could feel the hard evidence of Michael's own torment. She could feel the tremor that surged through him. He wanted her, whatever he might say. As much as she wanted him.

Other *Love Spell* books by Anne Avery:
**HIDDEN HEART**
**A DISTANT STAR**
**ALL'S FAIR**
**ENCHANTED CROSSINGS**
**FAR STAR**

# ANNE AVERY

# The Snow Queen

LOVE SPELL NEW YORK CITY

LOVE SPELL®

December 1996

Published by

Dorchester Publishing Co., Inc.
276 Fifth Avenue
New York, NY 10001



Printed in the United States of America.

# AN EXPLANATION TO THE READER

Hans Christian Andersen's classic fairy tale, "The Snow Queen," is, above all, a tale about the power of love to triumph over the dark forces that torment the world we live in.

Once upon a time, you see, a malevolent demon created a looking glass that showed only the dark side of whatever was reflected in its surface. One day, the demon's servants dropped the looking glass, breaking it into millions of tiny pieces, each of which has the same unhappy power to distort reality as the original looking glass. The pieces scattered about the world and whenever a piece lodged in someone's eye, it made them see only the dark side of whatever they looked at, and whenever a piece lodged in someone's heart, it made them accept only the dark half of whatever they felt.

Now as it happened, one of the pieces lodged in the eye of a little boy named Kay and another piece lodged in his heart. Kay had always been a sweet, happy boy whose closest and most beloved companion was his little friend, Gerda. Kay and Gerda had grown up together, for their families' houses were side by side in the town, and their rooms were at the very top of the houses, joined by two large flower boxes where they could sit and enjoy the roses that grew there.

Once the pieces of the mirror had lodged in Kay's eye and in his heart, however, he turned away from his beloved friend and went to play with the boys in the street. As he was sledding with them, he saw a beautiful white sleigh bearing a lovely lady who was half hidden under her rich white furs and fine white cap. As the sleigh passed him, Kay grabbed hold, thinking he would ride with it only to the edge of town. The sleigh did not stop at the edge of town, however. It went on and on, faster and faster, until the town was far behind them. Kay became frightened and tried to let go, but found to his dismay that he could not. Even worse, when he tried to pray, he found that all he could remember were the multiplication tables.

At last the lady in the sleigh heard Kay's cries and stopped to take him up in the sleigh with her. It was the Snow Queen who had carried him away. She was so beautiful that suddenly Kay forgot all about the town he had left behind and his little friend, Gerda. As they went along, Kay told the Snow Queen about the multiplication tables and said that he could do fractions in his head, but when she looked at him, he thought he did not yet know anywhere near enough.

The Snow Queen took Kay to her great palace of ice and

snow and showed him the frozen lake at the center of the palace where she sat when she was at home and which she called "The Mirror of Reason." Kay was shivering and blue with cold, but he was so entranced by the many patterns he could make out of the oddly shaped pieces of ice he found by the Mirror of Reason that he didn't even notice when the Snow Queen flew away and left him all alone in her frozen palace.

Now, Gerda wept when Kay did not come back, but she was a brave little girl and she loved Kay very much, so, although she was very frightened, she set out in search of him. Her journey was a long one, and in the course of it she met many people and had many strange adventures, but her heart was true and eventually she came to the vast, frozen palace where the Snow Queen had left Kay all alone, playing with his shards of ice by the Mirror of Reason.

At the sight of him, Gerda cried out in joy and ran to him and threw her arms around him, but Kay simply sat there, still, and stiff, and cold, and did not move. Then Gerda wept hot tears and clung even more tightly to him. The tears fell on Kay's breast and warmed the lump of ice that had frozen around his heart and washed away the splinter of looking glass that had lodged there. Kay stirred, and when he realized that it was Gerda who held him so tightly, he threw his arms around her and wept until the pieces of the looking glass that had lodged in his eye floated away on his tears.

Then Kay and Gerda took each other by the hand and came out of the Snow Queen's frozen palace together. To their amazement, they found they had grown to become a man and a woman, but they were still children at heart, and for them it was summer—warm, beautiful summer.

# The Snow Queen

# *Chapter One*

*Boston, Massachusetts—June, 1896*

A handful of thrown gravel clattered against the dining room window, startling Hetty and making her slop lemon polish on the battered oak table. She expelled a quick sigh of exasperation, but even her irritation at the mess she'd made could not stop the smile spreading across her face. There was only one person who would throw gravel at her windows.

She tossed her cleaning rag onto the spreading polish and set the still-open bottle on the newly shined surface, heedless of the ring it might leave. She hastily wiped her fingers on her apron, tucked in the errant strands of hair that had worked free of her prim bun, and shoved up the sash, which always stuck just when you didn't want it to.

He was standing outside on the grass, just as she'd known he would be, feet firmly planted an undignified distance apart and hands thrust deep in his pockets. Not even the sober black coat and conservative waistcoat he wore could disguise the lean, masculine grace of his body. His head was tilted up at an insouciant angle, blue eyes alight beneath intimidating black brows. The spring breeze tossed an untidy lock of black hair across his forehead, and Hetty felt her fingers twitch with the urge to brush it back for him. At the sight of her, he grinned, and the stern, dark lines of his face softened and lightened, like storm clouds touched by the sun.

Scarcely able to stifle the laughter that threatened her, Hetty thrust her head out the window. "Why, Michael Ryan! You've interrupted me at my work. I trust you have a good excuse, sir!"

"That's *Doctor* Ryan to you, wench," he said, laughing up at her in a way that made her feel flushed and uncomfortably constrained within her stays and petticoats, "and I've as good an excuse as a man could want. It's a beautiful day and I have an even more beautiful fiancée, and I've come to take her for a walk."

"And what of the dusting?" Hetty demanded, feigning indignation. "Have you thought of that?"

"Not a whit, and neither have you, if I know my Hetty," he fired back. His grin widened and he cocked his chin up at her, like an arrogant blackbird who had claimed possession of her garden and was daring her to chase him off.

"Come on, Hetty. Don't tell me you'd rather spend an hour with a dust rag than with me. The sun is shining, the birds are singing, and Payham's meadow is buried in flowers. I'll even take you to Gearson's for a soda afterward. A chocolate soda, with an extra scoop of chocolate syrup, just the way you like it."

Hetty bit down sharply on her lower lip, striving not to give in to his enticing blandishments. There was nothing she would rather do than spend time with Michael Ryan. But there was the housework, and supper to fix, and her mother would probably want her to read to her this afternoon. If she was to be a doctor's wife, she owed it to Michael to behave as a doctor's wife was supposed to behave. At least, she ought to *try*.

"What would the members of the Ladies' Circle think if they came for a visit and discovered that Dr. Ryan's fiancée hadn't dusted?" Hetty demanded. She was fighting a losing battle, but at least if she protested, she could put some of the blame for her dereliction of household duties on him.

"Damn the Ladies' Circle. I'll buy you *two* sodas." Her unrepentant lover grabbed the edge of the flower box mounted beneath the window sill and tried to pull himself up. The nails holding the box to the sill squealed alarmingly and the pansies quivered.

"Michael Ryan, you stop that!" Hetty commanded, swatting at his hands. "I'll make you dig up the whole meadow if you ruin my flower box."

"Two meadows, for a kiss!"

"You're exceedingly generous today, sir," Hetty said primly, grabbing the sash and tugging it downward, "but what would the neighbors think?"

Unfortunately, the warped old sash chose that precise moment to stick, just when Michael had managed to transfer his grip to the much more solid sill on either side of the narrow flower box. His head appeared over the pansies, only slightly flushed from the effort of maintaining his awkward position.

His coat strained over the lean muscles of his arms and shoulders, and Hetty was instantly conscious of a vivid and intensely unsettling memory of how those same muscles felt when he took her in his arms for a kiss. Face flaming, she abandoned her grip on the sash and leaned forward to plant a quick peck on his cheek. Even this early in the afternoon, the dark stubble of his beard pricked her lips, rousing a quick, unsettling heat within her.

"That's it?" he objected plaintively, one eyebrow arching in protest. Hetty could hear the scrape of his shoes against the clapboard siding as he tried to take some of his weight off his arms and hands. "The neighbors will think you're a very poor kisser, Hetty Malone, if that's the best you can do."

Hetty bent lower to brush a kiss across his lips, but he was ready for her. His mouth opened. The tip of his tongue teased her lower lip, tempting her further.

By the time she retreated, she was scarlet-faced and breathless, and her nipples had pricked into sharp points beneath her tightly buttoned bodice. Flustered, she straightened abruptly and cracked the back of her head on the sash.

"Ooof!" she said, and immediately retreated to rub the abused spot. "Michael . . . !"

The warning brought a bright laugh in response. He'd already dropped down from his absurd perch so that all she could see of him from this angle was the rebellious crest of black hair. "Five minutes, Hetty!"

Five minutes. Michael grinned. She'd be out in ten . . . if he was lucky. He craned back to look at the open window above his head, but Hetty was gone. He wondered if she'd remember to close the window before she left.

Suddenly nervous, Michael crammed his hands into his pockets. The action made the letter in the inside pocket of his coat crackle ever so faintly.

He should have told her about the letter earlier, should have discussed his plans with her.

Should have . . . but he hadn't. He'd been afraid to. He didn't want her to say no or to protest. He didn't want to hear her doubts because he had more than enough of his own.

Once more he glanced up at the open window. In his imagination, he could see her, gold-green eyes alight with the joy of seeing him, a lock of hair the color of golden oak curling in an undisciplined twist across her cheek. Her hair was always working its way free, as beautiful as Hetty herself and just as unwilling to be confined.

He thought of running that silken strand through his fingers, and ached.

He thought of leaving her, and flinched.

He'd never been separated from Hetty for more than a week in all his life and now . . .

Michael tensed his shoulders against the thought. The hidden paper rustled accusingly.

It would only be for a couple of months. He'd told himself that a thousand times. Just until he got settled and could send for her. Hetty would approve, once she understood how important this was to him.

He just hoped she would forgive him for having kept it secret from her for so long.

Five minutes. To tidy her hair, straighten her clothes, gather her hat and jacket, not to mention finish the . . . polishing! Hetty gave a squeak of dismay and dove for the abandoned polishing rag and bottle.

The rag had absorbed most of the heavy lemon oil she'd spilled, leaving only an irregular dark blotch that blended well with all the other blotches, gouges, and nicks that decorated the worn surface. The bottle, however, had left a neat black circle that would take days of sunshine and polishing to disguise. Her mother and the members of the Ladies' Circle would spot it instantly.

Her mother would merely smile, easily guessing the cause, but Hetty shuddered to think of the discreetly lowered glances from the ladies, which would say, more clearly than words, that poor Dr. Ryan would have a deplorably incompetent housekeeper for a wife.

With a sigh, Hetty gathered up the oil-soaked rag and the equally oily bottle and, holding them carefully out in front of her so they wouldn't drip on her clothes or the floor, bore them to the kitchen and tucked them out of sight on the high shelf that contained her other cleaning supplies.

The simple movement of stretching to reach the shelf made her nipples rub against the ribbed cotton of her vest and the harder line of her corset over that, reminding her of Michael's kiss and the quick, sweet heat of her response. The gloom that had descended on her at the thought of the Circle's disapproval vanished instantly.

She had loved Michael for as long as she could remember, since before she could remember, perhaps, when their mothers had taken them out for the air in their baby carriages, side by side. Soon she would marry him, and then she'd be free to love him for every hour of every day of the rest of her life.

The joy of it was, he loved her in return. As passionately and deeply as she loved him. She was sure of it. If the Ladies' Circle found her lacking, he, at least, did not. And that was all that mattered.

Her heart singing, Hetty flew about the little house, tidying up the last obvious traces of her aborted attempt at housekeeping, tucking the recalcitrant strands of her fine hair back in their proper place, gathering her hat and a proper jacket. Almost, she forgot the dining room window. She was halfway across the hall when she recalled it was still standing open, a blatant invitation to any bothersome fly that might wander past.

The sash's protesting squawk brought another, softer protest from her mother's bedroom.

"Hetty? Is that you? Whatever are you doing to make so much noise?"

"I'm sorry, Mother," Hetty called. With one last, firm shove she forced the window closed, then gathered up her abandoned jacket. As she passed her mother's bedroom door, she poked her head inside.

"I'm just going out for a walk with Michael, Mama. A walk and maybe a soda at Gearson's. I won't be gone long. Do you need anything before I leave?"

Her mother, looking especially thin and frail in the big wooden rocker beside her bed, smiled and shook her head. "No, dear. I'm sure I'll be fine. You have a nice walk and give my love to Michael."

For an instant, Hetty hesitated, caught between love and guilt. Ill health, a weak heart, and a naturally timid, clinging nature had turned Madeline Malone into an invalid almost from the day Hetty's father died over ten years before. The neighbors and the ladies from the church were good about stopping by for visits, but Madeline depended on her daughter for companionship as much as for everything else and felt lost whenever she was left to her own devices for very long.

"I'll ask Michael to read to you when we come back, Mother. Would you like that?" Hetty said now, hoping to make her mother smile. "He could read that new book by Mrs. Clay that we got, *The Duke's Secret.*"

Madeline laughed. "Michael does a lot of things well, but reading romances isn't one of them. Why don't you give him our *Medical Companion* instead?"

"What? And have him ignore us for hours?"

The laughter disappeared from Madeline's eyes. "Well, you'll have to get used to it. It was hard enough for you when he was a student. What do you think he'll be like now that he's a real doctor?"

Hetty laughed. "Don't worry! I have no intention of letting him forget me, no matter how much he gets caught up in his medicine!"

"Then you'd best not keep him waiting, Hetty. Go on now. Get!" Madeline made a little shooing motion with her hand.

Michael was waiting, one hip propped on the wooden porch railing, his father's gold pocket watch open in his hand. At Hetty's appearance, he grinned with the rare, lopsided grin that always made her heart turn over, and glanced down at the watch. "Eleven minutes and seventeen seconds. You must have torn through the house like a madwoman, Hetty."

Hetty sniffed in disdain.

Michael laughed and snapped the watch shut, then tucked it into its pocket and rose to his feet. "You look beautiful. Though I'm never sure," he added teasingly, gathering her into his arms, "whether I prefer the elegantly prim and proper lady you've become, or the hoyden who used to go racing across the fields with her pinafore up around her knees and her braids flying behind."

He held her tightly, as if he were afraid she'd slip away from him. His breath tickled her ear, warm and enticing. He pressed a gentle kiss to the sensitive flesh just beneath the angle of her jaw, then let his lips trace a tormenting line of kisses down the arc of her throat to the collar of her shirtwaist and back up again.

Hetty couldn't help it. She arched into him, inviting more kisses, almost dizzy with the strength of him and the warm, heady smell of starched linen and bay rum and man.

"Ah, Hetty," he breathed, "I do love you so."

He didn't have a chance to say anything else.

"Oh, lookee! Miss Hetty's spooning!"

"Hey, Doc! My big brother can do better than that! Do yuh want him to show yuh?"

"Kiss, kiss, Hetty missed. Aimed for her fellow, but he turned yellow and ran awaaay!"

Four boys were draped over the picket fence like a flock of scruffy jaybirds come to heckle the hen yard. One, a teasing, red-haired fiend in knee pants, swung on the gate with all the cocky confidence of a king.

"Hey, Miss Hetty! How many of those big sugar cookies of yours is it worth for us not to snitch on you and the Doc?"

Michael choked. Hetty dug her fingers into his

arm as a warning, then edged around him to confront their tormentors.

"Thomas Butler," she said in awful tones, "are you trying to blackmail me?"

She was met with wide-eyed, utter innocence. "No, ma'am. I'm just askin'."

"Just asking, hmmm?"

"Yes'm." The boy's raffish grin widened until it threatened to swallow half his freckles. "An' we're *real* hungry."

"As hungry as you were for the cherry pie that disappeared off Mrs. Hitchins's back porch last week?"

That shot struck home. Their faces suddenly assumed expressions of extraordinary innocence—all except for little Jimmie Goudge's, which twisted into a suspicious frown as its owner realized he'd been excluded from a productive raid.

Tommy beamed. "Well, I don't know 'bout *that* partic'lar pie, Miss Hetty, but Mrs. Hitchins does make *awful* good ones!"

Michael snorted and his face turned red. Hetty dug her elbow into his midriff in warning. He spluttered once or twice, sucked in a steadying breath, and turned to face the miscreants perched on Hetty's fence.

With the gravity proper to a doctor and a pillar of the community, he said in a voice that was only slightly shaky, "Are they better than Miss Hetty's sugar cookies?"

That was clearly a puzzler. Sound political wisdom favored a negative since Hetty was standing right in front of them, but they all knew it wouldn't be wise to let Mrs. Hitchins hear her culinary efforts weren't properly appreciated.

"Man to man, now," Michael said. As if to reassure Hetty of his loyalties, he clasped his hands around her waist and added, "Merely as a point of scientific inquiry, of course!"

Hetty might not have found that last so unsettling if he hadn't whispered it into her ear so that the faint, warm pulse of his breath set her nerve ends tingling.

"Quit that," Hetty said, ducking her head, then slapping Michael's hands away from where they had embarked on some rather distracting explorations beneath her jacket.

Tommy grinned. "You really want to know, Doc?"

"Of course he doesn't." Hetty clamped her hands over Michael's, pinning them in place above her hips. "It doesn't matter, anyway, because I'm fresh out of sugar cookies."

Four faces fell precipitously.

"But I might have some tomorrow."

Wild whoops greeted this announcement—and were immediately squelched when little Jimmie lost his balance and flipped headfirst over the fence. Hetty tore free of Michael's grasp and flew off the porch, but Jimmie was already struggling to sit up by the time she reached him.

Michael, accustomed to the disasters that befell little boys, followed her down the front path at a more dignified pace. He squatted in front of

Jimmie, who looked as if he wanted to cry but didn't dare in front of witnesses, and calmly surveyed the damage.

"A little scratch," he said, brushing back a heavy lock of blond hair. "You'll probably have a bruise by supper time."

Jimmie pressed a tentative finger to the spot. He winced. "That's all?"

Michael looked grave. "Well, in extreme cases there's a tendency to lose all interest in baseball, sugar cookies, and cherry pie—"

Jimmie's eyes widened in horror.

"—but we won't know for sure for several days."

For an instant, Jimmie wavered between disbelief and despair. His comrades' hoots of laughter decided him.

"Naw," he said. "That don't happen." The tone was appropriately dismissive, but the expression on his face was clearly one of relief.

Michael grinned. "Naw. It don't."

He lifted the boy to his feet, then stood himself. "But just to be sure, I'm going to prescribe a couple of pills." He plunged his hand into his coat pocket and rummaged through the miscellany he always carried there. The boys clustered around him, eyes wide.

"Ah, here it is." Michael drew a crumpled white paper bag out of his pocket and solemnly inspected the contents. With great care, he shook two horehound drops into Jimmie's eager, outstretched hand. "Take one now, and one as soon as the first one's gone. And here are two each for the rest of you." His eyebrows scrunched into a warning frown. "Just in case the problem's contagious."

An instant later the boys galloped off down the road, their shouted thanks muffled by the candy in their mouths. Michael stood at the gate watching them, grinning wickedly.

The lopsided grin was dangerously appealing. It made Hetty think of that kiss on the porch and his hands at her waist and . . .

"Michael David Ryan! I hope you realize you are totally without shame! What do you mean by embarrassing me by . . . by . . ."

"By kissing you?" Michael peered at her from beneath his devil-black eyebrows, his blue eyes dancing.

"Well, that, to begin with," Hetty said, determined to be stern.

"And afterward? Could you show me? Just to jog my memory, you know?"

"Will you be serious?"

The corner of his mouth tilted upward irresistibly. "Not if it means I'm supposed to quit kissing you, Hetty. I don't think I could give up that for anything."

"Well, no one's asking you to," Hetty said reasonably, dodging his efforts to kiss her again as she tried to tug his tie and waistcoat into some semblance of order. "But you're a doctor now and a respectable man. What would your patients think if they caught you misbehaving in public?"

"They'd think I had a damned pretty fiancée and that I'd be a fool not to take advantage of—

*urk!"* The last came as Hetty tightened the knot of his tie in reproof for his unacceptable language. The instant she loosened the knot, he added, "Either that, or they'd pity me for marrying an abusive shrew."

Hetty patted his tie approvingly and slipped from his arms. "I'll accept the abusive part, Dr. Ryan. It's the only way to keep you in line. But take care you don't drive me to the rest!"

"Yes'm," he said, with all proper meekness. He slid his arm free of her grasp and slipped it around her waist, pulling her tightly against him. "Thank God I have you to tell me how to go on, Hetty! I don't know how I'd manage otherwise!"

How *would* he manage without her? Michael wondered.

He glanced down. She was walking beside him, but all he could see was the top of her straw hat bobbing at his shoulder. The hat tilted as she turned to watch a robin fly past, then tilted again as they came abreast of a rose hedge just starting to bloom.

"Oh, look, Michael! Mrs. Jirgin's roses have come out. Before ours! Mama will be so disappointed." Without releasing her hold on his arm, Hetty stopped and bent to smell the roses.

Like a ship swinging around on its anchor chain, Michael came about on her command. He couldn't help it. God himself wouldn't be able to divert Hetty if she were intent on something, so what chance did he have?

Not that it mattered. He'd do anything Hetty

asked of him. He always had. The trouble was, she never asked for much. Not for herself, at any rate. The people she loved always came first—her mother, him. Her neighbors, even, including scruffy little boys with a passion for sugar cookies.

Michael thought of the letter hidden in the inner breast pocket of his coat and felt some of the brightness go out of the day.

She glanced up and something sweet and hot caught in Michael's chest, in spite of his doubts. The pink of her cheeks rivaled the pink of the roses; he could happily have lost himself in the spring-green depth of her eyes.

"Smell them, Michael. Aren't they sweet? Sweeter than ours, too. Do you think Mrs. Jirgin would let me have the petals to make a pomander for Mama's wardrobe?

Michael was no expert on rose petals or pomanders, but he obediently bent to sniff at the lush blossom. The scent was almost dizzying, the silken caress of a petal against the tip of his nose a disconcerting reminder of how soft and silken Hetty's skin had been when he'd trailed his kisses down her throat.

He jerked back. "Lovely."

Hetty laughed. "Oh, Michael."

"What do you mean, 'Oh, Michael'?"

His eyebrows arched, but she compressed her lips, eyes twinkling, and refused to answer.

"Come on, Hetty," Michael said, suddenly impatient. "Let's go. You can ask Mrs. Jirgin about the pomander later."

She came obediently. Not, he knew, because she had no will of her own—there was no one more hard-headed than Hetty if she was determined on something—but because she was always willing to do whatever he wanted if it would make him happy.

The thought roused guilt, and with the guilt came even more doubts. Michael shoved them into the farthest corner of his mind. She was bound to suspect if he kept worrying about them. And why should he worry, after all? He'd spent enough time thinking about this, considering all the obstacles, all the disadvantages. It wouldn't be easy for either of them, at least at first, but an opportunity like this didn't come along every day.

Frowning, Michael glanced down at Hetty. For the first time he noticed the slight fraying of the woven straw of her hat. The fraying wasn't really noticeable, especially since the cluster of ribbons and silk flowers that adorned the hat were obviously new. Hetty hadn't had the money to buy a new straw hat for everyday use so she had refurbished her old one.

That thought was enough to drive back the doubts. Soon, Hetty wouldn't have to worry about such things. She'd be able to buy a new hat every year. Two, if she wanted them!

All because of the promise in the letter in his pocket.

Michael's brow cleared and he felt his earlier eagerness return. Straw hats were trivial things, but there was so much he wanted for Hetty—for them both!—that was neither trivial nor easily achieved. And if they had to be apart for a few months, well, surely Hetty would recognize that the sacrifice was worth it when compared with all they had to gain.

As Michael had promised, Payham's meadow was full of flowers and the birds were singing happily under a bright afternoon sun.

Michael charged into the meadow like an eager young savage suddenly set free and Hetty followed breathlessly in his wake, laughing and scurrying to keep up with his long strides.

He led her up a hill that was knee-deep in wild grass and clover and daisies, and when they got to the top, he grabbed her hand. "Come on, Hetty! Faster! Don't slow down now!"

With a whoop as wild as any Tommy Burton might have given, Hetty lifted her skirts and plunged down the other side after him. To the devil with all her lecturing on dignity and proper behavior! She would go anywhere Michael wanted to go, as fast as he wanted to go there, regardless of the consequences.

They were halfway down the hill when Hetty tripped, undone by long skirts and high-button boots. As Hetty pitched forward, she jerked Michael off balance. He grabbed for her. She grabbed for him. An instant later they were tumbling over and over, shrieking like a barrelful of banshees.

They rolled to a halt in a thick patch of daisies and clover. For a moment, Hetty just lay there, sprawled on top of Michael with her hat tossed over her eyes and her nose pressed flat against his chest.

She blinked and stared at his top jacket button. Then she started giggling.

Beneath her, Michael's chest heaved as he struggled to catch his breath and keep from laughing.

Her giggling burst into laughter. An instant later, they were both roaring. Michael's arms tightened around her, anchoring her to him so that she shook with the power of his mirth. Her hat slid down over her nose, hairpins worked their way free, her bun uncurled down the back of her neck, and Hetty didn't care. Not even a little bit.

"What was that . . . you said . . . about . . . dignity?" Michael got out at last.

Hetty planted a quick kiss on his lips and levered herself up so she could look into his face. "I haven't the slightest idea."

She was, however, getting other ideas, ideas that were making her muscles melt and something in the middle of her belly go hot and hungry.

Michael snorted in disbelief. "Well, if I look half as undignified as you do, my career as physician to the rich is over before it's ever begun."

"Pooh!" Hetty said, flipping her hair out of her eyes. Her hat tumbled off and rolled into the grass unheeded. "You'll never cater to the rich and you know it, Michael Ryan. Half your patients will be too poor to pay, you'll forget to charge most of the rest, and whatever you *do* earn you'll give away by handing out horehound drops to everyone you meet."

Michael opened his mouth to protest, but Hetty didn't give him a chance. "Don't argue with me! You know I'm right. Mr. Gearson said he's never seen anybody go through horehound drops like you do. Says it's like to become half his business, just keeping you supplied."

The corner of Michael's mouth curled upward. "Miracle drug of the nineties! Just look how quickly they got little Jimmie back on his feet!"

When she didn't reply, he said, more seriously this time, "Trust me, Hetty. I'll soon have my debts paid off. Then we can marry and—"

"Oh, Michael, I don't care about your silly debts. Let's get married now. Right now."

"Now?" Michael studied her doubtfully, his eyes oddly troubled, then angled his head back so he could stare up the trail of crushed grass they'd left. "Who were you planning on marrying us? That fat robin in the willow over there?"

Hetty frowned at his levity. "You know what I mean. We could get married next week. The week after, if you absolutely insist. We could live with Mama—you *know* I can't leave her—and with the money you'd save by not having to pay Mrs. Bartlett for that horrid, dark room and those awful meals she serves, you could open your own office instead of assisting Dr. Stevenson. You could—"

"Whoa, Hetty!" A shadow crossed Michael's face. Abruptly he lifted her off him, then twisted into a cross-legged position in front of her.

Hetty made no effort to straighten her hair or

rearrange her skirts into a more ladylike order. All her attention was fixed on Michael.

Bits of grass and leaves were tangled in his hair. There was a green smudge on his cheek, his tie was askew, and his jacket didn't sit straight across his broad shoulders. Outwardly, he looked like a man who had just rolled down a hill with a woman in his arms, laughing all the way. But there was something in his voice, in his eyes . . .

Hetty drew in a deep, trembling breath. Suddenly—she wasn't sure why—she felt afraid.

"Why *can't* we get married next week, Michael?" she demanded, fighting to control her voice. "We've been engaged since you entered medical school. How much longer do we have to wait?"

Because she couldn't bear to be this close to Michael and not touch him, Hetty leaned forward and placed her hand on his black-clad knee. He refused to meet her eyes.

"I don't need a fancy house or a showy carriage to be happy, Michael," she pleaded. "I just need you. That's all. How long do we have to wait before we can allow ourselves to be happy? First we were too young. Then you had your studies, and then your debts, and now Dr. Stevenson doesn't want you to be distracted by a wife. How many more reasons can there possibly be for us not to get married?"

The words came tumbling out so quickly that she was breathless. Her stays cramped her sides, bits of grass had worked their way down her back, and a rock was digging into her bottom, but none of it mattered except her sudden, desperate need to convince Michael.

Michael sat silent. His mouth worked as if he wanted to speak, but couldn't. His jaw clenched. He frowned so hard that lines appeared in his forehead, half hidden beneath the rakish spill of his hair.

The silence stretched, broken only by the faint rustle of the grass as a light breeze moved past.

"Michael?" Hetty said at last, hesitantly. "Don't you . . . don't you want to get married?"

His eyes widened in horror. "Of course I do, Hetty. I want to marry you more than anything in the world, but . . . but . . ."

Suddenly he shifted around until he was kneeling before her. He stretched to take her hands in his. Hetty immediately buried them in her lap, out of reach. How could he say he loved her and wanted to marry her, then put two "buts" right after his words?

"But what, Michael Ryan?" she demanded sharply. "What is more important than the fact that we love each other?"

"Nothing, Hetty. But . . ." Something in her face must have warned him against one more "but." He reached into the inner pocket of his jacket and pulled out a much-creased sheet of heavy, cream-colored paper.

"Take a look at this letter, Hetty. You'll see. No, don't," he said an instant later, yanking it back before Hetty could take it from him. "It will take too long."

With an expression of almost boyish pride only

slightly marred by nervousness, he rocked back on his heels, placed his hands on his thighs, and said, "I've been offered a position in Colorado, Hetty. Not as an assistant. As a doctor with my own practice."

He drew in a breath, obviously waiting for her to cheer at the marvelous news.

Instead, Hetty said doubtfully, "In Colorado? But Michael, that's so far! Why—?"

"This would be a regular practice, Hetty. Not an assistantship, my own practice!" He hesitated. "Well, a partnership, anyway. We could get married, buy a house—"

"But we don't have to go to Colorado to get married, Michael, and we already have a house to live in. Mother's house. Why would—" Hetty cut off her words abruptly. She'd missed the connection, but suddenly Michael's enthusiasm was all too easily comprehensible.

"Colorado Springs? Isn't that where all the consumptives go, Michael? To Colorado Springs?"

He nodded. "That's right. A good number of them, anyway. They say it's a beautiful place, and with its high, dry climate and clean air, a lot of tuberculosis patients seem to do better there. Dr. Cathcart—you remember him? My first professor? The one I've corresponded with for the past few years?"

Hetty wasn't sure Michael even noticed her nod.

"He went there because his wife was ill. She died, but he decided to stay. He's getting old and it's getting harder for him to keep up with a full practice. Especially since he's conducting research on a possible cure for tuberculosis, too. But he's not quite ready to retire, so he started thinking. About taking a partner, I mean. He doesn't have children, and only some distant cousins or some such to inherit when he dies. And that's when he thought of me!"

Michael paused and looked at her expectantly, as if he was waiting for her to start cheering.

All Hetty could think of was, no, dear God, not this. Please not this. Please . . . please . . . *please* not this.

She looked away, unable to face the eagerness that radiated from him. Her gaze fixed on the bright clover and brilliant daisies bobbing in the tall grass at her elbow. Without thinking, she grabbed a handful and wrenched off their heads, then stared at them, shocked by her desecration.

Memories swamped her. Of a bone-chilling winter wind that seeped under her clothes and bit at her nose and froze her tears on her cheeks. Of snow piled knee-deep in the streets outside the narrow Boston row houses where the Ryans and the Malones had lived side by side since before she'd been born. Of Michael, just turned seven, standing stiffly beside her on the stoop and trying desperately to be brave while they waited for his father to carry his mother down.

Slowly, blindly, Hetty shredded the flowers she held, letting the pieces drift into her lap like the snow that had covered the world on that long-ago day when Michael's mother, in the last stages of pulmonary consumption, had gone away to die.

Mr. Ryan had carried his wife out of the house and set her in the waiting sleigh. Hetty remembered how frail and wasted she'd looked, as white as the snow that was already coating the heavy blankets that covered her to the chin.

Mrs. Ryan hadn't even glanced at her son as he stood there on the stoop. Instead, she'd stared sightlessly at the empty white street in front of her, blinking against the flakes that brushed her lashes. Hetty had wondered then what she was seeing, wondered if she was thinking about the cousin's farm in Georgia where she was headed and the warm southern sun they all hoped would heal her, because everything else they'd tried had failed and now there was nothing else left to try.

With infinite care, Mr. Ryan had tucked the heavy blankets and carriage robes around his wife, then climbed into the sleigh beside her. As he'd gathered up the reins, he'd glanced over at the little huddle of well-wishers on his front steps, then nodded at Michael. "I'll be home soon, son. Soon as I see your mama off on the train with the Wetherels. Until then, you mind your manners, you hear?" And with that, he'd driven off without even waiting for his son's hesitant nod.

Michael's mother hadn't even waved good-bye.

The sleigh was halfway down the street when Michael had broken away and gone running after his mother, crying and calling to her not to go. He'd tried to stay in the tracks left by the sleigh, but the snow was too heavy. It spilled over the cuts, tripping him and dragging him down until at last he'd just given up and collapsed face down in the path, choking on his own sobs and futilely battering his fists against the unresisting drifts.

His mother hadn't looked back, too wrapped up in her own misery and fear to see what she was leaving behind forever.

"Hetty?" Michael's puzzled query broke into Hetty's thoughts. "What do you say? It's a wonderful opportunity, don't you think? And Dr. Cathcart has said he wants to leave it all to me when he finally steps down. His house, his practice. Assuming it works out between us, of course. But it will! I know it will!"

Hetty gathered another handful of clover and daisies and started shredding those, too.

"Hetty? Hetty! Say something!"

Hetty blinked. Her hands stilled; her fingers tightened around the flowers, crushing them. She looked into the lean, shadowed face she loved so much, into the sapphire eyes where Michael's soul gleamed, naked and vulnerable, and her heart quaked.

"Dr. Cathcart didn't just happen to think of you, did he, Michael?" she said at last, reluctantly. "This isn't something you've been thinking about for a few days. You've been thinking about this, planning for it for a long time, haven't you?"

With each word she spoke, she ripped at the flowers she held, tearing them into tinier and tinier pieces.

He didn't respond. He didn't need to. The answer to her question was there in his eyes. The answer she didn't want to hear.

Hetty bent her head to stare, unseeing, at the

messy mound of lavender and white confetti on her skirt. "I wondered sometimes why you corresponded with Dr. Cathcart. Knowing how much you dislike writing letters, it seemed strange, but I thought . . ."

Her head snapped back up. "Why would you want to go so far?" she burst out. "You know I can't leave Mama. And why consumptives, Michael? Why something so . . . so hopeless?"

"It's not hopeless, Hetty! Haven't you been listening when I've been telling you about the advances—"

"But you tell me about everything, Michael! About a new kind of sticking plaster, or a better stethoscope, or a new surgical technique! You never said you wanted to work with consumptives! And most of the people you'd tend would be dying, wouldn't they? Just like your mother? How would you deal with that?"

Goaded, Michael leapt to his feet. "I'm a doctor, Hetty. A doctor! That's the sort of thing I'm *supposed* to deal with!"

For a moment, he towered above her like a dark and wrathful god, and then he started to pace.

"It's been, what? Fourteen, fifteen years since Koch discovered the cause of tuberculosis. Everyone thought it was hereditary, a weakness passed in the blood from mother to child. That's what they said when my mother died. Hereditary. But Koch proved them wrong."

He stopped for an instant to glare down at her. "Fifteen years, and still there's no cure for a disease that's responsible for as much as a quarter of all deaths in this country, Hetty. None! Lives are being destroyed by a bacillus we can't even see except through a microscope, and we're helpless to stop it!"

"But what does that have to do with us, Michael?" Hetty demanded. "We love each other. We want to get married. If you go to Colorado—"

Michael dropped to his knees before her. "It would only be for a little while, Hetty," he pleaded. "Just a few months, I swear. Just until I get settled and save enough money to bring you and your mama out to join me. I won't even worry about paying off my debts. I promise. I love you, Hetty, and I want to marry you. More than anything in the world."

"Then don't do this, Michael. Please. Let's get married. Now. Today. This week. You can talk to Dr. Stevenson. Maybe some of your professors . . ."

Tears were running down Hetty's cheeks, but she ignored them as she stretched out her hands to Michael.

"Please, Michael. Don't go to Colorado."

Michael's hands tightened over hers, crushing them in his sudden, desperate grip. "I'm going, Hetty. Because I have to. Don't you understand that? I *have* to."

# *Chapter Two*

*Colorado Springs, Colorado—December, 1898*

It had taken forever to cross Kansas and eastern Colorado. When stout Mrs. Fisk had first identified the ragged blue line on the horizon as the fabled Rocky Mountains, Hetty had blinked in disappointment. They didn't look nearly as impressive as the articles she'd read in *Harper's Magazine* had made them out to be. She hadn't realized they would grow and grow as the hours passed until they seemed to swallow half the sky.

And Pikes Peak! She hadn't needed help in identifying that! There was no mistaking that bold profile. Imagine a peak that was high enough to have snow on it, even in summer! Michael had written her that there were other peaks in the state even higher. Hard to believe, but true.

She'd checked in the big atlas in the lending library, just in case he'd been teasing her.

Hetty pressed her cheek against the coach window, straining to see more, but a rocky, pine-covered hill suddenly cut off her view. Reluctantly, she settled back into her seat. If only Michael were here beside her!

He'd written often, but his letters were seldom more than hastily scrawled notes dashed off at the end of a long and grueling day. Short or not, she had read them again and again, treasuring their invariable closing lines—"I love you, Hetty. Soon."

Hetty's fingers tightened over the bag in her lap with its precious bundle of letters.

"Soon" had stretched far longer than either of them had anticipated. Dr. Cathcart had died unexpectedly less than two months after Michael had joined him, leaving Michael with a house and office, the medical practice, and not much else. By the time Michael had sorted out his sponsor's tangled affairs and saved enough money for Hetty and her mother to join him, Madeline was too ill to travel. The journey would have put far too great a strain on her weakened heart, the doctors had said, and Hetty had reluctantly accepted their judgment. Her mother's welfare had to come first, regardless of her own desires.

For two years she had stayed in the little house on the outskirts of Boston and cared for her mother and tried not to blame Michael for having gone so far from her just when she needed him most. It hadn't been easy, especially during those last hard months when her mother lay so still and quiet in her bed, waiting for the relief that death alone could grant her.

Now Hetty struggled with guilt, as well as grief. For feeling relieved, sometimes, that her mother's sufferings were over and she was free to rejoin Michael. For being happy, in spite of everything.

She must have smiled, for Mrs. Fisk, who occupied most of the seat across from Hetty, gave her an apple-cheeked smile in return.

Mrs. Fisk had cheerfully served as Hetty's self-appointed tour guide and advisor ever since she'd boarded the train in St. Louis and discovered where Hetty was headed. The woman was an unabashed gossip and more than willing to recount for Hetty's benefit all the scandals, pecadillos, and general goings-on of the citizens of Colorado Springs.

Despite her prying ways, Clarabelle Fisk had a generous heart and was more than willing to spend an hour entertaining a fussy baby when its exhausted mother had given up the struggle, or to share paper-wrapped sandwiches with three hungry little boys when there were still hours to wait until the dining car opened.

In contrast, Hetty had decided that tall, lean Mrs. Scoggins, who had boarded in Kansas City and now sat beside her like a wood carving done up in brown bombazine, had no heart at all. Even though she and Mrs. Fisk were old friends and belonged to many of the same ladies' clubs, Lettitia Scoggins said little and sniffed disdainfully if she disapproved of whatever was under discussion, which was often. If it hadn't been for the long, colorful cock feathers that stuck up from Mrs. Scoggins's drab felt hat like flags on a circus tent, Hetty might have doubted the woman's humanity altogether.

"You'll be able to see the city itself soon, Miss Malone," Mrs. Fisk assured Hetty. "I'm sure you'll be impressed, even if you *are* from Boston. Mr. Fisk's pharmacy is a perfect example of just how modern we are. We have running water and gas lights, of course, and we're on the telephone, and—"

Mrs. Scoggins sniffed disdainfully. "That's all well and good, Clarabelle, but the city's still nowhere up to Kansas City standards. I've never seen a place that had more problems figuring out which way the public tram lines should run. Seems as if they're forever tearing up the streets and changing the schedules and inconveniencing the public. *Most* annoying!"

"True, quite true, Lettitia." Mrs. Fisk nodded so emphatically that her double chins became triplets. "Still, I worry more about all the consumptives chasing the cure. Did you know, Miss Malone, the Chamber of Commerce spent twelve thousand dollars on their first campaign to attract tourists and publicize the benefits of our mountain air? Imagine that! And us with no place to put them!"

She sat back to the accompaniment of protests from her overworked corset and looked solemn. "Thank heavens there are knowledgeable pharmacists like Mr. Fisk to help all those poor souls."

"That's as may be," Mrs. Scoggins said repressively. "It's certain the doctors don't know it all. Not by a long shot." She leveled an accusatory glare at Mrs. Fisk. "But neither do the pharmacists, if it comes to that!"

"I'm sure we all feel for your loss, Lettitia," Mrs. Fisk snapped, goaded, "but—"

"But what? My husband and son had the finest doctors and the latest medicines from the best pharmacists in town. And what good did it do them?" The answer was there in the hollow look of pain in Mrs. Scoggins's pale eyes. "I'll tell you what good it did them! None at all. The consumption killed them, regardless."

Neither Hetty nor Mrs. Fisk could respond to that. Hetty stared at her hands and the bag that contained her treasure trove of letters. Her heart ached for the pain of a woman she scarcely knew.

Mrs. Scoggins broke the silence first. "Humpf," she said, glaring at the front of the coach. "Not even to the edge of town yet and folks think they have to get in an uproar about their bags."

Excitement raced through Hetty, driving out the gloom. For one wild moment, she considered pulling down the window and sticking her head out and shouting, just as the little boy five rows back was doing, but one glance at Mrs. Scoggins's disapproving countenance discouraged her.

Soon. The word beat in time with the wheels on the tracks. Soon, soon, soon . . .

The train slid down the hill and chugged its way through an area of small, rather shabby houses half hidden behind the winter-stripped trees and scrub willows that lined the tracks. Sheds and outbuildings stood stolidly as they passed, their bare wood siding already graying from the sun. Freight cars and empty passenger coaches and engines and cabooses occupied the sidings, their markings identifying the companies that owned them. Denver & Rio Grande. Union Pacific. The Rock Island and the Colorado Midland. The Atchison, Topeka, and Santa Fe.

As if in salute, the engine hooted its warning, then hooted again.

The sound made Hetty clutch her purse tightly and lean forward in her seat. Almost there! She craned for a glimpse of the station and Michael, and realized too late that she was on the wrong side of the coach.

Like cattle packed too long in a cattle car, passengers surged to their feet at the sound of the whistle, gathering their bags and bundles while they bent to peer out the windows at the approaching station. They filled the aisle, chattering and exclaiming eagerly and blocking Hetty's view of the platform sliding past.

The train came to a stop with a sudden squeal of brakes and a teeth-rattling jerk. Passengers who were standing staggered and grabbed for the back of a seat, then immediately moved to the doors at either end of the car, anxious to be gone.

"Run a body over, give them half a chance," Mrs. Fisk said, trying to peer around the passengers who were blocking her view of the platform. "I don't see Mr. Fisk. I wonder where he could have got—ah! There he is! I hope he brought the wagon. I've no desire to be traipsing across town on foot, even if it is only a few blocks. And there's the trunks, of course, and . . ."

Before Hetty could explode with frustration, Mrs. Scoggins finally, and with immense dignity, rose to her feet. She pulled a card from her bag and handed it to Hetty. "Please feel free to call on me when you are settled, Miss Malone," she said.

"And you can always find me by asking Mr. Fisk," Mrs. Fisk chimed in over her shoulder. "Fisk Pharmacy. Everybody knows it."

To Hetty's immense relief, Mrs. Scoggins at last condescended to make her way down the aisle, cock feathers bobbing with every step. Mrs. Fisk followed, and Hetty brought up the rear, excitement shooting through her like a Fourth of July rocket. For an instant she hung on the last step of the coach, anxiously scanning the crowd.

Michael hadn't seen her. He would have been waiting right here if he had. Not that she'd expected him to spot her through the press of people and the dirty windows of the coach, but she did feel a twinge—just a twinge!—of disappointment that he wasn't scurrying up and down the length of the platform in a desperate effort to find her.

"Miss?" The harried conductor took her carpetbags and helped her down, then turned to help the passengers behind her. Hetty strained up on tiptoe, desperately trying to see over the crowd, anxiously searching for that one precious, familiar face among the many.

Nothing.

She moved a few feet into the throng, then came to a halt, uncertain. The broad brick platform wasn't *that* big. Surely Michael would have found her by now if he'd been looking. If he'd been there in the first place.

Her fingers tightened their grip on the top of her bag. She could feel the straight, stiff edge of the bundle of letters, even through the heavy crocheted covering.

He knew she was coming and when. She'd written him twice—no, three times—with all the details, so anxious and excited about their coming reunion that she hadn't wanted to risk any mistake. And he'd written her to confirm that he would be there, that he was as anxious and eager as she was.

"Miss Malone?" Mrs. Fisk was at her side, a tall, thin man who looked as if he suffered from dyspepsia firmly in tow. "Isn't Dr. Ryan here?"

"I don't see him," Hetty admitted reluctantly. She forced a smile on her lips. "Probably caught up with a patient at the last minute. I'm sure he'll be along any minute."

Mrs. Fisk's brows creased in a doubtful frown. "Mr. Fisk and I will just keep you company, then, shall we?"

"Oh, no, I'm sure that's not necessary. Really," Hetty added with more certainty than she felt.

"Let's check with the stationmaster at least," Mrs. Fisk urged. Her husband nodded dutifully, though his gloomy expression made it clear he didn't hold much hope for the effort.

At that moment, Mrs. Scoggins stalked out of

the crowd followed by a harassed porter pushing a handcart loaded with a large trunk and three heavy bags. "What? Not here yet?"

"No. He must have been delayed by a patient."

"Humpf!"

"I suggested we consult with the stationmaster," Mrs. Fisk said, more firmly this time.

Mrs. Scoggins once more led the way. Hetty was swept along and deposited in front of the high counter with the wooden grill that divided station employees from the common press of travelers. Her escorts clustered about her protectively as they explained her predicament.

"Dr. Ryan?" The man behind the ticket counter peered out at them over his spectacles. "Haven't seen him." He studied Hetty dubiously. "You his be-trothed?" he asked, putting the accent on the first syllable.

Hetty nodded.

"Dr. Ryan oughta be here. Been pesterin' me for a week about the schedules, makin' sure nothin's changed. Said you was comin' in this afternoon."

"Well, I'm here now," Hetty said, buoyed by the knowledge that Michael had been checking on her schedule. "Unfortunately, Dr. Ryan is not. We were hoping you might know where he is."

"Nope. I don't keep track of folks' comin's and goin's. But he's a doctor, ain't he? Who knows with a doctor where he'll be, what with folks gettin' sick and dyin' and havin' babies without consultin' anyone beforehand."

"Of course," Hetty said, trying hard to ignore

the biting little voice inside her head that said Michael should have gotten someone else to take care of his patients, at least long enough for him to meet her train and take her home. "I'll just wait for him here. He's bound to show up any minute."

Hetty brushed aside her newfound friends' concern, and felt a load lift from her shoulders when they eventually gave way to her insistence on remaining at the station alone. Their worries aggravated her own uncertainties. Besides, she preferred to greet Michael without having two interested observers on the scene. Three, she amended silently, thinking of Mr. Fisk.

It wasn't until she peered into the small mirror above the porcelain sink in the ladies' rest room that Hetty realized there were reasons to be grateful for Michael's tardy arrival. A half dozen troublesome curls had escaped from the chignon she'd fashioned with such care that morning. Her bangs, already less than perfectly frizzed for want of a proper curling iron, had started to straggle in damp wisps across her forehead. Her once neat green skirt and jacket were rumpled from hours in the cramped seats, the collar of her shirtwaist had wilted in the heat of the car, and her face . . . !

Hetty grimaced at the dirty face that peered back at her from the mirror and hastily ran cold water into the basin.

When she emerged a quarter of an hour later, considerably refreshed, it was to find the station emptied of all but the man at the ticket counter and a couple of porters who were busy sorting through the packets and boxes and trunks that had arrived with the 3:45. Since there was still no Michael anywhere in sight, Hetty collected her two carpetbags and made arrangements for the temporary storage of her trunks, then settled on one of the hard oak benches near the entrance to await Michael's appearance as patiently as she could.

An hour later, she was still waiting. The porters had finished their sorting; Mr. Davidson, the man at the counter, had given up asking her if she wouldn't like to have someone escort her to a nearby hotel or a boarding house; and Hetty had passed from uncertainty, to doubt, to irritation, and beyond. She was now struggling with a growing urge to box Michael Ryan's ears the first chance she got. The kisses she'd dreamed of for two years could come later.

Mr. Davidson was in the process of sorting through a pile of colored invoices when Hetty marched up to the counter to demand directions to Michael's house.

"Miss?" Mr. Davidson asked, startled. "Are you sure you don't want someone to show you to a good hotel instead?"

Hetty flushed at the unexpressed hint of something scandalous in her request. "No, I don't. Dr. Ryan said he had made arrangements for me to board with a neighbor. Going somewhere else will just confuse things more. So if you know where Dr. Ryan's house is, would you please be so kind as to tell me how to get there?"

"Of course, miss. Whatever you say." Mr. Davidson pushed his glasses back up his nose and came around the counter. From the front of the station, he pointed up the hill to the vast redstone building to the east. "That's the Antlers, ma'am. General Palmer's hotel. They'd likely find you a room, though the price is a bit steep, of course."

The expression on her face must have warned him, for he added hastily, "The Doc's house is right up near the college. Not that far, really. You just go up the hill, then it's maybe . . ." He scrunched up his face, calculating rapidly. "Oh, nine or ten blocks farther north. Or you can take the streetcar on Tejon. Comes by every twenty minutes or so, though it don't go clear to where you're headed. Anyways, Doc's got a little yellow clapboard place used to belong to Doc Cathcart. Can't miss it. It's an . . . er . . . unusual shade of yellow. I understand the paint's a bit of an issue in the neighborhood, but at least it's easy to spot."

Hetty's curiosity was tickled, but she didn't care to take the time to indulge in more questions. "Thank you, Mr. Davidson. If Dr. Ryan should appear, would you please tell him where I've gone?"

"Sure thing, ma'am. Sure you don't want someone to carry your bags, at least?" he added when she retrieved her two well-stuffed carpetbags from in front of the bench where she'd spent the past hour.

"No, thank you, Mr. Davidson. I can manage quite well on my own."

She was regretting her words before she'd gone

four blocks. The hill up to the Antlers had been as steep as it looked, but everything else was flat, with sidewalks and well-tended streets.

The problem was, Colorado Springs seemed to be seriously short on air. Hetty was puffing like a steam engine, and her heart was going even faster by the time she'd gone halfway. Michael had warned her that the higher altitude took some getting used to—Colorado Springs was even higher than Denver, which boasted of its mile-high altitude—but she hadn't really noticed the difference between Boston's sea-level, oxygen-rich air and Colorado's far thinner stuff . . . until now.

But then, she hadn't engaged in anything more strenuous than walking to the dining car until now, either. It was something else altogether to haul two heavy carpetbags filled with clothes, books, and the miscellany she'd considered absolutely essential for survival when she'd packed her things in Boston.

Not that she hadn't had offers of help—the majority of them quite respectable, too. But as Hetty's bags grew heavier and her discomfort increased, so did her irritation with Michael and his failure to at least arrange for her to be met. She declined the respectable offers of assistance, ignored the disreputable, and trudged on, plotting dire revenge on her hapless betrothed.

Mr. Davidson hadn't exaggerated about the house's paint. Hetty suspected that even a dark, moonless night would have been insufficient to disguise the garish yellow-orange color of the siding. The brilliant blue trim at windows and door and the dark green railings on the porch simply added a cheerful note of piquant bad taste to the scene.

If she'd had any lingering doubts that she'd found the right place, there was a small, weather-worn sign tacked to the wall beside the front door. SHERMAN CATHCART, M.D. BY APPOINTMENT ONLY.

So much for keeping up to date. Dr. Cathcart had been dead for almost two years. Michael had written that the majority of his work was tied to the local hospitals or individual referrals for consumptive patients. Judging from his letters, he had more than enough work to keep him busy regardless of whether he kept regular office hours or not. Maybe he hadn't thought it necessary to put up a new sign.

The front door was standing half open, as if inviting her to step inside for a cup of tea and a chat with the house's occupant, but there was no sound from inside, and no indication that anyone was around.

This was Michael's house, but where was Michael?

With a sigh, Hetty pushed open the gate and marched up to the house. Since her hands were full and the door was open, she didn't bother about the social niceties of knocking. She just shoved the door farther open and went right in.

The outer room must originally have been intended for a parlor. Michael—or more likely, Dr. Cathcart—had converted it into a small waiting room furnished with six solid oak chairs, each of venerable provenance and much the worse for wear. One door, firmly shut, led toward the back of the house. A second, half open, led off the makeshift waiting room into what must be Michael's office and examining room, since Hetty could clearly see the edge of an equally battered oak desk through the shadowed opening.

Hetty didn't hesitate. Bags still firmly in hand, she shoved open the door and swept through, only to be brought up short by the sight of Michael, head pillowed on the stack of papers and journals on the desk before him, fast asleep.

# *Chapter Three*

Hetty dropped her bags. The thud they made as they landed should have wakened the dying. Michael didn't so much as twitch.

With deliberate care, Hetty took off her gloves, then her hat, and set them atop her bags. She patted her hair, straightened her jacket, and shook out her skirts. There wasn't much she could do about her dusty hem, but she didn't intend for Michael to have the chance to notice that—at least, not at first.

"Michael Ryan," Hetty said loudly, propping her fists on her hips. "Wake up!"

This time Michael twitched. Then he snorted, shifted position, and immediately fell back asleep.

A jumble of journals, medical texts, and printed extracts covered the desk, creating a hard, untidy pillow for Michael's head. His arms were splayed across the desk on either side. His left hand lay, palm up, on top of the *Colorado Medical Journal*, while *Obstetric Medicine* peeked out from underneath. His cheek was pressed flat against another open journal at an article titled "Complications and Challenges in Dealing with the Premature Birth."

Hetty frowned. No wonder he'd fallen asleep. The titles alone were enough to cure a serious insomniac.

All her doubts and frustrations of the past couple of hours seeped away at the sight of him. Even asleep he looked exhausted. A rough black stubble of day-old beard darkened his jaw, making him appear older than he really was, harder. The bones of his cheek stood out sharply under his skin, his eyes had sunk deep in their sockets, and his eyelids seemed shadowed and heavy, as though weighted down by the short, thick lashes that rimmed them. His thick hair was as black and unruly as ever, but now it was plastered against his skull at the temples and across the brow, as though he'd been sweating and the damp strands had dried there, glued to his skin.

Hetty gently brushed her hand over the thick locks, trying to restore them to order—a hopeless task, even at the best of times. Her fingers trembled.

Two years, yet he hadn't changed. He was still pushing himself too hard, demanding too much of himself, letting others demand even more. And she hadn't been there to protect him, to chide him and tease him and make him laugh, as only she was capable of making him laugh.

Not that she'd had any choice. But now . . .

"Oh, Michael," she whispered, and felt a sudden, intense happiness bubbling up inside her, even as tears stung her eyes. She was here, now and forever. She would protect him from himself and make him laugh and see that he ate properly and slept and took some time for himself. And she would love him, which was all she'd ever wanted to do, for as long as she could remember.

Her heart pounding, Hetty bent and pressed a gentle kiss to his forehead, his cheek, the corner of his mouth.

He stirred then, muttering indistinguishable nothings, and his shoulders shifted beneath his crumpled coat.

"Michael?" Gently, Hetty shook his shoulder, willing him to wake and welcome her. "Michael?"

His eyelids fluttered and opened, but he remained where he was, staring at nothing as awareness slowly returned. Eventually he let out a long, long sigh and slowly raised his head and shoved himself away from the desk. For a moment, he merely sat there, blinking at the untidy pile of papers on his desk like an owl suddenly thrust into the light; then he yawned and started to run a hand through his hair.

Hetty smiled and clasped her hands tightly together, fighting against the urge to laugh that was building within her. In a moment he would come to full consciousness, and then . . .

"Hetty?" His hand froze on the top of his head.

"Hetty!" The last came out in a roar of delight. He surged to his feet. His chair tipped on its back legs, teetered for moment, then crashed to the floor.

Neither of them paid the slightest attention.

Hetty threw herself into his welcoming arms, her sore feet, bedraggled clothes, and earlier abandonment forgotten. He rained kisses on her mouth, her face, her hair, her throat, choking on tears and laughing and repeating her name, over and over and over.

Until that moment, Hetty had thought she knew what true happiness was, but she'd been wrong. She trembled with the sheer joy of his touch, his voice, his lips on hers. Her heart expanded until it threatened to burst her stays in one great explosion of utter wonder.

In all her dreams, in all her hungry rememberings, she had forgotten just how strong he was, how solid and secure his arms felt when they were around her, how incredibly *alive* his slightest touch could make her feel.

Hetty briefly surfaced for air. "If you're trying to apologize for leaving me at the station, you're doing a very good job."

He traced the curve of her jaw below her right ear with the tip of his tongue and made her gasp. "A *very* good job."

His arms tightened around her, crushing her against his chest. "God, Hetty, I'm sorry. I never meant—"

He laughed, but his laughter held a harsh, self-accusatory note that made Hetty flinch and tilt her head back so she could see his face.

"I've been annoying Davidson for days, making sure the schedules hadn't changed, and then—" His hold on her loosened as he met her questioning gaze. "Two years I haven't seen the woman I love and look at me! I haven't bathed—"

Hetty's lips twitched. "I noticed."

"—or shaved."

"I noticed that, too."

"I haven't even brushed my teeth! And don't you dare say you noticed that!" he added, glaring down at her.

Hetty chuckled. "It's a little hard not to, what with all those kisses and—"

"Hetty!" He stared at her for a moment, as if disconcerted by her readiness to agree with his catalog of failures. Then he started laughing. Really laughing, until his face lit up from the happiness inside him. "Oh, Hetty, you're incredible."

"That, too!" Hetty said, dimpling and nodding in ready agreement.

"And you're a fool, Michael Ryan," she chided, drawing his arms around her waist so that there would be no mistaking her meaning. "You not only need to shave and brush your teeth and take a bath, you need to comb your hair and change your shirt for one that doesn't look like you've slept in it for a week. And I don't care about any of it. Not unless it means you won't kiss me some more and hold me tight and—"

A fool he might be, but he was more than willing to comply with her demands.

He was right in the middle of a very convincing

demonstration of just how willing he was, when the sound of someone clearing his throat broke through their concentration.

"Excuse me, Doctor Ryan. I don't mean to interrupt, but you said . . ."

The man standing in the office doorway grimaced, clearly uncomfortable at having interrupted their lovemaking, but equally determined to complete the mission that had brought him there in the first place. Hetty reluctantly slid from Michael's embrace.

"No, please, come in, Mr. Rheiner." Michael hastily tried to straighten his clothes, then gave it up as an impossible task. "How is Mrs. Rheiner? And the baby?"

Hetty blinked, startled by the sudden cool detachment in his voice. It didn't sound like him at all—distant, professional. Emotionless.

She glanced at the visitor, wondering if there was something about the man that would produce such a reaction in Michael.

Mr. Rheiner was short, scarcely taller than Hetty herself, and thin. From overwork and stress, she guessed, rather than from any natural tendency to thinness. His face sagged with the combined effects of exhaustion and worry. His coat hung on him like a sack, even though it must originally have fit across his disproportionately wide shoulders.

He looked, Hetty thought, like a man struggling against adverse circumstances.

He shifted uncomfortably under her scrutiny, then abruptly dragged his worn cap off his head, as though just now realizing he was indoors and in the presence of a lady, regardless of the compromising position in which he'd found her.

"Ruth—Mrs. Rheiner—was sleeping when I left her," Mr. Rheiner said. His work-worn hands twisted and tugged at the cap he held. "The baby." He shrugged, as if dismissing any concern for the baby. The agony in his gray eyes told another tale. "We're keeping her warm. No drafts, like you said, and olive oil for her skin. But she doesn't cry and won't take the cow's milk, no matter what we do. Even if we put honey on the nipple, she won't take it."

He strangled the cap. Michael frowned, but said nothing. Mr. Rheiner shrank under the silent, considering gaze, as if the coldness of it was enough to shrivel him. He swallowed, then reluctantly thrust back his shoulders like a man facing his executioner. "You said there was medicine, Doctor? Something that might help?"

Michael nodded curtly, then leaned past Hetty toward the far corner of his desk where an odd collection of bottles and boxes and small yellow envelopes stood in precise array, like little soldiers in Michael's private army.

"I can't guarantee it," he warned, picking up a small paper packet and a vial of green liquid from the far side of his desk, "Mix the powder with honey and put it on her tongue. The syrup is for Mrs. Rheiner's cough. One spoonful, four times a day. It's new, but it seems to help some people. If that doesn't work . . ."

Michael frowned down at the man. "It's going to be difficult, Mr. Rheiner. Your wife is too weak from her own illness, and the baby . . ." He breathed deeply, then let his breath out through his nose in a gust of frustration. "The baby is much too early."

Mr. Rheiner gulped, too battered by Michael's clipped orders to respond.

If Michael noticed, he gave no sign. He shook his head angrily, as if shaking off a bad dream, and said, "I'll be by later this evening to check on them both."

Mr. Rheiner reached for the medicines Michael extended toward him, then hesitated and looked up into the dark, weary face above him. "I will pay, Dr. Ryan," he said nervously. "As soon as I can. I know my bill's been running up, but Mr. Harrelson at the depot, he said he might have work for me next week. And I have some day work promised—"

Michael brushed his explanation off the way he'd brush off a pesky fly. "I know you'll pay, Mr. Rheiner. That's not important now. What is important is your wife and baby. Use the money you're earning to buy good food for them. Milk and eggs and meat. Fresh fruits and vegetables. You remember?"

Mr. Rheiner nodded unhappily. "I remember." He carefully tucked the precious medicine in his coat pocket. His thin mouth twisted, caught between a hopeful smile and a frown. "I am learning to cook. Samuel, too, even though he's only eight. My wife . . ." He grimaced, embarrassed. "My wife says we are doing much better."

Michael smiled encouragingly, but there was no warmth in it. "Better than I would, I imagine. Now go on. Mrs. Rheiner is probably worrying about you. I'll come by later, I promise."

Michael managed to keep his forced smile up all the way to the front door, but the minute he closed it behind his visitor, the smile vanished and he slumped against the wall, his eyes empty and flat.

Hetty had followed them as far as the office door. Now her gaze met his across the little waiting room.

The silence stretched, filled with a hundred questions and two long years of separation.

"His wife is consumptive," Michael said at last, his words as hard and flat and unemotional as if he were addressing the paint on the opposite wall. "They sold almost everything they had, which wasn't much, and came out here for her health. But ever since the farm they were working on was sold, he's had a hard time finding anything except poor-paying day work. They're living out of their wagon and a shabby tent with a son who should be in school and now a baby who was born too soon. Too soon . . ." He shrugged, as if it didn't matter.

Hetty could feel his fear for the child and its mother. So where did this detached, icy calm come from?

Michael shoved away from the wall, but instead of crossing to her, he turned to stare out the window, as if he expected to see Mr. Rheiner still. His back was to Hetty, his shoulders tense.

Hetty waited.

"I don't know how they'll manage," Michael said at last, his voice flat. "The farmer who owns the land where they're camped isn't charging much, but it's still more than they can afford." He shrugged again. "Better than nothing, I guess. It's not easy to find a place to stay. A lot of folks around here are leery of the 'lungers,' as they call them. There are so many of them, especially families like the Rheiners who don't have much money and no special skills to help them get a good job. They come because they've heard there's a chance, that the air, the mountains—"

The words hung suspended, as if awaiting completion, a fairy-tale ending to the story that only Michael could provide. Instead, Michael suddenly slammed his hand against the wall and spun around to face Hetty.

"Do you know what they find, Hetty?" He was almost shouting. He didn't wait for her to answer.

"Nothing! Nothing but maybes and what-ifs and possibilities that are as likely to fail them as not. They find doctors like me with a hundred journals and not one answer. We grope and flail around and offer a pill or a potion or a prescription for eggs and milk and rest. That's it!"

His mouth twisted in an ugly sneer, but still the words spilled out. "That's all we have, you know. That and our sanctimonious platitudes. And then we send the bill for our services and we say all the right things to the family and maybe we go to the funeral. If we have time. There's nothing else we *can* do. Nothing!"

He stared at her as if he expected her to challenge him, attack him for his failures and those of the medical science he'd dedicated his life to.

She didn't speak or move, too shaken by this unexpected outburst to know what to say or do.

Two long years lay between them, years when she had tended a dying mother and dreamed of a life together and he . . . What had he been doing? What had happened to change her gentle Michael into this cold, angry man?

He shook his head like a man rousing himself from a bad dream. Then, his anger spent, he slowly walked over to one of the battered waiting-room chairs and slumped down in it, shoulders bent, his elbows propped on his knees as if he were too tired to sit upright any longer. He looked up, peering at her from under his disordered thatch of black hair like a repentant sinner asking for understanding . . . or forgiveness.

"She's twenty-eight, Hetty," he said at last, dispiritedly. "Just three years older than you. She's been fighting tuberculosis for the last seven of those years, and she's been losing the fight. They wanted a baby, but she was too weak. I tried to tell them, but . . ."

He shook his head angrily, as if he were trying to shake off the memories of all his futile arguments. "When she got pregnant, I told her she had to rest, lie down. But what was she supposed to do? They needed the money from the laundry and the sewing she took in. And now the baby . . ."

His words trailed off. His gaze dropped and he stared at the floor.

In an instant, Hetty was kneeling beside his chair. "You need a meal, Michael Ryan," she said. "A meal and a bath and a bed. When was the last time you slept?"

"What?" Michael blinked and looked down at her, as if he were seeing her for the first time.

"I said, when was the last time you slept?"

He frowned with the effort of remembering. The corner of his mouth lifted in a wry little smile. "This afternoon about three forty-five. As you should know, Miss Malone."

Hetty smiled back. "I'm surprised you'd risk reminding me. Besides this afternoon, I mean. When was the last time you got a chance to sleep?"

He dragged a hand down his cheek, considering. Hetty could hear the scrape of his palm across his day-old beard and sternly repressed an urge to run her own hand across that beloved cheek and along that lean jaw.

"I'm not really sure," he admitted at last, reluctantly. "Last night I spent delivering the Rheiners' baby, and the night before that . . . Well, I got a couple hours of sleep, anyway, before I was dragged out for a crisis." The shadows deepened at the memory. "And before that—"

"Just as I thought," Hetty said briskly, before he could dwell on whatever failure he was going to accuse himself of in that case. "And instead of getting a proper meal and some decent sleep, when you came back from the Rheiners' this morning you dragged out your journals and started studying, just in case you'd missed something that might help Mrs. Rheiner or her baby."

He started guiltily.

"That means, unless I miss my guess," she continued, "that you didn't get any supper last night, or breakfast this morning, or probably anything else, for that matter. But we can remedy that, I think."

She sprang to her feet, but Michael was quicker. In one smooth motion he wrapped his arm around her and dragged her into his lap.

"Bossing me around already, are you, Hetty Malone?" he demanded. He grinned down at her wickedly, but there was a hunger and a longing in him that ran far deeper than the laughter. Hetty could see it in the tension at the corner of his mouth, in the way his brows tightened into furrows over the sharp bridge of his nose.

His mouth came down over hers before she had a chance to reply. His lips were hard and demanding and they marked her instantly.

Like spark to dry tinder, his heat ignited hers. With a moan that was an admission of her own longing, her own need for him, she threw her arms about his neck and pulled him closer still, as demanding in her need as he was in his.

Hetty had thought she knew what kissing was. She'd thought that she and Michael had explored all the possibilities that were available to a man and a woman who were not yet wed.

She'd been wrong.

Two years and two thousand miles made a lot of difference in what a man expected out of a kiss . . . and what a woman found in it. Their kisses in that first startled, joyous embrace had been mere prelude. These were kisses that spoke of hunger and hope and longing, of all the promises they had made and that yet lay before them, awaiting fulfillment. These were kisses of fire, and salt tears, and a deeper, more passionate need, a woman's need . . . and a man's.

It was Michael who broke off at last, and Hetty who whimpered and sought to draw him back to her. He wrapped his arms about her and drew her head against his shoulder. His chest heaved with his efforts to draw breath, and his hand trembled as he pressed it against her cheek to hold her tightly against him.

"Ah, Hetty! It's been so long, and I've missed you so much! So much!"

"I have your letters. All of them," Hetty said to his vest, suddenly too shy to face his scrutiny. Her voice trembled with her own inner tumult as she clung to him, shaken by the power of the need that had taken her by storm.

"They were sorry little scraps, I know," Michael said, settling her more comfortably in his lap with her legs dangling over the worn wooden arm of the chair. "I always meant to write more, but somehow . . ." His words trailed off.

"I loved every one of them. I've read them so often, the oldest ones are worn thin at the creases," Hetty admitted. "Though I probably shouldn't tell you that, because then you'll get a swelled head and start thinking too much of yourself."

"No chance of that, now you're here to keep me in line. Two years . . ." The last word came out almost as a sigh. Hetty could feel his breath stirring her hair, the way a faint breeze stirred the grass, gently, gently.

Hetty laughed, because she didn't want him to be sad, and pushed herself away from his chest so that she sat as upright and dignified as was possible, under the circumstances. "Well, now I *am* here—no thanks to you, I might add!—and I mean to make sure you don't leave me at the train station ever again!"

She blinked and gently touched a finger to the edge of his mouth, tracing its curve. His beard grated against her finger. The sound of it sent a hungry shiver down her spine. "I won't let you leave me ever again, Michael Ryan. And that's a promise!"

"It's not one you'll have much trouble keeping, Hetty." His gaze fixed on her brow, her eyes, her nose. It fixed on her mouth, and he smiled. It slid down her throat, her breast, her legs, so indecorously propped over the chair's arm.

Michael got to his feet and with one easy tug drew her back against him.

Hetty could feel the hard length of him, the comforting width of his shoulders as his arms enclosed her. She wrapped her hands about his and gladly leaned into his warmth.

"We'll never get you fed at this rate," she said,

trying to be practical even though she would happily have starved as long as Michael was holding her.

"I'm feasting on you." He sighed and let his chin rest on the crown of her head.

"I'm so glad you're here, Hetty. So very, very glad."

# Chapter Four

Michael's tiny kitchen was stocked with an old stove, a small table with three mismatched chairs, a much-used coffee pot, a couple of apples, and dust. The shelves in the narrow pantry offered up more dust and one rusted, battered muffin tin.

Only the bath, tucked in a tiny room that opened into the back hallway, was modern and clean. Better yet, it was equipped with a small gas water heater that connected to the kitchen, as well as to the bath and sink. In Hetty's eyes, that more than made up for the kitchen's deficiencies.

While Michael shaved and tried to restore some order to his appearance, Hetty made a fresh pot of coffee. Her own ablutions at the train station would have to serve until she was installed in Mrs. Spencer's boarding house, where Michael had reserved a room for her and to which he would conduct her as soon as he was once more fit to appear in public.

Hetty frowned down at the cup in her hand. He needed a decent meal and some sleep, but he'd been adamant that coffee would be enough, just to tide him over until he could join her for dinner at Mrs. Spencer's.

"Are my sins really *that* grave, Hetty? You're frowning as hard as a preacher at a revival meeting."

He stood in the doorway, freshly shaved and neatly attired in a crisp white shirt and properly pressed, dark gray vest. He'd even managed to comb his hair into some semblance of order. But a shave and clean clothes could not erase the dark shadows around his eyes and in the hollows of his cheeks. He looked . . .

Hetty drew in a deep breath. He looked like heaven.

For a long, long while, he simply stood in the open doorway looking back; then his eyes crinkled into a smile. He sniffed the air.

"That coffee smells good."

Hetty started to rise, but he waved her back into her chair.

"I'll get it." He picked up the cup she'd set out for him and poured some for himself. Black, without sugar or cream. Hetty winced as he took a swig of the hot liquid. She'd intentionally made it strong, for his sake, but she'd been grateful to find a small bowl half-filled with crusted sugar to sweeten her own cup.

"Ah, that's good. You always did make good coffee, Hetty."

"Not that strong."

"No?" He studied his cup, one eyebrow cocked inquisitively. "Well, it's good, regardless."

With one easy motion, he pulled out the chair beside her and sat down. He cradled the cup of hot coffee in his hands, but his gaze was fixed on her. The very faintest of smiles touched his lips as he stared.

Hetty smiled back, suddenly uncertain what to say next.

"I was just thinking," he said at last. "About how wonderful it is to have you sitting at my kitchen table. And how much more wonderful it will be when I can see you sitting at it every morning for . . ." His voice trailed off, as if the words he'd found were too precious to be given up so easily.

Hetty waited.

"For forever," he said at last, with satisfaction.

She smiled. "For forever." She lifted her heavy crockery mug in a toast. They clunked—the cheap, heavy porcelain would never clink—and drank to the future.

"And in the meantime, you need to eat." Hetty pushed the chipped blue plate with the two apples she'd polished in front of him, then handed him the knife she'd dug out of the drawer in the table.

Michael laughed. "You aren't going to turn practical and sensible on me in your old age, are you, Hetty?"

"You'll never know if you die of starvation and exhaustion first," she retorted. "Eat."

She'd sliced thousands of apples in her lifetime and watched her mother and neighbors slice thousands more, so why, Hetty wondered, did she suddenly find the simple act of watching him slice the first apple so . . . compelling?

His long, beautifully shaped hand cradled the apple as he cut it in half, then half again. Juice beaded on the shiny red surface and dribbled down his fingers. He set the quarters on the plate, then, one by one, picked them up and neatly trimmed out the seed-speckled cores before slicing them again into three tidy slices each.

Hetty watched as he bit into the last slice he'd cut. His teeth, so white and even, snapped the slice in half. The muscles of his mouth and jaw worked as he chewed, their movement visible beneath the smooth-shaven skin.

"Hmmm. Good apple." He sighed, then bit into another slice. "I hadn't realized how hungry I was."

He licked the juice-stained tips of his fingers, and Hetty jumped, startled by the burst of heat the slight gesture roused in her.

The motion caught Michael's attention. "Would you like one? It's very good." He picked up a slice and offered it to her.

Hetty eyed it, acutely conscious of his nearness and her own intense awareness. Her hesitation was a mistake. Michael's eyes widened as he suddenly realized the potent possibilities of his simple gesture.

Slowly, and with infinite care, he lowered the slice of temptation to his plate. For a moment his hand hovered, the tips of his fingers almost touching the abandoned half-moon of fruit.

To Hetty, it seemed as if time had slowed until each second dripped past like honey, thick and slow and heavy with its sweetness. Details stood out. The sharp lines of bone beneath the surface of his hands. The hard knob of each knuckle. The springy arc of dark hairs against lighter skin, which made the starched white stiffness of his cuff seem even stiffer and whiter.

Hetty realized suddenly that she could hear the faint, starchy crackle of his shirt as his broad chest rose, then fell with each breath he took.

His fingers trembled, ever so slightly. He took a gulp of air, like a drowning man fighting back to the surface. His hand clenched into a fist an instant before he snatched it off the table and shoved it into his lap, out of sight.

He took a deeper breath, then another. Then he swallowed, hard, and met her wide-eyed gaze.

Hetty hung suspended, like a honeybee trapped in that golden, timeless honey, and all she could think was that she wished she'd taken that slice of apple. Her mouth watered at the thought of the juicy flesh.

"Hetty?" He said it hesitantly, as if he'd had to force her name past a throat grown suddenly tight.

"Yes?"

"How soon . . ." He swallowed and Hetty

watched, fascinated, as his Adam's apple bobbed. "How soon do you think we can get married?"

The streets between Michael's and Mrs. Spencer's boarding house were as dry and winter-brown as everything else, but Hetty floated all the way over nevertheless.

A marriage license. A church. She and Michael had discussed them all while sitting in his shabby little kitchen sharing the coffee, the meager portions of apple, and a love they'd found had stretched across two years and half a continent.

Mrs. Michael Ryan. Hetty rolled it around in her mind, savoring the sound of it. The Doc's wife. She smiled and glanced up at Michael. His head was up and he was staring straight ahead with the slightly vague air of a man whose thoughts were elsewhere, the faintest trace of a smile on his lips.

The inside of her mouth tingled suddenly with the memory of the long, deep kiss he'd lavished on her there at the kitchen table. The taste of it still lingered on her tongue—coffee and tart apple and the faintest trace of mint tooth powder. And beneath it all, the dark, heady taste of Michael himself.

If it wouldn't have made entirely the wrong impression on anyone watching, Hetty would have skipped. She would have jumped up high enough to click her heels together. She would have shouted from the sheer excitement of it all.

*I'm going to be Mrs. Michael Ryan! I'm going to be married!*

For Michael's sake, however, she would try to restrain herself. She had his reputation to think of, after all. It wasn't going to be easy, but she really would try.

At the unspoken promise, Hetty straightened her shoulders and held her head just a little higher. Dignity. That was the ticket. All the doctor's wives she'd known back in Boston had said so, and they ought to know, because most of them had been married to their husbands for forever.

It was Michael who shattered all her good intentions.

He chuckled. Just a little chuckle, as if it had popped up in his throat by mistake. Hetty looked up at him. He glanced down at her.

That faint smile he'd been wearing widened and the chuckle grew louder, until it rattled around in his chest like a rambunctious genie trying to get loose. He stopped square in his tracks, beamed down at her like a man demented, and then suddenly gave a terrific, wild whoop and swept Hetty into his arms, despite the two heavy carpetbags that he held in his hand.

"Hetty, Hetty, Hetty," he laughed, swinging her in a circle while her bags bumped and thumped against her fanny and the backs of her legs. "Married! At last!"

Hetty would have said "Amen!" to that, but he didn't give her a chance. Right there, in front of God and the neighbors, he gave her a kiss hot enough to make her shoe buttons sizzle.

By the time they arrived at Mrs. Spencer's front

door, Hetty was flushed and disheveled, but she didn't care. Not, that is, until she faced the round-faced woman with the crimped bangs and starched lace collar who opened the door to them. That stern visage made her sober immediately.

"Dr. Ryan! And you must be Miss Malone!" With immense dignity, the woman swung the door wide. "We've been waiting for you. Indeed we have! Come in!"

Blinking against the abrupt transition from sun to shadow, Hetty stepped into the dark-paneled hallway. She repressed a strong urge to peek into the mirror of the massive oak hall tree to assure herself that Michael had left no visible traces of his kisses even if he *had* set her hat slightly askew, but she couldn't help glancing around at the somber, imposing residence that was to be her home for the next few days.

To her left was a large parlor, filled to overflowing with dark, velvet-covered sofas and carved wooden tables covered with bric-a-brac. Heavy velvet drapes backed by sheer lace curtains cut down the light from the tall windows. To her right, sliding double doors had been drawn shut, further blocking the light. From behind the doors, she caught a soft murmur, as if someone on the other side were reading aloud, but she couldn't make out the words.

Mrs. Spencer shut the front door firmly behind them, then moved close and said in a low voice, "Actually, I'm very glad you're here, Dr. Ryan. I have some new guests you should see. Two brothers. The eldest is extremely ill."

Her stern face took on a grimmer cast as her gaze turned to the sliding doors, then back to Michael. "Normally I wouldn't have taken in someone who's that far gone, but . . . well, he said that you were to come see him. I wouldn't want to turn away one of your patients. Not if I have room, you understand."

All the happiness drained out of Michael's face, to be replaced by an expression of horror. "I forgot. I was called away for Mrs. Rheiner and when I got back late this morning, I . . ."

His features hardened, and his expression grew cold. "If you will introduce me, please, Mrs. Spencer?" He set Hetty's bags down; then, without a word or a glance for Hetty, he followed Mrs. Spencer into the room on the right.

Just before she slid the doors shut behind her, Mrs. Spencer threw Hetty a stiff, apologetic little smile and motioned her into the parlor.

Hetty settled on a ponderous stuffed chair that gave her a view of the sliding doors. When Mrs. Spencer slipped out of the room a few minutes later, Hetty caught a glimpse of the room's occupants. One sat propped up against pillows in a high bed. His face was so pale and wasted that for a moment Hetty thought he was dead. The other, only slightly less cadaverous-looking than his brother, stood at the head of the bed, his attention fixed on Michael, who was taking the bedridden man's pulse. Mrs. Spencer coolly slid the doors shut behind her, cutting off Hetty's view.

Something of Hetty's shock must have shown

on her face, for when Mrs. Spencer settled onto the sofa near Hetty's chair, she said, "You needn't be concerned, Miss Malone. They won't be with us much longer. The one won't last more than a few days. His brother won't survive him by a month."

Hetty stiffened, shocked at the blunt comment.

Mrs. Spencer didn't notice. Her attention was focused on the closed doors across from them. "I don't like to take them when they're that ill, you understand. My other guests don't like it. They don't like it at all. Unfortunately, there aren't many places they *can* stay, and if Dr. Ryan says he will attend them . . ."

She shrugged. "At least I can usually count on Dr. Ryan to come when he's called. That's better than some."

"Do you mean to say that people would deny those poor men a place to stay?" Hetty demanded indignantly.

Mrs. Spencer looked at her, eyes wide with surprise. "But of course they would. When they're that far gone, you understand. Even the hospitals don't like to take them because there's nothing they can do but watch them die."

The gold pendant watch pinned to her bosom glinted as she gave a sigh that was carefully calculated to hint at the tribulations she suffered. "It can be very difficult. Of course, these gentlemen have the money to pay for the additional care they need and to cover the trouble they cause. I wouldn't have taken them in, otherwise. Not everyone is so . . . fortunate."

Hetty bit back the words of shock and disgust that threatened to spill off her tongue. The uncaring, calculating tone of Mrs. Spencer's words appalled her, but there was nothing she could do to change matters. At least, not yet.

"But that's neither here nor there," Mrs. Spencer added briskly. "They won't bother you. You'll probably never see them, except maybe when you're going in and out. I've given you a lovely room at the back. Very quiet, and there's a nice view of the Peak through the trees. I'm sure you'll be very comfortable."

Mrs. Spencer's eyebrows arched. "Until you get settled elsewhere, that is."

She looked at Hetty expectantly, clearly anxious to hear all the details of the coming nuptials.

The stark contrast between her curiosity toward Hetty and her cool indifference to the brothers' suffering made Hetty's gorge rise.

Was this what happened, Hetty wondered, when a city had so many invalids? Did people become indifferent to the sufferers themselves and begin to think of them only as customers and boarders, desirable if they weren't too ill and could pay their bills, unwanted if they were dying and poor?

Before she could betray herself, the doors slid open again and Michael emerged. Once more Hetty had a quick glimpse of the room's occupants. She looked away before Michael could close the doors behind him, suddenly ashamed for having intruded, even as an observer, on the agony and the despair that were so clearly graven on the brothers' faces.

Without a backward glance, Michael came across the room toward them. Hetty cringed at the angry self-condemnation in his eyes.

"I have to fetch my medical bag. You'll be all right, Hetty?" He didn't wait for an answer. "I'll rejoin you for dinner."

"Yes, all right." Hetty wasn't even sure he heard.

Without another word, he turned and left. Hetty flew out of her chair after him. She reached him just as he stepped out onto the broad front porch.

"Michael, wait," she said urgently, drawing the door shut behind her. She kept her voice low so her words wouldn't carry to any listening ears. "You were distracted, Michael, exhausted. You wouldn't have forgotten to come, otherwise."

He flinched as if she'd struck him, then swung around to face her, his lean body rigid with fury. "But I *did* forget, Hetty. They asked for my help and I forgot them."

Hetty quailed under his anger, even though she knew it was not directed at her. "Will they . . . Will they be all right?"

Michael stiffened. For a minute, she didn't think he'd answer. "Tell Mrs. Spencer it won't be long before she can rent that room again. A few weeks, at most."

With that, he turned and stalked away.

* * *

Michael didn't come for dinner. Mrs. Spencer even agreed, reluctantly, to set aside a plate in the warming oven at the top of the vast black stove in the kitchen, but he still didn't come. At ten, Hetty despondently trailed up to her room.

She'd missed him when he'd returned with his medical bag. He'd spent a half hour with the Turner brothers, then slipped away without a word to her. There was his promise to visit the Rheiners again, of course. Hetty tried not to think of what disaster might have befallen that poor family to keep Michael with them through a second night. Or perhaps he'd been called to yet another patient's bedside, and then decided that it was too late and he was too tired to call on her again that evening.

Of course. That was it. Hetty plucked the hairpins from her hair, one by one, and carefully laid them in the small bowl set on the top of the dressing table in her room. He'd simply returned too late. Mrs. Spencer wouldn't approve of his disturbing the household past nine o'clock.

Somehow, even that thought didn't ease Hetty's loneliness. Until she'd boarded the train in Boston, she'd never slept any place except in her own home, her own bed. Now she was alone in a houseful of strangers. The comfortable room with its promised view of the Peak felt unwelcoming and cold in spite of the afternoon heat that still lingered here at the top of the house.

Hetty tried not to think about it as she dutifully brushed her hair the requisite hundred strokes, then braided it and, with one last check to be sure she'd put her things neatly away, turned off the gas lamp and crawled into the high, narrow bed.

Around her, the darkness pulsed, alive with the faint sounds of the house and its occupants as they settled for the night. From down the hall she heard the roar as the toilet flushed, then the creak of the bathroom door and soft footsteps padding along the hallway until another door creaked open, and closed. Voices murmured near the top of the stairs, then died away.

With trembling hands, Hetty drew the blankets up to her chin. Michael would come for breakfast, of course. Mrs. Spencer had said he'd asked her and she'd told him he could. Not that Hetty really wanted to see him with so many other strangers gathered around the same table, but it was something to look forward to, something that could help her get through the still, dark hours of the night that lay ahead.

Tomorrow he would arrange for their marriage license. Tomorrow . . .

She drifted into sleep, clinging to that thought.

Mrs. Spencer's was dark when Michael pulled up in front a little after eleven. Not even one small light glowed behind drawn curtains to relieve the stark black bulk of the boarding house.

The horse from the livery stable blew noisily, then cocked his hip and drooped in the traces. Michael knew how he felt.

He didn't mind a long, hard day if at the end of it he could be sure his efforts had counted for something. He thrived on that kind of challenge.

But the past few days had been as long and hard as any he could remember, and his efforts hadn't amounted to a hill of beans.

Forget the sleepless night he'd spent attending Mary Rheiner and her baby. Forget his having slept through Hetty's arrival.

Michael winced. No, don't forget that, even if Hetty had forgiven him for it. Two years. Two long, lonely years without her laughter, and he hadn't even managed to meet her train.

He dragged a tired hand down his face, then dug his knuckles into his eyes and rubbed hard, trying to rub out the grittiness and ache of too little sleep.

He ought to go home and go to bed. Forget about today and yesterday and the day before that. Forget about everything, at least for a while.

Except Hetty. He didn't want to forget the way she'd felt in his arms when he'd kissed her, the way she'd tasted. He didn't want to forget the wide-eyed wonder of her as she'd watched him slice the apple she'd polished with such care.

His tired body ached, suddenly, with the hunger that had tormented him ever since he'd left her to come West. He shifted on the hard seat and arched his back, tensing his muscles against the ache and the cold and the exhaustion.

There had been times when he'd thought he'd give up. Abandon his patients, the practice Dr. Cathcart had left him, everything . . . just so he could go home. So he could go back to Hetty.

Michael stared at the black, blank facade of the house and wondered which room was hers. The one at the top, maybe, in a corner where she'd catch the breeze. Or maybe on the first floor—

Michael's fingers tightened around the reins, but the horse was too tired to notice. Not the first floor. Mrs. Spencer only had one room on the first floor to let, and the Turner brothers were occupying that. The two brothers he'd forgotten. The brothers who had come West too late for the dry Colorado air to have a chance of healing their damaged lungs.

Michael stared at the unlit windows, thinking of the two young men behind them whose futures could now be measured in days and weeks, seeing again their strained and hollowed faces, the way they'd clung to each other as he'd told them what they already knew and had not dared admit, even to themselves.

Perhaps there was something their doctors hadn't tried, something that—

Michael savagely cut the thought short. There was nothing. No medicines, no treatments, no miracles. James and Jacob Turner would die of tuberculosis and there was nothing he could do for them except ease the pain of their dying.

The horrible waste of it all made him angry. And when he was angry, he tended to dig in his heels and fight even harder.

But how did you fight an enemy you couldn't even see?

# *Chapter Five*

Michael presented himself on Mrs. Spencer's doorstep the next morning at precisely a quarter to seven. He'd shaved with care, put on a freshly starched shirt and clean suit and tried, albeit without success, to plaster his hair into place with White Rose hair oil. In one hand he carried a small bouquet of dried flowers he'd begged from his neighbor. He hoped it would encourage Hetty to overlook the medical bag in his other hand.

Before he could knock, the door swung wide.

Michael's breath caught in his throat. He'd expected Mrs. Spencer to open the door, but it was Hetty who stood there, caught in the morning sunlight streaming through the open door. Like an angel at the heavenly gates, he thought, then wondered if the thought was blasphemy. He took a closer look, and decided it was not. The angels would be flattered by the comparison.

"I was watching from the parlor window," she admitted shyly, a hint of pink in her cheeks. Her smile was as radiant as a blessing, and Michael felt the glow of it melt the accumulated doubts in his breast.

But Hetty, shy?

Footsteps sounded in the depths of the hall behind Hetty, shattering the moment. Michael stiffened. He'd forgotten that his beloved was not welcoming him to her home, but into a boarding house where unseen strangers could observe them from dark corners and his every word would be fodder for gossip and speculation.

The reminder took some of the sparkle out of the morning. Breakfast with Hetty would not be the simple, intimate meal he'd been imagining all morning, but a clattering circus with the two of them the main attraction.

"Michael?" Hetty said gently.

Michael awkwardly thrust the flowers at her. "I . . . I'm sorry, Hetty," he faltered. The paper around the stems rustled in protest at his death grip. "About last night, I mean. And about forgetting to meet you at the station. And—"

"That's all right," Hetty said, rescuing the abused flowers before he crushed them utterly. "I understand."

She dropped her gaze to his peace offering. "They're very pretty."

It *wasn't* all right. Michael could feel her lingering hurt and confusion, even if she hadn't set them out on public display.

Explaining his plans for the day to her was going to be more difficult than he'd anticipated.

"You'd better come in," she added, more briskly this time. "Mrs. Spencer doesn't like to let the cold in."

It was only when he'd set his black bag down on the seat of the hall tree and reached for his hat that Michael realized he'd forgotten that essential item of masculine attire.

"I don't know why you bother. You're always losing them, anyway," Hetty said at his elbow, the barest hint of laughter in her voice. She'd come close, so close she had to tilt her head back to look up at him.

Somewhere deep inside Michael a hungry fire sprang to tormenting life. He drew an unsteady breath, fighting for control.

More footsteps echoed, this time in the upper hall. Michael was vaguely aware of the smell of biscuits baking and bacon frying, of voices in the kitchen at the back of the house and the steady thunk-thunk-thunk as the housemaid set the breakfast plates around the table in the dining room. Not two feet away, the door to the Turner brothers' room stood closed, so near that he might almost hear the rustle of bedsheets if he tried.

The combination made an uncomfortable counterpoint to his intense, unsettling awareness of Hetty . . . and the lustful thoughts it engendered.

"You know what your problem is, Michael?"

Hetty's eyebrows arched upward over eyes that sparkled, even in the dim hallway, and her mouth curved in a teasing smile. "You need coffee. Hot and black."

She dragged him into the parlor and, after firmly instructing him to sit, disappeared in the direction of the kitchen, bearing the mangled flowers with her. She reappeared a couple of minutes later with a steaming mug in her hand.

"You're not to speak another word before you've drunk that," she admonished him sternly. "I'll have to remember that, once we're married. No conversation before the first cup of coffee."

Michael abruptly buried his nose in his mug and took an enormous gulp. The coffee almost burned his throat on its way down, but even its heat couldn't compete against the thought of marriage and Hetty and mornings. Or rather, what would precede those mornings once they were man and wife.

The announcement that breakfast was served, immediately followed by a stampede of hungry boarders headed for the dining room, prevented Michael from making any greater fool of himself than he already had.

Hunger—the empty-belly kind of hunger—helped Michael survive breakfast, but even a full belly didn't make it any easier to face Hetty's indignation when he explained his plans for the day.

"What do you mean you will be occupied all day, Michael Ryan?" she demanded sharply. "I didn't come two thousand miles just so I could sit in Mrs. Spencer's parlor, you know."

They had retreated to the barren flower garden at the side of the house where they were less likely to be overheard, but even the tangled shadows cast by the bare limbs of the elm at the side of the plot couldn't disguise the stubborn set of Hetty's chin.

"I have patients, commitments, responsibilities, Hetty," Michael said, just as sharply. "I can't ignore them, just because they're inconvenient."

"But you can ignore *me*, is that it?"

"I'm not ignoring you!" Michael exploded. "I told you—"

"Right. You told me. You also forgot me at the train station, didn't show up for supper last night, and now you're saying you're going to be busy all day and I'll just have to find something to do to entertain myself in the meantime. Well, it's not going to work that way, Michael Ryan, no matter what you say!"

"Hetty—!"

"Don't 'Hetty' me!"

"Look," Michael said, striving to keep his voice at a reasonable level. "I have to check on the Turner brothers, visit Mrs. Rheiner, then—"

"So why can't I go with you to the Rheiners?"

"But—"

"I'll bet Mr. Rheiner could use a little help. I could fix them a meal, maybe, or help wash out a few baby clothes. There are probably a dozen things you men have never thought of that need doing. I—"

"Hetty!" Michael roared. "Would you please let me get a word in?"

Hetty's chin set more firmly still and her eyes narrowed distrustfully as she glared at him. "Not if you're going to keep being unreasonable, Michael Ryan."

"I'm not—"

"Of course you are."

"Hetty!"

This last was directed at her back because she'd already stalked off. She stopped at the edge of the garden and turned to glare at him.

"I'm going to get my hat and my bag, Michael Ryan. I'll be waiting on the front steps for you as soon as you've finished with the Turners."

And with that she turned back around and marched off.

Michael stood glaring after her, speechless.

He didn't want her with him on his rounds. It wasn't right. It wasn't proper. It wasn't professional.

It wasn't . . . safe.

And it wasn't the risk of infection that worried him.

Hetty sat beside Michael on the narrow buggy seat, but they might have been at opposite ends of the universe for all the pleasure Michael seemed to take from the situation. He had emerged from the Turner brothers' room in a grim mood, and all her efforts to divert his thoughts into more cheerful channels had failed.

His withdrawal puzzled her. They'd seldom

quarreled, but when they had, Michael had always been more than willing to hold up his side of the argument. When pushed, he could shout louder, stomp harder, and swear longer and far more fluently than she could, but he hadn't resorted to any of those tactics to get his way this time.

She'd half expected him to drive out the opposite end of the livery stable and leave her, so when he'd pulled the horse to a halt and held out his hand to help her into the buggy, she'd concluded—erroneously, it seemed—that he was willing to make peace.

He wasn't even willing to talk.

His reticence worried her, more especially because she didn't think it was really due to her insistence on accompanying him. There was something more than that, something deeper, but she didn't have the slightest notion what it might be, and she didn't have a hope of finding out if he refused to talk to her.

The day was too beautiful, the scenery too breathtaking, and Michael's company too welcome, silent or not, for Hetty to worry much. She'd figure out what the problem was eventually. So long as Michael loved her—and she was very sure he did—everything else, no matter how terrible, was manageable.

By the time they reached the farm along the Fountain River where the Rheiners were staying, Hetty had fallen irretrievably in love with her new home. There was a raw grandeur, a sweep about this country that was as different from Boston as night from day. This late in the year, the wild grasses that swept away to the horizon were dried to a golden brown, but above it all towered the purple-blue bulk of Pikes Peak, traces of snow visible on its crest.

The Rheiners had chosen a grassy, protected clearing for their camp. Huge cottonwoods on all sides would cast welcome shade in the summer, while the lazy rattling of the dead leaves that still hung on the branches made a soothing background harmony with the nearby river. Two rawboned sorrel draft horses were staked out at the far side of the clearing, hips cocked and heads drooping. The only sign that they were alive was an occasional twitch or a lazy swish of their tails.

A farm wagon with a canvas cover stood near a large, square tent. A black chimney protruded from the top of the tent, the outlet, no doubt for a camp-sized cookstove. On the open ground between the tent and the wagon, a ring of stones marked the regular site of a campfire. Someone had made the effort to drag the massive trunk of a fallen cottonwood to one side of the fire. At night the trunk undoubtedly served as table and chairs for the family, but right now its surface was covered by a collection of ragged towels and indeterminate scraps of cloth that were draped over it, drying in the sun.

At the sound of the buggy rattling across the hard ground, a tousle-headed boy poked his head out of the wagon. A moment later, Mr. Rheiner emerged from the tent and stood, one hand shading his eyes, watching their approach.

"Miss," Mr. Rheiner said politely as he helped her out of the buggy. The minute she was firmly on the ground, he stepped away and reached for a hat that wasn't there. The discovery that he would have nothing to hang on to seemed to unsettle him even more than her unexpected arrival. After an instant's painful hesitation, he shoved his hands into his pockets and hunched his shoulders, careful not to meet her gaze.

Michael climbed down behind her. "How are they?" he asked, turning to pull his medical bag out from under the seat. "Is there any change from last night?"

"The baby took a bit of milk this morning out of the dropper, but she spit it right back up. We've been giving her the syrup and putting that honey and powder on her tongue, just like you said."

"Is there any change?"

The man hesitated. "She's still breathing."

A muscle at the corner of Michael's jaw jumped, but all he said was, "I see."

Without another word, he strode toward the tent, lifted the flap, and ducked inside. Mr. Rheiner followed behind uncertainly, as if debating whether his presence was required—or even wanted.

Hetty stared after them, troubled by the exchange between the two men, uncertain what it meant and if there was anything she could do about it.

"Ma'am. Ma'am?"

The boy who had poked his nose out of the wagon on their arrival was now hovering near the back of the buggy, wary as a rabbit out of its burrow but clearly anxious to have a word with her.

He was thin and gawky and beautiful in the way all young boys are beautiful. His blond hair looked as if it had been combed by a high wind, his shirt sleeves missed reaching his wrists by an inch, and his pants, carefully patched at the knees, gaped a good three inches above his scrawny ankles. He looked like any gangly boy his age except for the shadows that lurked at the back of his pale blue eyes.

One of Hetty's heartstrings quivered. How old had Mr. Rheiner said his son was? Eight? She held out her hand and smiled. "Hello. My name's Hetty Malone. What's yours?"

"Samuel," the boy said shyly, coming forward to take her hand. "Samuel Rheiner. Pleased to meetcha."

Hetty waited, wondering what would come next, but Samuel's reserves of courage had evidently been tried to their maximum in confronting her in the first place. He fidgeted and chewed his lower lip and stared at her, wide-eyed, as if pleading for help.

"I'm sorry to hear your mother isn't feeling well," Hetty said, choosing her words with care.

Samuel's neck sank into his shoulders and his eyes grew wider still, but he didn't cry. The great big gulp he took sucked the tears back down where they wouldn't embarrass a grown-up, eight-year-old boy.

"Da says she'll be all right, her and my sister," he said, clearly anxious to reassure himself as much as her. "He says Dr. Ryan's the best there is, better'n everybody else for folks as are sick like my mom. That's what Mrs. Carter says, too, and the other ladies from the church who come visitin' every week. And Da says . . . He says it's gonna be all right 'cause Dr. Ryan gave us the medicines and all and told him what to do."

Another heartstring quivered, then broke. Hetty nodded. "I'm sure Dr. Ryan will give you the very best advice possible."

Samuel nodded back. "Yup. That's what Da says. And Ma, she says even old Dr. Franklin back home never helped her half as much as Dr. Ryan. Not half! And he never came to visit as often as Dr. Ryan, neither."

"Well, I'd say your mother's pretty lucky to have you around to help, too. I met your father yesterday, and he said you were even learning to cook! That's mighty impressive for a boy your age!"

That was entirely the wrong thing to say. To Hetty's dismay, Samuel's pale eyes started to glitter with incipient tears. He blinked them back, however, and plunged forward.

"Well that's sorta . . . I'm tryin', but . . ."

Hetty placed a comforting hand on his shoulder. "It's not easy. You should have seen the messes I made when I was learning. But you'll get the hang of it eventually. You'll see."

Samuel brightened. "I was hopin' . . . That is, I wondered if you'd help me, ma'am. If it's not a bother. Da says it's not right to bother folks, but I thought—"

"Of course I'll help if I can. Just lead the way."

He led her to the wagon, then climbed up over the high tail gate as quick as the monkey Hetty had seen once in a circus, years before. He appeared a moment later with a fat book and a thin journal with frayed edges and a broken spine in his hands. A moment later he was on the ground and offering the journal to Hetty.

"It was my gran's," he said. "She kept all her receipts and stuff in there and Ma says there's nobody cooked as good as Gran." He blushed. "I didn't know her. She died before I was born, but that's what Ma says. An' I thought maybe I could make up one of her receipts. You know, like Da and me have been learnin' to do outta this book."

He waved the fat book he held, which Hetty recognized as one of the modern cooking and household management books that had become so common.

"Trouble is," Samuel added forlornly, "I can't read nothin' in Gran's book. I thought maybe it'd be like Ma's, but . . ." He shrugged, embarrassed by his failure. "I thought maybe you could help me figure it out, so's I wouldn't have to bother Da about it."

Hetty nodded in understanding and opened the aged journal. Neat lines of script marched across the yellowed pages in ink that had turned a pale purple-brown with age. The script *was* hard to read, but when she tilted the journal to get a different angle of sunlight, she realized the problem wasn't the pale ink.

"I'm sorry, Samuel. I can't read it either. It's in German. Maybe you can find a lady in church who can read it for you. I'll ask around, but I'm new in town and I don't know many people, so . . ."

Samuel's shoulders drooped. "That's okay. I just thought—"

"Hetty? Could you come here, please? Mrs. Rheiner would like to meet you." Michael stood before the open flap of the tent, as stiff and expressionless as a well-trained butler, his black suit and vest grimly out of place in the sun-drenched meadow.

Samuel's worried gaze fixed on Michael, but he didn't say anything, just took the journal from Hetty and climbed back into the wagon to return it to its place.

Michael didn't follow Hetty into the tent, and the minute she entered, Mr. Rheiner slipped out with a silent nod.

Inside, the air was heavy, hot, and still, suffused with the buttery light that shone through the worn canvas roof and sides. Most of the heat came from the small fire in the two-lid stove set in the back corner of the tent. Beside the stove stood a large wooden rocker. A sturdy camp table in front of the stove bore a deep wooden dresser drawer that had been put to use as a cradle. The dresser itself was nowhere in sight.

A tall iron double bed had been set in the opposite corner of the tent from the stove. Its wheels were chocked with river stones; short boards set under two of the wheels compensated for the unevenness of the packed dirt floor. It was a solid, practical bed, the kind a young couple bought when they hadn't much money and were planning for a long, loving future together.

The occupant of the bed didn't look as if she had much of a future at all.

Ruth Rheiner must once have been beautiful, but illness, hard work, and suffering had claimed their toll. The colorless skin of her face stretched across her bones like parchment, delicate, almost translucent. Her hair needed to be washed, but her bedgown and the worn sheets on the bed were all spotlessly clean. A faded pink ribbon, carefully pressed, held the neck of her gown closed.

"Miss Malone." Her smile, faint as it was, illuminated her face. "I wanted to thank you. For coming. And you just arrived. It was kind."

Her voice was fainter even than her smile, slightly roughened by the chronic cough of the long-term consumptive. She spoke with a slight German accent that was totally lacking in her son's speech and had to pause to catch her breath after each short sentence, but there was a dignity to her that Hetty found very moving.

"Dr. Ryan was very worried about you, and I wanted to see if there was anything I could do to help." Her little lie made Hetty flinch. Her reasons for coming had been purely selfish. She hadn't wanted to let Michael out of her sight. The small basket of food and fresh eggs that she'd talked Mrs. Spencer's cook into making up for her had been an automatic gesture, the sort of thing one always did, under the circumstances. Now she was glad she'd come, for the sake of these people whom she would very much like to have as friends, even if Mr. Rheiner never got up the courage to look at her directly.

Now she crossed to stand by the bed. "I met your son, Mrs. Rheiner. What a . . . a *wonderful* little boy! You must be very proud."

Mrs. Rheiner beamed; a faint flush of pleasure stained her pale cheeks. "Thank you. He is a good boy. And my Robert. A good husband. A *good* husband. I have been . . . very fortunate."

"And now a daughter. May I see her? I know she's very frail right now, so I won't disturb her."

"Yes. Of course. Dr. Ryan says she's . . . doing well . . . for her size." As Hetty bent over the dresser drawer, she added, "Would you . . . check her? Please? The pad beneath her. She's . . . too small . . . for clothes right now."

Ruth Rheiner's voice was growing weaker and hoarser under the strain of talking. Glad to be of some use, however little, Hetty pulled aside the flannel blanket mounded in the center of the drawer. Someone had made a warm, protective nest for the infant by layering flannel sheets at the bottom of the drawer, then padding the sides with baby blankets, clean cloths, and a worn shawl.

At the center of the nest lay the tiniest baby Hetty had ever seen. The infant was bald, wrinkled, and red, yet there was a delicate perfection to her that took Hetty's breath away. She'd been washed with sweet oil, and a soft flannel belly band had been tied across the knot of the umbilical cord. She'd been placed atop a flannel pad that would serve in the place of the diaper she was far too small to wear.

"She's dry and sleeping quite happily," Hetty said, carefully tucking the flannel blanket around her so that it protected her from any drafts without touching her fragile little body.

"She's very beautiful," Hetty added softly, turning back to the bed. "What have you named her?"

"Anna. After her grandmother. My mother." Worry immediately drove out the glow of pride. "But she's only . . . three and a half pounds. It is . . . not very much."

"No, but we had a neighbor back in Boston who had a baby smaller than that. It was very difficult at first, just as it is for you, but the baby grew up to be one of the terrors of the neighborhood. Truly!" she added, seeing the struggle between hope and disbelief that Mrs. Rheiner was waging with herself.

Hope won. Mrs. Rheiner smiled. "And we have . . . Dr. Ryan. He has been . . . so good to us. To me." Even hope was not enough to combat the weariness that was beginning to claim her, however.

"Well," Hetty said briskly, "he won't be very good to me if he finds I've been tiring you out by talking too much. I'll come again, if I may?" A nod. "Is there anything special I can bring you next time?" A weak shake of the head, but the denial was softened by another smile.

Hetty patted the thin, pale hand that lay upon the coverlet. "Then you just rest and I'll go out and harass your menfolk for you."

She almost couldn't hear the faint "thank you" that came in response, but she didn't miss the tiny hint of a twinkle that shone in Ruth Rheiner's eyes. If she'd had the breath for it, Hetty rather thought Mrs. Rheiner would be laughing.

# Chapter Six

Hetty emerged from the tent to find Samuel seated on the cottonwood trunk morosely pitching pebbles into the campfire ashes. His head snapped up at her appearance, and he jumped to his feet as fast as if someone had shoved hot coals beneath him. From the anxiety darkening his young eyes, Hetty suspected he'd been expecting the worst. When she smiled at him, instead, relief washed across his face like sun across black clouds.

"Your mama's tired," Hetty told him, gently squeezing his shoulder in wordless sympathy, "but your sister's as pretty as a little elf baby."

Samuel swallowed nervously. "She's awful tiny."

"Yes, she is. But she has a mother and father who love her, and a big brother to protect her.

That's important, you know." She couldn't honestly reassure him and tell him everything would be all right, but she refused to go around with the same grim, haunted expressions that Michael and Mr. Rheiner had adopted. The situation was bad enough without that.

"Did Dr. Ryan give you that basket of food out of the buggy?" she asked, thinking it would be better to change the subject entirely.

Samuel's mouth narrowed ever so slightly. He might be only eight, but he already had his father's pride, and, as with his father, the pride was warring with their indisputable need for help right now.

"Yes'm, I got it," he said at last. "Thank you very much."

"My momma was sick for a long time. Years, in fact. I always appreciated it when the neighbors brought over a dish or a loaf of bread or whatever. It was just a little thing, you know, but it helped when there were so many other things I had to do. I'm always glad when I can help others, like they helped me. I expect you'll do the same, too, one day."

Her words must have taken the sting out of the gift, or at least given him another perspective on the matter, because Samuel almost smiled. Almost.

Michael evidently had finished whatever he'd been discussing with Mr. Rheiner. "Hetty?" he called from beside the buggy. "Ready to go?"

Neither of the men said a word as she and Samuel crossed to them. As Michael moved to her side to help her into the buggy, Hetty leaned close and whispered, "Give me some of your horehound drops."

His head jerked back as if he were dodging a fly. "What?" he demanded, frowning down at her.

"Your horehound drops. For Samuel."

"Don't be foolish, Hetty. Just get in the buggy." Once more he held out his hand and this time, after one hard, doubtful look, Hetty took it and climbed into the buggy, then scooted across to her side of the seat. He followed her and gathered up the reins.

"Mr. Rheiner," he said, nodding curtly. "Remember about the goat. Your daughter might take that milk where she won't the other." He didn't wait for an answer, didn't even wave at Samuel, just snapped the reins and set the horse in motion.

Hetty kept silent until they were far beyond the little meadow and long out of earshot. Then she exploded.

"How can you be like that, Michael Ryan?" she demanded.

"What?" Michael jerked around on the seat, startling the horse. "What the devil are you talking about?"

"Like . . . like a block of ice on legs, that's what. You've got those poor people scared to death of you."

He frowned so hard, his eyebrows looked as if they'd crashed together at the top of his nose. "Don't be ridiculous."

"I'm not being ridiculous. And why don't you have any horehound drops?"

"What do horehound drops have to do with you calling me a block of ice?"

"You used to carry a bag of drops in your pocket everywhere you went," Hetty said, stubbornly setting her chin. "You weren't a block of ice then. I figure there has to be a connection."

Michael snorted in angry exasperation. "I was an assistant, then, Hetty, not a doctor with more patients than I know what to do with."

"So that makes it all right to ignore that poor boy? I'd bet even one horehound drop would help. Just a little one!"

"Samuel? He's not my patient. His mother and sister are. And they're both pretty damned sick, in case you didn't notice."

"Anna's not sick, she's premature. There's a difference."

"Anna? Is that what they named her?"

Hetty gaped. "You didn't know?"

He shrugged, clearly uncomfortable. "I didn't ask and they didn't say."

"You didn't even *ask*?"

For a moment, Hetty wondered if the world had dropped out from under her feet. Michael hadn't bothered to find out the name of a beautiful, delicate baby he'd helped bring into the world? *Her* Michael?

Michael bristled. "Look, Hetty, my job is to save lives . . . if I can. I'm not here to carry on trivial conversation over tea."

"You know what *you* need, Michael Ryan?"

Hetty demanded. "A big dose of horehound drops, that's what. I swear this high altitude has affected your brain. Since when is knowing a baby's name 'trivial'?"

"I didn't say it *was* trivial! I said—"

"I heard what you said! I also know what those poor people think about you. Besides being scared to death of you, they happen to think you walk on water. If you—"

*"I do not walk on water!"*

The explosion almost tipped Hetty off the seat. Michael could have thrown dynamite and not startled her half as much.

"Michael! What—?"

"I'm not a damned miracle worker, Hetty!" Michael roared. His face was turning red under his tan. "I'm a man! Do you understand that? A man!"

"Nobody said—"

"And there aren't any neat little miracles. Not for people like Ruth Rheiner. Don't you think I'd have used them by now if there were?"

"Of course, but—"

"We can't vaccinate against tuberculosis. We don't have a cure for it. We don't even have a proper sanatorium like the ones they're building back East. Not yet, anyway. Maybe soon, if someone can get the funding and the land and . . . Hell, there's so damn much we need, Hetty, and even then there's no guarantee. But it would be a start. Better than leaving her in that hot little tent with all the worries she's facing now. She's not strong enough to take care of herself, let alone her son and her baby and her husband, like she tries to do. But if we had a decent sanatorium, even a few shelters, a lab, a kitchen—*something* besides what we have now—it would help. We—"

"Michael!" Hetty finally broke in, dazed by this sudden flood of words. "I haven't the faintest idea what you're talking about!"

"I'm talking about a sanatorium, Hetty! A place where people like Ruth can be cared for properly without having to worry about everything else. They're having some good results back East. Hell! The first one was built in Saranac, New York, by a doctor who went up there to die of TB and got well instead. If he can do it, why can't we?"

Michael's face was suddenly alight with eagerness. Hetty didn't try to interrupt. She wasn't even sure he was talking to her so much as thinking out loud.

"Good food, rest, medical care, clean air. That's what Ruth needs, and all the other patients like her. I can give her the care and she's got plenty of clean air—if I could get her out of that tent and away from her baby—but until she can rest, *really* rest . . ."

For a moment he was silent. Hetty could see the eager light fade in his eyes as he said, "But it all takes money. Money and land and support and staff and—"

He shrugged. "There's your miracle, Hetty. Getting the resources to establish something like that."

"Miracles can happen, Michael," Hetty said softly.

"So they say."

"Sometimes they just go by another name."

"Well, at least I know the name of the next patient—and the last, I might add, that you're going to be visiting this morning. His name is Fred Meissner, and he is far too old for horehound drops, so you needn't worry that I've been depriving him."

"Humpf," said Hetty.

"And what is that supposed to mean?"

"No one's ever too old for horehound drops, Michael Ryan, which just goes to show how much *you* know!"

Fred Meissner sat canted to one side of an ugly, overstuffed chair, straining to get more light on the open book in his hand. His gold-rimmed spectacles rode on the prow of his nose like a metal insect about to take flight, and he shoved at them every now and then as if they annoyed him.

At the sight of Hetty and Michael standing in the parlor doorway where his housekeeper had left them, his eyes lit up and his dried-prune face gained another dozen wrinkles from a grin that must have spread from ear to ear. At least, Hetty assumed it had. She couldn't tell for sure because the old man possessed the biggest, bushiest white mustache she'd ever seen.

He slipped a bookmark into his book and set it aside, ran fingers as gnarly as old roots over the glory on his upper lip, then painfully levered himself to his feet.

"Doctor Ryan," he said, extending his hand. "Good to see you, boy. Beginning to wonder if you'd forgotten this old man."

"Not at all," Michael said stiffly, gesturing Hetty forward. "I wanted you to meet my fiancée, Hetty Malone."

"Mr. Meissner," Hetty said, taking his huge, twisted old hand in hers. "I'm delighted to meet you. Dr. Ryan told me about you, but he never said anything about that gorgeous mustache of yours. Now why do you think that might be?"

The old man's eyes lit up. Without letting go of her hand, he leaned toward Hetty conspiratorially and winked. "Worried I'll cut him out. Ladies always did go for a man with a mustache. Told him so a dozen times, but he keeps on shaving it off."

He chuckled, then released Hetty's hand to stroke the silver strands complacently. "Between you and me, I think it's 'cause his grows in straggly. Happens sometimes, even to the best of us." He twitched his upper lip so Hetty could get a better look at his own masculine achievement.

Michael snorted, but Hetty pointedly ignored him. "Yours obviously didn't."

"Nope. 'Course, my wife complained at first. Said it tickled when I kissed her. So I shaved it off. She took one look at my homely puss and told me to grow it back again. Never had any complaints about the ticklin' after that." He waggled his eyebrows when Hetty laughed, then reluctantly levered himself back into his chair.

"How are you doing, Mr. Meissner?" Michael

asked with formal dignity, settling into the chair beside him.

Mr. Meissner scrunched up his chin and looked thoughtful. "Not bad. Not bad for ninety-three."

"Ninety-one last March," the housekeeper called from the kitchen. "You tell the truth, Fred Meissner!"

The old man craned around in the direction of the warning voice and shouted back, "Ninety-three, woman. You just tend to the coffee pot." He eased back into his seat, cackling. "Madder'n a wet hen, she is. Told her this mornin' a good-looking woman like her had ought to get married again. She's only sixty-seven. Got a lot of wear left in her yet. Damned shame to waste it."

"Mind your manners," the housekeeper said sharply, emerging from the kitchen with all the necessities for a sociable cup of coffee. "Next thing you know, you'll be saying something you'll regret, and then I'll hear you mumbling about it for a week after."

"At my age, woman, it's a waste of time to be regretting my mistakes. Besides, I've made way too many of 'em for it to matter now."

"Well, I won't argue that. Cream or sugar, Miss Malone? How about you, Doctor Ryan?"

They settled with their coffee. Fred Meissner was an outrageous flirt, and he relished having a new "filly" on whom to practice his charms. He'd been born in Germany, but had come to America as a young man in search of adventure. He had eventually found it in the gold fields of California, where he managed to loose his German accent and get a wife, even if the big strike always eluded him. He'd remained in California during the war between North and South, then returned to the East and taken up work as a surveyor and engineer for the railroads. As the railroad had moved West, so had he. He had a wealth of wild tales about laying the first lines across Colorado and Kansas, then down through New Mexico Territory, where he claimed to have left dozens of beautiful señoritas in tears on his departure.

"Never told my wife about 'em, of course. She wouldn't have approved. I'd never of left her, anyhow, no matter how much those pretty señoritas begged. My Ida made the best flapjacks from here to the Mississippi, and there wasn't anyone could touch her when it came to roasting a haunch of venison."

Some of the light went out of his face at the memory of his wife, and for a long while he simply sat stroking his mustache, his rheumy old eyes unfocused as he stared into a past that had left him marooned at the closing of the century without the wife and friends who had shared so many years and so many adventures with him.

It was Hetty, bending forward to put her cup and saucer on the tray the housekeeper had left, who inadvertently roused him from his reverie.

"What . . . What was I saying?" he asked, shaking off his memories.

"You were telling us how well your wife roasted venison," Hetty said gently.

"Was I? Yes, yes she did. I miss it, you know. The venison." His mustache curved upward with his grin. "No teeth. Takes me so long to chew it these days, I fall asleep before I finish."

Hetty laughed, which pleased him, but Michael was grimly disapproving.

"Just as well. I've told you to stay away from foods like that." He leaned forward to set his cup and saucer beside Hetty's. "One of these days you might start listening to me."

"Not if you're gonna keep telling me I oughta eat that damned—'scuse me, miss!—that danged pap you set such store by. You and her"—he hooked a thumb in the direction of the kitchen—"are bound and determined to put me in my grave."

"And that's where you're going to be if you don't start following Dr. Ryan's orders, you ornery old coot," rang out of the kitchen, clear as a bell. The housekeeper hadn't abandoned the battlefield—she'd been keeping her ears open for rebellion.

"Mrs. Scott is a good cook, and she's just trying to keep you healthy, you know," Michael chimed in sternly, just as if Fred Meissner were a troublesome schoolboy instead of a man who'd seen a good sixty years more of hard living than he had. "You'd be a lot better off if you'd listen to us every once in a while. Whether you like it or not," he added on a note of warning when Mr. Meissner scowled back.

Hetty debated the wisdom of boxing Michael's ears for him, right then and there. He seemed to have forgotten his patients needed more than just medicine to stay alive and to find life worth living.

Whatever his age and physical infirmities, Mr. Meissner clearly had all his wits intact. It was a darned shame that the very people who cared most about keeping him alive didn't seem to think it was necessary to listen to what *he* wanted for himself.

"No sense arguing about it now. We need to be going, anyway," Michael said, rising, as formal as if he'd been taking tea with the governor. "I just wanted to see how you were doing and introduce Miss Malone to you."

"Best get along then, boy. Don't want to keep you from peddlin' your pap to somebody else. *They* might need it!"

That hit pleased the old man. His irritation evaporated instantly. He cocked his head to one side and gave Hetty another conspiratorial wink. "These young fellers get nervous when they're up against competition, you know. 'Specially if they can't manage even a fringe on their upper lip."

Hetty laughed. "I do believe you're right, Mr. Meissner. But after all, the poor things can't be blamed for something that's beyond their control, now can they?"

Mr. Meissner considered the question. "No, I suppose they can't. And I suppose you do have to be gittin'. But before you go, if you wouldn't mind pourin' me out another cup of coffee, miss?"

He shifted awkwardly in his chair and pulled a small silver flask from his back pocket. "And add a little of this," he said, extending the flask to her. "Helps the rheumatiz in my hands, you know."

Michael was there in an instant. "Now, Mr.

Meissner," he said sternly, taking the flask from the old man's hand. "You know I told you not to touch this stuff." He frowned down at the flask, then at his unrepentant patient. "In fact, I could have sworn you told me you didn't have any more around the house."

"Hell, boy . . . er, beggin' your pardon, miss. I've been drinkin' since I was nine and snuck some of my daddy's from where he'd hid it in the barn. Seeing as how it hasn't killed me yet, I don't think it's likely to now. Trouble with you doctors," he said, poking a lumpy finger into Michael's flat belly, "is that you think you can hold that old bugger, Death, at bay. Well, you can't. He'll come when he's danged good and ready, no matter how much you kick against it, so you might as well enjoy what you got right in front of you. Sooner you find that out, happier you'll be."

"Humpf," said Michael.

Before he could say more, Hetty slipped the flask out of his grasp and unscrewed the top. "You just say when, Mr. Meissner," she said, starting to pour.

She stopped after pouring the equivalent of a couple of teaspoons full, long before Mr. Meissner said "when." She didn't think the old man noticed. He was too pleased with having outmaneuvered Michael to care if she paid any attention to him. Hetty set the doctored cup of coffee on the table beside Mr. Meissner's chair where Michael couldn't reach it unless he shoved her out of the way.

From the grim, set look on his face, she suspected he was considering doing just that. Mrs. Scott sailed in before he had a chance to move, clearly anxious to show them out.

They left, then, but only after Hetty had solemnly promised to return for another visit. At the front door, she glanced back. Fred Meissner was still there, elbows propped on either arm of his chair, his crippled hands dangling uselessly above his lap. He didn't notice her because he was staring straight ahead, his eyes focused on something far beyond the limits of the sun-drenched room.

And all the while his liquor-laced cup of coffee steamed on the table beside him, forgotten.

"What did you think you were doing, pouring that liquor in his coffee?" Michael demanded as he handed Hetty into the buggy.

"Pooh!" said Hetty. "He's right, you know. It can't hurt him now, and it probably does help the pain from his rheumatism."

Michael bit down on a sharp retort. He felt insulted and betrayed, as if she'd openly mocked his medical skill.

"Just who went to medical school, you or me?" he demanded, climbing into the buggy behind her. The livery horse flicked an ear at an annoying fly and ignored them entirely.

"You, for all the good it did you. Either you weren't paying attention, or they left out a couple of important items in your education."

"Such as?"

"Common sense and a little human understanding."

Michael stiffened. "I beg your pardon."

She shifted around to face him, her green eyes as dark as a summer leaf, fair warning that she was roused.

"Oh, Michael. He's an old man. His wife and most of his friends are dead. His bones hurt, he can't see well, and I'm sure he doesn't get out much anymore. He certainly can't do any of the things he used to, and that has to be awfully hard on him. How can it possibly hurt if he has a little nip of whiskey with his coffee every now and then if that's what he wants?"

"You sound as if you don't think I care about him," Michael said stiffly, stung by her criticism.

"No, I think you care very much. I just think you've put the cart before the horse when it comes to what really matters, at least as far as Mr. Meissner is concerned. At ninety-three—"

"Ninety-one."

"See, you're just like his housekeeper. Trying to make him stick to facts when he'd rather flirt and tell outrageous stories and lie about his age. What the devil—excuse me!—what difference does it make if he's ninety-one or ninety-three? He's still an old man who likes to make the discomforts of old age a little less uncomfortable by putting a drop of whiskey in his coffee. What is so terrible about that, for heaven's sake?"

"It's not good for him, that's what! It upsets his digestion, damages his liver—"

"Oh, bother his liver," Hetty burst out. "I don't need a medical degree to know that when he dies, Mr. Meissner is going to die of old age, plain and simple. I rather doubt his liver is going to have much to say about the matter."

"How can you be so . . . so callous? I expected better of you, Hetty."

"And I expected better of *you*, Michael Ryan! All you're thinking about is your precious medicine and not the patient at all."

Michael exploded. "That's absurd!"

The livery horse, spooked by the shouting, threw up his head and shied. A lady halfway up the block jumped and turned around to stare.

Michael ignored the horse and turned his shoulder to the lady. He managed to lower his voice, but he couldn't control the angry tension that vibrated in his words. "That's absurd, Hetty, and you know it."

She raised one eyebrow doubtfully, but refrained from answering. Instead, she settled more firmly on the seat, then neatly arranged her skirts so they fell in becoming folds about her feet.

"You *know* it's absurd, Hetty," Michael insisted, unwilling to leave the matter alone. He felt as though she'd shot him.

"You'd best take up the reins," she advised him calmly. "Your horse has just taken a bite out of what's left of the neighbor's flower garden."

Michael yanked his horse's nose out of the garden, but not before it had left a noticeable hole among the dried leaves, and flicked the reins to set the beast in motion. He didn't care in what direction.

"I'll leave you at Mrs. Spencer's," he said at last, when he had his voice under some degree of control.

"I don't care to return to Mrs. Spencer's just yet," Hetty responded coolly.

"Then where *would* you like to go?"

"I would like to be set down at Mrs. Scoggins's," she said at last. She pulled a small card out of her bag and read the address. "Will that be convenient for you?"

Cool as you please. Michael ground his teeth. If that was the way she wanted to play the game, it was fine with him. He had more important things to do, after all. Much more important.

"That will be *quite* convenient," he snapped, and urged the horse into a rattling trot.

Hetty ignored Michael's grudgingly offered assistance in climbing down from the buggy. Once she was on the ground, she dismissed him as coolly as if she'd hired his services at the stable; then she stood, head high, while he glared silently down at her, anger visible in every taut line of his body.

"I believe you said you had other patients to see?" she said at last, provoked.

He growled—there was no other word for it—and jerked around on the seat. An instant later he'd slapped the horse back into a trot, leaving her to choke on the dust his wheels kicked up behind him.

Disgusted, Hetty retreated to the scrolled iron gate that guarded Mrs. Scoggins's front walk and the impressive three-story brick home that stood at the end of it. She shook out her skirts and brushed off her jacket and tried very hard not to worry about what had just passed between her and Michael.

She could only guess at what had caused the change in him, but she loved him too much to let him go on as he was. Medical degree or no, Michael clearly had a few things to learn—and she was just the person to teach him. She'd bang it into his thick head if she had to.

Hetty sagged against the gate, troubled. This was not the way she'd envisioned their reunion. It seemed as if nothing had gone right, starting with her first step off that train when he hadn't been there to meet her.

No, it wasn't quite true that *nothing* had gone right.

There were the kisses they'd shared, for one thing. She hadn't forgotten about those. Not by a long shot. And the apples . . .

Hetty smiled, a small, secret smile, and felt an odd little warmth start somewhere low in her belly.

She'd have to remind herself of the apples the next time she got worried.

With a brisk shove, she opened the gate and marched up the walk to Mrs. Scoggins's front door.

A girl of sixteen or so opened the door at Hetty's knock. Her plain black dress and starched white apron identified her as the maid, but she giggled when Hetty asked if Mrs. Scoggins was at home, then immediately pressed her fingers to her mouth and blushed.

" 'Scuse me, ma'am. Yes'm, Mrs. Scoggins is at home. Was you wishin' to see her?"

Hetty clamped down on the smile that threatened. "Yes, please. If she's available."

The girl frowned thoughtfully. "Well, yes'm, I guess she is. It's just her and Mrs. Fisk, you know. In the closet."

Hetty hastily covered her mouth and coughed. "Of course."

"But I don't think that'll matter," the girl added cheerfully, swinging the door wide. "Won't you come in, please? And who should I say is calling?"

Hetty gave her name, then watched, amused, as the girl walked off, trying hard to maintain the demeanor proper to a well-trained maid. Her natural ebullience overtook her near the top of the grand staircase. She giggled—Hetty heard it all the way at the front of the hall—and bounced up the next step, then the next, until she abandoned all effort to conform and simply dashed up the remaining stairs and disappeared in the shadowed hallway at the top.

While she waited, Hetty stared about her at the house Mrs. Scoggins occupied in such solitary splendor. The furniture and appointments were expensive and elegant and not nearly so oppressively dark as Mrs. Spencer's, but there was an uncanny stillness about the place that Hetty found unsettling, as if everything had been chosen with care, then, for some unfathomable reason, suddenly put away under glass, never to be used again. The thought of living here with no one for company except a servant made her shudder.

Before she had time to dwell on it, the maid came rocketing back down the staircase. Halfway to the bottom, the girl stopped in mid-stride, like a runaway horse pulled up by a masterful hand, and descended the remaining steps with careful dignity.

"Mrs. Scoggins asks, would you mind joining her upstairs, ma'am. Her and Mrs. Fisk."

The girl led Hetty to a bedroom whose tall brass bed had almost disappeared under a heap of folded linens and towels and sheets.

"This will do, I think, though it is not the best," Mrs. Scoggins was saying, holding a slightly worn sheet up to the light for inspection. "The corner needs mending, but that would be good training for a young girl learning to sew."

"They do say the heathen creatures are good with their hands," Mrs. Fisk said, squinting approvingly at the frayed corner. Her corset creaked as she bent to examine the jumbled contents of several large boxes on the floor between them. "That will make two, possibly three boxes, then, and Mrs. Grove said the Auxiliary only promised five."

"I'm sure—ah, Miss Malone, do come in." Mrs. Scoggins gathered up the sheet she held and handed it to the maid, who had preceded Hetty into the room. "Here, Betty. If you would fold this, please, and these others we've set aside," she said, gesturing to the boxes.

Mrs. Scoggins's stiff, old-fashioned brown silk was softened by a touch of lace at the throat and a small pink cameo pinned to her collar, but her demeanor was as rigidly proper as ever. "We were just sorting through the contents of the linen closet for donations to a medical mission to Brazil. The organizers are sending urgent requests for linens for the hospital and school they are building. Mrs. Fisk brought word of it."

The words were stiffly formal, almost cold, but the sheets and towels Hetty could see sticking out of the boxes were not the shabby, worn-out cast-offs usually included in such charity boxes. A number of the items looked brand-new.

Such generosity made her bold. "Will you be sending all of it to the mission?" she asked, indicating the tumbled pile that Betty was rapidly putting to rights. "I know a family here that could use a little help, too."

She told them about her visit to the Rheiners that morning. Mrs. Fisk tsked and clucked at Hetty's tale while Betty sniffed mournfully but discreetly in the background. Mrs. Scoggins was made of sterner stuff. At the mention of Samuel and his efforts to translate his grandmother's book of "receipts," she blinked and her eyes grew suddenly hollow-looking, but that was all.

"Humpf," she said, when Hetty came to the end of her tale. "Totally inadequate arrangement. I should not care to eat a meal cooked by an eight-year-old boy."

She frowned at the boxes she and Mrs. Fisk had been filling, then at the untidy stacks of linen still piled on the bed for inspection. "Betty, you have a sufficiently large family to know what these Rheiners might need. Sort out a box for them, please. But first," she said with the majestic air of someone pronouncing a royal decree, "we shall have some tea."

They took their tea in a small, sunlit room at the back of the house. It was the first room Hetty had seen that looked as if it might actually be used on a regular basis.

The most noticeable item in the room was an ornately framed photograph that stood on a small table at one side of the room. In a house where every flat surface had long ago disappeared under a fashionable array of expensive clutter, this photograph stood alone in its place of honor.

Even from her seat halfway across the room, Hetty could identify the much younger Mrs. Scoggins who stood stiffly at the back of the picture, garbed in all her finest. Her hand was possessively placed on the shoulder of a distinguished, muffin-faced man who sat, straight as a ruler, in a heavy chair placed square in the center of the picture. A boy of perhaps four stood beside his father's chair, one arm engagingly propped on his father's leg, one little leg carelessly crossed in front of the other as if he took his father's solid support for granted.

Beloved husband and adored son, both dead

years before from consumption and only this photograph and Mrs. Scoggins's memories left behind to mark their passing.

Hetty's heart twisted within her. She couldn't help noticing that Mrs. Scoggins, despite her apparent air of calm, kept glancing at the photograph as she poured the tea and passed the plate of shortbread around. As if the photograph were a talisman, or a spur to memories that were growing more distant with each passing year.

"Betty's learning," Mrs. Fisk said, interrupting Hetty's thoughts. The stout lady took a bite out of the shortbread she held, then another. "They're quite good, Lettitia," she added, chewing diligently. Her multiple chins quivered with the effort. "Really quite good."

Mrs. Scoggins set her china cup in its saucer and nodded. "She actually *walked* up the stairs yesterday morning. It almost gives me hope she'll learn to control her exuberance."

"Do fine," Mrs. Fisk mumbled around another mouthful. Her eyes crossed slightly as she tried to wipe away a crumb that had attached itself to the tip of her nose.

"I hope so. She'll certainly need some sort of skill. Twelve children, Miss Malone!" Lettitia Scoggins added, turning to Hetty. "Can you imagine that? There are twelve children in Betty's family, all of them younger than she is and with a father who's not worth much to himself, let alone his family."

The mere thought of it seemed almost too much to bear. Her mouth thinned. "Twelve!"

"I take it you're training her to become a maid?" Hetty asked.

"Maid? Good heavens no. Not but what," she added after a moment's thoughtful pause, "she hasn't benefited from the experience of serving in more . . . genteel surroundings than those to which she is accustomed. No, I employ her as a maid, but I am training her to be a bookkeeper."

Hetty's eyebrows shot up. "A bookkeeper?"

"Of course." Mrs. Scoggins voice grew positively frosty. "I served as my husband's bookkeeper for years." She glanced at the photograph as she spoke.

"Just the thing for a girl like Betty," Mrs. Fisk said complacently, holding out her cup for more tea and diverting Mrs. Scoggins's attention from Hetty's blunder. "There we were—our church group, you know—trying to think what to do to help, when Lettitia suggested the bookkeeping. Three lumps, please, Lettitia. That's it. And just a bit more cream. Betty's quick with her numbers, you see," she added for Hetty's information, "but what with her upbringing and the need to look after all her brothers and sisters, she'd never had a chance to learn proper manners and what not. And bright or not, a girl hasn't a chance of a decent job if she doesn't know how to behave correctly."

"Of course. I didn't mean—" Hetty cut short her fumbling attempt at an apology as Betty herself walked into the room.

"Beggin' your pardon, Mrs. Scoggins," she said,

"but there's Mr. Mersen on the telephone, ma'am. He says could he talk to you, please."

"My attorney." Mrs. Scoggins rose to her feet. "He was handling some matters during my absence. I'm sure you'll forgive me. It can be so difficult to get a clear line between here and Denver, you know, and even then you have to shout like a savage."

Hetty set down her cup and rose to her feet. "I really should be going. Thank you so much for the tea. And the things for the Rheiners. It was very kind of you. I'll try to pick them up tomorrow, if that's all right."

"Best be on my way, as well," Mrs. Fisk said, lumbering to her feet. "Wouldn't have come what with having been away and all, but Mrs. Grove was anxious about those mission boxes." She tucked two pieces of shortbread in her bag, then followed Hetty out of the room.

It wasn't until she and Hetty had shut the front gate behind them that she said, "Don't worry you've upset her. She's never got over the loss of her husband and son, you see."

"I certainly didn't mean to insult her." Hetty hesitated, wondering if she should say more. "I saw the photograph," she admitted at last.

Mrs. Fisk nodded, clearly troubled. "Lettitia Scoggins will never admit it, but she gets lonely in that big house. It's good for her to have Betty around, even if the girl does drive her to distraction sometimes."

Hetty thought of the chill, orderly elegance of

the house, and of the little boy in the photograph, leaning so confidently against his father's knee, and she shivered.

"Well, no sense dwelling on it," Mrs. Fisk said briskly. "Life goes on. All we can do is make the best of it."

And with that she marched off down the street, leaving Hetty to follow after.

# *Chapter Seven*

Hetty returned to Mrs. Spencer's to find the front door standing open and the hall in utter confusion. Someone new was moving into the front bedroom, and Mrs. Spencer was bustling around like a distracted hen, changing sheets and throwing the windows open for air and explaining to the new boarders, a middle-aged couple nervously perched side by side on a sofa in the parlor, the rules of the house.

Michael, it seemed, had arranged for the Turner brothers to be moved from the boarding house to a hospital where they could have better care—not an easy achievement, since even the hospitals didn't like to take terminal consumptives. From her exclamations and muttered comments, Mrs. Spencer was torn between delight at having the brothers gone and irritation at their abrupt departure.

When Hetty stopped her in the hallway to ask if Michael had left any word for her, Mrs. Spencer, half-hidden behind the rumpled mound of sheets in her arms, merely shook her head and hurried away, the trailing ends of the sheets billowing after her like sails in a gathering wind.

" 'Scuse me, ma'am." The maid edged around Hetty, a mechanical carpet sweeper in one hand, a broom and dust pan and feather duster in the other. Before Hetty could ask her if Michael had left any message, she darted into the bedroom and slid the door closed behind her.

Irritated, Hetty retreated to her room to wash and change for supper. She certainly didn't begrudge the Turner brothers Michael's attention and concern, but she didn't think it was unreasonable to expect Michael to leave her a message, either, even if it was just a note to say he'd join her for supper.

In the end, it didn't matter. Michael didn't appear in time for supper.

Throughout the interminable meal, Hetty kept her eyes on her plate and tried not to notice the curious glances from the other boarders. When they gathered in the parlor afterward to chat and let their meal digest, Hetty excused herself and slipped upstairs to her own room.

She read for a while, then went to bed early, wondering what had kept him. It was a long time before sleep came.

Michael didn't come for breakfast, either. By

that time, all the doubts and uncertainties of the previous day had disappeared under a growing irritation.

When Hetty marched up to the front door of the oddly painted house a little after nine, it was to find the door locked and the blinds on the windows drawn.

Hetty glared at the door, trying to decide what to do next. If Michael thought ignoring her was a good way to get her to apologize, he had another three thinks coming.

She couldn't ask the neighbors where he'd gone. Michael wouldn't appreciate it, and the neighbors would inevitably start to wonder why Dr. Ryan's newly arrived fiancée had been forced to ask. She didn't care to sit in Mrs. Spencer's elegant, oppressive parlor waiting for him to show up, and she hadn't the slightest idea where to begin looking for him.

On the other hand, there was more than enough to do to keep her occupied until he reappeared. She had a whole new town to explore, after all, and a beautiful day in which to explore it.

The downtown was bustling. Hetty stopped at the train station first to make arrangements for her trunks to be delivered to Michael's house. That chore attended to, she poked into drygoods stores and dress shops and discreetly peered in the windows of offices, exploring possibilities. She quickly found the Fisk Pharmacy, a solid, prosperous-looking building with a modern soda fountain proudly set up front.

Mr. Fisk poked his bald head out of the pharmacy at the back of the shop and gave her a gnomish little grimace that made his eyebrows wiggle. "Be with you in a minute, ma'am," he called, then popped back into his sanctuary before she had a chance to say a word.

While she waited, Hetty studied the well-stocked and carefully dusted shelves. A few of the products bore unfamiliar names, and she missed a few others she'd used regularly in Boston, but the Boston friends who had warned her about life in the wild and untamed West had clearly missed their mark by a mile. Colorado Springs might be smaller than Boston, but it was certainly no less modern.

"I'm sorry, ma'am. The boy is out making deliveries and I—well! Miss Malone, isn't it?" Mr. Fisk peered at her over the tops of his glasses. Then he slid the gold-framed spectacles up his nose and peered at her through them. His expression gave her no clue as to whether the change in perspective helped. "Dr. Ryan picked you up finally, did he?"

"We managed fine, thank you, Mr. Fisk," Hetty said, carefully edging around the truth. "But he's busy this morning, so I'm out exploring, so to speak."

"That man's always busy." Mr. Fisk didn't look as if he thought being busy was necessarily a virtue. "Patients all over the place. Consults at Glockner. For consumptives, you know. Seems to have good results even if he isn't as willing to try new ideas as he might be." The latter was clearly a source of some misgiving in Mr. Fisk's book.

Hetty nodded. "He does seem to have a bit more than one man can handle." She was perfectly willing to accept compliments on Michael's behalf and ignore the rest.

"And if he makes a dollar for all his efforts, I'll be surprised. Never knew a doctor so willing to take on patients, regardless of whether they can pay or not. Mind you, there isn't a doctor worth his salt that doesn't have a few patients who don't pay, but your Dr. Ryan . . ." The scrawny pharmacist cocked his head to the side and clucked disparagingly, like a dissatisfied old hen.

"Most doctors don't go into medicine in order to make money, Mr. Fisk," Hetty said tartly, irritated.

"True, true. But Dr. Ryan manages not to make it more than most." He stared at her as if challenging her to disprove his statement. His polished pate reflected the light shining through the windows behind him, making it appear as if a faint pink halo circled his skull. "Can't do much doctoring if you're broke, now, can you?"

"I wouldn't know, Mr. Fisk. I doubt the problem will ever arise, in any case."

"Yes. Well . . ." said Mr. Fisk doubtfully, unwilling to abandon his animadversions on Michael's character so easily. "Can't even find the man half the time. Stormed in here first thing this morning. Ordered some medicines mixed up and stormed out. You think my delivery boy could find him after?" He snorted. "Even his office was locked up. Boy had to bring them back. Wasted a good hour this morning, and we're busy today, too."

"If you like, I will take the medicines," Hetty said stiffly. "I'm sure I'll be seeing Dr. Ryan soon."

Mr. Fisk eyed her closely, then dug under the counter and produced a small, paper-wrapped bundle tied with string. "I suppose it will be all right. Don't much like handing out medicines like this to just anyone, but under the circumstances . . ."

Hetty started to reach for the bundle, then drew her hand back, thinking of Mr. Fisk's strictures on Michael's financial sense. "How much is it? I can pay now, if you like."

Mr. Fisk flapped his hand in front of his nose dismissively. "It's on Dr. Ryan's bill."

Hetty had a sudden, vivid image of Mrs. Fisk on the train, doling out the paper-wrapped sandwiches that were to have been her lunch to three hungry urchins whose mother was distracted with a newborn. The Fisks might look like Jack Spratt and his wife, but it seemed they both had kind hearts.

"Make a lot of money off Dr. Ryan's account, do you, Mr. Fisk?" Hetty asked, looking the balding pharmacist straight in the eye.

"Now and then, Miss Malone," Mr. Fisk said blandly. "Now and then."

Hetty smiled; then her smile widened. "Would you happen to have any horehound drops, Mr. Fisk? I'd like a large bag, please. No, two. And I will pay for them." This time, anyway, she thought. The next time around it would be Michael who paid. She'd make very sure of that.

When Hetty finally emerged from the pharmacy, the horehound drops and the packet of medicine were in her crocheted bag and her step was a little bouncier than it had been when she'd gone in.

The bounce slowly disappeared from her step as the day grew warmer and Hetty grew tired of exploring. Somehow, it wasn't nearly as much fun as she'd thought it would be. But, then, she'd always expected Michael would be there to show her around.

Hetty frowned down at a crowded display of kitchenware, plumbing supplies, and hand tools that filled the window of a hardware store. Why hadn't Michael made arrangements to spend at least these first few days with her? Would it really have been that hard to ask another doctor to take care of his most urgent patients for a day or two?

The door of the next shop stood open, and Hetty could hear the steady clankety-thump of a printing press coming from deep inside.

The thought of printing and paper increased her irritation. Michael could at least have left her a note this morning! Surely that wasn't too much to ask. A few lines telling her when she might expect him or where they could meet. Or he could have sent her an invitation to dinner. That would have been even nicer. Maybe at one of the more elegant hotels in the area. Just the two of them, without any of Mrs. Spencer's boarders lined up on either side of the long table, watching them.

At the thought of dinner, Hetty's stomach

growled. Since Mrs. Spencer served a morning and evening meal only, Hetty bought some crackers and a small piece of cheese, cut into smaller slices, then carried them to the tidy park that occupied a full block of the downtown area.

She found a bench in the shade of a tall pine tree. It might be December, but Colorado had turned on the sunshine full force to welcome her.

As she ate, she watched the steady stream of people, carriages, and carts in the streets around her and tried hard to ignore her growing resentment that Michael not only wasn't there, but she hadn't the slightest idea where he *was* or when she would see him next.

A nasty little voice somewhere in the back of her mind said it wasn't irritation she was feeling, but uncertainty. Or even, maybe, a little bit of fear. But that was absurd. Hetty didn't believe in listening to nasty little voices. They had an uncomfortable way of saying things she didn't want to hear.

His absence had nothing to do with their quarrel yesterday, and the coldness he'd shown to his patients had nothing whatsoever to do with her. Absolutely nothing. Michael loved her just as much as she loved him. If they found that each of them had changed a little in the past two years, that was only to be expected, wasn't it?

He was busy. That was all there was to it. Too engrossed in his work to realize how vulnerable she felt right now, and too dedicated to consider leaving his patients if he felt they needed him, even for a little while.

All very simple and straightforward. Eminently reasonable. Perfectly sensible.

Really.

Hetty chomped down on a cracker as hard as if it had tried to talk back. It shattered and rained crumbs down her jacket and into her lap.

"I would appreciate it if you would leave my packages at Fisk's where they belong."

It was the voice, not the words, that brought Hetty around with a jerk. "Michael! Where—?"

"Really, Hetty. I have far too much to do to spend my time chasing around town after something as important as that medicine."

Hetty sucked in her breath, startled by the ice in his voice. She squinted up at him, but the early afternoon sun was right behind him. The angle turned him into a forbidding, broad-shouldered silhouette cast in blinding light.

None of it seemed real. This coldly angry man was not the man she knew.

"Michael?" she asked, disbelieving.

"Who else would be chasing around town trying to retrieve that packet of medicine? Mr. Fisk doesn't need it back, now, does he?" His words had an acid bite that made Hetty flinch. He extended his hand, palm up.

Hetty angrily jumped to her feet. She tried to take a step toward him, but instead rammed her knee into the edge of the cast-iron park bench between them.

She gasped and backed off, blinking back tears at the jolt of pain that shot through her knee. The pain transformed her former irritation into outright anger.

"Just like that, you want your package back? With no apology? No word of explanation? No thanks?"

He frowned. She'd never seen such a cold, forbidding look on his face.

"I can't wait, Hetty. There are some pills I need in that packet, the last ones Mr. Fisk had until he gets his new stock in. I don't have time to run from one pharmacy to another to see if anyone else has them." Once more he held out his hand like a king demanding tribute.

Despite the day's warmth, Hetty shivered. This wasn't the Michael she knew. It couldn't be.

He had an emergency. That was it. Of course! How foolish could she be not to realize?

With clumsy haste she picked up her bag and fumbled among its contents, searching for the small, paper-wrapped parcel she'd taken from Mr. Fisk.

Michael took it from her with a clipped word of thanks, then spun about on his heel and started to walk away.

"Wait! Michael!" Hetty hated the sharp note of desperation in her voice, but her pleading words tumbled out the instant he stopped and half turned to face her. "How soon will you be free? Where will we meet? Will I see you—"

"I don't know, Hetty," he said. His words hit like shards of ice, cold and stinging. "There are things—I have—" He stopped and drew a deep, painful breath.

"I don't know," he said at last. And with that he was gone, striding away with the grim, erect posture of an executioner on his way to a hanging.

Stunned, Hetty watched his black-garbed form until it was swallowed up in the bustle of afternoon traffic. And then she stood a little while longer, motionless, staring at the place where he had disappeared and clutching her bag to her stomach as if it would protect her against the uneasiness that had settled in her middle.

All the emotions she'd been struggling with over the past hours came back in an awful rush—anger, resentment, uncertainty, doubt—harder and fiercer than ever.

Nervously, she dug her fingers into the crocheted covering of her bag, twisting and dragging at the intricate knots and trying to hang on to the items collected inside the taffeta inner lining, even though they insisted on shifting away, out of her grasp.

Just like Michael.

With an explosive, inarticulate exclamation of frustration, Hetty slammed the bag down on the bench seat. For an instant, she just stood there glaring down at the hapless heap of cloth; then she whirled around and thumped down on the bench beside it, hunched her shoulders, crossed her arms beneath her breasts, and glared at an inoffensive bush on the opposite side of the walk.

Just who did Dr. Michael Ryan think he was? She'd crossed half a continent to come here! Abandoned everyone and everything she'd ever known just to be with him. And for what? To be ignored, insulted, and talked down to as if she were some misbehaving, half-wit child?

She would, she decided, rent a horse and buggy at the nearest livery stable, pick up the box of linens that Mrs. Scoggins had set aside for the Rheiners, and take the box out to the little camp by the river. There were probably a dozen chores she could take care of for them. Unlike some people she knew, the Rheiners might even appreciate her efforts to help.

And when she came back, she would sit on Michael's front porch until he returned—all afternoon, if need be—so that she could give him a piece of her mind and demand an explanation.

And she would not, she absolutely would *not* let herself worry about why Michael was avoiding her.

Michael left the horse and buggy at the livery stables, then trudged the two blocks home. His black leather medical bag felt as though it weighed a good ten pounds more than it normally did. Inside he felt frozen, numb, and he was too exhausted to care much, one way or the other.

It was a long two blocks.

Three houses down from his own, he jerked to a stop.

Hetty was sitting on the top step of his front porch, head high, back straight, feet primly together. The bulky net bag she'd been carrying earlier was in her lap and her full brown skirts were gathered tidily about her legs. She held her hands clasped on her knees with the fingers twined as if in prayer and she looked as composed and dignified as if she were waiting for her ladies' church group to begin its weekly meeting.

Michael's heart sank. Hetty was the sunniest person he knew, but when she turned stiff and formal and dignified, a smart man ran for cover. Only trouble was, he didn't have the strength to dodge right now, let alone run.

The gate squealed as Michael reluctantly shoved it open, then banged shut behind him as he dragged up the walk. Hetty watched him, unmoving, her face still and expressionless and shuttered.

He came to a halt at the foot of the steps and wearily set his bag down at his feet. "Whatever it is, Hetty, it will have to wait."

Her eyes widened angrily and her chin came up. She jumped to her feet, her string bag in her hand. "Have to wait? I haven't been doing anything *except* wait since I got here!"

A spark of anger briefly flared in Michael, then flickered and went out. He was too tired to feel anger. He was too tired to feel much of anything except the painful gnawing of the ice inside him, the recognition of his failure.

He let his tired gaze slip from her face, down her throat and breast and waist, down the long length of her legs to where the neat, squared-off toes of her shoes poked out from beneath her skirt.

His exhaustion-drugged brain produced a muzzy image of him sinking down on the rough, weather-stained step beside her. He wanted to bury himself in her arms, to lay his head upon her breast and let her warmth surround him and drive out all the icy hollowness inside him. He wanted to weep and feel her gentle touch brush away his tears. He wanted to sleep while she lay beside him, ready to drive away the dark dreams that so often lay in the shadows, waiting to pounce.

He didn't move.

Neither did she. She just stood on the step looking down at him, waiting for him to respond to her challenge. Instead, he bent and picked up his medical bag, then slowly climbed the steps to stand beside her. For a moment he hesitated, wanting to bend and kiss her, knowing he couldn't bear so brief a taste of her. She returned his gaze, brow furrowed in confusion.

"Michael?" Tired as he was, he could hear the questions that weighted her voice.

He frowned, opened his mouth to speak, but couldn't find the words to explain. They were there, jammed behind the wall of ice that held him in its grip, but he couldn't get them out. He shook his head and walked past her.

The lock opened with a scraping protest. He shoved the door open and walked on through to his office without bothering to hold the door for Hetty. The house was stuffy after so many hours of being closed.

The journals he'd been reading when he'd fallen asleep at his desk the day before yesterday were still there waiting for him. One lay open, the page creased where his cheek had pressed against it. The rest lay strewn about, their pages marked with scraps of paper he'd ripped from a notebook to keep his place. He stared at the mocking stack of accumulated medical knowledge while the seconds ticked past silently.

From somewhere above his head, he heard a bird scrabble for footing on the roof. Another fluttered in the bush outside the window, making a branch scrape against the window before it launched into noisy flight.

Michael tensed, head cocked, listening to the familiar noises as the birds went about their lives, heedless of the humans around them.

The crow he'd heard outside the hospital shortly after dawn that morning had been just as unconcerned, the heavy downward beat of its wings clearly audible in the stillness of the stark room. He remembered stopping, listening. One beat, two, three, then nothing but a soft whoosh of air to mark its passing before it was gone.

Jacob Turner had tilted his head up to follow the sounds. The thin morning light filtering through the window shades had been pitiless, exposing the gaunt, gray emptiness of his face, the hollowness of his sunken eyes. For a long moment he'd simply sat, motionless; then he'd let his gaze drop back to the blanket-shrouded form on the narrow bed across from him.

"We should never have come," he'd said, his voice so weak that Michael had to strain to hear him, even in the silence of the little room. "The doctors, they told us. They said it was too late."

Jacob had turned his ravaged gaze on him

then, as if pleading for understanding. "We had to try, though. It was our last chance. We had to take it."

Michael had nodded. His mother had reached for that last, desperate chance at health, just like the Turners. But she at least had died among friends.

As though he'd caught Michael's unspoken thoughts, Jacob had shifted his bleak gaze back to the shrouded form of his brother. "We should never have come," he'd said.

He hadn't said another word, not even when the men from the undertaker's had come for his brother's body. Michael had at last forced him to take a sleeping draught, then stayed to be sure he was settled in another room, a room with only one bed this time.

Less than an hour later he'd been called to a seventeen-year-old TB patient who had suffered her first severe hemorrhage. She was an orphan, a housemaid who could no longer work and was now reduced to charity and a crowded ward with a dozen other young women just like her. And after her there'd been the five-year-old boy injured in a wagon accident whose crushed leg he'd had to amputate, knowing what it would mean for the boy, and for the man he would become. And after that . . .

A muscle in Michael's jaw jumped painfully, rousing him from his bitter thoughts. Very deliberately, he set his medical bag down in the middle of the jumbled journals on his desk, then took off his coat and folded it over the top of the bag, hiding everything.

Behind him he heard Hetty's footsteps crossing the room toward him. She swung around and came to stand behind the desk, right where he usually sat. There was a stillness about her that Michael found terrifying.

"We need to talk, Michael."

Michael sucked in air, then let it out slowly. "Not now, Hetty," he said, enunciating each word with care.

"Yes, *now*." She paused, worrying the side of her lower lip with her teeth, studying him. "I know you're tired. I know you didn't ignore me today because you wanted to. I know you have patients who need you. I *know* all that. But it's not good enough, Michael. Not anywhere near good enough."

He flinched. Not good enough. *Not good enough.*

"This isn't like you, Michael. This coldness. This . . . this . . ." She flung up her hands, frustrated at her failure to find the words she wanted. "It's as if you've gone away from me somehow and I . . . I don't know how to find you."

She moved closer and placed her hand on his arm, silently pleading for the explanation he refused her. Michael could feel the warmth of her even through his shirt, but it wasn't enough to thaw the chill inside him.

His eyes locked with hers. "Tomorrow," he said at last flatly, putting her hand from him. "Please, Hetty. We'll talk tomorrow."

Her lips thinned and her eyes narrowed, but she didn't press him, just picked up her bag and, head high, quietly walked out of the room.

Michael listened to the sound of her footsteps as she crossed the waiting room and drew the door shut behind her. The second and fourth porch steps creaked beneath her weight. He heard the faint click of her heels against the paved walk, the squeal of the gate opening, then closing behind her.

And still he stood there, aching in the silence.

Once, he could have told her everything, but two years of silence lay between them, and now he didn't know how to begin. He was afraid that, once started, the words would come roaring out like a river in spring thaw. How many of his failures as a doctor could he recount before she was crushed in the deluge?

And God! How many failures there were!

He'd been warned of this as a medical student. "They'll die on you, my boy," crusty old Doc Eggerts had said, thrusting out his thick lower lip and scowling at him. "Despite the best you can do, they'll die on you, and all you can do is stay with them while they do it. You'll have to learn to accept that and go on."

Well, he'd gone on, but he hadn't learned to accept it. He didn't think he ever would.

Michael's mouth narrowed in self-disgust. James Turner was dead and all he could think about was that *he'd* failed. Yet there *was* something he could do.

Shaking off his fatigue, Michael retreated to

the small second bedroom he'd converted into a lab after Dr. Cathcart's death. The room was as dim and stuffy as the rest of the house, yet the moment he crossed the threshold Michael felt a sense of calm descend on him.

He dragged up the cheap muslin shades that covered the windows and seated himself at the worktable that held his microscope, the cases of slides he'd made over the past year and a half, and the thick stack of journals in which he tracked his experiments and ideas and the case histories of his TB patients.

Over twenty years had passed since his mother had gone away to die of tuberculosis, the "white plague" that had tormented humankind for centuries. In that time medical science had identified the cause and means of transmission of the disease, but it was no closer to finding a cure than it had been when his mother joined the thousands of desperate sufferers searching for a miracle. Some had found their miracle, while others, like his mother, had not. No one understood why.

God knew there were enough people searching for an answer. His shelves were full of pills and powders and mechanical devices, all useless, that had been tried at one time or another. He subscribed to every medical journal published that dealt with pulmonary diseases of any sort, and tuberculosis in particular.

His laboratory was crude and his efforts limited to whatever time he had free from his own medical responsibilities, but here in this small room among his test tubes and his petri dishes and his journals Michael found comfort. No one suffered here, no one died. Instead, logic and the spirit of scientific inquiry reigned supreme, and Michael gladly immersed himself in the search, grateful to escape from the all-too-human troubles that awaited him outside the door.

Now he breathed deeply, dragging in oxygen to combat his weariness, then dragged his most recent journal in front of him and opened the pages, skimming his latest notes to remind himself where he'd left off. He stuck his elbow on the table, then propped his head on his hand and started reading.

# *Chapter Eight*

At half past seven the next morning, Hetty let herself into Michael's house with the key she'd purloined the evening before. Michael had been too tired and withdrawn to notice that he'd left the door ajar and the key conspicuously in the lock. When she'd left, she'd simply shut the door, locked it, and pocketed the key.

She took three steps into the waiting room and stopped, suddenly uncertain.

Silence hung like smoke in the air, oppressively still and heavy. The house smelled stale, as if it had been locked up for days instead of hours, and there was a faint bitter tang underlying the staleness that she found impossible to identify.

For a moment, Hetty considered calling out, then decided against it. If Michael was already gone, the effort was wasted. If he was here, he was asleep—he couldn't have missed the noise of her entrance, otherwise. And if he was asleep, she'd just have to wait until he woke up.

But what was she supposed to do in the meantime?

It took only a glance around the waiting room to decide. The hall door was closed, but the door to Michael's office stood open as if in invitation, and Hetty believed in accepting an invitation when it was offered.

Michael woke to the smell of frying bacon and brewing coffee. One eye snapped open. The other required more time. It took him a minute to figure out the problem—he was sprawled across his bed, belly-down, with his head half buried in the pillow.

He groaned, dragged his face out of the pillow, and awkwardly twisted around until he could prop himself up on one elbow. He sniffed the air. No doubt about it. Bacon and coffee. But how?

No answers came. He yawned and tried to sit up. He managed on the second try.

Slumped on the edge of his tumbled bed—he'd simply collapsed on top of the coverlet, fully clothed, the night before—he considered possibilities. Only one resolved itself into a probability.

With an effort, he shoved himself off the bed and walked over to the door in his stocking feet. Propping one hand on the door frame, he leaned out into the hall and shouted, "Hetty?"

An instant later, she emerged from the kitchen

wielding a fork and clad in an enormous white apron that looked as if it had just come off the store shelf. Her cheeks were glowing with the heat from the stove. There was a faint trace of dampness across her brow and on the tip of her nose, yet her sleeves were primly buttoned to the wrist and her shirtwaist even more primly buttoned to her chin. Her hair was done up on the top of her head in some curly arrangement that must have needed a hundred hairpins just to keep it in place. Michael had a sudden, intensely vivid mental picture of himself slowly pulling out all those pins, one by one, as the silky curls tumbled down over his hands and arms. The impact of the image made him stagger.

"I thought you'd be waking up soon, so I started breakfast." She fumbled at her waist for the small chatelaine watch she always wore, snapped it open, and frowned down at the face. "Actually, it's more like dinner, but I don't imagine that matters much."

Michael stared at her stupidly. In his imagination, he was still counting hair pins. "Dinner?"

"It's after eleven, Michael Ryan," Hetty said tartly, "so you'd best be moving. I fired up the gas water heater for you. I'd suggest you grab some clean clothes and get into that bathroom before the water cools. I won't put the eggs on until you're done."

With that, she spun about on her heel and disappeared into the kitchen. Michael stood a moment longer, gaping at the spot where she'd stood, before she called out from the kitchen,

"And if you think I'm going to kiss you before you've bathed, shaved, and brushed your teeth, you have another think coming!"

Thus admonished, Michael slowly drew himself erect and hauled himself off to do as she bade. The shave felt good, the hot bath even better, but Michael found himself drawing out the process far beyond the time required to make himself presentable.

Some of the previous day's sense of failure and despair had eased, but he remembered enough of her visit the afternoon before to worry him. It wasn't beyond the bounds of possibility that she would throw the skillet at him the moment he emerged. Not that she'd ever done anything like that before, but then, he'd never before snapped at her and demanded that she leave him alone, either.

To his intense relief, she didn't even throw the kitchen towel she had draped over her shoulder when he finally stepped into the kitchen. Instead, she pointed to the chair he'd occupied the last time they'd been in the kitchen together and ordered, "Sit!"

Michael sat.

A moment later, she was filling his cup with coffee. By the time he'd downed that and worked up the courage to ask for more, she had set a plate piled with bacon, three fried eggs, and two thick slices of fried toast in front of him. Then she whisked his coffee cup off and returned that filled, too.

All Michael's misgivings at the quantity of food

disappeared the instant he took the first bite. He was well into his third egg and sixth piece of bacon before he even came up for air.

"God, Hetty, this tastes—"

"Don't talk, eat," she admonished sternly, and plopped another piece of fried bread at the edge of his plate to replace the two that had somehow disappeared. She thunked a small Mason jar down in front of his plate. "There's some strawberry preserves, if you want them. Mr. Murphy at the grocer's said one of the local ladies made them." And with that, she cut two more sizable slices of bread and turned back to the stove.

Fortunately, one of the slices was for her. As she sat nibbling on the piece she'd doused in preserves, she openly studied him. Michael kept his gaze fixed on his plate and only now and then ventured to spy on her out of the corner of his eye.

He swallowed the last bite, sat back in his chair with a groan of satisfaction, and said, "That was wonderful, Hetty, thank you."

"You're welcome. In case you've forgotten, it's called eating. It's one of the things you're supposed to do regularly—every day, preferably." There wasn't a touch of amusement in her gold-green eyes as she added, "Sleeping is another."

She set her piece of bread on the plate. "You can't help anyone, yourself *or* your patients, if you don't take care of yourself, you know."

She was right. Of course she was right.

"You don't understand, Hetty," Michael objected, frowning at the jar of preserves. "I'm a doctor. There aren't any nice, tidy office hours when you're a doctor."

"And that gives you the right to be rude, on top of everything else?"

Michael winced and forced himself to meet her steady, questioning gaze. "I . . . it was a difficult day yesterday, Hetty. I just . . . I was just too tired to talk. I'm sorry."

Her mouth grew prim. The expression might have been a little more forbidding if it weren't for the trace of strawberry preserves that clung to the corner. "And what about yesterday at noon?"

"Noon?" The preserves were distracting him. His imagination kept suggesting ways he might remove them.

"Downtown, when you demanded your package without so much as a 'Hello, Hetty,' or a thank you, or a word of explanation."

Hetty on her high horse was a sight to get a man's blood stirring. Her eyes sparkled like peridots in sunshine while a faint pink flush traced the curve of her cheek. And then there were those damned preserves.

"And before that, not even a note tacked to your front door to tell me where you'd gone or when I could expect you back. And not one word of apology for not appearing at breakfast."

At her mention of the missed breakfast, all the reasons for his absence came flooding back, drowning Michael's pleasure in the moment and in Hetty. The familiar chill clamped hold of his vitals despite the warmth of the day and the stove with its dying fire behind him.

He couldn't tell Hetty about James Turner. Not here. Not right now. He couldn't tell her about the futile medicines he'd ordered for Jacob Turner, or the seventeen-year-old TB patient, or the five-year-old boy with the missing leg, or . . .

He couldn't tell Hetty any of it.

Furthermore, he didn't want to. There was Hetty and there was his work, and for the past two years he had lived with only the bright, shining memory of the one to keep him company as he confronted the hard, hurtful realities of the other. In some muddled way he could not yet comprehend, the two had become separated as they had not been before he'd left Boston. He saw no reason not to keep them separated still. He wanted Hetty protected, untouched by the harshness that he so often dealt with. She deserved that, especially after the long months she'd spent caring for her mother during her last illness.

Michael's heart swelled. His Hetty had endured so much and come so far, and he had done nothing to support her through any of it. Well, all that would change, starting now. He owed it to her. That, and more.

"I'm sorry, Hetty," he said, and folded his hand over hers where it lay on the shabby gingham tablecloth. "I . . . I guess I haven't really grasped the fact that you're finally here and not half a continent away. I've gotten so used to living like this that I don't know how to do it any differently. But that doesn't mean I'm not willing to learn. Or change. Honest."

As if of their own volition, his fingers curved

into the center of her palm. His fingertips tingled at the warmth of her and the smooth, delicately textured feel of her skin.

Her fingers tightened automatically, trapping his. She blinked, breathed deep, then let her breath out slowly. "Oh, Michael, I'm sorry, too. Not three days and already I'm complaining and trying to pick a quarrel."

"You have every right to the complaining, but you can't pick a quarrel if I don't fight back, now can you?" His hold on her tightened. "Ah, Hetty, I've done a horrible job of welcoming you to Colorado, but I'll make it up to you. I swear I will."

There was an odd little tremor at the edges of her mouth as she fought against the tears that threatened to betray her. "You'd better, Michael Ryan."

She sniffed, a very tidy, practical sort of sniff, and blinked again. "I don't suppose you remembered about the marriage license or anything, did you?"

Michael blenched. He'd forgotten, God forgive him. He'd forgotten entirely. Before he could make that damning confession, Hetty said, "That's all right. I know you had other matters that were more urgent. But I wish . . ."

"You wish . . . ?" Michael prompted when she didn't continue.

"I wish you'd let me help you, Michael. I can, you know. You can trust me. I—"

She didn't have a chance to finish. He was out of his chair and around the table before his heart had time for another beat.

And then she was in his arms, warm and solid and tasting of strawberry jam and Hetty, and that was all Michael could think of.

Hetty pulled back first, caught between laughter and tears and fighting for breath. "My!" she said in a shaky little voice. "Oh, my!" And then she got a better look at him, and the laughter won out altogether.

"What? Are you making fun of my kissing, Miss Malone?"

"It's . . . the . . . preserves. On your . . . chin."

"The what?" Understanding dawned. "You're the one responsible. You were wearing them first. *You* take care of it!"

Ever obedient, Hetty complied by rising on tiptoe to lick the tell-tale traces away.

"Ah!" Michael said a moment later. "Oh . . ."

Hetty retreated at last, trembling, and laid her head upon his chest. Michael gave a long, low groan of contentment.

"You'll have to make lots of strawberry preserves when we're married, Hetty," he murmured at last. "Lots and lots of strawberry preserves."

"Mmmmmm," said Hetty contentedly to his top vest button. "I don't know. We haven't tried plum or raspberry or—"

"Hetty!"

"Well, you're the one who started it!"

Hetty squirmed out of his embrace, and Michael reluctantly let her go. Holding her like this, kissing her, taxed his powers of restraint to the limit. He'd have to marry her soon—*very* soon—or risk going mad with wanting her.

She retreated beyond arm's reach and carefully tugged her apron into place, then tucked in a few errant locks of hair and fluffed her stylishly frizzed bangs. Once more presentable, she turned her sharp gaze on him.

"Your vest is twisted to the side," she said, pointing. "Your tie is crooked, and your hair is mussed."

"That's your fault," Michael grumbled, doing his best to rectify matters.

Her cheeks grew round with the impish smile that claimed her mouth. "I took care of the jam on your chin. You'll have to deal with the rest."

"Why, you—"

Michael lunged for her, but she was quicker. In a flash she was on the opposite side of the table and had pulled a chair out to block his path.

"Your hair is *still* a mess, sir," she said with great dignity.

Michael grabbed the chair, but she retreated around the corner of the table before he could reach her. "Maybe feeding you *was* a bad idea after all."

"That will teach you to meddle."

"What about your patients?"

Michael stopped short with a groan. Almost noon, and he hadn't given one thought to the patients who were waiting for him.

"I have a few visits I absolutely have to make, Hetty. I'm sorry."

"Of course," Hetty said. But for an instant, Michael thought a shadow had crossed her face.

"I think I can arrange for someone to take over

some of the others, though," he added hastily. "I have to make some calls . . ."

He shouldn't promise, Michael knew. He couldn't predict when an emergency would arise. No doctor could. But he owed it to Hetty to try at least.

"I'll be done by three, Hetty. I swear. We could . . . Ummm . . ." What could he possibly offer that would make up for his neglect and surly humor over the past two days? He wasn't even sure what there was in the way of entertainment out there. His work hadn't left him time to indulge in sightseeing excursions or evenings at recitals or any of the other things most folk seemed to fill their time with.

What would *Hetty* like? She liked flowers, he remembered, but December wasn't the month for picking flowers. They'd gone to the circus once, and she'd fallen in love with the elephants and the tigers and the ladies in their spangled tights, but there weren't any circuses in town right now, as far as he knew. She liked long walks and lemonade and chocolate and—

"I know!" Michael exclaimed in relief. "We could meet at Fisk's Pharmacy for a chocolate soda. How does that sound? And then we could go for our marriage license. Together."

For once, he'd said something right. Hetty's face lit up like a child's on the Fourth of July. "Oh, yes!"

"You don't mind about the wait?"

She hesitated, then shook her head, suddenly serious again. "Your patients need you, Michael.

I understand that. It's just . . ."

"It's just . . . ?" Michael prompted when the silence stretched uncomfortably.

Hetty's gaze locked with his across the table. "I need you too, Michael Ryan," she said softly. "Don't ever forget that."

Before he could respond, she clasped her hands together and squared her shoulders. "You have your patients to see to, and I'd best get these dishes done," she said briskly. "Is there anything I can do for you while you're out?"

Michael hesitated. He didn't want to drag her into his demanding life, but she'd said she wanted to help. Something simple, then; enough to serve as apology for having ignored her, but not too much. Nothing unreasonable. "Would you mind taking some pills to Mr. Meissner? I forgot to tell Mrs. Scott to pick them up, and I didn't have time to run them by yesterday."

Hetty smiled, obviously pleased at the small task. "I'd be delighted. I liked him very much. He's a wonderful old man."

"But no whiskey in his coffee! Understood?"

For an instant, Michael thought she was going to argue. Then her eyes started to twinkle and her mouth pursed up as she tried to suppress the wicked grin that threatened.

"Oh, go comb your hair and straighten your tie." As she turned to the sink, Hetty tossed one last order over her shoulder. "And I want the mirror after you're done. If I'm going to go calling on a gentleman, I need to look my best, you know."

Michael was halfway into the bathroom before

the significance of her remark dawned on him. "Hey! I'm a gentleman, too!"

"Humpf!" said Hetty, running water into the sink from the faucet set high in the wall above it. "That's what *you* say!"

Distracted, she inadvertently opened the faucet too far, until the water gushed down, splashing off the flat-bottomed sink and over the front of her apron. Hetty gasped and immediately shut it off, but the damage was done. She whirled about to glare at him, caught between laughter and indignation. "*Now* look what you made me do!"

Discretion being the better part of valor, Michael fled.

The telephone Dr. Cathcart had installed was one of the older models. Even though the door between the hall and the kitchen was shut, Hetty could hear the harsh metallic whir and grind as Michael cranked it. Good manners forbade her eavesdropping, but she would have had to abandon the house altogether to avoid hearing Michael's shouting.

"Number 41, please . . . Oh, hello, Mrs. Jeffers. Changed your duty hours, have you . . . ? Uh-huh . . . I see. Did you try that syrup I suggested . . . ? Oh, really? I'm sorry to hear that. . . . *I said, I'm sorry to hear that*. . . . Yes, yes, she arrived. . . . No, we haven't set a date. . . . Yes, I'll certainly let you know when we do. . . . Number *41* . . . Yes, I'll have other calls to make after."

Hetty grinned as grim mutterings came from behind the door. Her mother had refused to have a telephone installed in the house. Hetty hadn't minded in the least. She found it an intrusive, noisy, and undignified invention, but she supposed it made sense for Michael to have one. Given Michael's passion for science and scientific advancement, he probably would have had one installed if Dr. Cathcart hadn't already done so, no matter how obnoxious the contraption might be.

The telephone, however, didn't concern Hetty nearly as much as the small laboratory she'd found in her explorations before Michael had awakened.

The dark little room, with its marble-topped work space stretching from one side of the room to the other and the floor-to-ceiling shelves with their burden of chemicals and glassware and odd devices whose function Hetty couldn't begin to divine, had been worrisome enough. She didn't much care for the idea of the bedroom she would eventually share with Michael being right next door to a room filled with who knew how many dangerous things—especially if he was going to conduct noisome experiments like whatever had left the bitter smell in the air—but she could deal with that issue when the time came.

No, what troubled Hetty were the bound journals she'd leafed through, each one filled from first page to last with Michael's untidy writing. Most of the notations were totally unintelligible, scientific formulae and endless medical terms that held no interest for her; what little she had understood, however, made it clear that Michael was trying to find a cure for consumption, or tuberculosis, as everyone seemed to call it these days.

Each entry had been carefully dated. Sometimes the time was noted, as well. As Hetty skimmed entry after entry, journal after journal, it quickly became clear that for the last year and a half, Michael had devoted to his research whatever time he had available that wasn't already taken up by his work. He'd even found the energy to work in his lab last night, though he'd refused to talk to her, had almost physically thrust her away from him, in fact.

If she'd found Michael's dedication to his work frustrating these past two days, how was she going to cope with this?

She'd considered confronting him with it this morning, then decided there was nothing to be gained by discussing it now, when there was so much else they needed to sort out between them. Once they were married he would surely set aside this extra burden of work. It was only because she hadn't been here to keep him company that he'd immured himself in his work and his research like a monk sworn to eternal prayer.

"Dr. Stevens, I'm glad I caught you! About that scheduled surgery . . . The boy's receiving morphine, of course, but I'm worried . . . Rapid pulse, shallow respiration, what you'd expect. . . ."

Not prayer, Hetty reminded herself, listening to the awkward, one-sided conversation being conducted on the other side of the door.

Not prayer at all. Service. Michael had dedicated himself to medicine in order to serve others. To save lives. Surely there was no more noble calling than that.

Hetty thought of Samuel Rheiner and his father, so anxious to place their trust in Michael if only Michael would let them. She thought of Mr. Fisk, who worried that Michael took on too many patients who couldn't afford to pay, and of Mr. Meissner, who took a drop of whiskey for his "rheumatiz" and chided Michael about death.

She thought of Michael as she'd found him earlier, sprawled across his bed like a teenage boy. Only he wasn't a boy. Not any longer.

No boy possessed a beard that coarse and black or shoulders that broad and lean-muscled. No boy could have been that exhausted, or carried such shadows in the hollows of his eyes and the hard angles of his face where the skin was stretched too tight across the bone.

Kneeling there beside his bed, Hetty had ached to lay her hand on Michael's face and smooth away the lines of strain that seemed graven across his brow and at the corners of his mouth. She'd longed to touch the silver hairs at his temple, hairs so fine she'd almost missed them among the thick, disordered thatch of black. She'd been afraid to wake him, and yet she'd yearned to lie down beside him on the narrow bed and hold him until he relaxed into her warmth.

She had no idea how long she'd remained there, crouched at the side of the bed watching him sleep while her anger and resentment slowly seeped away. If he hadn't shifted in his sleep, turning away from her and burrowing his face deeper into the pillow, she might have been there still.

But he had moved, and she'd stood and quietly left the room, then just as quietly slipped out of the house to buy groceries so she could feed him when he woke, even if she couldn't comfort him when he slept.

"Yes, Mrs. Jeffers. . . . Thank you. . . . Yes, I'll do that. . . . No, no more calls. . . . Thank you!"

Michael returned the earpiece to its hook with an exasperated bang. For a minute there was silence; then he called out, "I'm just going to check my bag, Hetty. Make sure I've got everything. I'll be ready whenever you are."

By the time Michael emerged from his office, his medical bag firmly gripped in his left hand, his hair combed and his tie and vest properly in place, Hetty had been waiting for him for almost half an hour.

He stopped short when he saw her and his eyes grew wide. "Hetty!"

It was as if he'd forgotten her existence. Hetty suppressed the urge to snap at him, but only by an extreme effort of will. So much for all the promises he'd made not an hour before.

"I . . . I'm sorry. I was checking my medicines and thinking about a couple of my patients and I . . . I just forgot about you." A slow tide of crimson flooded his cheeks. "Used to be it was me who always had to wait around for you."

At least he had the grace to look ashamed, Hetty thought. The thought didn't bring much comfort.

"Seems some things have changed," she said, fighting not to show her hurt. She grabbed her bag and marched out the door, head high.

Abashed, Michael followed her onto the porch, then turned to pull the door closed behind him.

"If you can forget me this quickly, Michael," Hetty said coolly, "are you sure you'll remember to be at Fisk's Pharmacy at three?"

Michael wasn't paying any attention. He was fumbling about, patting his trouser pockets, then his coat pockets, then the hidden pockets in the breast of his coat. The longer he fumbled without producing anything, the deeper his frown grew.

Hetty sighed. She was wasting her breath asking for his assurances, anyway.

"Is this what you were looking for?" she asked, holding his door key up by its shank.

He jerked around, irritated. The minute he spotted the key, his jaw dropped. "Where—?"

"I took it with me yesterday after you'd left it in the lock and the door wide open. How did you think I got in this morning?"

Judging from his embarrassed scowl, he hadn't thought about it at all. He plucked the thing out of her fingers and neatly locked the door, then pocketed the key.

"The livery stable's that way," he said, pointing. He took her elbow and led her down the steps and out the gate. "I've got to remember to leave written instructions with the head nurse. Forgot yesterday. And I need . . ."

Hetty heard him talking, but she suddenly found it impossible to focus on the words. Michael wasn't talking to her, he was talking to himself. She might as well not have been there for all the attention he paid her.

She could feel the warmth of his hand, even through her jacket and shirtwaist. They were so close that she could hear the soft sound of his breathing as they walked. But as she looked up into his face, she realized that Michael had already moved away from her, back into his closed world of medicine, where she couldn't follow . . . and he didn't want her to.

Suddenly, all the brightness went out of her day.

# *Chapter Nine*

To Hetty's disappointment, Mr. Meissner wasn't any more interested in horehound drops than Michael seemed to be these days.

"Never touch 'em," the old man said, waving away the white paper bag Hetty had offered him. "My Ida used to swear by 'em, but I never did like 'em. Whiskey's better if you have the cough, you know." He winked at her, for all the world like a little boy sharing a delightfully naughty secret.

The little bit of whiskey she'd poured in his coffee the day before obviously hadn't done him a bit of harm. It was having company and an interested audience for his tales that made his watery old eyes light up. Hetty listened and laughed and wished Michael could have been there to laugh along with her.

"Mr. Meissner," Hetty said at last. "I have a big favor to ask you."

"Yes?" He straightened, obviously pleased that someone thought he could be of use.

Hetty fished several folded sheets of paper out of her bag. "These are recipes a little boy and I copied out of a German lady's cookbook yesterday. We need someone to translate them and I thought, if it wouldn't be too much trouble, that you might be willing to help us."

Mr. Meissner propped his elbows on the arm of his chair and leaned forward, listening intently as she told him about the Rheiners and Samuel's ambition to prepare some of his grandmother's dishes for his mother.

"I don't know if we got it all right or even what it is we *do* have," Hetty said, handing him the papers. "We just copied the first few pages of recipes as best we could. The ink's faded and some of the words were very hard to read, but I thought . . . that is, I hoped it would be enough to start with."

Mr. Meissner tilted his head back and peered down his nose at the pages, but no matter which way he turned them, his arms weren't anywhere near long enough. "Ahh," he said at last in disgust. "I need my glasses. But yes, I will translate them for you."

Hetty gave a very undignified bounce. "Oh, thank you!"

"It will take some time, you know," Mr. Meissner warned, carefully folding the papers and placing them on the table beside his chair.

"That's all right. We—Samuel and I—we appreciate whatever you can do!"

Hetty rose to leave when Mr. Meissner started to droop in his big chair. She kissed him goodbye, which pleased him, and promised she'd be back as soon as she was able, and warned him to behave himself until she did. The last admonition made him cackle with delight, but he refused to promise. "A man just never knows what might come up, you see," he said, lovingly smoothing his mustache into place.

Mrs. Scoggins was just as pleased to have her company, though she managed to cover her enthusiasm a great deal more effectively.

"Humpf," she said when Hetty told her how much the Rheiners had appreciated her gift of bed linens and towels. "They won't last long when they're boiled in a pot and scrubbed on a rock, I can assure you."

Hetty had an instant's disconcerting image of the Rheiners being tumbled about in an enormous tub of laundry before she realized that Mrs. Scoggins had been referring to the hand towels, not the Rheiners.

"I also suggested to Betty that she might go with you on your next visit. She's collected a few items that might be useful. And," she added sternly when Hetty started to interrupt, "you'll be doing me a favor by letting her accompany you. Really, I'm not at all sure where she gets her energy. If I have to remind her one more time that a lady *walks* up the stairs . . . ! Well! I really *can-*

*not* be held accountable for my tongue, under the circumstances!"

Since an excited Betty had greeted her at the door with a long list of all the foodstuffs and household items Mrs. Scoggins had instructed her to pack for the Rheiners, Hetty had a very good idea of just how much of a favor would be done, and by whom.

"It will be very hard for that poor family," Mrs. Scoggins said with a frown. "When we came—I believe I mentioned that my husband and son were consumptive, did I not?"

Hetty didn't think Mrs. Scoggins saw her nod, for she was looking at the photograph, not at Hetty, as she spoke.

"Mr. Scoggins at least had a sizable personal income besides the revenues from his business. We bought some land near the city and started building a house on it, but he grew too ill to manage the drive, so we bought this house, as well."

She gave a wintery smile. "I've never been able to let that first house go, even though it's more nuisance than anything else. Most of the land is leased by a nearby rancher, but there's still the main house and property and a smaller house for the caretaker—when I can find one. The last one left almost a month ago, and I've found no one I'd trust to replace him. I've leased it on occasion, but most people find it's just far enough from town to be a nuisance. Pity, really. The view from there is truly breathtaking."

For a moment she fell silent and her gaze turned inward toward her memories. Hetty wasn't sure Mrs. Scoggins even remembered she was there.

The sound of Betty clattering up the stairs jerked Mrs. Scoggins out of her reverie. The girl must have been three-fourths of the way up before she remembered her employer's injunctions against running. The clatter came to an abrupt halt. There was an instant's silence, then the sound of a dignified, measured tread upon the remaining stairs.

Mrs. Scoggins sighed, then smiled wryly. "My son was as bad as Betty, I'm afraid. Forever running up and down the stairs, even though we told him not to. It was only at the end . . ."

She caught herself, as if embarrassed at having said so much, but once the floodgates were lifted, it seemed she couldn't stop her memories.

"He used to play hide-and-seek. He thought it was so amusing to have us all chasing about, trying to find him. Once he jumped out at me from under the stairs, just like a little goblin, you know. It pleased him no end that he made me shriek in a *most* unladylike fashion. He liked sliding down the banister, too. Scared me out of my wits the first time I caught him at it, but he just laughed and ran up to do it again."

Her pale eyes fixed on Hetty. "Children think they'll live forever, you see. They don't know—how can they?—just how fragile life really is."

Hetty thought of a seven-year-old Michael, face down in the snow, flailing his fists and sobbing and desperately crying out to his mother not to leave him.

Mrs. Scoggins was wrong on that account, at least. Children *did* know how fragile life was. There just wasn't anything they could do about it.

Only adults like Michael were mad enough to think they could beard Death in his dark den, as if they had some say in the ordering of the world.

Fisk's Pharmacy was warm and welcoming after the long walk from Mr. Meissner's to Mrs. Scoggins's to the pharmacy. The bell at the top of the door jangled merrily as she walked in, rousing the resident spirit.

"Afternoon," Mr. Fisk called from behind his marble counter. "Didn't think to see you back so soon."

"Dr. Ryan is treating me to a chocolate soda." Hetty crossed her fingers and hoped she wasn't lying. According to her watch, there were still a couple of minutes to go to three o'clock. Michael would surely be walking in any minute now.

"That so?" Mr. Fisk pursed his lips and frowned at her. "Ginger beer would be better. Settles the stomach and cools the blood. Or lemonade, but that's not as good for the blood as ginger beer. But ice cream . . ."

He shook his head mournfully. "Can't say I approve of ice cream, even though I carry it for those as want it. All that cream and sugar's hard to digest. Blocks the bowels, you know."

Laughter suddenly formed at the back of Hetty's throat. "I'm afraid I'm partial to chocolate sodas, Mr. Fisk, no matter how dangerous they might be."

"Well, don't say I didn't warn you." His sigh was so deep, it seemed to be sucked up from his toes. After a moment's consideration, he said, a little more cheerfully this time, "Of course, Mrs. Fisk is fond of an ice cream soda now and then herself. Her bowels seem to work just fine. Maybe you'll be resistant to the deleterious effect of the ice cream, too."

"I . . . ahem! I certainly hope so, Mr. Fisk."

The bell rang suddenly. Hetty turned and almost broke into a jubilant jig as Michael walked in, closely followed by a boy of about sixteen trailing adoringly in his wake.

". . . I've been studying that book you lent me, Dr. Ryan, *The Cottage Physician,* and I think it's pretty interesting even if it *does* have a strange name, and I was wondering—" The boy suddenly caught the full force of Mr. Fisk's disapproving stare. His flood of words stopped as abruptly as if he'd swallowed them.

"Don't you be pestering Dr. Ryan, Joseph," Mr. Fisk said sternly.

"He's not pestering me, Mr. Fisk." Michael grinned at Hetty and tapped his pocket watch. "Three minutes late. Not too bad."

"No, not too bad," Hetty agreed, beaming up at him. With his cheerful teasing, all the doubts that had been troubling her for the past few hours suddenly melted away like ice in Arizona. "Guess I won't have any reason to complain, after all."

"I'm not pestering Dr. Ryan, Mr. Fisk," Joseph

said. "Honest! I just met him on the street outside and I was telling him—"

"Well, maybe you should be telling him some other time. He's here to see his fiancée, not listen to you, you know."

"His fia—" Joseph's eyes grew wide and his face flushed bright red as he glanced over at Hetty. "Oh!"

"I'm Hetty Malone," Hetty said, extending her hand. It didn't look as if either Michael or Mr. Fisk would have the good sense to introduce them.

The boy hastily wiped his hand on the side of his pants before shaking hers. "You're the lady who's going to be Mrs. Dr. Ryan?"

"Well, yes, I guess I am!" Hetty agreed, laughing.

"*I'm* going to be a doctor, too! Just like Dr. Ryan!" Joseph's shoulders went back and his chest expanded a good three inches with pride. "He's lent me lots of books, but my favorite so far is *Responsibilities of the Physician*. He said I should study it 'cause I'd have to be real sure I wanted to be a doctor, just like him. And I do!" the boy added, grinning up at Michael.

He turned back to Hetty. "You should have seen the way he fixed my pa's leg when Dr. Sherwood was just going to cut it off! I want to do that, too! Pa's up and walking now, you know. Says he's going to be back at work real soon and—"

"Things don't always work out as well as they did for your father, Joseph," Michael interrupted, clearly uncomfortable with the boy's enthusiasm.

"And don't forget," Mr. Fisk added, "if it weren't for the pharmacists, you'd be in a heap of trouble." For emphasis, he thumped his fist on the marble counter dividing his *sanctum sanctorum* from the rest of the world. "Drugs! Medicines! Vaccines! That's the ticket! Doctors are just fine for broken legs, but where would you be without the pharmacist? Surgeon's no good for a cough, now, is he?"

Michael nodded, but Hetty could see the sudden wicked gleam in his eyes. He glanced down at Joseph and winked. "I won't deny the pharmacist has an important job, but I don't recall ever seeing one at the patient's bedside at two in the morning. At least, not for any of the patients *I've* attended!"

"Humph! Folks took their medicine, they wouldn't *get* sick at two A.M.! You remember that, boy!"

"Yes, sir. And what sort of medicine are they supposed to take for babies, sir?"

Mr. Fisk gasped. Hetty choked. Michael studiously inspected a nearby display of Dr. Cook's Condition Powders for Horses and Cattle.

"To keep them from coming at all hours, I mean," Joseph added, the picture of perfect innocence. "Seems most of my brothers and sisters have arrived in the middle of the night. Makes it hard to sleep, what with all the commotion. Even if we do get sent over to the neighbors right off."

"Babies, is it?" Mr. Fisk snorted and wiggled his eyebrows menacingly. "Humph! Best you get back to work, *I'd* say, and stop worrying about babies. Babies!"

Joseph's eyebrows knitted together in a stubborn frown, but he'd been too well brought up to argue with his employer. He sighed. "Yes, sir."

"What can I get for you, Dr. Ryan?" he asked as Mr. Fisk retreated, muttering, into his den. It evidently hadn't occurred to Joseph that Hetty might have wanted to place her own order.

"A chocolate soda for Miss Malone," Michael said, struggling to control his laughter. "With extra chocolate sauce—right, Hetty? And a ginger beer for me."

Hetty snorted. Michael looked at her blankly, but she just smiled sweetly and didn't offer any explanation.

Michael claimed one of the four small, marble-topped tables that occupied the open area in front of the soda fountain while Joseph disappeared to work his magic behind the counter.

Hetty took the chair Michael held for her. "It seems you've been encouraging rebellion in the ranks," she said, very low so neither Mr. Fisk nor Joseph could overhear.

Michael gave her a wry grin and claimed the seat opposite. He stashed his medical bag under the table, out of the way. "I hadn't intended to. I didn't realize until it was too late that Mr. Fisk was grooming Joseph to be his assistant someday."

"And now you're leading him astray. Tsk."

"Me!"

"That bit about the babies. You can't tell me he

didn't know *exactly* what he was suggesting."

The corner of Michael's mouth twitched. "It's the medical books. There's one with a lot of diagrams, you see—"

"Diagrams?"

"Would you like me to show you?"

She shouldn't say it. Really she should *not* say it. No lady would ever dream of saying anything like it, in public *or* private.

"Actually," Hetty said, "I think I'd rather have a demonstration."

Michael's eyes lit up. Fortunately, Joseph saved her by suddenly appearing with a chocolate soda in a tall, fluted glass in one hand and a fizzing ginger beer in a regular glass in the other.

At sight of the ginger beer, Hetty snickered.

"What?" Michael eyed her warily, the glass halfway to his mouth.

"Mr. Fisk approves of ginger beer," Hetty said, striving for the same air of innocence Joseph had demonstrated earlier.

"Does he?"

"You should ask him sometime."

Michael grinned and took a long swig, then set the glass down on the table. "Ahhh. I didn't realize how thirsty I was. And just in case you were wondering," he added politely, "I've listened to some of Mr. Fisk's lectures on diet and good health."

"Have you?"

"I think I'll stick to bacon and eggs."

Hetty grinned and dug into the froth-covered ice cream, savoring the fizzy-sweet combination of soda water, ice cream, and chocolate sauce. "Mmmm. This is good." Throwing manners to the winds, she lifted her glass to sip at the foam on the top.

Michael laughed. "You have a chocolate mustache, Hetty. A big one." He leaned across the table and wiped away the traces of foam on Hetty's upper lip.

The tip of his finger barely touched her skin—just one quick stroke on the right side of her mouth, another on the left—yet Hetty felt the force of it clear down to her toes, with an extra-spectacular response somewhere right in the middle.

Deliberately—and very provocatively—she brushed her upper lip with the tip of her tongue. Michael's eyes widened and his mouth opened as he took a deep breath.

"You haven't properly appreciated a chocolate soda if you haven't made a mustache," Hetty said complacently, pleased with herself—and Michael's reaction.

What did it matter if she wasn't behaving like a lady? In an hour, two at most, she and Michael would have their license to marry. A day or so to make the final arrangements with a preacher and they could be married, man and wife till death did them part.

The thought sent a shaft of heat lancing through her body.

As if he'd just had the same thought—and the same reaction—Michael reluctantly leaned back in the small, wire-backed chair, watching her with deep, dark blue eyes. His long legs didn't fit easily under the small table, but he sat relaxed, like a man determined to enjoy the moment.

Hetty breathed deeply, trying to gather her scattered wits and still her suddenly racing pulse. It didn't work. And what was wrong with enjoying the moment, anyway?

"Mr. Fisk doesn't approve of ice cream or chocolate sodas," she said provocatively.

"No?"

"No." With great aplomb, she scooped a chocolate-and-soda frothed lump of ice cream out of the fluted glass and stuck it in her mouth.

"Stops up the bowels, isn't that right?" Michael inquired politely.

Hetty laughed, choked, then tried to scowl, but fell into a fit of coughing giggles, instead. "Don't *do* that!" she protested.

"Do what?" Michael bent to retrieve the spoon she'd dropped. "I wasn't the one who took too big a mouthful of ice cream. You didn't see me choking on my ginger beer, did you?"

"That's because you drank half of it in one swallow!"

"Efficiency. That's the ticket," Michael agreed amiably, setting the long-handled spoon back on the table.

It was such a silly conversation, Hetty thought, but if silly conversations could get Michael to forget his patients and his responsibilities, even for a little while, she would gladly talk nonsense, morning to night.

"Dr. Ryan!"

Hetty and Michael jerked around in their chairs to find Clarabelle Fisk bearing down on them from the back of the store like a locomotive with a strong head of steam.

"Miss Malone! How nice to see you!"

Michael rose to his feet. "Mrs. Fisk." He pulled a chair up to the table. "Won't you join us?"

Good manners prevented him from doing anything else, but it was all Hetty could do to keep from scowling.

"Don't mind if I do," Mrs. Fisk said, carefully settling onto the offered chair. "I see your fiancée has managed to make you take an hour off. Good thing. You work much too hard, you know. Much too hard. Mr. Fisk has said so any number of times."

Hetty's heart sank as she watched the good humor drain from Michael's face.

"Unfortunately, Mrs. Fisk," he said, "sick people don't take days off."

"They certainly don't seem to," Mrs. Fisk agreed equably. "I can't tell you the number of times Mr. Fisk has had to open up the shop special just because some child had developed the croup. You'd think young mothers would know that camphorated oil and a plaster of warmed onions would work as well as all those fancy syrups. Though I hope," she said, leaning forward and lowering her voice conspiratorially, "you won't tell Mr. Fisk so. He sets such store by his medicines, you know, and doesn't approve of all those old-fashioned remedies."

Hetty couldn't help smiling in spite of her irritation. "I understand your husband doesn't approve of ice cream sodas, either," she said.

Mrs. Fisk's double chins set stubbornly. "He's always lecturing me about them. Not that I pay it any attention, mind. I've never been sick a day in my life, ice cream sodas or no."

Even Michael had to smile. "Then you're just the kind of patient a doctor likes to have, Mrs. Fisk—one that never needs him."

She chuckled, clearly pleased. "Now, what would you doctors do if everyone were that healthy? Why—"

She never got a chance to finish. The doorbell suddenly started jangling wildly, the door itself banged open, then shut, and a black-coated whirlwind blew in.

"Doc? Doc! Thank God! They said you were here!"

The whirlwind abruptly resolved itself into Mr. Davidson, the clerk from the train depot. Tie askew and coattails flapping, he came rushing toward them.

Drawn by the racket, Joseph popped his head up over the shelves he was stacking and Mr. Fisk peered out from the pharmacy, eyes blinking myopically behind his glasses. Michael was already reaching for the medical bag he'd left under the table.

Hetty was the first to speak. "Mr. Davidson! Whatever in the world—?"

"You're needed down at the station, Doc. Quick! Gentleman, just come in with his family on the afternoon train. We've got him in the stationmaster's office, but he's coughin' up blood something awful. His wife's in fits and the kids cryin' and we don't know what to do. You gotta come!"

"Of course I'll come." Medical bag in hand, Michael was on his feet and digging in his pocket for coins to pay for their drinks. "I'm sorry, Hetty," he said as he tossed three nickels onto the table. "Probably best if you go on home. Back to Mrs. Spencer's."

One of the nickels started to roll toward the edge. Without conscious thought, Hetty slapped it flat just before it rolled over the edge and onto the floor. She started to speak, then stopped. Michael was already halfway out the door.

"Don't wait for me!" he called over his shoulder an instant before the door slammed behind him.

"Sorry to interrupt you, miss." Mr. Davidson grimaced apologetically. "Didn't have a choice. *You* understand." Then he, too, was gone, leaving Hetty gaping at the empty doorway while the clangor of the bell slowly died away.

"Well, good gracious." Mrs. Fisk sat staring, gape-jawed, at the empty doorway.

"Should have used the telephone," her husband said in disgust. "Frederick Davidson always goes off half-cocked like that."

Joseph, clearly excited by the commotion, came around from behind the tall display shelves. "Must be something pretty awful. Wish *I* could go. Dr. Ryan might need some help."

"Dr. Ryan can do just fine without your help," Mr. Fisk said sternly. "Sounds serious enough that he won't need any boy getting underfoot."

Hetty was only half listening. *Wife in fits and children crying,* Mr. Davidson had said. Michael, on the other hand, had simply told her to go home.

Go home when Michael would have his hands full with a sick man and there'd be no one to help the distraught wife or see to the children? Hetty's head came up and her jaw hardened. Not likely!

With brisk determination, she picked up her crocheted bag from under the table and rose to her feet. "Will fifteen cents be enough?" she asked.

Mrs. Fisk didn't even seem to hear her. She was still staring at the front door.

Joseph reluctantly turned his attention back to his work. "Fifteen cents? Oh!" His eyes widened at the sight of the three nickels on the table. "Oh, yes, ma'am! Fact is, it's too much. Soda and a ginger beer. That only comes to a dime. And you haven't even finished your soda."

He tried to return the extra five cents, then beamed when Hetty waved him away. "Thank you, ma'am. Tell Doctor Ryan I appreciate it!"

Hetty waved acknowledgment from the doorway an instant before the door banged shut behind her, too. Mr. Fisk was going to be a bit irritated with all the racket, but it couldn't be helped. Michael needed her.

Michael didn't know the woman before him, but he'd seen the look in her eyes countless times before. Desperation, hope, and anger, all hopelessly jumbled up together—and all aimed directly at him. The doctor. The man of science who was expected to have all the answers.

But what did the doctor do, Michael wondered, when he didn't have any answers? The muscles of his shoulders and chest tightened involuntarily. With careful deliberation, he shifted his medical bag to his left hand and extended his right. "I'm Dr. Ryan. Dr. Michael Ryan."

Her hand was cold within his, her skin rough and callused by years of hard work. Her fingers trembled, ever so slightly, then stilled an instant before she pulled away from him.

"I'm Jessica Lanyon." She glanced toward the far side of the room where a long wooden bench had been converted into a makeshift bed. "And that's my husband, George."

Under a heavy lap rug, his head supported on a pile of blood-spotted pillows, lay the thinnest man Michael had ever seen. His skin was colorless. Not pale, but completely drained of life until it seemed the fine white bone of his skull shone through. His eyes were closed, deeply sunk and shadowed, his brown hair dull and matted. His chest rose and fell in a shallow, unhealthy rhythm as his lungs strained to drag in air. His hands, sculpted into pale claws by the disease which was consuming him, clutched the rug as if they had tried, and failed, to lift its heavy weight, and he now lay still, resigned to ultimate defeat.

The symptoms were unmistakable—the wasted body, the bloodless skin, the lingering traces of bloody foam at the corner of the man's mouth, and the blood stains on the pillows. Most of all, the agonizing cough that brought up blood, followed by a desperate and failing effort to breathe.

Michael fought back the sick feeling of familiarity. He was a doctor and he had work to do—even if there was nothing, absolutely nothing, that he *could* do except ease the man's suffering in the last few hours left him on earth.

But first things first. He turned to meet the angry, watchful gaze of Lionel Harrison, the stationmaster and the office's usual occupant. Harrison didn't speak, but Michael had no trouble reading the big man's thoughts. Death and suffering were to be respected, but they weren't allowed to interfere with the work of the station. He wanted these interlopers out of his office, and he expected Michael to see to it as quickly as possible.

"I'll need that table, Lionel," Michael said, pointing. "And a chair. And you'd better bring a basin." He saw the quick flare of resentment but ignored it.

Reluctantly, the stationmaster dragged the heavy table across the floor, then grabbed a chair from the far corner while Michael removed his coat, opened his medical bag, and began laying out the instruments he'd need.

It wasn't until he turned to accept the basin that Harrison had rousted out from somewhere that Michael spotted the two children, a boy and a girl, who sat huddled together in the broad oak chair behind the desk. They'd been hidden earlier, protected by the hovering bulk of the stationmaster. Alone in their corner, they looked like rag dolls tossed out of the way and forgotten.

Michael blinked and looked away, unable to bear their beseeching, bewildered gaze. They shouldn't be there, but there was no place else for them to go and nothing he could do to help them right now.

At the first touch of Michael's fingers against his wrist, George Lanyon opened his eyes. Michael watched as the soul behind them slowly swam back to an awareness of its surroundings, then just as quickly retreated into the self-absorption of the dying.

The physical examination didn't take long.

Pulse weak. Breathing shallow and too fast. Skin cold and bloodless, eyes sunken. Only the tops of Lanyon's lungs produced the hollow echo that indicated they were still functioning. The rest, filled with blood, fluid, and diseased tissue, gave back a lifeless thud.

George Lanyon would be dead by morning . . . if he could last that long.

Michael let his stethoscope drop and sat back in the chair he'd drawn up beside the bench, struggling to keep his expression from revealing what he'd found.

As if in confirmation of the diagnosis, a sudden bout of coughing shook Lanyon. He hunched his shoulders against the spasms as his lungs tried to rid themselves of the blood and fluid that were drowning him, but he was too weak to do more than aim for the basin Michael held for him.

When the racking coughs finally eased, he collapsed against his pillows, exhausted. He didn't seem to notice that Michael's starched white shirt was now spotted with blood.

"Have you ever hemorrhaged before?" Michael asked, setting the half-filled basin under the bench, out of sight.

Lanyon ignored him. It was his wife who answered. "A few times, at home. And on the train. That's why they put us off. The bleeding stopped, but they still put us off."

Michael nodded. "How much?"

"Just a little, really," the woman said. Michael could see her lie—and her fear—in her eyes. He didn't respond, but looked at her steadily for a moment, willing her to tell him—and to face the truth herself.

She slumped in her chair and her hand tightened around her husband's. "A . . . a lot. I don't know how much. Seemed like he can't stop and he can't breath and—" She cut her words off sharply and took a deep breath. "A lot."

"I know it's very frightening, but at least you're here, instead of being jostled and crowded on the train."

Useless words that offered no comfort and no hope, but what else could he say? He couldn't lie and he wouldn't offer false hope. But he couldn't bring himself to tell her the truth, either. Not while that wild desperation gleamed in her eyes. Not while her children sat in a chair only a few feet away, listening to every word that was said. Just as he'd sat, all those years ago, hopelessly alone while the world he'd known shattered into a thousand unrecognizable shards around him.

Hope was the only thing Pandora had managed to keep in the little box she'd opened. Mrs. Lanyon wasn't going to abandon it until she had to, and he wasn't going to try to make her.

"We were headed to Arizona," she said, her eyes fixed on her husband. "Dr. Clancey—that's our doctor back home—said he thought the dry air might help. Brother-in-law to one of my cousins went West maybe twenty years ago for his consumption. He has grandkids now. George thought . . . we hoped . . ."

Her voice trailed off painfully. She couldn't go on, and she couldn't break down in front of her husband or her children. She couldn't afford to.

Hers was the heaviest burden, Michael thought, remembering the empty look in his father's eyes after his mother died.

Like his father, Jessica Lanyon would bear the responsibility for helping her children through the empty days that lay ahead, no matter how difficult her own struggles with grief might be. Unlike his father, she would have the additional trials that inevitably descended upon a woman who had lost her husband and her sole source of support.

Michael hoped to God she was stronger than his father had been.

The children would have to face a loss that they were still too young to understand fully, just as he had had to face the loss of his mother. They would turn to their mother for consolation, and

# Chapter Ten

Hetty found the station house buzzing like a beehive. Word had spread that a stranger, seriously ill and possibly dying, had been put off the train, and no one wanted to miss the excitement. Disaster, it seemed, had a stimulating effect on the populace.

Frederick Davidson was trying, rather ineffectually, to keep the gawkers back from the long wooden counter that divided the waiting area from his own narrow work space. Every so often he threw a nervous glance over his shoulder at a door which stood open behind his desk. According to a metal sign nailed to the wall beside it, the door led to the office of Lionel Harrison, Stationmaster.

Hetty hesitated, suddenly caught between her determination to offer what help she could and an uncomfortable sense that she was placing herself on the same level as the people around her by forcing her way in when she wasn't invited. She glanced at them, crowded in front of the counter like ghouls at the edge of a graveyard, and shuddered.

No, not ghouls, she silently amended, studying the faces around her. Most of these people knew what pain and suffering and loss were. But *this* pain, *this* loss, did not touch them. They could feel the brush of Death's robes as he passed without fear of being swept up in the suffering he brought.

Not that Death would stop here today, Hetty told herself firmly. Not if Michael could help it.

A breathless voice at her side startled her.

"I came quick as I could," Mrs. Fisk said, pressing her hand to her heart. "Had the horse and buggy out back. Where's Dr. Ryan, then?"

"Back there, I think," Hetty said, pointing toward the open doorway.

"Lionel Harrison's office." Mrs. Fisk's mouth drew into a tight line. "He won't be pleased about that."

Because of the press of the crowd, Hetty had to force her way to Mr. Davidson's side. "Dr. Ryan needs me," she said. Without giving him a chance to stop her, she opened the wooden gate set into the counter and sailed across to the office at the back. Behind her, she heard Mrs. Fisk's protests as Mr. Davidson moved to block the gate, but she wasn't going to waste time interfering.

A big, barrel-chested man glanced up at Hetty's

entrance. He was leaning against the desk, arms crossed, his back to the rest of the room. No one else paid her the slightest attention.

Hetty moved close so she could keep her voice low. "Mr. Harrison?"

He nodded warily.

"I'm Hetty Malone, Dr. Ryan's fiancée. I'm here to help him."

His shaggy eyebrows lifted, and his broad chest swelled as he took a deep breath of relief. While Hetty was taking in her surroundings, Mr. Harrison took advantage of his opportunity and slipped out of the office.

Hetty didn't try to stop him. Her attention was fixed on the opposite end of the room, where a man lay half-buried under a heavy lap rug. A woman sat beside him, desperately clinging to the lap rug and watching him with eyes grown so round and hollow that she seemed to be devouring him with her gaze. Hetty didn't need to be a doctor to know the man was dying of consumption.

She could see the grim admission of Michael's impotence in the tension that gripped his tall body. His coat was off, his vest hung open, and he was standing, his back half turned to the door, beside a table that had been shoved near the bench. His medical bag gaped open on the table and he was in the process of mixing some sort of liquid in a finger-smeared glass, probably the only thing that could be found in the office at such short notice.

Evidently satisfied with the potion he'd concocted, Michael turned back to the makeshift bed, glass in hand. To her horror, Hetty saw that the starched white cuffs and sleeves and breast of his shirt were spotted with blood, just like the pillows.

He threw her a glance that seemed to say, "We'll talk about this later," then bent and lifted the suffering man's head and held the glass to his lips.

"Drink this. It will ease the pain a little and perhaps stop the coughing."

The man opened his eyes, but he didn't seem to be fully aware of either Michael or his wife. Instead, he stared into the floating dust motes as though striving to see what lay beyond them and the dull gold light that held them. At the first touch of the liquid against his throat, he burst into a wet, racking cough.

Hetty was at Michael's side in an instant. She took the glass from his hands while he held the man as the stranger retched into an enameled metal basin that had been placed on the floor by the bench.

Unable to bear the pitiful sight, Hetty turned her head away and found herself looking straight at two small children, huddled together in Mr. Harrison's big desk chair, clinging to each other as they watched their father's helpless battle for life. The eldest, a boy, couldn't have been more than five, but he'd wrapped his arms around his little sister with fierce protectiveness. The little girl's plump cheeks were streaked with the tracks of her tears.

The child wasn't crying now. She huddled in the shelter of her brother's arms, her little legs drawn up as she tried to make herself into as small a ball as possible. As if, thought Hetty, she hoped that God might not shatter her life if she made herself too small to be found.

Hetty was on the point of setting aside the glass and going to comfort the children, but the man's desperate coughing had eased enough so that Michael was settling him back on the narrow bench. "Let's try again," he said, as gently as a mother comforting a child, and stretched out his hand for the glass Hetty held.

"Nothing stops the cough," the woman said, watching her husband feebly struggle to sip from the glass. "Nothing. That's why we were going to Arizona. We'll never make it now." She burst into tears at that and slid off the chair onto her knees beside her husband, limp and sobbing as if her heart was breaking. "Oh, George! George!"

Hetty knelt beside her. "Ma'am. Dear ma'am. Shush now. Shush," she said, scarcely knowing what she was saying. She wrapped her arms about the woman, trying to draw her away, but grief had given the other a strength out of proportion to her thin, care-worn frame.

"What are we to do?" she demanded of her husband in a voice choked with the tears streaming down her face. She wrapped her work-hardened hands around his and held on, as if she hoped to anchor him beside her so he couldn't slip away. "You can't leave us. Not here. Not like this. Please, George. Please. Oh, God! Please!"

At her mother's panicked cries, the little girl began whimpering again, but Hetty couldn't afford to worry about that now. It was all she could do to keep the woman from throwing herself across her husband.

"Come, now. Let Dr. Ryan help your husband," Hetty soothed, tugging at the woman's shoulders, trying to draw her away. "You mustn't cry. Not now. He needs your strength, don't you see? You have to be strong. For his sake. And the children's."

Hetty couldn't tell if the woman understood her or not, but she allowed herself to be drawn back to her chair, too weakened by grief and fear to fight against Hetty's insistent pull.

Michael was too busy tending to the dying man to spare them a glance. He shifted the pillows, plumping them up and rearranging them so the man's head was raised and slightly tilted back, freeing the airways a little. A very little.

With his gold pocket watch open in one hand, Michael counted the man's pulse. Hetty saw his lips move, ever so slightly, as he counted. He frowned, snapped the watch shut, and tucked it back in its vest pocket. His grim expression was gone as quickly as it had appeared, hidden behind the coolly professional expression of a doctor who was determined to keep the worst from his patient.

Carefully, he laid the man's hand on his chest. His long fingers, usually so refined and pale-looking, appeared unusually strong and coarse against the stranger's bony, wasted wrist. Neither his patient nor his patient's wife heeded the contrast. The former had once more withdrawn into his blind, hopeless struggle to breathe, and the latter was slumped in her chair, sobbing into her hands.

Hetty met Michael's somber gaze. His eyes were almost colorless, the brilliant blue that had been there earlier washed out by the pain of helping a man to die.

An anguished sniff reminded her that there were others in the room in need of care. Hetty glanced at the frightened children, huddled in their chair. They were so young! She shuddered to think what they'd had to bear in the past months, and how much more would weigh upon them in the days and weeks to come.

She rose and drew Michael aside. "Can he be moved? Surely there's a boarding house close by that could take them in. I don't think they could afford a room at the hotel, but *this* place . . ."

A shadow passed over Michael's features. "No, he can't be moved. He doesn't have much longer, and the jostling if we tried to lift him . . ." He shook his head. "I won't consider it unless we can be sure there's room and he's willing to try. Besides, Mr. Davidson said they'd already tried, even before they came to get me." His mouth thinned to an angry line. "Nobody wants them, under the circumstances."

"I'll find somebody. Leave it to me." Hetty lightly touched his hand in reassurance. "And the children. They shouldn't be here."

Michael's brows knitted in a sudden fierce

frown. "He's their father. They have the right—"

"Of course they do. But they're so young, Michael, and so frightened. Their mother doesn't have time for them right now, and that only makes it worse."

Michael sighed and his broad shoulders sagged. "I know. Perhaps Mrs. Spencer . . ."

"Don't worry about it. You have enough to do as it is."

"You shouldn't have come, you know," he said. Yet despite the admonition, he placed his hands on her shoulders, as if to reassure himself of her solidity, then bent to brush a kiss on her forehead. "But I'm glad you did."

"Yes," Hetty said. "Well." She would walk through hell and back for him. Knowing that it mattered to him made the journey easier. "I'll see if I can find someone to help."

As Michael turned back to his patient, Hetty crossed to kneel in front of the children. "Hello," she said, very gently so as not to frighten them. "My name's Hetty. What's yours?"

The little boy protectively drew his sister closer. "Our daddy's sick, isn' he? Real sick," he said, fighting manfully against the quaver in his voice.

"Yes, I'm afraid he is. That's why Dr. Ryan's here. To help him as much as he can."

The boy's lower lip quivered. Then his jaw hardened. "Doctors don't do him no good," he said truculently. "Ma said so. That's why we're goin' to Arizona."

"Well . . ." Hetty said helplessly. How could she respond to that?

"I gotta go pee," the little girl said plaintively, studying Hetty with round, tearful eyes. "I'm a big girl now. Momma says so. She says I shouldn't make more work for her by not bein' a big girl, but I gotta go pee."

She hiccupped and her face started to crumple at the pain and confusion of being caught between the need to be held and comforted and her desperate need to be a "big girl" so she wouldn't cause any trouble and anger her parents.

"I'll take you, Sarah," the boy said defensively, as if he expected Hetty to accuse him of neglecting his sister. "Don' you worry. But hang on a little longer, okay?"

"Yes, just for a little bit," Hetty said soothingly. "I'm going to ask a very nice lady to take care of you. Only for a little while," she added hastily as the boy bristled. "Just until your mother is free. Will that be all right?"

"Ma told us to sit here." The responsibilities of being the oldest weighed heavily on a five-year-old's shoulders.

"And you're being very good about it, too." Hetty gave them what she hoped was her most encouraging smile. "I'll ask your mother first, shall I? And perhaps . . ." She glanced back at Michael and the children's father and mother. "Perhaps you would like to talk to your father?"

Hetty had to swallow hard against the tears that threatened to claim her, too. Their father was lost in his own private battle against death and, for the moment, he had forgotten the existence of his children. But this might well be their last chance to speak to him. Their last chance to say good-bye.

Little Sarah nodded eagerly. Her brother, determined to play the grown-up role assigned him as best he could said, "Yes, please. If it's all right," and threw a troubled glance at his parents, as though uncertain whether he was demanding too much, under the circumstances.

"Wait here, all right?" Hetty gave the two her most encouraging smile and rose to her feet.

Their mother started guiltily, then gnawed on her lower lip as Hetty explained what she proposed. Yet even as she listened, she never took her eyes off her husband, who lay, eyes shut, struggling for breath.

When Hetty finished, the woman leaned forward and gently clasped the skeletal hand that lay so still on the heavy lap rug. Her fingers trembled, ever so slightly, but her voice was surprisingly steady. "George?" When her husband gave no sign of having heard her, she said, a little louder, "George?"

George's eyes opened at that. He blinked, as though uncertain of where he was; then his gaze cleared as he focused on his wife. "Jessica?"

Hetty could hardly make out the single word, his voice was so low and rough, yet even that small effort appeared to exhaust him.

Michael had taken up a position at the head of the crude bed, and though he looked as if he were struggling as hard as George for each breath his patient took, he made no move to interfere. Hetty could feel his futile anger at his helplessness as sharply as if it were her own.

Jessica gently squeezed her husband's hand. "The children," she said. Her eyes suddenly filled with tears. She swallowed, fighting to keep them from spilling over. "I think . . . I think you should speak to them."

"David? Is he . . . there? And . . . little . . . Sarah?"

"Yes, they're here." Jessica sniffed, fighting back the tears. "They . . . they'd like to talk to you. If you're strong enough."

"I'd like . . . I'd like . . . that . . ." George gave up and clutched at his wife's hand, desperately seeking to draw strength from her familiar touch.

Hetty didn't wait to hear more.

She helped Sarah down from the chair, but David stiffly rejected her proffered hand, and as she led them across the room, he stopped once to gently but firmly prevent his little sister from shoving her thumb in her mouth.

Jessica held out her hand to her children and attempted a watery smile of encouragement. "Come and say good—come see your father. He wants to talk to you, but he's very weak and can't say much."

Hetty glanced at Michael, who nodded in approval and stepped away from the family. They had little time left to be together. He wouldn't leave them, Hetty knew, but he would try to give them at least the illusion of privacy. As Hetty slipped out the door, Michael was feigning utter absorption in the train schedule chalked on the blackboard near Mr. Harrison's desk.

The stationmaster had put the time to good use by taking charge of the matters he was more accustomed to dealing with. The gawkers who had crowded the waiting area so short a time before had been summarily evicted.

To Hetty's relief, they hadn't gone far.

She spotted Mrs. Fisk at the center of a gaggle of gossips. At her appearance, their heads came up alertly and they watched her approach with the eagerness of a flock at feeding time.

A gossip and a busybody she might be, but no one had a kinder heart than Clarabelle Fisk. The instant she understood what was needed, she crossed her hands over her stomach and nodded.

"Of course I'll take care of the poor things. A good meal. That's what they need. A good meal and someone to hang on to until their mother can take them over." Her eyes narrowed and she tucked in her two chins with stern determination. "And don't you worry any about Lettitia Scoggins refusing to take them in. She may not be used to the racket, but she's got a good heart, just like you said. She won't turn them away when she knows there's no place else for them to go."

"But Clara," a prune-faced lady protested, scandalized. "The man's consumptive! His wife and children have been exposed. Surely you don't expect Lettitia to take them in. Even considering the circumstances. Think of the risk of infection!"

A couple of the other ladies nodded in agreement, their expressions pinched tight with sudden anxiety. It was one thing to have a stranger dying of a communicable disease if he was kept well away from the members of the community, quite another to have people who had been exposed to the dread disease running loose among them.

Clarabelle Fisk wasn't one to be deterred from helping others in need, however, not even strangers. "I certainly *can* expect her to take them in, Abigail Bowman!" she retorted. "What's more, if you didn't spend so much time worrying about what horrible new disease you and your Jed will catch, I'd suggest *you* take them in. The good Lord knows *you* have more than enough room, rattling around like you do in a house that's *far* too big for just the two of you!"

"Well!" Abigail Bowman drew herself up indignantly. "Just because your Robert wants to stay in that little cracker box of yours doesn't mean—"

"If you wouldn't mind coming right now, Mrs. Fisk," Hetty said, hastily grabbing the older woman's arm and pulling her away. "The gentleman is very weak and won't be able to talk to them for long, and the little girl really does have to go."

"Humph," snorted Clarabelle Fisk, stumping along in her wake. "Twenty years ago, when they thought you just inherited it, they'd have been mooning about how tragic it was to die of consumption. Now that they know they can get it too, they're as flustered as an old spinster being asked to dine with a doxy."

Hetty managed not to choke, but just barely.

"You'll forgive my being so blunt, Miss Malone, I'm sure, but you mark my words. Half those fine ladies will be gone by the time I come out with those poor children. Just see if they aren't."

Clarabelle Fisk was right. Half the ladies *were* gone by the time she emerged from the station with David and Sarah in tow, and a couple of the others, too curious to retreat, drew up their skirts and kept a careful distance as the trio passed.

Hetty fought back tears as she watched from the waiting room door. If those ladies were any example, Jessica and her children would be shunned as long as they remained here.

But not by all, Hetty thought as Clarabelle stooped to pick up little Sarah, then took David's hand in her own. Not by all.

Squaring her shoulders, she turned back to the almost empty waiting room. Mr. Harrison, adrift without the anchor of his work, had claimed his clerk's desk as replacement for his own. The clerk and the errand boy had been dispatched to deliver the family's belongings to Mrs. Scoggins's house. Clarabelle Fisk had stoutly declared that a room *would* be found for the family, that Lettitia Scoggins wouldn't turn away folks in need no matter what others might do, and Lionel Harrison had had the good sense not to argue.

He looked up as Hetty stopped beside the desk. "They're off, then."

Hetty nodded. "Yes."

The stationmaster glanced at the open door of

his office. There was nothing to be seen but his blackboard with its neat grid of train schedules and the early-evening shadows that were beginning to fill the station. His gaze dropped, then fastened on a paper file whose long metal spike was half hidden in its load of colored freight tickets. Distracted, he picked the file up by its point and twirled it between his thick fingers so the weighted base spun first one way, then the other, then back again.

"I've seen men die," Lionel Harrison said at last, his voice harsh, but low, so it wouldn't carry. "I've seen them shot and crushed and mangled. I've seen them suffocated under a coal slip and drowned in a river like a dog. I dug my own father's grave when I was fourteen because there was no one else to do it."

He snapped the file down on the desk and sat back, still without meeting her gaze. "Even after all that, I can't say I care to see a stranger dying like this. Not in my office."

"He's far too weak to be moved. You saw that for yourself."

She might as well not have spoken, for all the attention he paid.

"How long?" he demanded bluntly.

Hetty stiffened, shocked. "Not long. Or so my—so Dr. Ryan says."

"Humpf. Well, the preacher should be here any time now. And I told my clerk to alert Hiram Beadle soon as they got rid of those bags. Hiram's the closest undertaker," he explained when Hetty looked blank.

At the mention of the undertaker, Hetty felt something inside her shift, then squeeze tight. He said it so coldly, but he wasn't a cold man. He was, quite simply, a busy man who had work to do and who wanted these strangers out of his office and out of his life as quickly as possible, even though he knew as well as Hetty that they wouldn't leave until Death had claimed his prize. The hard, practical side of Mr. Harrison merely said, the sooner the better.

Hetty glanced at the empty doorway and thought of Michael. He needed her. She had to get back. But there were still a few things she could tend to first.

"We'll need more towels," Hetty said, "and tea for . . ."

She frowned, irritated that she kept forgetting to ask their names. Jessica and George. That was all she knew. It was disrespectful to address adults by their given names if she didn't know them well. The impropriety bothered Hetty, for their sake.

"We'll need tea," she said firmly. "And coffee for Dr. Ryan. And perhaps some bread or soup. I don't think she's eaten." She wasn't likely to, either, but Hetty couldn't think of anything else.

"Yes, all right," he said, clearly irritated at having yet another task thrust at him that he didn't want. He shoved his chair back from the desk and stood, towering over Hetty. "He should be in bed. The man has a right to die in a decent bed."

"He'd die before we got him there."

"Then he shouldn't have left his own in the first place." With a growl of disgust, Harrison grabbed his hat and stalked out of the station. From the way he threw back his shoulders the moment he passed through the door, Hetty suspected he was glad to be gone, even if it meant leaving his precious train station in incompetent hands.

Hetty stared at the shadows that were swallowing the station platform behind him.

Lionel Harrison was right. It *would* have been better if this stranger had stayed in his own bed in his own home, wherever that was. Instead, he'd made a desperate bid to regain his health in the West's higher, drier climate. He'd uprooted his family and spent their savings and suffered God knew what physical agonies, all so he could die in a barren station house among strangers.

Standing as he was just inside the office door, Michael could hear the soft murmur of voices in the waiting room, but he couldn't make out the words. He found himself straining to pick out Hetty's low tones under Harrison's rumbling half-whisper, wondering what she was saying, how she was coping with the stationmaster's resentment of this unexpected disruption of his routine.

He wished she'd go home. He didn't like her being exposed like this.

At the same time, he wished Hetty were standing beside him right now. He could use a dose of her sensible courage.

He'd had years of training and hard work and practical experience, and none of it meant anything.

Oh, he'd conducted the proper physical examination, useless as that was under the circumstances. He'd taken a pulse, percussed the chest, listened to his patient's medical history, and administered some morphine. And that was it. That was all he could do. That was all anyone could have done.

"At times like this, Ryan," that old crow, Crooven, had told him once when he was in training and attending a terminal patient, "the only thing you can do is look solemn. Not worth much, that, but it makes the family feel you appreciate the seriousness of the situation, don't you know?"

Michael rubbed his hands on the sides of his trousers, then leaned back against the wall behind him, trying hard not to look toward the far end of the room where Jessica Lanyon sat clutching her husband's hand.

Crooven's advice had angered him then. Now, he wished he'd paid more attention. If he'd learned how to hide behind false solemnity, he might not be so uncertain now. He'd said all the right things, done all the right things, yet all the while he was back in another room in another time, and it was his mother lying on the bed and his father, distraught, bending over her. And he . . . he was a little boy forgotten in the corner, just as David and Sarah had been forgotten, God forgive him.

He hadn't been present when his mother died.

Like George Lanyon, she'd gone in search of a cure she never found. Unlike him, she'd gone alone.

He'd been exactly six years, eleven months, and twenty-three days old. His mother hadn't even waited to share his seventh birthday with him. He suspected now that she'd forgotten all about it.

He'd often wondered if she'd forgotten about him, too, there at the last.

George Lanyon died at 10:37 P.M.

By then, Michael had ceded responsibility to the minister who had come in answer to Lionel Harrison's summons, and eventually the minister, when even prayers were exhausted, ceded responsibility to the undertaker.

Hiram Beadle was ready. With respectful, unsentimental dignity he murmured his condolences to the widow, then tended to transferring George Lanyon's body to the polished black hearse he'd left standing outside the station.

Jessica Lanyon, who had risen to her feet when Hiram first approached her, bore it all with white-knuckled calm until the moment when he and his assistant inadvertently bumped the draped litter as they tried to maneuver their burden out the narrow office door. A quickly suppressed curse from the assistant, a rough shuffling of feet, and the two were gone.

With a low moan, Jessica collapsed in her chair. Hetty was beside her in an instant. She bent and wrapped one arm protectively around the older woman's shoulders, but there was nothing she could say that could offer comfort.

From outside came the thump of heavy footsteps, another curse, the scrape of the litter as it was shoved into the hearse. Jessica flinched at each slight sound but said nothing, just sat and stared blindly at the dark, shuttered windows, straining to follow what was happening beyond them.

They heard a slight thud as the back door of the hearse was slammed shut, then the jingle of harness and a soft command to the horses, immediately followed by muffled creaks and rattles as Hiram drew away from the station.

As the sounds faded into the night, whatever raw courage had supported Jessica through the long hours faded, too. Her head bent, her shoulders drooped, and the rigid tension that had held her melted away, leaving her limp and shaking. She twisted and tugged at the sodden handkerchief she held, oblivious to Hetty's ministrations and the minister's words of condolence.

Only Michael roused her from her misery. She started when he touched her hand, and her head jerked up. Her too-thin body stiffened as she pulled away.

Hetty ached at the sight of the ashen shadows around Michael's eyes and the way his skin stretched, drum-taut, over the bones of his cheek and jaw. Out of respect, he'd straightened his tie, buttoned his vest, and pulled on his jacket, but the somber black of his clothes only made him appear all the more gaunt and worn.

"Mrs. Lanyon," he said, clearly struggling to

find the right words, the right tone. "I just wanted to tell you that I'm sorry. I—"

"Sorry? Why should you be sorry?" Jessica Lanyon's words cut at him with sudden, bitter fury. "You just came in at the end, as useless as all your kind who poked at my poor George and dosed him with your useless medicines and sent your bills afterward, no matter if you did him good or not."

She surged to her feet, bristling with the anger and fear and grief she had repressed for so long. "It was a doctor sent us out here, did you know that?" she demanded, glaring up at Michael like a little banty hen gone mad. "A doctor, just like you. Said it might help. Might! For 'might' and 'maybe,' we sold our house, our furniture, everything! Just so George could . . . could die . . . oh, God. *George!*"

The last came out in a keening wail as Jessica Lanyon suddenly broke for the door through which her husband's body had been taken. Michael caught her, but his touch was like tinder to a fire. She screeched and reared back, fighting to break free of his hold.

She didn't fight long. With a cry that might have been torn from the throat of a dying animal, she collapsed as suddenly as she'd begun. Michael managed to catch her before she slumped to the floor, but it was Hetty who held her as tears flooded her face and her slight body shook with the wracking sobs that claimed her.

While Hetty knelt beside her on the floor, rocking her and murmuring soothing nothings, Michael and the minister stood helplessly by, unable to act and unable to leave, in a room where death still hung heavy in the air.

To Hetty, it seemed as if time had slowed to a painful, crippled crawl. At least she had something to do in trying to comfort Jessica, no matter how little comfort she was actually able to give. Michael had nothing to occupy him now except to glare at the contents of his medical bag, which lay strewn about the table, as if they had somehow betrayed him by failing to provide the miracle that George Lanyon had needed, and never found.

Even tears eventually had an end, but it was some time before Jessica Lanyon was capable of standing on her own. She refused to look at Michael and shook her head vehemently when Hetty suggested they escort her to Mrs. Scoggins's. In the end, she accepted the minister's offer to accompany her and help break the news to her children.

The two slipped out of the office like somber wraiths, leaving Hetty and Michael alone in the disordered, silent room. Hetty could hear the sound of their footsteps crossing the waiting room, then Lionel Harrison's low, rumbling voice as he unlocked the outer door for them. The gaslights wavered in a passing draft, making the shadows in the corners quake.

Hetty glanced at Michael. He stood still and silent, like one of the mythical warriors Hetty remembered reading about, turned to stone by Medusa's glance. Jessica Lanyon's refusal of his offer of assistance had frozen him in his place, as drained of life as if he really were cold stone and not a living, hurting human being.

"You couldn't have done anything more, Michael." Hetty clasped her hands around his arm, willing him to look at her. "Nobody could have."

"No." He didn't look at her, didn't respond to her touch. His voice sounded hollow, as though it came from someplace empty and echoing inside him.

"These last hours might have been far worse for him if you hadn't been here. The heroin syrup helped. Mrs. Lanyon could see that. It really did help."

"Yes."

Yes. One flat, unexpressive word, nothing more. Hetty shivered. "Michael—?"

"The syrup helped, but it couldn't stop the hemorrhage. It couldn't stop the disintegration of his lungs. It couldn't save him. Nothing could. At least, not anything that medicine could do. None of us have the skills or knowledge to help him. Not me. Not the doctors that tended him. Not anyone."

Something tore the words from deep inside him, like hot pincers tearing flesh. He might as well have been confessing to murder, instead of admitting that there were limits to modern medical knowledge.

"It's so damned much chance, Hetty. Some live, some die, and we don't know why. It's as if being a doctor were simply a matter of tossing the dice."

His eyes went blank suddenly, and the tension in his shoulders gave way to a discouraged slump. "If we only knew more, if only . . ." His voice trailed away into discouraged silence.

The solid thump of heavy boots on a wood floor startled them both. Hetty jumped and tightened her grip on Michael's arm, but Michael merely lifted his head and squared his shoulders, once more assuming the heavy dignity of his calling.

"God, Doc. You look like hell." Lionel Harrison's big body filled the narrow doorway. When Michael didn't respond, the stationmaster's gaze shifted to take in the rest of the room—the chairs and desk shoved out of the way, the table where Michael had spread out his equipment and his useless medicines, the bench.

The tumbled blankets that had been piled on the bench in lieu of a proper mattress still bore the imprint of George Lanyon's body. The blood-flecked pillows still showed where his head had lain.

Harrison grimaced and looked slightly sick. He glanced back at Michael. "This place looks worse than you do, if that's possible. Damned if I know how I'm going to work here tomorrow, and with half a day's work already lost . . ."

He started to swear. Hetty could see him biting the words back as he remembered, just in time, that he was in the presence of a lady and that he'd already said far more than he ought.

"Don't worry about it," he said before she could speak. "I'll have Jed clean it up first thing in the morning. Except that." He pointed to the overflowing basin that had been shoved under the bench, out of the way. "I'll get rid of that tonight."

He almost swore again, but this time, rather than restrain himself, he turned and stomped away muttering something about a bucket and gloves.

Michael sighed and glanced down at Hetty guiltily. "I need to take you home. I hadn't intended . . ."

His voice trailed off; then he swiftly bent to press a light kiss to her forehead. "I hadn't intended for you to endure this, but I'm glad you were here, Hetty. It . . . it helped. Thank you."

Before Hetty could respond, he broke away and started gathering up his instruments. "I'll clean them tomorrow," he said, as if to himself. "Tomorrow. Not tonight."

He straightened at last and snapped his bag shut, but he continued to toy with the leather-covered handles, as a man will when his thoughts are elsewhere but his hands need something to do. While he collected his things, he'd deliberately kept his eyes fixed on his task, but now his gaze strayed to the bench with its tumbled coverings.

For a long, long moment he simply stood there staring. Hetty held her breath, watching him.

His hand clenched around the handles; his nails dug into the curved side of the bag. The bag was his proudest possession. She'd saved and scrimped for a year so she could give it as a graduation gift to him, yet he was digging deep, white gouges in the polished black leather.

Abruptly he leaned forward and grabbed a corner of one of the blankets. With one ferocious jerk, he dragged it up over the pillows, tumbling blankets and pillows into an untidy heap, erasing any sign that a man had lain there just a short while ago.

With equal ferocity, he grabbed his medical bag, then swung around to face Hetty. His eyes glittered in the unsteady light from the lantern, cold and colorless and empty.

"Are you ready to leave?" he demanded, as harshly as if she'd challenged him.

Hetty nodded, fighting against the tears that threatened her. "Yes. Let's go home, Michael. Let's go home."

# *Chapter Eleven*

Not even a single light softened the black bulk of the boarding house. Hetty drooped on the buggy seat.

"Mrs. Spencer's gone to bed, then. I won't be able to get in." She found it vaguely surprising that the thought of being shut out didn't bother her. "She told me that first day, 'in by ten or out all night.' As if it were a children's rhyme."

"It's almost midnight now." They were the first words Michael had spoken since they'd left the station. His voice sounded flat and faint, as if he spoke from a long way off, but Hetty could hear the dragging weariness underneath.

"Yes." Hetty tilted her head back, easing the strain in her neck and shoulders. Overhead, through the arching branches of the elms, she could see the stars. The stars George Lanyon would never see again on this earth.

She brought her head back down quickly.

"I could take you to Mrs. Scoggins's."

"No. She has enough to deal with. I wasn't even sure she'd agree to take the Lanyons in. I can't add to her burden. Not tonight."

The silence stretched. Hetty felt brittle, her nerve endings as fragile as glass since Michael had withdrawn into his private anguish, leaving her alone and uncertain. Except to hand her into the buggy, he hadn't touched her, hadn't spoken, had scarcely moved even, except for the necessary directions to the horse. It was as if he'd deliberately withdrawn from everything around him, including her.

"A hotel, then," he offered at last.

"No." The word came out so fiercely, it startled even Hetty. "No," again, this time more calmly. She suddenly knew what she wanted. "I want to go home with you, Michael."

"With me? But Hetty, we're not—"

"We're not married, and I don't care. I want to go home with you. *Now*."

The rightness of it was almost stunning in its simplicity. She *needed* Michael . . . and he needed her even more.

Hetty slid closer and wrapped her hands around his arm. He jumped; then his muscles went hard and still, as though he was fighting against any response, however slight.

"Take me home, Michael," Hetty said, very softly.

His arm trembled beneath her fingers, ever so slightly. "There's a cot . . ."

"A cot will be fine."

"For me. You . . ." He cleared his throat, then tried again. "You can have the bed."

Michael didn't say another word. Because she didn't want to wait in the house alone, Hetty insisted that they return the horse to the stable first. They walked the one and a half blocks back through the silent dark, side by side, unspeaking.

This time Michael remembered to close and lock the front door behind him. For a moment he simply stood there, letting his eyes adjust to the deeper dark. Only for a moment, the space of a couple of heartbeats, no more. It was enough to set Hetty's senses aching with a sudden, almost overwhelming awareness of his nearness.

In the night silence of the house, she listened to the soft in-out of his breathing. He was nothing more than a darker shadow in the black, but she could hear the scrape of his sleeve against his coat, the almost imperceptible rustle of his shirt beneath his vest.

All the normal sounds that a decently clothed man would make, and they made her intensely, achingly aware of the naked male body beneath.

With the awareness came a hot flush of shame. A man had died tonight. It was wrong—indecent, even—to indulge in such wanton thoughts so soon afterward, but Hetty found she couldn't stop. Her body insisted on reminding her that she was alive, regardless of what had happened.

"Wait here. I'll light the lamp." Michael kept his voice low, yet to Hetty's straining nerves it seemed to echo in the little room. He crossed to the wall-mounted gas lamp on the opposite side of the room. The soles of his boots grated against the worn wooden floor. A board creaked beneath his weight, then another, and Hetty felt her own body shift and tense in response to his movements.

There was a hiss and the faint, acrid odor of gas, then light flared in the little room, almost blinding after the dark.

Michael glanced at her, then as quickly looked away. "I'll set up the cot in my office," he said. "You can have the . . . the other."

Hetty followed him down the hall and waited at the door of his bedroom while he lit the gas-light there, too.

The soft, golden light gave a welcoming glow to the little room, but there was nothing welcoming in Michael's stiff refusal to meet her gaze.

"The sheets are this week's laundry," he said to the wall behind the bed. "Since I ended up sleeping on top of the covers last night, I guess it won't be too bad."

"It will be fine," Hetty said, and tried not to think about how he had looked sprawled across the bed, tried not to remember how broad his shoulders had seemed, how warm his skin had been when she'd touched him.

"There's a clean towel on the shelf." Michael pointed toward the corner where wooden shelves and several clothes hooks were half hidden behind a simple calico curtain. "I'll start the water heater, if you like."

Like a tired and resentful clerk in a half-rate hotel, Hetty thought, and realized, suddenly, that Michael didn't want her here. The knowledge hit her like a blow from a fist.

"That won't be necessary." He started to slip past her, but she held out her hand to stop him.

"Michael? If you'd rather I didn't stay, I . . . I won't. I just thought . . . But if you think the neighbors would mind, or that it will hurt your reputation—"

"*My* reputation?" He looked at her blankly. "Don't be ridiculous."

He shoved past her, then, but stopped in the doorway leading to the kitchen, bracing his hand against the jamb as if he were physically preventing himself from disappearing into the blackness beyond.

"Let me know if you need anything, all right?" He didn't bother to turn and look at her as he said it.

"Yes, all right." Hetty flinched at the snap of the latch as he shut the kitchen door behind him, effectively closing her off from the rest of the house—and from him.

Stunned, Hetty retreated into his bedroom. The little room was uncomfortably cool, though the gas light was enough to help warm the small space.

Her stomach rumbled, reminding her she'd had nothing to eat since her half-finished soda at

Fisk's. It didn't matter. She'd have to be a whole lot hungrier before she'd venture into the kitchen for leftover bread and preserves, because she could hear Michael moving about out there, even through the walls and doors that divided them. Retrieving his cot, no doubt.

At the thought, Hetty glanced guiltily down at the bed he'd given up in exchange.

It was a low, iron-framed bed, wider than the single bed she'd left behind in Boston, though not so wide as the beds she'd surreptitiously inspected in stores when she thought no one was looking and she could indulge her indecorous imaginings. The light coverlet was rucked into untidy ridges and rumpled valleys where Michael had shifted in his sleep, and the pillows, unlike the fat new feather pillows Hetty had pinched and priced and fantasized over for so many years, were wearing flat. They still showed the hollow where Michael's head had pressed.

With a choked sound that wasn't quite a cry, Hetty bent and tugged the coverlet flat, then grabbed the pillows and pummeled them into shape. She wouldn't think about it. She would *not* think about it!

The towel was where Michael had said it would be, right next to two neatly folded nightshirts that looked as if they had never been used. Hetty pulled the towel down, then hesitated, and pulled one of the nightshirts down, as well. It was muslin, white with blue stripes, and long enough to reach to her toes. She could wrap herself up in it if she wanted.

With a rough, convulsive movement, Hetty crushed the nightshirt and towel against her breast. What she really wanted was for *Michael* to wrap his arms around her and hold her tight against him and tell her that he loved her, over and over and over. She wanted his warmth and his strength, like shelter against a storm, and his kisses to chase away the dark.

For a long while Hetty simply stood there, staring at the newly straightened bed and fighting against the urge to break down and cry.

She wanted so badly to cry. For herself. For Michael. For George and Jessica Lanyon. For little Sarah and brave big brother David. She wanted to cry for all the stupid, senseless pain that living brought, and the even more senseless pain that dying left in its wake.

In the end, she merely sniffed and blinked and trailed sadly off to wash her face and brush her teeth as best she could with some tooth powder and the tip of her finger. It wasn't what she would have preferred, but then, not much was these days. Not much at all.

The cot was a heavy canvas and wood affair that was awkward to set up and not all that comfortable to sleep in. A bedraggled pillow and coarse blanket had been stored with it. Both had a dry, dusty smell to them, but Michael shook them out as best he could. Better to endure the discomfort than run the risk of retrieving something better from his bedroom. The bedroom where Hetty would soon be asleep.

Michael groaned and sank down on the end of the cot.

He should never have let her remain at the station tonight. He should have sent her away with the children and given orders that she wasn't to be allowed back.

That he hadn't ate at him like acid. God forgive him, he had *wanted* her there. Not just to help him or for the support she could give Mrs. Lanyon, but because *he* needed her.

Selfish bastard.

The door to the bedroom opened. He could hear its protesting grate even through the walls and closed doors between. A board in the hallway creaked; then the bathroom door clicked shut.

She was so close. He could go to her, take her in his arms and kiss her and—

No! He wouldn't think of that. Didn't dare think of it. He was too afraid of what might happen if he did.

Yet still he sat there listening as she crept back to his bedroom and shoved the door shut. An eternity passed before he heard the creaking protest of the bed as she settled into it.

His body easily remembered the feel of the lumpy mattress, the sheets, the shabby pillows. It was his mind that insisted on conjuring images of Hetty, soft and warm beside him, of Hetty—

Michael leapt to his feet. Fool! *Fool*!

Two years of loneliness and longing and pure, unsatisfied lust exacted their toll in the tormenting fire that raged through his veins and made his limbs tremble and burn with wanting. He thought the buttons on his trousers might shoot off like bullets from the strain and his skin burst into flame from the heat.

He started to pace, then stopped, glaring at the opposite wall like a caged lion suddenly confronted with his bars. Hetty would hear him.

Once more he sank down on the cot, but this time his groan of protest came from the very center of his soul.

This was wrong, all wrong. Hetty being here, his lust, everything.

He knew what lay beneath it. It was the need to shake his fist in the face of the dark specter that claimed his patients like so many prizes won on the carnival midway, laughing at him as if he were a carney who had tried to rig the game, then lost to a cleverer cheat.

He couldn't drag Hetty into his private war with Death. If he were to go to her now, he would be using her, hiding behind her love like a cowering dog trying to avoid the blows of an angry master. He was supposed to protect her, shield her from the ugliness of life, not use her to ease his own anguish.

When he could no longer stand the silence and the still angry fire in his blood, Michael got clumsily to his feet. He knew from experience that a dunking in cold water would drive out some of the aching need within him. Not much, not enough so he could sleep, but enough that he'd be able to think again, to focus on something besides wanting Hetty.

He needed to record the medical details of

George Lanyon's last hours before he forgot them. One more set of data to add to all the other data he'd collected over the past two years in the hope that somewhere in the growing mass of information he would find a clue, something that would lead him to a weakness in his enemy's defenses.

He had no idea if he'd ever find that clue, or if it even existed. He only knew he had to keep looking. Despite the cruel, irrational disorder that Death wreaked on human lives and hopes, Michael believed—passionately and devoutly believed—that there was an order and a logic to counter it, if only he could find it.

If only . . .

When she finally climbed into bed, Hetty was wearing Michael's nightshirt. It was bigger than her nightgowns. The hem dragged on the floor when she walked, and she'd had to roll up the sleeves two turns even after she'd buttoned the cuffs.

Hetty had thought it would comfort her to sleep in a shirt that Michael had worn, but it didn't. She thought she could detect the very faintest hint of Michael's scent on the pillows. She could feel the hollow his body had worn in the lumpy mattress. But she couldn't believe he'd ever worn the nightshirt. The fabric was still too stiff and new.

But if Michael didn't wear the nightshirt when he went to bed, what *did* he wear?

The question brought her eyes open wide. The

dark, which a moment before had seemed so vastly cold and unfriendly, suddenly seemed too warm and almost smotheringly close. Hetty turned on her side and tried to snuggle into the hollow in the mattress, but all that did was make her more intensely aware that this was Michael's bed, Michael's pillow, Michael's shirt.

As if to confirm his ownership, light spilled under the door and across the floor as Michael opened the door between the hall and the waiting room, then crept to the bathroom on stocking feet. His efforts at quiet were wasted, for the water roared through the pipes like a river in flood, no matter what. Hetty knew he was gone when the light beneath her door disappeared as abruptly as it had come.

But Michael didn't go to bed. Hetty could hear the faint creak of floorboards every now and then as he moved about his lab. The intermittent reminders of his presence drove sleep away, leaving her wide-eyed and aching.

He didn't want her, Hetty reminded herself. He'd made that clear. He'd retreated into silence and his work and left no place for her.

Maybe that wasn't true, though. Maybe he needed her as much as she needed him, but didn't know how to admit it any more than she did. Maybe the problem was that they'd fallen out of the habit of relying on each other and didn't know how to begin again.

But that didn't mean they couldn't learn.

She found him in his workroom hunched over one of his journals. The pencil in his hand moved across the page with jerky impatience, as if it wanted to go faster and Michael was holding it back.

He didn't hear her crossing to him. When Hetty touched his shoulder, he jumped and his fingers clenched, snapping the pencil. He swung around to glare at her, and for a moment Hetty wasn't even sure he recognized her.

"Hold me, Michael. Please."

She hadn't planned on saying it. She hadn't really planned on saying anything, but the words were right and as honest as she could make them.

"Hetty?" he asked, as if he were just rousing from a trance.

Without thinking about it or stopping to wonder if she ought, Hetty bent forward and kissed him.

It was an awkward kiss and it went awry, but the second one did not, and when Michael rose to gather her in his arms, their bodies melded together with the easy, heated grace of two flames born of a single fire.

"Hetty," Michael murmured as he trailed kisses across her lips and chin, down her throat to the primly buttoned collar of his own nightshirt. "Oh, Hetty."

He swept the unbound mane of her hair aside and dug his fingers into the hard plane of her shoulder blade and the more yielding curve of her waist, as if he were afraid she'd slip free of him without so secure an anchor. His arms tightened about her possessively, drawing her closer against him.

Hetty arched into him willingly. Only then did she realize how great a difference there was between kissing Michael when she was bound in corsets and collars and God knew how many layers of clothing, and kissing him when all that covered her suddenly sensitized skin was one thin layer of blue-striped muslin.

She gulped in air. She had no choice in the matter because she would have exploded otherwise, but the simple, automatic movement made her chest swell and pressed her breasts so tightly against Michael's chest that for one mad moment Hetty wondered if they might be joined like this forever.

Michael was quick to take advantage of the change. His hand at her waist slipped lower, pressing her hips and belly against him until she could feel the hard, unmistakably male outline of him through the too-thin layers of cotton and wool and muslin that divided them.

The very marrow in her bones began to melt with the heat of her wanting.

Like a starving man suddenly given food, Michael pressed rough kisses against her mouth. She coiled her fingers in his hair and pulled him closer to claim even more. She nipped the soft curve of his earlobe, and he let out a breath that was half moan, half sigh, then bent a little more to let her trace the labyrinth of his ear with the tip of her tongue.

She tilted her head so he could reach the sensitive flesh at the curve of her jaw, just below her ear, then arched back so he could trace again the curve of her throat with his lips.

And all the while there were little gasps and incoherent murmurs and pleas that were answered, only to create newer and even more urgent demands. Their hands and bodies strained for union until Hetty was dizzy and dazed and wild with a hunger she had never known before.

Abruptly Michael broke free of her exploring mouth and her searching hands. For an instant, he held her away from him, staring at her from under his devil-black brows with eyes grown wide and wild.

But only for an instant. Then he bent and swept her into his arms.

"Oh, Michael. I do love you! I do!"

He kissed her once more, so hungrily that her body arched in response and the very soles of her feet burned. One kiss, then he carried her through the house with the gaslight casting a gold-white glow across his dark features and the floors creaking softly beneath his stocking feet.

Even to Hetty's heated eye, the bed she'd so recently abandoned looked like a slattern whose petticoats were showing. The pillows were bunched into an untidy heap against the iron rail at the head, and the covers were thrown back to reveal suggestively wrinkled sheets whose edges had come untucked and now hung down in sluttish disarray.

At the sight of it, Michael stopped as abruptly as if he'd run into an invisible wall. Hetty tilted her head to look up at him, startled by the sudden tension in him. He wasn't looking at her—his gaze was fixed on the tumbled sheets.

Suddenly he gave a groan that seemed torn from somewhere deep inside him. With his arms still tightly clasped about her, he turned and collapsed onto the hard edge of the bed. The frame squealed in protest at the weight, but held.

For a moment he merely sat there staring blankly at the opposite wall, his throat working with emotion; then he shifted his hold on her so she was sitting on his lap, the nightshirt indecently bunched up around her knees.

"I can't, Hetty. Not like this. I can't." The words emerged in a strained whisper. He refused to look at her.

He tried to brush a lock of hair behind her ear, but his hand shook so that he slid his fingers through the heavy mass and grabbed hold, instead.

Hetty hissed as his grip tightened painfully. "Not like this?" she demanded, roused to anger. "And what is this *like,* I'd like to know?"

She shifted on his lap, and this time it was Michael who hissed at the pain of it. Or was it the pleasure? His mouth opened and for an instant his eyes went unfocused.

Hetty didn't care. She grabbed two fistfuls of shirt and shook him. "Michael?"

That caught his attention. His eyes snapped back into focus.

"Hetty, you don't understand. I . . . I'd be using you. I want you so much, I think I'll explode if I can't have you, but it's not *right*. Not tonight. Not like this. Don't you see?"

Hetty squeezed her eyes shut and tried not to scream. This was a fine time for Michael to remember his scruples.

"No, I *don't* see. How could you be using me if I love you? If I want you as much as you want me?" Hetty let go his shirt and slid her hands up to his shoulders, fighting to control her frustration. "Anyway, we'll get that marriage license sooner or later and then we'll be married and—"

Michael gritted his teeth. The muscles and cords of his neck tautened like ropes under strain. "It's not because we're not married."

"No?" Hetty slowly worked her hands up the sides of his neck, letting her fingers probe the tight muscles at the back while her thumbs stroked and rubbed along the cords in front.

He shook his head, fighting for breath. "No."

She slid her hands into his thick black hair, cradling his head as she traced the curve of his jaw and the hollow of his cheek with her thumb. "What, then?"

"Hetty." It was half groan, half plea.

"What, Michael?" Hetty insisted.

She almost didn't care if he answered. She was too fascinated by the ease with which she had reduced him to this quivering, incoherent lump of male. She'd always assumed it was the man who ruled in matters of physical love, but obviously she'd been wrong. The knowledge gave her a heady sense of power.

Hetty shifted her weight on his lap, leaning into him until her hip ground into his belly. He gasped and his fingers dug into her back and side, but that didn't stop her from tracing the outline of his mouth with her tongue, then pressing her lips to his in a hot, demanding kiss.

Michael's mouth softened under hers and his hands slid up her back, drawing her so close that her breasts brushed against his chest. At that brief, erotic touch, he suddenly wrenched free and clamped his hands on her shoulders, forcing her back.

His eyes met hers, but this time there was a haunted look in them that made Hetty cringe.

"A man died tonight, Hetty."

She stiffened. "Michael—"

"There was nothing I could do. I know that. But—" He bit the word off sharply, as if whatever came after burned his tongue.

"When I followed you out of that room," he said at last with difficulty, "I knew what you were thinking. You were thinking of him, and his wife, and his children, and you were grieving for them."

Hetty nodded, uncertain what he was driving at.

"Do you know what I was thinking?" He looked at her with an expression as bleak as if it were her death he was discussing, not a stranger's.

Hetty shook her head.

"I was thinking about making love to you," he said. Self-loathing made his voice rough as sandpaper. "Right there in the waiting room. And all the way here, and when I showed you this room, and—God, Hetty! It was indecent how much I wanted you! How much I want you now!"

For a moment, Hetty simply stared at him, suspended between tears and exultant laughter.

"It's no sin to be alive, Michael," she said at last, tenderly.

"But Hetty—"

A kiss cut his protest short.

Michael almost gave in. Almost. Then he abruptly shoved her away and tried to get to his feet.

Hetty was quicker. She wrapped her arms around his neck and pulled him down onto the bed beside her.

# *Chapter Twelve*

They tumbled into the hollow of the mattress, off balance and awkward. Since the nightshirt was already indecently rucked up around her thighs, Hetty had no trouble in swinging a leg over Michael and pinning him to the bed. Her hair tumbled down in disarray, spilling across the sheets and over his throat and shoulder like heavy silken cords. Hetty didn't bother to brush it back.

"We're *alive*, Michael," she said, her voice fierce with conviction. "That's our gift, to do with whatever we will. Are you going to waste it just because you can't save the world, no matter how hard you try?"

He lay looking up at her, his face shadowed by the curtain of hair that enclosed them. Hetty could see the doubt and guilt wash across his face, warring with desire. His lips twisted in a self-mocking grimace.

"Ah, Hetty," he said, "it's always been so easy for you, hasn't it? The loving, I mean. The laughter." He worked one hand free and delicately looped a heavy lock of hair behind her ear. "Do you have any idea what a rare and precious blessing that is?"

"I know." She leaned closer. "Because I know what a blessing loving you is."

It was more than that, Hetty realized. It was torment and temptation. The muscles of her arms and shoulders trembled, taut with urgency, and there was a hot, tight wetness between her legs that refused to be ignored.

It frightened her, this sudden, aching need, and yet it set her free in ways she could not begin to comprehend.

Pressed tightly against her she could feel the hard evidence of Michael's own torment. She could feel the tremor that surged through him. He wanted her, whatever he might say. As much as she wanted him.

She bent forward to shower him with kisses even as she fumbled with the buttons of his shirt, the fastenings of his trousers. Short, choked animal sounds came from her, and her hips began to thrust against him in an untutored, yet strangely familiar rhythm.

Michael arched under her in mindless response, then abruptly dragged her off him and rolled on top. For a moment he simply hung there above her, his chest heaving, eyes wild, before he lowered his head and began his own tormenting exploration.

Somehow they worked their way fully onto the bed without letting go their hold on each other, graceless and eager and fighting for breath, trying to squirm onto the pillows without stopping their frenzied exploration. The sheet twisted under Hetty. The nightshirt caught beneath her, pinning her as effectively as if she'd been roped and tied.

"Let me," Michael said, propping himself on one elbow and tugging at the nightshirt's hem.

She lifted her hips just as Michael gave a second, more forceful tug. The nightshirt sailed upward, exposing her thighs and hips and belly and mounding over her chest until all she could see was the shadowed ceiling above her and Michael's face, suddenly gone rigid.

Almost reverently he laid his hand on her belly. His palm was warm and firm against her soft flesh, unsettling. Slowly he stroked upward, letting his fingers curve into her waist, over her ribs, then under the mounded muslin to shape her breast.

Hetty breathed deeply and held on, as if that one breath might be her last.

Downward he stroked. Over her breast, tugging at the sensitive nipple, back along her ribs and over her belly and down her thighs, then up again. And down again. And up. And each time his hand moved closer to that heated ache between her legs, until Hetty feared she would be reduced to pleading for release or go mad.

He gave her no chance to plead. He eased down beside her and once more claimed her mouth, teasing her, demanding that she open for him. In that same instant, he gently stroked down the slippery cleft that was at the heart of all her torments, then pressed his fingers tightly against her and slipped deeper still.

Hetty had thought she understood what it meant to kiss a man and be kissed by him. She'd thought she understood what desire was.

She'd been wrong.

"Oh," she breathed, and "Oh!" again, an instant before she was incapable of saying anything at all.

"It . . . it didn't hurt *too* much, did it?" Michael asked anxiously a great while later, levering himself up on one elbow, as if that way he'd be able to see more in the dark.

The bed creaked as Hetty rolled back against him. She couldn't help it. They were both nestled deep in the hollow of the mattress, her back and hips curved into his chest and thighs. It was the only position they'd found that would accommodate the two of them in the narrow bed without their being stacked one on top of the other like so much lumber.

Not that the double layering didn't have its attractions, Hetty thought with rather muzzy-headed satisfaction. It just wasn't practical for sleeping, and right now going to sleep with Michael pressed warm and solid and naked against her back was what she wanted more than anything in the world.

"It didn't hurt very much at all," she said at last. "A little, maybe, but only the first time. After that, it was"—she caught herself on a yawn—"it was wonderful."

Wonderful wasn't nearly enough to describe it, but it was the only word Hetty could think of at the moment. She was so tired, so sore, and so satisfied that she wasn't sure she'd ever be able to move again . . . or would want to if she could.

"I'm glad," Michael said softly. He laid his palm against the side of her face and gently brushed back the sweat-soaked strands that clung to her cheek and temple. His skin felt warm against hers and damp.

"Michael?"

He slowly traced the line of her throat and continued up over the curve of her shoulder. "Hmmm?"

Hetty blinked, trying to remember what she'd wanted to say. His touch was so light and sure and sensitive, so soothing. "Aren't doctors supposed to know about that sort of thing?"

"About the pain, you mean?"

"Uhmh." She shifted slightly on the pillow so she could peer up at him, so close above her. All she could see was the dark bulk of him, almost invisible in the dark. "And . . . other things."

He laughed, but Hetty, as sleepy as she was, could have sworn there was a faint note of embarrassment under the laugh.

"We . . . we learn about some of it, of course, but . . ."

Hetty could feel his shrug. "But?"

He pressed her head back against the pillow and sank down beside her. "Go to sleep, Hetty."

Hetty ignored him. "But?"

Michael sighed. "One of the first things you learn in medicine," he said at last, reluctantly, "is that there's a lot of difference between textbooks and . . . reality."

"You mean . . ." Hetty's brain was too tired to make immediate sense of his confession. "You mean you've never slept with a woman before?"

His hand gently, reverently cupped her bare breast. "No, I never have. I've delivered dozens of babies, but I've never, ever slept with a woman. Until now."

Hetty considered that. "Oh," she said. She blinked into the darkness, then considered it some more. "I thought men were supposed to learn with . . . with other women. Before they married, I mean."

He was silent for a long while. "Some do, but they don't have you to love."

Hetty smiled into the pillow. "Oh."

"Go to sleep, Hetty."

His thumb slowly brushed over her nipple, back and forth in a soft, exquisitely soothing gesture. In spite of herself, Hetty found herself relaxing into him. Strange, she thought sleepily, how a simple gesture could be so erotic one moment, so comforting the next.

"Michael?" Hetty mumbled.

"Yes?"

"Do you think we could buy a new bed?" She yawned, a deep, eye-watering yawn, and snuggled closer. "I don't think this one will survive your education."

He laughed.

His laughter was the last thing Hetty heard as she drifted into sleep.

Hetty snored. Very softly and without any interesting whistles and snorts, but she definitely snored.

Michael found the sound strangely comforting—almost as comforting as the soft, warm body pressed so close against him and the drift of silky hair that tickled his chin and throat and chest.

Hetty had fallen asleep over an hour ago, as easily and as innocently as a child. Michael envied her her peace of mind. For a while, she'd helped him forget. For a very little while.

Despite his dragging weariness, sleep eluded him.

The silence was too full of whispers.

*We're alive,* Hetty had said. *It's our gift.*

Our burden, Michael thought, and closed his eyes against the accusatory dark. *My* burden.

It would have been easier if he could have simply buried the dead and gone on. He couldn't, because the dead left the living behind them to stand in judgment of his failings.

Even when his eyes were closed, he could see the stricken faces of the Lanyon children. What were their names? David. He remembered that. David and . . . Sarah. Two lost souls huddled together on that hard office chair. He hadn't been able to face them then. He couldn't bear to see them now.

Hetty mumbled something in her sleep and rolled back against him. Michael shifted, trying to give her more room, but she merely cuddled closer, leaving him precariously balanced at the very edge of the bed.

Michael shook her gently. "Hetty?"

She burrowed deeper into the pillows, as comfortable and relaxed as if she'd lain beside him for years. Even asleep, Hetty trusted him.

The mere thought of that trust was frightening. What if he failed her as he'd failed so many others?

Choking back a groan, Michael rolled away from her and off the bed. Moving cautiously in the dark, he found the top sheet wadded at the far edge of the bed and gently pulled it over her.

It wasn't easy finding his clothes. His shirt was on the floor near the head of the bed, his pants kicked into the corner at the foot, and his socks and drawers and undershirt were scattered everywhere in between. They made an untidy armful, but he managed to slip out of the room without waking Hetty.

He finished the final notation in his journals just as dawn began peeking under the drawn shades.

* * *

She was awakened by the shrill clamor of the telephone.

Hetty jerked upright in bed, heart pounding, desperately trying to figure out what that atrocious noise was and where it was coming from. It took her a moment to realize that she wasn't in her little bed in Boston . . . and that Michael was no longer in *this* bed.

The tinny clanging stopped as abruptly as it had begun. Hetty slumped back against the wall, her head whirling.

In all her muddled daydreams about the morning after, she'd never once imagined waking up to a telephone or a bed that looked as if a storm had swept through it.

Someone—Hetty wasn't sure if it had been she or Michael—had kicked the coverlet out of the way so that it now dangled mournfully over the foot of the bed. The top sheet straggled off the side and the lower sheet lay wadded up in the center of the bed, exposing the drab gray-and-blue striped ticking of the mattress.

For a moment, Hetty stared stupidly at the small white knots where the mattress had been stitched and anchored, front to back, like a quilt. There was something vaguely absurd about that tidy little bit of white cord amid the tangle of stained sheets and rumpled bedclothes.

Hetty supposed she ought to feel at least some slight twinge of shame for her wanton behavior, but all she could dredge up was a little soreness, a strong desire for a hot bath, and an even stronger satisfaction with herself and Michael and life in general.

So this was what it meant to be a married lady! Or same as, if you disregarded the little matter of the wedding ceremony.

To Hetty's immense satisfaction, she found she definitely liked it.

She drew her legs more comfortably under her and languidly stretched. She could feel the way each muscle and bone meshed, some protesting more than others, as she bent first to one side, then the other. The sheets had left an untidy network of wrinkles impressed in her skin, her hair was a mass of snarls and tangles, and she could smell Michael and the traces of their lovemaking on her skin.

If anyone had told her about such details, she would have thought it all repulsive. To her surprise, Hetty found the smells and the disorder stirred a slow heat within her, a heat that could easily be fanned into something more exciting . . . assuming Michael could be enticed into an early-morning indulgence.

Michael set the telephone's earpiece in its cradle with the greatest of care.

It was either that or rip the damn thing off the wall altogether.

A gentle touch on his shoulder startled him out of his thoughts. He jerked around to find Hetty standing behind him.

Her hair fell in a wild tangle about her face and shoulders, giving her a dangerously tempting air of innocence and wanton womanhood, all in one. She'd pulled on his nightshirt but hadn't bothered to button it. The collar gaped in a narrow vee all the way to the bottom of her breast bone. From this angle he could see the soft curve of her right breast and the beginning of a faint trace of shadow beneath it.

"What is it, Michael? What's wrong?"

Michael hesitated. "Nothing's wrong. Go back to bed. It's too early for you to be up yet."

She met his lie with silence and an unwavering stare that was more unnerving than any accusation could have been.

He shouldn't tell her. Last night had been more than enough. She didn't deserve to be troubled with anything more.

If she sensed any of his doubts, she didn't show it; she just stood there waiting, her generous heart more than willing to share his burdens with him, no matter what they were.

"Jacob Turner died last night," he said at last. The confession brought an odd sense of relief, immediately followed by anger at his own weakness. "He just gave up and . . . died."

Hetty's eyes widened in shock. "Oh, no! And I didn't even think to ask about them. How terrible! And his brother? James, wasn't it? Is he all right?"

Michael reluctantly shook his head. "James died yesterday morning, shortly before dawn."

"Before—" Hetty clamped her mouth shut, studying him anxiously. "Is that where you were? With him?"

"Hetty, it's too early. Why don't—"

"It is, isn't it? You were with them, and you never said a word." Her forehead creased into a troubled frown. "But I thought that—that Jason still had several weeks to live, at least. That he wasn't—"

"He gave up, Hetty," Michael said sharply. "He was alone. He didn't have anything left to live for, and he knew there wasn't a damn thing I could do to help him. There wasn't anything *anybody* could do. So he just gave up. It happens sometimes."

For a moment he just stood glaring down at her, torn between the urge to rage at an uncaring universe and the need to drag her back into the bedroom and make love to her, again and again and again. Either way, he'd be running from reality . . . and using Hetty to do it.

"Oh, for God's sake, Hetty. Go get dressed. I have patients waiting for me."

Hetty tried to slam the door to the bedroom, but it refused to cooperate. It squealed, then stuck. She had to shove it closed and that only made her angrier.

Ignore her, would he? Treat her like a child who wasn't capable of understanding adult problems in an adult world? Tell her to get dressed as if she were a disobedient schoolchild? The guilt she felt for having forgotten the Turner brothers disappeared in a rush of frustration and resentment.

The sight of the bed stopped her cold, just as it

had stopped Michael the night before. The dark red stain in the center of the indecently crumpled sheet was clearly visible, mute evidence of what had occurred.

Blood, lust, and love. That was what they'd had last night.

Well, the love was still there, but Michael had chosen to ignore it.

The wet ache between her legs told her lust was lurking, ready to pounce—not that it did her much good if Michael refused to cooperate.

That left the blood.

She hadn't even noticed it when she'd awakened. There wasn't nearly as much as she'd expected. When Michael had gently cleaned her legs and belly with a wet towel after that first time, she'd been too embarrassed to look. Too embarrassed and too shaken by the unexpected intimacy of the act, by the concern and wonder and love she'd seen in his face as he'd tended her.

He'd shut off the gaslights afterwards and made love to her again, more gently this time, but no less urgently. In the dark, Hetty had found her senses heightened so that each caress, each unintelligible murmur had taken on an unexpected potency.

The third time had been brief. They'd both been sore and tired, yet they'd giggled like schoolchildren and found they fit together more easily, that the narrow bed suddenly wasn't as cramped and uncomfortable as they'd first thought.

And then she'd fallen asleep, only to wake to anger and cold rejection.

No, that wasn't right. Michael's anger had been directed at himself, not her, and his rejection . . .

Hetty slowly sank onto the edge of the bed, her eyes unfocused. She shoved her hands through her hair, pushing it back from her face, tugging at it until her fingers snagged in the tangles, trying to think.

Michael hadn't rejected her. He'd shut her out. There was a difference.

Not that his excluding her hurt any less or was any less worrisome than if he'd rejected her outright, but at least it was easier to understand.

Last night she'd seen firsthand what he faced. Though he'd said nothing, she'd felt his anguish and his soul-deep anger at the human suffering he was powerless to prevent. What kind of courage and commitment did it require for a man to confront such tragedy on a daily basis?

But Michael had tried to hide Jacob's death from her this morning, hadn't even mentioned James Turner's death yesterday, and had tried to prevent her from accompanying him on his visit to the Rheiners the day before. It didn't take a genius to see that he'd decided to build a wall between her and his work, or that he was resisting her attempts even to peek over the edge.

The thought disturbed her.

Much as she had as a child when she was troubled, Hetty drew up her legs under the nightshirt and wrapped her arms around her ankles until she was huddled into a tight little ball. Her hair tumbled about her like a curtain as she propped her chin on her knees and stared at the opposite wall, considering.

Part of Michael's reticence, no doubt, was a desire to protect her from the more unpleasant realities of his work. But that wasn't the whole of it.

Somewhere along the line, Michael seemed to have forgotten that she was supposed to help him in his practice. They'd agreed on that long ago, when he was still an eager medical student with dreams. Evidently, he wasn't going to abide by that agreement.

After the events of the past three days, Hetty had the feeling he'd decided to divide his life into two very separate parts, his work and his private life. The only trouble was, he didn't seem to have left any time free to *have* a private life!

And if he was going to continue to work from the moment the sun came up until he dropped from exhaustion at the tail end of the day, what would it mean for her? For them?

Surely he wasn't expecting her to fit into some comfortable little cubbyhole of his existence, ready to be brought out whenever it was convenient for him, then shoved back whenever it wasn't? But what other possibility had he left her? He hadn't even bothered to arrange for another doctor to handle his patients so they could have these first few days free to get to know one another again!

Her unhappy thoughts were interrupted by a peremptory knock on the door.

"Hetty? Are you in there?"

Where else *would* she be? Hetty thought in irritation as she climbed down off the bed and crossed to the door. She had to tug to open it, which didn't help her temper any. She yanked so hard, that once it came free of the jamb it flew open and hit the wall behind it.

Michael's eyes widened as he took in her disreputable state. "I thought you'd be dressed by now."

"Well, I'm not, but I see you've managed." Hetty didn't much like the note of pique she heard in her voice, but she was powerless to prevent it. It hurt that he'd slipped out of bed this morning without waking her. It hurt even more to realize that he intended to abandon her to her own devices now, just as if nothing had changed between them.

A muscle at the corner of his mouth jumped. "I have rounds this morning, Hetty."

"This early?"

"Yes. If I'd known . . ." His eyes glittered, ice-blue and bleak. Hetty had the unsettling impression that he was looking through her, rather than at her. "If I'd known what would happen, I would have asked someone to cover for me this morning. But I didn't know."

An involuntary burst of heat made Hetty's muscles clamp tightly in her belly. She glanced at the bed, then back at Michael.

His gaze was fixed on the small, telltale stain that was visible even from across the room. His throat worked as if he were trying to swallow, but couldn't.

The anger Hetty had wanted to fling at him a moment earlier suddenly turned back on her. He'd lost three patients in the past day and a half, and though there was nothing he could have done to save them, she knew him too well not to realize their deaths troubled him deeply.

She reached out blindly to touch him. Her hand came to rest on his chest, right above his heart. "Michael?"

He forced his gaze back to her. "Hetty, I'm sorry. I—"

Before he could say more, Hetty pressed her finger to his lips. "Don't! Don't you dare apologize, Michael Ryan. Not for last night."

Tears started in her eyes, but she blinked them back fiercely. "Don't apologize for anything . . . except leaving me this morning."

She slid her hands behind his neck while he stood frozen, as if he were afraid to breathe. She was so close, she could feel the warmth of him on her lips when he finally bent to claim the kisses she so willingly offered.

Michael pulled free first. He was panting and his tie was askew. His lips gleamed wetly, even in the shadowy hallway. He ran his tongue over them, tentatively, as if he wasn't sure what he'd find.

Slowly he released her and stepped back. There was a dazed wonder in his eyes that Hetty knew reflected the wonder in hers.

"It's different, isn't it?" he said, touching his fingers to his mouth.

Hetty nodded and licked her own slightly swollen lips as she watched him trace the edge of first his upper lip, then his lower. He wasn't touching her, yet her body responded as eagerly as if he had. She tensed, startled by the shaft of heat that pierced her.

It *was* different—she wasn't sure how.

The why was easy. She'd never made love to Michael before, nor he to her. That simple, glorious, primitive act had changed what lay between them forever.

Even though her back was to the room, Hetty was intensely aware of the disordered bed behind her. Michael glanced at it, then quickly looked away.

"I have to go, Hetty."

Hetty drew herself up straight. "Yes, of course you do. You had breakfast first, I hope?"

He smiled at that, genuinely amused. "Yes, ma'am. Some bread and preserves, anyway."

Another shaft of heat lanced through Hetty. Either Michael guessed at her reaction, or something showed in her face, because he suddenly drew in a sharp breath.

"Next time," he said, clearly fighting for control, "I'll remember to let *you* lick the jam off."

Before Hetty could respond, he was gone.

# *Chapter Thirteen*

It was only after the front door had closed behind Michael that Hetty realized he'd once again slipped away without saying when or where he would appear again.

Hetty bit back an exclamation of irritation and turned her attention to more useful matters, such as lighting the water heater so she could indulge in a long, hot bath.

The bathtub was an ugly, zinc-lined model that lacked even a wooden cabinet to disguise its ponderous iron body. Hetty didn't give a hoot how it looked. After a lifetime spent heating water over the stove, then scrambling to bathe in the small copper hip bath her mother had always used, being able to stretch out her legs and still have water to her chin was sheer luxury. To her delight, she even found a box of bath salts on the wooden shelf over the sink.

Between the hot water and the salts, she'd managed to work out almost all the lingering aches by the time the cooling water finally forced her to climb out and get dressed.

Although Michael undoubtedly had his sheets and towels done at a laundry, Hetty stripped the bed and set the stained sheets to soak in the kitchen sink. Just touching the sheets roused distracting memories and brought a flush to her cheeks.

Bathing, dressing, washing sheets, making a bed. They were prosaic tasks, things she'd done thousands of times without wasting a moment's thought on them, yet today Hetty found herself intensely aware of her body as she moved about tending to what needed doing. Each slight movement reminded her that she had slept with a man, felt his naked body pressed hard and sweaty against hers, felt him move within her and known the sweet bliss of fulfillment. It was a strange, slightly wicked sensation, and she savored every bit of it and hungered for more.

While the sheets soaked, Hetty warmed up the coffee left in the pot Michael had prepared that morning, then sat at the kitchen table to work out the snarls in her hair. It wasn't an easy task, but Hetty found it soothing because it kept her hands busy while her thoughts tumbled dizzily.

She'd have to return to Mrs. Spencer's, of course. For the sake of Michael's reputation. She didn't much care about hers. If Michael neglected to get the marriage license today, she'd tend to the task herself.

Michael had left a key to the house on the kitchen table with a note that it was his extra key and she should keep it, so it would be easy to come and go as she needed over the next few days.

Her trunks had already been delivered. She'd seen them, sitting on the covered back porch, waiting for her. There were things in them—pictures, her mother's favorite china teapot and six silver spoons, her favorite fry pan—that she would need to turn this stark bachelor's house into a home for her and Michael.

They didn't have a parlor. Dr. Cathcart had seen to that when he'd turned the old parlor into a waiting room. But they could make other arrangements. Her mother's rocker would fit beside the stove and her pie safe could go in the corner. The other things she'd shipped could be stored somewhere. For now, at least.

But they had to buy a bed. A decent, sturdy, *large* bed with a good mattress and sheets that fit and two fat feather pillows to fill the linen cases she'd embroidered with such care over the years.

Thinking of the bed made Hetty flush again and stir uncomfortably on the hard kitchen chair.

Enough of daydreaming.

More than anything else, she had to stop by Mrs. Scoggins's this morning. After foisting a grieving family on her without so much as a by-your-leave, she owed it to her friend as well as to Jessica Lanyon to offer whatever help she could.

She only hoped Mrs. Scoggins was still willing to speak to her.

Hetty pinned up her hair, then finished washing the sheets. She left them in the sink to drain as best they could since she couldn't possibly hang them out for all the neighborhood to see, clean or not.

She would, she decided, stop at Mrs. Spencer's first. Michael might be able to provide soap and towels and nightshirts, but he'd lacked an extra toothbrush—a lack she intended to remedy the next time she was in Fisk's Pharmacy. Mrs. Scoggins would be next, and there was no way of telling how long that visit might take or what might be needed.

The rest would have to wait.

"Indecent. That's what I call your behavior, Miss Malone. Positively indecent. And I won't stand for it. Not for a minute."

Mrs. Spencer sat, back rigid, nostrils flared as though she smelled something foul. Hetty suspected she was enjoying herself and that at least some of her indignation was staged for the benefit of the cook and the maid, whose ears were no doubt pressed tightly against the parlor door.

For her part, Hetty was finding it very difficult to control her own temper. Only the knowledge that she had, in fact, indulged in exactly the activity that Mrs. Spencer was accusing her of kept her from saying what she *really* thought.

"In other words, Mrs. Spencer," she said as coldly as she could manage, "you would simply have abandoned that poor family. I find that attitude . . . contemptible."

Mrs. Spencer reared back and her eyes spat fire. "Contemptible, is it? Well, you may think what you please, but you will do it somewhere besides my boarding house. I run a respectable establishment, and I will not tolerate either your insolence *or* your indecent behavior!"

She rose to her feet with the air of a hanging judge who had just pronounced sentence. "Pack your bags. Your bill will be waiting for you. I expect it to be paid in full before you leave—and I trust you will *never* darken my door again!"

Hetty stood, caught between anger at the woman's arrogance and the uncomfortable feeling that she'd been plunged into the middle of a badly written melodrama. "I can assure you, Mrs. Spencer, I don't *want* to 'darken your door.' If you will excuse me?"

She didn't wait to be dismissed, but stalked out of the room, head high, and up the stairs to retrieve her possessions.

A half hour later she carried her two carpetbags into Michael's bedroom and set them in the corner, out of the way. Despite the short walk, she was flushed and hot. Tendrils of hair had slipped down to curl damply about her face and the collar of her shirtwaist was threatening to wilt.

Hetty was too excited to care. She wouldn't deliberately have chosen to move in with Michael until they were legally married, but since Mrs. Spencer had forced the issue, she fully intended to take advantage of the situation.

She glanced at the now neatly made bed.

And she'd make sure Michael took advantage of it, too.

For the first time since becoming a doctor, Michael found his patients unbearably trying. He didn't want to listen to their complaints, didn't want to worry over why they weren't responding to treatment, and absolutely did *not* want to spend time explaining their condition to nervous family members who seemed determined to be obtuse, overly emotional, and difficult.

What he *did* want was to be back in bed with Hetty.

It was almost as if his body had turned traitor, as if some devilish imp had taken control of it with the express intention of mocking him. After all, he'd had all night to savor the warmth and softness of her. Instead, he'd skulked away like a thief in the dark, driven by memories and his own grinding self-doubts.

Would it always be like this? he wondered, gritting his teeth against the uncomfortable, disconcerting ache. Wanting her when he couldn't have her? Running from her when he could?

He'd always thought it would be so simple. Loving Hetty. Marrying her. Having a family.

He'd pictured himself coming home at the end of the day, his work done and Hetty waiting for him to spend the night in whispered secrets and seduction.

He'd never imagined his dreams would be

haunted or that he'd see faces in the dark even when she was lying next to him asleep.

And now he'd found that they were, and he did, and suddenly it didn't seem simple at all.

To Hetty's surprise, it was Mrs. Scoggins who answered the door, not Betty. The older woman put a finger to her lips in warning and carefully shut the door behind Hetty.

"The children are upstairs." Her thin lips compressed into a frown. "Little Sarah cried herself to sleep, and David keeled over in spite of trying not to. They're exhausted, but I don't imagine they'll be asleep long. Bad dreams, you know."

"And Mrs. Lanyon?" Hetty asked, following Mrs. Scoggins toward the kitchen at the back of the house.

"Making arrangements for the funeral. Clarabelle Fisk is with her. I was just fixing some tea to take upstairs with me. Would you like some?" She added more tea and hot water to the pot that was steeping before Hetty had a chance to say yes.

"I sent Betty out to do some shopping, though none of them has much appetite," she said with a little cluck of disapproval. "That's to be expected, I suppose, but it's still worrisome. Especially with the little ones."

Mrs. Scoggins moved about the kitchen with a dignified efficiency that surprised Hetty even more than her opening the front door had earlier. Somehow, she hadn't pictured Lettitia Scoggins doing anything besides directing meetings of the ladies' club and issuing orders to Betty, no matter how kind a heart she had. Obviously, she'd been wrong. Again.

"It's been a rather difficult morning, I admit. Mrs. Lanyon and the children, of course. Calls from my lawyer, who still can't find me a respectable caretaker." Mrs. Scoggins set an extra cup and saucer on the small tray she was arranging without missing a beat in her litany of grievances. "The butcher sent the wrong cut after I'd *clearly* told him what was wanted, the grocer's is out of the brand of pickling spice I prefer, and the gardener says he can't come next week to clean out the flower beds as I'd asked." At the thought, she set the teapot on the tray with enough force to make tea slop out the spout.

She glowered at the spot on the well-starched linen doily, then firmly set the sugar bowl on top of it. "I'm trying to ignore all the irritations, however, at least for the moment. I don't like to leave the children alone for long. In case they wake up, you know. Though I can't imagine what I'll offer them to eat for dinner if Betty doesn't get back soon. Not that they ate anything for breakfast, mind you, and probably won't touch any supper tonight."

"I . . . I hope you don't think it was a terrible imposition," Hetty ventured nervously. She wasn't quite sure how to take Mrs. Scoggins's sudden torrent of talk. "Sending the children to you, I mean. But none of the nearby boarding houses would take them in and—"

"No need to apologize," Mrs. Scoggins said sharply. Her mouth thinned. "It wouldn't have been at all proper to leave those children in a boarding house. Not proper at all."

Hetty agreed, knowing it wasn't propriety Mrs. Scoggins was thinking about, but two small, frightened children who had tried so very hard to be brave. Not that Lettitia Scoggins would ever admit to having quite so soft a heart, Hetty thought, following her hostess up the back servants' stairs to a small sitting room on the second floor.

Mrs. Scoggins set the tray down on a spindly looking table; then, motioning Hetty to keep silent, she led her on tiptoe into the next room.

David and Sarah Lanyon lay nose to toe on a four-poster bed that half filled the room. Pillows had been stacked along the outer edges of the bed to keep them from falling off, but neither one so much as twitched as she bent over them. They were sprawled in heavy, slack-limbed sleep, their faces pressed deep into the pillows. Tear tracks marred Sarah's plump cheeks and dark shadows were visible beneath the thick fringe of David's lashes, but other than that, Hetty could detect no hint of the ordeal they'd just gone through.

It wouldn't show on the outside, anyway, she thought, straightening. But on the inside . . .

She tiptoed out of the room after Mrs. Scoggins, then waited as the older woman carefully closed the door behind them, leaving just a crack so they could hear if either of the children stirred.

"Poor things," Mrs. Scoggins whispered, as if to herself. "Poor little things. Whatever is to become of them and their mama now?"

By one o'clock, Michael had completed his regular rounds. There were a number of home-care patients he needed to see, but none of the visits was urgent, and after the trouble he'd had concentrating this morning, he wasn't ready to put himself through another round of consultations this afternoon. By tomorrow he might be capable of paying more attention to his work than to his fantasies and frustrations. He certainly wasn't capable of that feat now.

But deciding what he was not going to do that afternoon didn't help him decide what he *would* do. There was the matter of the marriage license, of course. But after that? He'd walked out of the house this morning in a daze, too angry with himself and too shaken by the effect of Hetty's kisses to think straight enough to make plans, or find out if she had any of her own.

On the off chance that Hetty might still be lingering at the house, he turned his horse down his own street, rather than the one which led to the stables. He was half a block away when he began to wonder if his eyes were playing tricks on him.

A wide straw hat popped into view just above the top of his picket fence, then immediately ducked out of sight only to bob up a couple of feet away a moment later.

As Michael pulled his horse up in front of the gate, the hat reappeared again. Only this time he could see Hetty's face under it, her attention fixed on something out of sight behind the fence. At the sound of his wheels, she glanced up, then rose to her feet with a smile on her face so wide that it made the day seem brighter.

They erupted into speech at the same time.

"Whatever are you doing here?"

"I didn't expect to see you back so soon."

"I thought—"

"I wondered—"

Hetty cut her words off short. So did Michael. Then they both burst into laughter.

Michael hooked his reins and got down from the buggy. He didn't bother to take out his bag, just left it under the seat and strolled over to the fence.

"*What* are you doing, Hetty?" he asked. Not that he really cared, so long as he could feast on her sunlit face and dancing eyes.

"Gathering flower seeds. See?" She held up a battered pan so he could inspect her meager harvest. "I hope you don't mind. I didn't have anywhere else to go, and it's such a beautiful day and—"

She stopped short, embarrassed, then raised her eyes to meet his. Her smile disappeared even as the green in her eyes seemed to deepen. The corner of her mouth twitched invitingly. "And I wanted to," she added. "Gather the seeds, I mean."

"Did you?" Michael asked, too fascinated by the delicate color the sun had put in her cheeks and the shadow her hat cast along her face to know what she was saying, or care.

"Yes," Hetty said. She gently shook the pan she held, making the dried seeds rustle and scrape against the tin. "Your garden has gone to ruin, but some flowers came up in spite of the weeds. I thought I'd collect their seeds for next year, when I'll be able to make a tidier bed."

The word "bed" brought them both up with a guilty start. Hetty blushed, but her eyes met his. Her mouth curved into a smile full of unspoken promises.

The smile was almost Michael's undoing. In a desperate bid for distraction, he grabbed hold of the fence and peered over the top.

At one time, a neat flower garden had been laid out along the base of the fence. Now dead weeds and uncut grass filled the space, almost burying the four or five species of flowers that had managed to grow over the summer, in spite of everything.

"Are you sure it's worth the effort, Hetty? That's the sorriest-looking garden I've seen in a long time."

Hetty laughed. "Have you even been looking?"

Michael couldn't help grinning in return. "Actually, no. I don't recall having noticed it at all, to tell you the truth."

For an instant, he thought about leaning over the fence to kiss her. If she'd been two feet closer or he'd been two feet taller, it might have been possible, but not otherwise. He'd impale himself if he tried, and that wouldn't do either of them any good.

His grip on the worn pickets tightened. He wanted to kiss her so badly, it hurt. Her innocent mention of untidy beds had stirred the same dangerous images he'd been trying all morning to ignore, and now that she was so close and the front door stood open and—

"You don't have to do this, you know," he said, wrenching his thoughts away from more temptation. "I hire a boy to mow the lawn every week in the summer. He'd be happy to tend the flower—"

He barely caught himself in time. "Er, clean out the weeds, too," he finished lamely.

Hetty's mouth pinched up and her eyes glittered wickedly. "But I rather like taking care of beds, Michael," she said provocatively.

Michael squeezed his eyes shut and groaned.

His beloved patted his hand soothingly. "I won't tease any more, I promise," she said.

He might have had more faith in her promise if he hadn't heard the underlying laughter in her voice. Michael ventured to open one eye, out of which he glared at her suspiciously. "Promise?"

Hetty nodded primly. "Promise. Cross my heart and hope to die," she said, crossing her heart.

Unfortunately, the childish gesture drew Michael's gaze in a direction that wasn't conducive to childish thoughts. He opened his other eye and determinedly fixed his gaze on the porch railing.

Hetty turned to follow the direction of his gaze. "I don't mean to be critical, Michael, but I can't help wondering who chose this . . . ummm . . . particular combination of colors."

He'd long ago stopped noticing the garish paint scheme, but Michael couldn't deny that the house stood out from among its decorous neighbors. "I rather like the blue, actually."

"It goes so well with that yellowy-orange on the siding."

The corner of Michael's mouth twitched. "Not to mention the green on the porch."

"*I* wouldn't mention it! Not if I could help it, anyway!"

"But think of the conversational possibilities, Hetty!"

"I am!" Hetty's green eyes twinkled distractingly. "According to Mr. Davidson down at the train station, your house generates quite a lot of conversation in the neighborhood."

"Does it?" Michael's eyebrows shot up in surprise. "I didn't know that."

Hetty shook her head despairingly. "Do you pay attention to *anything* except your work, Michael?"

She meant to tease him, but Michael couldn't help catch the real note of reproach underneath. He shoved away from the fence, suddenly irritated. The last thing he wanted right now was to be reminded of his work and the demands it made on him. The demands that his patients had the *right* to make on him, so far as he was concerned.

"Never mind that," Hetty said hastily, evidently sensing his sudden change in mood. "But I really would like to know why Dr. Cathcart—I assume it was Dr. Cathcart!—painted his house such an outrageous combination of colors."

Michael shrugged. "The house looked like this when I got here. I asked Sherman about it one afternoon, then had to explain why I was asking."

Hetty's eyebrows shot up in disbelief.

"He was color-blind," Michael explained. "He thought he was having the house painted in some sort of respectable shade of tan and brown. Either the painter didn't have the sense to realize he couldn't judge, or thought he'd found a good way to get rid of paint he couldn't give away, otherwise."

"Oh!" said Hetty. She turned and studied the colorful facade.

"And if the neighbors don't like it, they never told *me*," Michael added, irritated that Hetty should be the one to tell him his neighbors objected to the house. "Or Dr. Cathcart, for that matter!"

She wasn't paying the least bit of attention to him. "Tan and brown, hmm? Odd, isn't it?"

"The color?"

Hetty shook her head, her gaze still fixed on the house. "How you can look at something without realizing you're seeing it all wrong."

Michael frowned back. "What's that supposed to mean?"

She shrugged as if shaking off a troublesome thought and turned back to him. "Nothing of any use."

Suddenly, she smiled up at him. The corners of her eyes crinkled enticingly. "Do you realize I could have given you a dozen kisses by now if you'd come through that gate instead of hanging over the fence?"

Michael grabbed for the gate latch and was just about to lift it when the sound of a galloping horse coming up the street caught his attention. He glanced over his shoulder at the approaching horseman, then abruptly released his hold on the latch and dashed into the street.

Samuel Rheiner, mounted bareback on one of his father's big farm horses, barreled toward them. The sound of the animal's heavy hooves echoed in the quiet street.

"Dr. Ryan! Dr. Ryan!" the boy called. He sawed on the reins. The horse threw up its head and swerved, then dropped from a gallop to a bone-jarring trot so abruptly that Samuel pitched forward onto its withers. Only a quick grab at its mane kept him from tumbling into the street.

Michael moved to catch the bridle, but the lathered horse, more accustomed to a plow than a rider, readily stumbled to a halt not three feet away, sides heaving and nostrils flaring.

"Dr. Ryan! Da says, come quick! Please!" The boy's face was drawn and white, his eyes large with fear. He threw a leg over his horse's withers, ready to jump, but Michael grabbed him by the waist and swung him to the ground.

Michael set the boy on his feet and knelt before him. He was aware of Hetty coming to stand beside him, but he couldn't worry about her. Not now.

"Take a deep breath," he commanded. "All right, now tell me. Is it your mother?"

Samuel nodded anxiously. "She's coughing up blood. Da says, worse than she's ever done. I didn't know. I . . . I've never seen her that way." He gulped, fighting for an adult control that was beyond him. "She's not going to die, is she?"

Michael shook his head. "No, she's not going to die. Not—" He bit back the words on his tongue. *Not this time.*

Somewhere at the back of his mind, memories of his own mother's illness were banging on his consciousness with insistent force, demanding his attention. He refused to acknowledge them. They were much too painfully close to what Samuel was facing, and he couldn't allow himself to be distracted. Not now.

"No," he said again, "your mother's not going to die. But I'll go see what I can do to help her now, all right?"

Samuel nodded dumbly.

"All right." Michael rose to his feet. "You can stay here with Miss Malone and I'll—"

"No!" Samuel, eyes blazing, set his jaw in stubborn determination. "I'm going back with you. Da needs me."

"Of course he does," Hetty said.

Michael glared at her, but she ignored him. All her attention was focused on the boy.

"Besides, I'm going to go with you. Your father and Dr. Ryan will be so busy with your mother, they won't be able to tend to the things we can. Isn't that right?"

Samuel nodded warily, clearly surprised to find someone on his side.

"Good. Why don't you tie your horse behind Dr. Ryan's buggy, then? I imagine the three of us can fit on that seat if we try. I'll just get my bag and lock the door . . . unless you need to get anything first?" she added, glancing at Michael, brows raised in inquiry.

Michael shook his head. There was no sense fighting her. He didn't have time to waste arguing, and he wouldn't win, anyway. The last thing he wanted was to have her involved, but he needed her help. He didn't want to admit it, but he needed her . . . and so did Samuel and little Anna.

# *Chapter Fourteen*

Samuel squirmed on the buggy's leather seat, too anxious to sit still. Hetty tried to distract him by telling him about Mr. Meissner and the promise to translate his grandmother's recipes, but he refused to listen to any of it.

Michael said nothing. Over Samuel's objections, he'd left the boy's horse at the livery stable and kept his own horse at a spanking trot, regardless of the roughness of the roads outside the city limits. Only when they came to the crude track leading to the clearing where the Rheiners had set up their camp did he slow to a walk.

Hetty glanced at him out of the corner of her eye. All trace of the laughter they'd shared earlier was gone, wiped away as completely as if it had never been. His sharply sculpted profile now seemed carved in stone. More than once she caught Samuel looking up at him nervously, but Michael ignored the boy, just as he'd ignored her and everything else except the horse and the road in front of them.

The clearing looked much the same as it had before, with the sole exception that this time, a small black-and-white she-goat was staked out in the dried grass not far from the tent. At the sound of the carriage, the goat bleated and swung around on her tether, waking the fawn-colored kid sleeping in the grass at her feet.

Michael drew up near the fallen cottonwood. He was already on the ground and reaching for his medical bag under the seat when Mr. Rheiner emerged from the tent.

Samuel took one look at his father's stoop-shouldered figure and scrambled from the buggy before Hetty had even gathered up her skirts. He dodged around Michael and under the carriage horse's nose.

"Da! I was quick as I could be, just like you said. Honest. Honest I was." His anxious gaze flicked between his father and the closed tent flap.

"Now then, boy," Mr. Rheiner said gently. "Now then. You did well. Your Mama's resting. It's all right." He bent to fold his son in his arms, but Samuel slipped away from him and darted over to peer into the tent.

"Mr. Rheiner?" Michael gave no sign that he was even aware of Samuel's presence.

Mr. Rheiner met his ice-blue gaze with a worried frown. "Thank you for coming, Doctor. Ruth—well, you'd best see for yourself." With that, he turned and pulled the tent flap back so Michael could precede him. He didn't even glance at his son. His attention was focused on the shadowy back corner of the tent where the bed stood.

Samuel sniffed and retreated two steps, but the instant the flap fell into place behind them, he angrily dug the heels of his hands into his eyes, wiping away the tears.

Hetty quietly came up beside him, ready to offer whatever meager words of comfort she could. Samuel turned away and stalked over to the fire pit between the tent and wagon. For a moment he just stood with his back to her, stiff as a rod; then he squatted down on his skinny haunches, hunched his shoulders, and stared at the ring of ashes and fire-blackened river stones as if he expected to find the secrets of the world hidden somewhere beneath them.

So intent was he on his own misery, he didn't seem to hear the thin wail that suddenly arose inside the tent. Hetty glanced at the closed tent flap, then at Samuel, and decided her presence would be more welcome elsewhere.

Hesitantly, she poked her head into the tent.

Little had changed. The stove and bed and rocker were as they'd been before. Even the camp table with its dresser-drawer cradle stood in the same place. But this time the hot, heavy air snapped with tension as if before a gathering storm.

Michael and Mr. Rheiner stood close beside the bed. Hetty caught a glimpse of Mrs. Rheiner, eyes shut, head wearily tilted back against the pillows; then Michael moved and all Hetty could see was her thin, pale hand on the coverlet. As the pathetic wailing from the drawer increased, both men glanced over their shoulders, clearly torn as to where they were needed the most.

"Do you want me to take the baby?" Hetty asked, meeting Michael's glance.

Michael glanced at Mr. Rheiner, then at the woman on the bed. In the dim light inside the tent, his face seemed darker, harder, more like hewn granite than warm flesh. Another wail from the drawer settled the matter.

"Yes, please. Take the whole drawer, but if you pick her up, keep her well bundled. No drafts, remember, even if it is warm out. And wash your hands first. There's a basin by the stove with warm water and soap."

Hetty nodded her understanding, suddenly conscious of a nervous lump in the pit of her stomach. She'd handled plenty of her friends' and neighbors' babies, but she'd never handled any as tiny as Anna Rheiner. She washed her hands as ordered and dried them on a towel that looked as if it might have come from Mrs. Scoggins's box of linens, then turned to the drawer on the camp table.

Anna was on her back in the middle of her nest of blankets, her delicate hands balled into fists and her mouth wide open in protest at the unfairness of the universe. A quick check showed that the pad beneath her was clean and dry, that nothing was pinching her, and that the flannel belly band was firmly in place and wasn't rubbing. Which left one possibility.

Hetty found a baby bottle with a black rubber nipple sitting at the back of the camp stove, half-filled with milk. A quick squirt on her wrist proved the contents were warm enough. The question was, could Anna even get the nipple in her mouth? Hetty frowned at the little mouth, still wide open in protest, then at the nipple. She thought she remembered Michael mentioning a dropper, but no dropper was in sight, and why would anyone have fixed the bottle if it wasn't intended to be used?

Well, nothing ventured . . .

She tucked the bottle into a corner of the drawer where the wadded blankets would prevent it from tipping over, then folded down the edges of a couple of other blankets so they formed a tent over Anna. The blankets muffled the baby's wailing a little, but not enough.

"My Anna . . . ?" Ruth Rheiner's voice was weaker than her infant daughter's.

"She's all right," Mr. Rheiner murmured soothingly. "She's hungry."

"Hungry?"

Hetty thought she detected a faint note of satisfaction in the whispered query.

"That's right. Miss Malone is going to take care of her for you, so you're not to worry. Not right now. All right?" Even a seriously ill woman could not mistake the stern, authoritarian note in Michael's cool voice.

"Yes . . ." Mrs. Rheiner said. Her hand

clenched on the coverlet—more in anger and frustration than in pain, Hetty thought—then slowly relaxed. "All right."

Hetty got a good grip on either end of the drawer, then cautiously lifted it off the table and carried it out of the tent. The movement didn't seem to disturb Anna. Her wailing continued unabated.

Samuel was watching as she emerged, as wary as a deer waiting to flee into the underbrush. As Hetty walked toward him, he slowly rose to his feet.

"She's not s'posed to be out of the tent," he said, studying the tented mound of blankets disapprovingly.

"Dr. Ryan said it was all right," Hetty said, setting the drawer down beside the cottonwood. The huge trunk would serve as a windbreak if any breeze came up. "She's sort of fussy and your mother needs some rest."

He looked up at her, then, his eyes dark hollows of doubt. "How's my ma? Is she okay?"

Hetty forced herself to meet his worried gaze directly. "I don't know, Samuel. I know she's tired, but Dr. Ryan's with her and so is your father. They'll take care of her."

The corners of his mouth twitched and quivered as he fought against the threatening tears. Rather than risk speaking, he settled for squatting down a couple of feet away from Hetty and his sister, his back propped against the solid trunk. He refused to come any closer when Hetty suggested that he move over.

Her heart ached for Samuel, but Anna needed her attention more. Hetty dug out the bottle and carefully rearranged the blankets so nothing but Anna's eyes and minuscule nose and wide-open mouth were exposed. At the first touch of the rubber nipple against her lips, Anna jerked away, angrier than ever.

Hetty tried to follow her, brushing the edge of the nipple against her lower lip, but Anna kept turning away, as if she found the ugly rubber nipple an insupportable insult. After four fruitless tries, Hetty sat back on her heels and wondered what to do next.

"Squeeze some on her tongue," Samuel said. He was still seated, back against the trunk, but his head was tilted so he could get a better view of Hetty's operation. The scowl on his face said more clearly than words that he wasn't impressed so far. "She don't seem to have figured out it's food yet, so you gotta show her."

"Oh," Hetty said. She placed the tip of the nipple against Anna's lower gum and gently squeezed the base of the nipple, just above where it was stretched over the top of the bottle. "Like this?"

Samuel edged upward and craned his neck so he could get an even better view. "Yeah, like that."

Anna screwed up her mouth as if to protest, then gave a little smack and clamped down on the nipple and started sucking.

"It works!"

Samuel sank back down until he was sitting squarely on the ground. He shrugged and looked away. "Yeah, sometimes."

The nipple was too big and Anna was still too small and weak to be able to suck well. She tended to tug on the nipple for a moment or two, then fight against it as if struggling for breath, then come back and tug on it again. It wasn't a very efficient process, but she was obviously taking enough to keep her alive. Hetty watched, fascinated by the child's delicacy—and her determination. Anna Rheiner might not weigh four pounds, but she was a fighter. She wouldn't have lived this long, otherwise.

Hetty didn't know how long she watched Anna before she again became aware of Samuel. He was still sitting against the tree trunk, legs folded tightly against his body, skinny arms covered in two layers of flannel shirts and wrapped around his knees, skinny ankles sticking out of too-short pants. Like a shabby little cricket all alone at the end of the summer, Hetty thought, and felt a sharp tug of sympathy for a little boy who was having to grow up much too fast.

"That was very brave of you," she said, "riding all the way into town like that."

He frowned and hunched his shoulders. "I'm not a baby, you know. 'Sides, Da asked me to. For Ma."

"I'd say your mother is lucky to have a son like you. When I met her the other day, I could tell how proud she is of you, of all you've done to help her."

He looked up at that, wary once more.

Before he could say anything, Michael

emerged from the tent and came toward them. Hetty could read neither satisfaction nor worry in his face, but Samuel twisted around to stare at him, fixing him with a gaze so anxious and penetrating that Hetty was surprised Michael didn't flinch from the force of it.

He didn't seem to notice. He didn't even glance at Samuel, but came to stand beside Hetty, towering over her while he watched Anna suck.

Hetty glanced at Samuel. He was staring at Michael, his young face strained with worry.

"She's doing better than I expected," Michael said after a long, uncomfortable moment.

"You mean . . . Ma?" In that one word was compounded all the hope and fear that an eight-year-old boy could feel.

Michael's gaze flicked to Samuel, then away. "Your sister," he said at last. "Your sister's doing better than I expected."

Hetty caught that brief glance. She looked at Samuel, so small and frightened; then she looked at Michael, standing tall and tense and still beside her. Suddenly, understanding dawned.

*He's afraid!* she thought. *He's afraid for Samuel* and *for himself. He's afraid he'll lose Ruth Rheiner, and he doesn't know how to tell Samuel.*

*He doesn't know how to deal with the boy's fear because he never learned to deal with his own.*

Michael had drawn away from his patients, not because he didn't want to become involved in their problems, but because he was too much involved, because he was unable to separate the doctor who had to deal with unpleasant truths from the man who had to live with them . . . and who suffered for it.

A faint sputtering sound brought Hetty's attention back to her infant charge with a jerk. Anna had fallen asleep in the middle of a mouthful of milk. A trickle of white ran out the corner of her mouth. Her forehead scrunched up and her nose wrinkled; then she turned her head to the side, gave a couple of satisfied little smacks, and fell even more deeply asleep.

Hetty couldn't help smiling at the wrinkled little face in its cocoon of blankets. She wiped away the milk, then tucked the bottle into its corner and covered Anna up again.

"She's asleep?" Michael asked.

"Sound asleep and with a full tummy," Hetty agreed. The satisfaction in seeing Anna fed and asleep drained away at the sight of Michael's grim face.

"Why don't you sit here," she said to Michael, patting the ground beside her, "and tell us how her mother's doing."

Michael took one step backward, as if preparing to run away. Hetty grabbed his pant leg and tugged. "Samuel wants to know," she said firmly. "He rode all the way into town to fetch you, remember."

From the look on his face, Hetty suspected that Michael would have run away if she'd let go of his trousers. Her grip tightened. She gave another tug. "Sit."

Michael refused to sit, but he did, reluctantly, go down on one knee beside her. He braced one hand against his thigh and propped his elbow on his other knee, as awkward as if he were steeling himself against blows to come.

"Your mother's resting, Samuel. She's . . . she's very tired, you know. The coughing wears her out, so I gave her a draught of something that will help her sleep."

Samuel might only be eight, but he was no fool. Michael had skirted around the truth and he knew it. "She was spittin' up blood this morning. She's never done that before. Leastwise, not near so much."

Samuel hugged his knees tighter against his chest and glared up at Michael as if he expected him to deny it. "I *saw* it!"

"It happens sometimes, Samuel." Michael's voice sounded brittle, as if it might shatter at any moment.

When he got no response, he added carefully, "Your mother has finally agreed to try something I've been suggesting for quite a while now. We're going to move her out of the tent, set her up outside so she has lots of fresh air, all day long."

"You're gonna leave her *outside*? Just like . . . like one of the horses or somethin'? What if it snows?"

"Then we'll move her back into the tent until it stops," Michael snapped.

Hetty stretched out a hand to calm him. He angrily shook her off, but he did take a deep breath, and when he spoke again, he was once more in control.

"We'll put up some protection for her, Samuel.

But she has to get out of that stuffy tent and get some fresh air."

"An' that will make her all well?"

Michael's fingers dug into the muscles of his thigh. "It's helped a number of people with the same trouble your mother has," he said with careful precision.

Samuel knew a dodge when he heard one. His jaw set stubbornly, but his eyes looked hollow and haunted. "Missus Prichard, the lady up the road what loaned us the goat, she says . . ."

The words seemed to stick in his throat. He swallowed, a big gulp that didn't go down easily. "She says when folks get to bleeding like that, they . . . they die."

Silence. Michael's hand clenched into a fist. Hetty could see the tendons on the inside of his wrist tense and shift as his fingers dug into his palm.

"Sometimes," he admitted at last. "If the bleeding gets worse, yes, sometimes they die. But sometimes—a lot of times!—they get better."

Hetty could feel the effort he made to meet Samuel's searching gaze without flinching. "You have to believe me, Samuel. They get better, too."

Samuel looked away first. His lips thinned as he turned to glare at the drawer where his sister lay. "Missus Prichard says my Da put her,"—he poked his chin out to indicate the drawer—"in Ma's belly." He swung his head back to glare at Michael. "Is that right? Did my Da do that?"

His question caught Hetty by surprise.

Michael nodded cautiously. "Yes, he did. Just like he put you there."

Samuel's face darkened suddenly. "Ma never coughed up blood before. Not before *she* came along."

He sprang to his feet, his thin body quivering with anger and pain and fear combined. "If my ma dies, then it's my da's fault. Isn't it? *Isn't it*? His and . . . *hers*."

He spat out the last word as if it burned his tongue, then abruptly turned tail and ran. By the time Michael scrambled to his feet, Samuel had disappeared into the trees at the far side of the clearing.

For what seemed an eternity, Michael simply stared blindly at the spot where Samuel had vanished. Then he exploded.

"Damn all meddling busybodies!"

His fist crashed down on the unheeding tree trunk, again and again.

"Damn them! Damn them! *Damn them*!"

While Mrs. Rheiner slept, Hetty helped Michael and Mr. Rheiner construct a simple shelter that would be Mrs. Rheiner's new parlor and bedroom combined for all but the very worst weather. The shelter was patched together out of worn canvas, supported by four sturdy saplings felled near the river and guyed by an assortment of old ropes Mr. Rheiner dug out of the bottom of the wagon.

Samuel never came out of hiding.

When Mr. Rheiner wanted to look for his son, Michael lied and said he'd told Samuel to go exploring for a few hours, that the boy needed the exercise and a chance to get away or he'd risk getting sick himself.

Samuel's father accepted the explanation readily enough. With all the crushing burdens he was already struggling under, he didn't have any energy left to notice his son's sufferings.

Other than his lie for Samuel, Michael kept silent. He roughly dismissed Mr. Rheiner's stumbling explanations about his continuing inability to find a job or to pay him, refused to meet Hetty's questioning, worried glances, and concentrated on the job at hand with a cold efficiency that was almost terrifying.

Only once did he give any hint of the turmoil inside him. Against Mr. Rheiner's protests, Michael insisted on felling the four trees they needed by himself.

Though he'd had no experience with chopping down trees, Michael attacked them furiously. With each vicious blow, the trees shivered and rained down dead, dried leaves. As the ax bit deeper, the trees swayed, then slowly started to tilt until their own weight brought them crashing down.

Michael watched each one fall, the heavy ax ready in his hands for another stroke as if he thought the trees would rise up against him in one last mad convulsion. He trimmed and cut each one to size with the same ferocity, swinging the ax upward with surprising ease, then slamming it downward in a deadly arc that sent leaves and wood chips flying in all directions.

As Hetty watched him, she could almost hear his curses ringing in her ears. Damn them! Damn them! *Damn them!*

As soon as the shelter was finished and Mr. Rheiner had ducked into the tent to check on his wife and daughter, Hetty drew Michael aside.

"You have to find Samuel, Michael. You have to talk to him, make him understand."

"Understand?" He laughed, but there was no humor in the sound. "How can I make him understand when *I* don't understand? There's no reason to any of this suffering, Hetty. There never has been."

"No, but that doesn't mean we have to give in to it."

"You don't give in to it, Hetty. Didn't you know that? It just swallows you up, regardless of what you do."

"Michael!" Frustrated, Hetty grabbed hold of his sweat-stained shirt and shook him once. Hard. "Why do you always have to look at the dark side of everything?"

His fingers closed around her wrists like iron shackles. He pulled her hands away from his shirt but made no move to release her.

She tilted her head back, ready to blast him, and shivered instead at the wintry chill of his gaze. Never had Hetty seen him like this, his wild black hair and thick black brows shadowing eyes of ice, his shirt damp and dirty, with the sleeves rolled to his elbow and the collar open to expose his throat and a fringe of sweat-dampened black curls at the collar of his undershirt.

"Tell me, Hetty," he demanded angrily, "where's a bright side to any of this?" He nodded at the makeshift shelter, but his gesture encompassed the whole of the camp and its occupants. "Where's the bright side when a young mother is sick, maybe dying. When a baby's born too soon, and a man is working himself to death, and a little boy—"

He broke off with an ugly grimace, fighting for breath. "Well, Hetty? Where's the bright side of that?"

Hetty wrenched herself free of his grip, feeling as angry as he was. "I'll tell you where! It's in the love that holds this family together in spite of everything. In the love that wanted to bring a new life into the world, no matter what the risk. You may not think it's much, Michael Ryan, but it's a whole lot more than some people *ever* have!"

"And a lot of good that will do Samuel if his mother dies!"

His words were cold and sharp and they cut like flying glass, but his eyes—

Hetty froze, trapped in that icy glare. His eyes were fixed on hers, the pupils black holes in hard crystal, but somewhere in those pale blue depths Hetty sensed his plea—mute, impassioned, desperate.

Once, he'd leaned across her mother's kitchen table in the hush of a winter's night and told her of his dreams of being a doctor, of his belief that medical science would soon conquer the disease that had claimed his own mother all those years ago. She remembered his eyes then, wide and eager and so blue that the irises were almost indistinguishable from the black pupils.

Now his eyes were the blue of winter frost, and instead of talking of dreams, he had to find words of comfort for a boy as lost and frightened as he'd once been, knowing that the medical science he'd believed in, the science to which he'd dedicated his life, offered no more answers than it ever had.

All Hetty's anger drained away in a rush. She stretched out her hand and gently touched his sleeve.

"You have to help Samuel through this, Michael. He's scared and he's all alone and he trusts you."

"He wants me to produce a miracle, you mean."

For an instant, Hetty thought he would say something more, but he didn't. As abruptly as if she'd burned him, he turned away to stare across the clearing.

As if it sensed Michael's stare, the nanny goat looked up from where she'd been grazing and bleated at him. The kid, startled, kicked up its heels and darted around its mother, then ducked its head and began to nurse greedily, tugging at its mother's teat so roughly that she finally kicked him away and moved over. The kid gave a *baa* of protest and dived right back.

"There are all sorts of miracles, Michael," Hetty said.

When he refused even to look at her, she added softly, "Did you ever think that, to Samuel, what you say might not be nearly as important as what you do?"

Michael threw up his hands and jerked back around to confront her. "All right then, Hetty, what am I supposed to do? Do you have any good suggestions?"

She frowned, considering, then thrust her hand into the pocket of her skirt.

"Here, take these," she said, dragging out a small, slightly crumpled paper bag and holding it out to Michael.

Michael eyed the bag suspiciously. "What is it?"

Hetty grabbed his hand and slapped the bag into his palm. "Horehound drops. To give to Samuel."

She watched as his fingers reluctantly closed around the bag, then added, "And take a few for yourself. I think you're going to need them."

# Chapter Fifteen

Samuel came creeping out of the underbrush like a frightened rabbit, scenting the wind for danger.

Michael spotted him the instant he emerged, but rather than risk scaring the boy off again, he kept his attention on the task to which he'd dedicated the better part of the last half hour—flaking bits of bark off the fallen cottonwood, one after the other. Oddly shaped chips lay scattered on the ground around his feet, in some places inches deep. They'd be useful for starting fires, he supposed, if anyone wanted to bother with picking them up.

Reassured by Michael's seeming distraction, Samuel edged into the clearing. When no one pounced, he defiantly sauntered across to the end of the trunk farthest from Michael's perch.

"I'm back," he said, propping his hip against a rough knob where a branch had once sprouted. "How's Ma doing?"

"Much better," Michael said, prying off another chip. He inspected the piece with care, then tossed it on the growing heap at his feet and reluctantly turned his attention to Samuel. "She's awake. She had a little soup and a boiled egg and she said it made her feel a whole lot stronger."

He hesitated, uncomfortably conscious of the tension in his shoulders and the tightness in the pit of his stomach. The bag of horehound drops in his pocket weighted him down like sins on his conscience.

*You have to help Samuel,* Hetty had said. He supposed she was right—no, he *knew* she was right—but that didn't make the job any easier. He hadn't the faintest notion how to begin or what to say once he had and—

And he was gut-shakingly terrified by the whole damned idea. He'd been terrified ever since that first time when the Rheiners had come into town to consult with him and Samuel had sat outside, a lost and lonely little boy who was as frightened as he himself had once been.

He pried off another bark chip, this time with such violence, it went spinning out beyond the farthest chip.

"Your mother asked for you, Samuel," he said at last.

Samuel's head came up at that.

"I told her you were off fishing."

Samuel's mouth narrowed into a straight, hard

line of self-condemnation. "I shoulda been here."

He sprang to his feet and took two quick steps toward the tent, then stopped dead in his tracks. "Can I go in? Can I see her?" he asked, eyeing Michael doubtfully. The tone was belligerent. The look in his eyes was not.

Michael knew that look. He remembered the doubt, the constant wavering between resentment and guilt, fear and denial, as he'd struggled to come to terms with his own mother's illness. He remembered how much it had hurt when the adults around him had kept him from her, no matter how good their reasons for doing so.

"You can't see her right now," he said at last, reluctantly. "Miss Malone and your father are helping her wash up and change her gown and—and what not. As soon as they're done, we'll move her out to the shelter. See?" He gestured to the newly constructed shelter, but Samuel was not going to allow himself to be distracted.

"She don't wanta see me." It wasn't a question.

"Of course she does!" Michael protested, jerking upright on the trunk. "As soon as Miss Malone and your father are through—"

"They're takin' care of my sister, too?"

"Well, yes—"

"Ma's got time for Anna."

"No, she doesn't. Your father's taking care of Anna. Your father and Miss Malone."

Samuel chewed on the corner of his lower lip while he stared at Michael through narrowed eyes. As if he expected him to confess a lie.

He hadn't lied, Michael reminded himself. Yet.

Nor would he if he could possibly help it, but somehow he had to make Samuel understand what he himself had never understood. What he wasn't even sure he understood now.

"Samuel, your mother isn't sicker because of Anna," he said, choosing his words with care. "She's tireder, yes, but that's all. The sickness—"

"Consumption!" Samuel snapped, standing his ground.

Michael nodded, understanding. Samuel didn't want lies, and he didn't want an adult's condescension, either. "The consumption develops in different ways. Your mother was already tired with all the work she was doing and—"

" 'Cause of me," Samuel said, stricken. "She was working 'cause of me."

"What?"

"All that work she took in before—before Anna. It was my fault, wasn't it?" He staggered over to the trunk and sagged against it. His eyes, huge and hollow in his thin face, never wavered from Michael's face.

"No! Of course it wasn't your fault!" Michael was almost shouting. He couldn't help it. The boy's self-blame was as sharp as the blame he'd shouldered all those years ago—and just as mistaken.

He swung off the trunk and moved toward Samuel, but the boy shrank back, away from him. Michael froze. Guilt knifed through him. Guilt and fury. He, of all people, ought to have known. How could he have been so damnably stupid, so clumsy? If only he'd—

He cut the self-recriminations short and slowly sank down on his haunches about three feet away, until his eyes were on a level with Samuel's.

"It wasn't your fault, Samuel. Believe me. It wasn't *anybody's* fault."

"Then why—?" Samuel's lower lip trembled, just for an instant before he bit down on it so hard that Michael winced. The boy ducked his head, struggling against the emotions that were threatening to swamp him.

Michael stared at the mop of shaggy, golden hair. A bit of dead leaf drifted down from where it had caught at Samuel's temple and a tiny twig stuck out at the crown—remnants, no doubt, of his earlier plunge into the underbrush. Michael repressed the urge to pluck out the twig. After all, eight-year-old boys *should* have twigs in their hair. And dirt on their hands. And a hole in the knees of their pants from where they'd caught them climbing a tree, or digging after a fox, or whatever else it was little boys that age got into trouble for doing.

*Why?* That was all Samuel wanted to know. One simple, sensible explanation for his mother's illness. An explanation that he could understand so he could stop blaming himself or his father or his infant sister and get on with living. Just . . . *why?*

Michael's leg muscles started to tremble with the effort of balancing on his heels. He braced his hand against the trunk, steadying himself against the protest of his calves and knees and thighs.

Samuel wanted to know why, but Michael

didn't know why. He'd never known why. But he did know how. That much, at least, he'd mastered. He could tell Samuel how even if he never, ever knew the why of it.

"You see, Samuel," Michael ventured, "tuberculosis—consumption, as you call it—is a disease that can strike anyone. It's caused by a tiny little thing you can't even see called a bacillus. A tubercle bacillus."

As the words flowed out, calmness flowed in. He'd thought, once, that medicine would have had a cure for tuberculosis by now. Well it didn't. Not yet. But they understood the cause and its destructive mechanism. That was the key. With it, the cure could not be far away.

It was all he had to offer Samuel. All he had to offer himself.

"The bacillus lodges in a person's lungs," he continued. "Like a little speck of dirt in your eye. You know how that is, don't you, Samuel?"

Samuel raised his head to meet Michael's questioning gaze. Was it only his imagination, Michael wondered, or did the boy look a little less tense, a little less frightened?

"Those little specks get in your eye and sometimes they wash right out. Other times, they start to hurting you and your eyes get teary and you rub them, trying to get that speck out."

Samuel simply stared, his expression unreadable.

"Well," Michael said, warming to his explanation, "that's the way the tubercle bacillus is. It gets in a person's lungs and sometimes it gets thrown right back out, so to speak. Other times, it starts irritating the lungs and the person starts to cough, just like your eyes watering up. Just a little cough, you know. Not much at first."

At the thought of the cough, Michael remembered the bag of horehound drops Hetty had given him.

Fishing the drops out of his pocket was a little awkward because of his crouch, but Michael managed. He opened the bag and pulled out a drop.

"Horehound drops aren't any good for that kind of cough, Samuel, but they still taste good," he said, smiling and popping the drop into his mouth.

Hetty had been right. He *could* help Samuel understand. The horehound drops were simply an extra little touch. He'd almost forgotten how helpful they could be in easing a child's nervous fears.

He held out the bag to Samuel. "Would you like one, too?"

Samuel's gaze dropped to the bag of drops, then swung back up to meet his.

With a choked cry, the boy grabbed the bag and hurled it away, as far as he could fling it.

Michael watched, stunned, as the bag tumbled through the air, spilling candy drops in its flight. It came to earth near the rear wagon wheel and burst open, scattering horehound drops like round, brown gems across the packed, brown earth.

* * *

Mrs. Rheiner—Ruth, she'd insisted Hetty call her—endured Hetty's and her husband's ministrations with fortitude, too tired and battered to do more than fret about the indecency of being moved, bed and all, to a makeshift shelter where all the world could see her in her bedgown. Neither Hetty nor her husband ventured to remind her that the only people who were likely to see her were the neighbors and the ladies from the church who helped out whenever they could and who had already seen her at less than her best.

The arrangement disturbed Hetty almost as much as it did Mrs. Rheiner, but for a different reason. It seemed so crude and uncomfortable and . . . and *cruel* to leave a woman who was so ill to the mercy of the weather's vagaries.

Michael had frowned down her protests when they'd built the shelter and scoffed at Hetty's mention of Ruth's qualms about the arrangement's respectability. Much good being respectable would do her if she died, he'd snapped, drawing one of the guy ropes taut. She'd already refused to follow his advice for far too long and look where it had landed her.

For Anna's sake, the tent had to be kept warm and free from drafts, but Ruth needed fresh, clean air and plenty of it if her damaged lungs were to heal, winter or no winter. The established sanatoriums in the East were generally open to the air, he'd irritably explained. If there was three feet of snow on the ground, they bundled their patients under a half-dozen blankets and rolled them out to take the sun, regardless of the temperature.

"It's going to be rather nice, really," Hetty tried to reassure Ruth now. "The sides of the shelter can be let down if it gets too windy or it storms or you need some privacy, but otherwise you'll have a much nicer view than the ugly old walls of this tent. You'll be able to see the sun come up, and the moon. It will be just like going to the theater, for all the show you'll have!"

Ruth gave her a weak smile. "And I won't risk . . . waking Anna . . . when I cough."

"Don't you worry about Anna," Mr. Rheiner said gruffly. "I'll take care of her just fine, and you'll have Samuel if you need him."

"Poor Samuel," Ruth whispered. She closed her eyes and sank back in the pillows. She didn't even notice when Hetty, after one last check to be sure everything was ready, slipped out of the tent to go fetch Michael.

One glance at the scene outside the tent was enough to tell her Ruth Rheiner had been right. Poor Samuel indeed.

At the far edge of the clearing, Michael paced like a caged beast, his head down and his hands shoved deep into his pockets as if he didn't trust himself not to hit something if they were free.

Samuel was at the opposite side of the clearing, hunkered down in the grass beside the goat and her kid, his back pointedly turned to Michael and the camp.

Hetty tensed and repressed the urge to duck

back into the tent, wondering what had gone wrong. At her call, Michael's head came up and he immediately moved toward her, but there was an awkward reluctance about him at striking odds with his normal lean-limbed grace. Samuel ignored her for as long as he could, then reluctantly abandoned his companions and came dragging over, head down, as awkwardly tense as Michael.

Whatever had passed between Michael and Samuel, there was no time to worry about it now, Hetty reminded herself, trying to keep her worry from showing in her face. While Mrs. Rheiner huddled in her rocker by the stove, Hetty helped Michael and Mr. Rheiner and Samuel maneuver the tall, iron-framed bed over the boards they'd laid between the tent and the shelter, then fetch Samuel's bed from the wagon, since he'd be sleeping in the shelter, too, in case his mother needed him during the night. Michael spoke only when it was absolutely necessary and Samuel, who deliberately stayed as far away from Michael as possible, said nothing at all. He grunted or nodded as the occasion demanded, and once the task was done, immediately retreated to his spot near the goats while his father carried his mother out of the tent and tucked her back into bed.

Michael waited just long enough to assure himself that Ruth hadn't suffered from the move; then he headed off in the opposite direction from Samuel, intent on hitching the horse back up to the buggy, anxious to be off now that there was nothing more for him to do.

Hetty helped Mrs. Rheiner get settled, then fussed over making up Samuel's truckle bed at the foot of his mother's. There was little else she could do. A neighbor had left a pot of stew that morning, Anna was fed and contentedly asleep in her drawer in front of the stove, and Mr. Rheiner now sat in a chair beside his wife's bed, her hand protectively cradled in his, his gaze fixed on her pale, drawn face. Though Hetty was making no effort to keep quiet, he didn't even glance at her as she finished tucking in the corners of Samuel's blanket.

With a last, quick check to be sure everything she could do was done, Hetty turned and walked away.

When they'd pulled Samuel's bed out of the wagon, she'd seen the scattered horehound drops and the crumpled bag that had been blown against the wheel by a stray gust of wind. The sight of it, the careful way Samuel ignored it, and the quickness with which Michael bent to retrieve it and thrust it into his pocket had told her all she needed to know about the failure of her little ploy.

She'd meant to help—only that!—but in her meddling she'd somehow managed to drive Michael and Samuel farther apart than before.

The recognition of her mistake tormented her. How much else had she not understood? How many other things would she make worse by her well-intentioned interference?

A wooden bucket sat on the ground at the far side of the tent, half filled with water Samuel had fetched from the river. The sand had already settled out; after sitting in the sun so long, the water was surprisingly warm. She scooped out a cupful and splashed it on her face and hands, enough to rinse off the worst of the afternoon's sweat and grime, then used the worn towel looped around a tent pole to dry off. She tried not to think of the hot bath she'd taken . . . was it only that morning?

Michael already had the horse hooked up to the buggy and was waiting for her, ready to be off. She could see him out of the corner of her eye, standing as still and dark as the elongated shadow the late afternoon sun cast at his feet.

Hetty straightened, ignoring him, and pressed the heels of her hands into the tired muscles of her lower back, rubbing at a spot where a stay had pinched. With a precision the crumpled fabric no longer warranted, she rolled her sleeves back down and buttoned them at her wrists, then fastened the three small buttons at the collar of her shirtwaist.

She was tired and hungry and dirty, but despite her discomfort, she was reluctant to leave. The thought of the drive back to Colorado Springs while Michael was in this grim and silent mood was more than she could bear right now.

"Hetty?"

It was Michael calling. He stood at his horse's head, one hand on his hip in obvious impatience. Reluctantly, Hetty turned and waved to indicate she was coming.

But first, she had to say good-bye to Samuel.

The boy didn't even look up as she came across the shadow-streaked grass toward him. He was sitting close to the little nanny goat, his fingers buried in her coarse hair. He wasn't quite petting her, more like hanging on to the little creature's bony, animal warmth. The goat didn't seem to mind. She was grazing, clipping the dried grass off with her teeth, then chewing busily.

The kid, which had been sleeping beside Samuel, awoke with a start at the sound of her skirts dragging across the grass. It staggered to its feet, then hopped out of reach as its mother swung around on her tether protectively.

Deprived of his friends, Samuel let his hands drop in his lap and waited for her to come up to him.

"Samuel," Hetty said, going down on one knee beside him, "I'm leaving now."

He nodded politely, but refused to look at her.

"I . . . I just wanted to tell you that I made up your bed for you, but your father said, if you didn't like sleeping outside, you could sleep in the tent with Anna and he'd sleep with your mother, instead."

"I want to be with Ma," he said. The hard set of his jaw made it clear that he'd fight anyone who tried to stop him.

Hetty awkwardly patted his shoulder. "And she's glad to have you there."

He resentfully shrugged away from her hand.

"I'll let you know when Mr. Meissner is done with those recipes, shall I?" She was groping for something to say, Hetty knew, but she couldn't bear to leave him like this. "Next time you come in to town with your father, I can take you to meet him. I'm sure you'll like him. I know he'll like you."

She got no response.

"And maybe we could . . . oh, I don't know. We could get a chocolate soda at Fisk's Pharmacy! Would you like that?"

This time she got a scowl, followed by a hesitant nod.

The nod, Hetty thought, was probably the best she could do. And what had she offered him anyway? A sop to her own discomfort rather than any solace, a distraction rather than any real help.

Hetty gathered her skirts about her, preparing to rise. Instead, urged by her heart's promptings, she fell on both knees and grabbed Samuel up in her arms and hugged him tightly against her.

For an instant, his wiry little body arched in protest. But only for an instant. Then he flung his arms around her shoulders and squeezed her as tightly as she was squeezing him.

"Oh, Samuel," Hetty whispered, pressing his head against her shoulder. Her eyes stung with sudden tears. "It's so hard, sometimes, isn't it?"

If Samuel heard, he gave no sign of it, just clung all the more tightly, his pain and fear too deep for the tears that threatened her.

Hetty had no idea how long they remained like that, but Samuel eventually eased his grip on her and cautiously drew away. Hetty let him go, but before she did, she planted a quick kiss on the top of his tousled head.

"You take care of yourself, Samuel Rheiner," she said, looking him straight in the eye. "You hear?"

Samuel nodded and gave her a watery little smile. "Yes'm," he said. "I will."

"Good." Hetty gave him the best, most encouraging smile she was capable of, and rose to her feet. The kid, which had cautiously edged closer, jumped back with a bleat of alarm and went scurrying.

Hetty laughed and Samuel's smile turned into a wide, relieved grin.

They rode back to town while the setting sun made an indecent display of pink and orange across the aquamarine sky. Hetty watched in awe as the colors spilled and spread, casting the bulk of mountain into a purple evening stillness. Somewhere in the dying grasses at the side of the road, a bird called mournfully, then fell silent. Even the rattling of the buggy wheels couldn't disturb the evening's tranquility.

Nothing could except Michael, sitting as cold and silent as a block of ice on the seat beside her while the sunset faded and the night came on.

Hetty let the silence stretch, all the way from the little camp by the river until they came into the city, whose streets were filled with early evening traffic. People going home, people going out to a meeting, or a visit with friends, or to the theater.

There was no sense in trying to speak. She didn't know what to say. She wanted to ask Michael what had happened between him and Samuel, but now was not the time, and Michael, she knew, would not tell her anyway. He'd drawn into his silence like a crab into its shell, pincers warily out front in case someone came prying.

It wasn't until Michael turned down the street leading to Mrs. Spencer's boarding house rather than to the livery stables that Hetty roused herself. She'd forgotten all about her eviction this morning and her move to Michael's house.

"Michael?"

"Yes?" He didn't look at her.

In the distant, dull-yellow light of the street lamps, Hetty could make out the intersecting lines of his nose and brow, the ridge of his cheekbone. Everything else was cast into shadow, indistinguishable except through memory.

"I can't go back to Mrs. Spencer's." The words came out in a rush, startling her.

He turned to look at her, his eyes black hollows in the dark. "It's not ten yet. Not anywhere near."

"I know, but . . . Mrs. Spencer kicked me out this morning. Because I didn't come in last night. She said . . ." The words were far more difficult to say than Hetty had expected. "She said she wouldn't tolerate my 'indecent behavior.' "

Michael didn't move, but Hetty could have sworn he flinched as if she'd struck him.

She laughed, trying to make the insult into a joke. "You should have seen her, all hoity-toity and nose in the air, putting on a show for the servants. I—"

*"Damn!"*

Michael's curse cut through her mockery, all the more potent for being almost inaudible.

The cold, quiet ferocity of it startled Hetty.

"I *knew* I should have taken you to a hotel," he said, gritting the words out one sharp syllable at a time. "I knew it! No matter what you said."

"No! Michael! How can you say that?" Hetty clutched at his arm. "Last night was . . . it was *wonderful!* Who cares about what a narrow-minded old biddy like Mrs. Spencer thinks?"

"*I* do, Hetty. Because that's what they'll all think. You know that as well as I do."

"But we're—"

"We're going to be married. Right. And I haven't even gotten the marriage license." His voice was acid with self-condemnation. "How many days has it been? Four? Five? And *still* I haven't gotten it."

"Michael, there have been emergencies, you—"

"*I'm* responsible for your reputation, Hetty. Me! The man who says he loves you and who still exposes you to insults and the rudeness of people like Mrs. Spencer."

"But—"

"I go off this morning just as if nothing had happened and leave *you* to deal with the consequences."

Fear hit Hetty, for Michael, for the fury he was directing at himself like a madman bent on destruction.

"Bastard," he said fiercely under his breath, his gaze fixed on the rump of the tired horse in front of him. "Self-centered, unfeeling *bastard.*"

"Michael! *Listen* to me!" She grabbed hold of Michael's arm and shook it. "Do you realize what you're saying?"

"Of course I realized what I'm saying! And it's nothing to what I *would* say if you weren't around!"

"No! You're saying it's all your fault. Well, it's not! It's *not!* Why do you think you have to be the one who's always responsible for everything? Just who do you think you are, anyway? God?"

His head swung around at that. Hetty could have sworn his eyes glittered, even in the dark.

"No, I don't! Because if I were, I'd sure as hell do a lot better job of it!"

And with that, he jerked the horse into a turn and refused to say another word until he drew up in front of the house.

He insisted on leaving her there, in spite of Hetty's protests. After a moment, Hetty gave in, knowing she'd gain nothing by quarreling or by pigheadedly insisting on accompanying him to the stable.

Besides, there were things she could do in the meantime. Light the gaslights, start a meal—she'd bought canned ham and canned beans the day before. She could put coffee on and light the water heater, which was rapidly becoming the chief indulgence of her life. Those things, simple as they were, would help make things more comfortable for Michael when he returned.

Michael escorted her to the front door and opened it, then stepped inside to light the gaslights, the first task that Hetty had promised for herself. He didn't look at her, didn't speak, and the minute he was done, he turned around and walked out of the house and drew the front door closed behind him.

# *Chapter Sixteen*

They ate in silence—ham and beans with toast Hetty made from the heel of day-old bread. There wasn't much else in the house. As she was setting the table, Hetty had picked up the small jar of preserves, then just as quickly set it back down and pushed it to the back of the shelf.

Michael sat across from her, silent darkness in the golden gaslight, black hair in disarray with the one rebellious lock at the crest arching up defiantly, black brows drawn low, dark shadows along his cheek and jaw and chin. Hetty's fingers itched at the thought of how his beard would grate against her skin if she were to lay her hand on the side of his face, of how it had scraped last night against her throat and breast and belly.

The thought brought heat and a slow, dull ache that made the hard chair she sat on a torment.

With the ache came a sharp awareness of the space around her and the walls between them and the bed with its fresh, clean sheets and neatly laid coverlet and the pillows that flattened far too quickly beneath the weight of her head . . . and his.

Hetty laid down her fork, listening to the soft hiss of the gaslights, the faint click of Michael's fork against the plate. The house and its empty spaces seemed to narrow until there was only the two of them and the table between and she thought she could almost reach across the intervening distance and touch him, reassure herself of his warmth and solid strength.

They had quarreled, confused by weariness and all the guilt and worry the day's events had inflicted on them, but the quarrel was not about *them,* not about what had bound them to each other long years before they could even think of marriage licenses and weddings.

Hetty told herself that, over and over, and tried to ignore Michael's silent absorption in his plate.

She watched as he lifted a forkful of beans and the dark, grainy ham to his mouth, watched his jaw work as he chewed and his throat move as he swallowed.

He'd buttoned his shirt, retied his tie, and put on his jacket and vest before they'd even left the clearing. If it weren't for his unruly hair and beard-shadowed cheeks, he might have been any proper, respectable doctor returned from a call on a patient, hungry at the end of a long day, and tired.

Yet beneath the neat black facade, Hetty knew, was a stained and crumpled shirt and a hard male body that made her think of things that weren't respectable at all.

Things like the smell of him that had surrounded her when she'd grabbed his sweat-soaked shirt and shaken him. Things like the damp, black curls that had peeked from his open collar and the heat of him beneath her hands.

She'd shaken him then. Shaking wasn't what she wanted to do to him now.

When she'd lit the water heater in the bathroom earlier, before Michael had come back from the stable, she'd happened to glance at the big iron-and-tin bathtub. Though it was a frivolous indulgence to bathe twice in one day, she'd been thinking that she wanted a bath, and that Michael would probably want a bath, as well, and suddenly the two ideas had coalesced into the most shocking—and shockingly tempting—idea she'd ever had.

Hetty ripped her gaze off Michael and fixed it firmly on her plate.

It was a ridiculous idea.

An absolutely depraved idea.

An extraordinarily tempting scheme, for the two of them to share a bath and wash away not only the dirt of the afternoon's labors, but also the unsettling emotions that had come with it. To begin the night afresh, free of the tensions their quarrel had set between them.

But how to suggest it? How to breach the stern

wall of silence Michael had willfully set between them?

Hetty studied him from under her lashes.

The minute he'd walked back in from the stable and hadn't kissed her, she'd known he'd decided to blame himself for everything that had happened during the day—for her eviction from the boarding house, and his inability to mend the breach with Samuel, and Ruth's attack, and . . . and whatever else he'd decided to blame himself for in the past hour or two.

It was a rather comprehensive list to indulge in for one night, but Hetty had no doubt he'd do his best to torment himself with every possible point. And if she couldn't get him to kiss her, how was she ever going to broach the idea of sharing a bath?

It might have been easier if she'd ever had any skill at flirting, or a little more experience in seduction, but she had neither. The relationship between them had always been so open and honest that she'd never felt the slightest need of either.

Now she wished she had both, and maybe a little something else, besides.

Hetty shoved her plate away, suddenly anxious. She'd never before had the need to flirt or seduce, but Michael had never before borne the kind of responsibilities he now carried—for her, for his patients, for himself.

Was she wrong in thinking that life was so much simpler than everyone else was trying to make it? Was she being simpleminded or blind or insensitive to believe that there ought to be some joy, even in the grim uncertainties of Michael's work?

Or was it just her own weariness and worries that were making her feel so . . . so lost? And so much in need of Michael's touch, Michael's kisses?

A metallic scrape caught Hetty's attention. She glanced up to find Michael aimlessly running his fork around an empty plate, as if he expected a stray bean to suddenly pop up out of nowhere.

The corner of Hetty's mouth twitched in the beginnings of a wry smile. She'd been thinking lascivious thoughts and he'd been gobbling down his dinner with a fine masculine disregard for anything except his belly. "Do you want any more?"

His head jerked up and his eyes focused on her as if he were forcing his thoughts back to the present. "What?"

"More," Hetty repeated patiently. "Do you want anything more to eat? There's one can of ham left, if you'd like some."

His eyebrows drew together, as if he were irritated by the effort of having to concentrate on her words. "No." He shook his head. "No, thank you. It was a good dinner."

Hetty couldn't help laughing and was almost grateful for the release of it. "Liar! Either you haven't been paying much attention, or your cooking is even more abominable than I suspected."

He had the grace to blush, at least, but his smile

held self-mockery, not humor. "A little of both, I'm afraid. Some day you can ask Mrs. Ives, the old lady in the blue house next door, about my pot of boiled potatoes."

Which nicely avoided the issue of what he'd been thinking about, Hetty realized. She studied him, wondering if she ought to ask, or if it would be better to skirt the issue altogether.

Michael didn't give her a chance to try. He scowled at his plate, then laid his fork down and pushed both away from him. "I've been worrying about Mrs. Spencer," he admitted reluctantly. "About what she might say."

"Who cares what she might say?" Hetty shot back, angry that any mention of Mrs. Spencer should intrude between them now. "She's just an old busybody who has nothing better to do than—"

"She's a respected lady in the community, Hetty. Someone who could make life unpleasant for you if she started gossiping about . . . about us."

"About me, you mean."

"That's right, about you," he said, his voice like a cracking whip. "I'm supposed to be a respectable man, but if I step over the line, no one's going to mention it. If *you* step over the line . . ."

They both knew there was no need for him to finish.

"Michael, we've already discussed this, remember?" She might as well have harangued the kitchen table for all the attention he paid her.

"I've been thinking."

"Michael—"

"It's too late to find a place for you tonight, but Mrs. Scoggins might have some room left."

He was fighting for control. She could hear it in his voice, see it in the set of his jaw, in the taut, square line of his shoulders.

"Or maybe Mrs. Fisk. Their house is rather small, but there's only the two of them and—"

"You're joking! Aren't you?"

". . . they do have an extra bedroom. On the other hand, Mrs. Scoggins could probably use some help as long as the Lanyons are with her. It wouldn't be for long, just until—"

"Michael!" Hetty slammed her hands on the table so hard that the glasses rattled. "Will you listen to me?"

He stopped talking. Hetty wasn't at all sure he intended to listen.

"I am *not* going to move in with Mrs. Scoggins or Mrs. Fisk. I am also not going to go to a hotel, another boarding house, or anywhere else except to bed. With you. Right now."

She rose, awkward with anger and urgent need and the sudden realization that she wasn't at all sure what she was going to do next. It was so much easier to throw yourself into a man's arms if you weren't divided by the length of a kitchen table.

For an instant she swayed, unsteady on her feet and slightly breathless. Then she caught her balance and moved around the table toward him.

As he got to his feet anger was evident in every line of his body. His gaze locked on her, but there was no welcome in it, no warmth. Hetty faltered, then stopped, close enough for him to take her into his arms . . . if he wanted.

Michael made no move toward her. His hands hung at his sides, half curved inward toward his thigh, not quite a fist. His body seemed to quiver in the light, like a plucked string vibrating from a finger touch, yet it might have been no more than her fancy, a trick of the light.

Hetty tensed, fought for breath. His eyes held her, their shadowed, crystalline depths a turmoil.

It would be so easy for him. To stretch out his hand and touch her sleeve. To whisper her name. Just that.

Instead, he closed his eyes and tilted his head back, away from her, and this time she was absolutely sure that he trembled, but whether from anguish or from anger, she couldn't tell.

Like lightning flashing from point to point, an answering anger arced through her. She'd understood his reluctance last night, but not now, not over this.

Last night she'd gone to him, needing his warmth and his strength as much as he'd needed hers.

Tonight . . .

Tonight it was his turn. Tonight he would have to come to her.

With sudden resolution, she reached out and touched his sleeve. He jerked as if she'd shot him and his eyes snapped open to fix on her.

Hetty met his gaze unflinchingly. "Ever since I arrived, Michael, you have shut me out, pushed me aside—*forgotten* me, for heaven's sake! And each time it's happened, I've tried to understand and make excuses and adapt."

She brought her chin up higher. "Well, not tonight. Tonight, I am going to bed. I want to share it with you, and I know—I *know*—you want to share it with me. But it is your decision. Yours, Michael, not mine. Tonight, *you* will have to adapt to *me.*"

With that, she turned and walked out of the kitchen, head high.

Just as he had the night before, Michael sat on the edge of the cot, his head down, his hands anchored on his thighs, and tried not to listen to the sounds Hetty made as she moved about, preparing for bed.

The task was even more impossible tonight than last. Tonight he knew secrets he hadn't known before, sweet, rare treasures that nearly drove him mad, now that he possessed them.

A burst of heat rocked his body. His fingers dug into the muscles of his thighs in an involuntary spasm at the spine-rattling force of it.

He would *not* think of those secrets. He wouldn't listen to the footsteps, the opening and closing doors, the little creaks and groans from the floorboards and the door hinges and the bed. He wouldn't make it worse by trying to imagine what she was doing when he could hear nothing at all.

His body betrayed him. His sense of hearing

had become so wickedly acute, his thoughts so tormentingly carnal, that he couldn't shut them out, no matter how hard he tried.

Last night, as long as he was safely immersed in his work, he'd found the courage to resist temptation—for Hetty's sake. Then she'd come to him and kissed him and all his brave intentions had slunk away like cowards from the battlefield.

Well, not tonight. He'd caused enough harm for one day. The thought of Hetty subjected to insults and eviction because he hadn't had the strength of will to find her a better place to stay made him writhe with shame.

If it were just a matter of gossip, it would have been easier because then a quick marriage might have quelled the petty rumors and snide comments. The damage was done. Even if they'd never slept together, common opinion would say they had.

It wasn't just a matter of gossip.

It was a matter of how much more harm he might cause Hetty if he gave in to her ultimatum and his own desire.

Michael stared into the dark of his office. He wasn't at all sure exactly what additional harm he would do, but he didn't dare risk finding out. He hadn't expected the disaster that talking to Samuel had caused, either, and all because he'd let Hetty talk him into it in spite of his doubts.

Well, Hetty wouldn't succeed in talking him into anything. Not tonight. Not now. No matter what.

* * *

She had both pillows all to herself, yet despite the additional softness, Hetty found small comfort in the narrow bed. At least last night Michael's scent had lingered on the cases, soothing and disturbing, all at once. Tonight the linens smelled of soap and sun and nothing else. It didn't seem a fair trade at all.

She'd taken her bath, but she regretted every minute of it. The feel of the rough sponge on her skin, the wet slide of soap and water had been a poor substitute for Michael's touch.

He wasn't going to come. She'd thrown down her challenge and he, for all the crack-brained reasons of honor and respect and guilt and whatever else he'd chosen to torment them both, had refused to accept it. By now, he was either asleep on that appallingly uncomfortable-looking cot, or he was once more draped over his journals and his research, shutting her out of his life so he could wallow in his damnable commitment to his damnable medical science.

Well, tonight she was not going to rescue him, no matter how much she suffered or how lonely and empty the dark-draped bedroom seemed without him.

The telephone woke Hetty, just as it had the day before. Like an exhausted miner trudging out of the depths, she struggled back to consciousness from the pit of bad dreams and restless wakefulness where she'd spent one of the longest, most miserable nights she had ever endured in her life.

The room was flooded with the morning sunlight streaming past the thin window shade. Hetty scowled at the welcoming light and blinked at the room around her, disoriented and grumpy.

She'd left the bedroom door open last night, just in case, but at some point Michael had pulled it shut. It muffled his conversation now so that she couldn't make out any of the words. Not that it mattered, of course. She had no doubt the call would be yet another excuse for him to leave her here while he went about his day untroubled by her presence.

Hetty lay there a moment, considering. There was no way she could stop Michael from going out, but she *could* make sure his day wasn't nearly as untroubled as he undoubtedly hoped it would be.

She tossed back the covers—without the two of them to tangle the sheets, the bed had remained remarkably tidy—and swung her feet to the floor.

In the hope that Michael might give in, she'd left her hair unbound and worn one of her prettiest nightgowns, an indecently sheer muslin gown with a mass of frothy lace and tiny tucks and fine Hamburg embroidery across the bodice and at the cuffs. The gown covered her from head to toe, but in the right light, it didn't hide anything at all. With her hair falling loose and seductively tangled about her shoulders and the morning sun behind her so that it filtered through the muslin of her gown and outlined her body, she ought to be a sufficiently wanton presence to shake even the most resolute saint.

Let Michael get a taste of what he'd missed, she thought, padding across to the door and tugging it open.

He was standing in the hallway, his back to her with one shoulder propped against the wall beside the telephone, listening intently to whoever was on the other end of the line. He was dressed in trousers and starched white shirt, but hadn't yet put on his vest or jacket. His braided suspenders traced the curve of his spine, then split halfway up his back in a Y that made his shirt bunch in an oddly enticing way, emphasizing his lean hips and waist and the breadth of his shoulders.

The sight of him made Hetty's breath catch in the middle of her chest and that sensitive spot at the juncture of her legs suddenly blossom with heat.

At the sound of the bedroom door opening, Michael tensed, ever so slightly, then glanced over his shoulder at her, the black earpiece still firmly affixed to his ear.

That first glance was enough to freeze him right where he stood. His eyes widened, his jaw dropped, and for a minute, Hetty was afraid he might stop breathing altogether.

She smiled. The sweetest, most innocent smile she could manage. "Good morning," she said, and stretched. As she arched upward, she managed to push the door open wider until there was nothing to block the sunlight behind her except the sheer muslin of her gown.

Like a rusty marionette on strings, Michael came upright and edged around to face her.

He was definitely breathing. Fast and shallow and rather unsteadily, to judge by the quick rise and fall of his chest. Even from this distance, Hetty could see the pupils of his eyes widen until they seemed to swallow all the blue.

Hetty stretched again, arching her back and shoving her shoulders back until her breasts and belly pressed against the fullness of her gown at the front. Then she wriggled, just a little, and dragged her hands up behind her head, letting her fingers trail through the mass of her hair so the heavy locks spilled over her arms and shoulders in a silky tangle. The tension and stretch in her muscles was exquisite, but not half so satisfying as the dazed look on Michael's face.

At the apex of her stretch, she even allowed herself one long, low groan of contentment, such as any woman who had slept well and awakened to a beautiful new day might give after a wonderfully sensual stretch.

Michael didn't groan. He sucked in air like a man who'd been gut-punched.

Hetty let her smile widen; then she batted her eyes as if she were batting off sleep and walked past Michael toward the bathroom. Since Michael's shoulders were very wide and the hall wasn't wide at all, it was a bit of a squeeze. Especially since he seemed incapable of any movement except watching her.

"Excuse me," Hetty said, and forced her way past him. Her breast grazed his arm and her hip and belly brushed against his hip, but she really couldn't help that, under the circumstances.

"Wha—?" he croaked, then gasped and edged around so he could speak into the telephone's mouthpiece. "No, no. Of course I'm listening!" he shouted, a great deal more loudly than Hetty would have thought absolutely necessary. And all without taking his eyes off her.

"Sorry," she said. She smiled up at him, then disappeared into the bathroom and quietly closed the door behind her.

"I'm sorry," Michael said into the receiver. Even through the bulk of the door he sounded a little breathless. "I didn't realize I was yelling . . . No . . . Yes, yes, we'll be there. Thank you. Good-bye."

He slammed the earpiece down on its hook.

It could have been her imagination, of course, but Hetty thought she heard heavy breathing on the other side of the door. If she did, it wasn't for long, because Michael shoved himself away from the wall hard enough to make the mirror above the sink jiggle, then stomped down the hall toward the front of the house. He slammed the door between the hall and the waiting room so violently that the mirror rattled on its hook, then tilted off plumb completely.

Hetty stared at her disheveled image in the mirror and smiled in satisfaction.

Vengeance was sweet.

* * *

The sweetness didn't last long.

Hetty was struggling to fasten her corset when Michael knocked on the closed bedroom door.

"Hetty?" He didn't wait for an answer. "That was Mrs. Scoggins on the telephone. She called because she thought we would want to know that the funeral for George Lanyon is this morning at ten. She asked me to let you know, since Mrs. Spencer isn't on the telephone. I explained the situation and asked if you could move in with her for a while. She said yes."

Hetty sucked in a deep breath, ready to object, and the last fastener slipped into place.

"I'll take you over early with your bags. And don't try to argue!" he added sharply before she could do just that. "If your bags aren't packed when you come out of there, I'll pack them myself."

By the time Hetty had managed to cross the room and yank the door open, he was almost in the kitchen. She stuck her head out into the hall, but kept the rest of herself decently out of sight. She'd had more than enough time to be appalled by her wanton behavior earlier and didn't care to make a lewd spectacle of herself twice in one morning.

"Michael!"

He turned to face her, his sharply carved features caught between sunlight and shadow. "You are going, Hetty, if I have to throw you over my shoulder and carry you there myself."

This time it was the kitchen door he slammed behind him.

Hetty sat at the kitchen table, cradling a heavy pottery mug of coffee in her hands as she watched dust motes sliding peacefully down a sunbeam.

Michael had gone out over an hour earlier to make a quick check of his patients before he returned to take her to Mrs. Scoggins's. Once she'd washed the abandoned supper dishes and packed the few items she'd unpacked the night before, Hetty had retreated into her mug of coffee and her thoughts. Neither one had brought her any comfort.

In the silence of the echoing house, both her anger of the night before and this morning's flippant mockery had slowly congealed into an unsettling disquiet.

Unlike her girlhood friends, she had never believed that marriage would change a man, any more than it would change a woman. Not in any important way. Certainly not at the fundamental level of who and what each was as a person.

It hadn't mattered, because she hadn't wanted to change Michael. She had loved him exactly as he was—intense, dedicated, but always kind, always responsive to the emotions and needs of the people around him.

She wasn't sure how to cope with this new Michael she was discovering, this driven man who could laugh one minute, then retreat into an almost destructive absorption with his work the next. She wasn't sure she *could* cope with him. Not for the rest of her life.

George Lanyon's death had shown her the why of the changes in Michael, allowed her to understand, as she never could have otherwise, why what he did was so important, and so very, very difficult emotionally.

But understanding the why didn't help her understand the how.

How could Michael have let his dedication and concern consume him until he was unable to see anything of life beyond the demands of his profession? How could he have let his compassion be buried under layers of ice so thick that he couldn't cope with the fears of a boy facing what he himself had faced so long ago?

At the thought of Samuel, Hetty's grip on the mug tightened until the coffee-warmed pottery seemed to burn through her palm. Brave Samuel, all alone and frightened.

Hetty thought of the horehound drops spilled across the ground beside the wagon and the crumpled bag that Michael had so hastily whipped out of sight.

Michael had been right. Horehound drops couldn't solve Samuel's problems.

But why, oh why, was it so impossible to take a moment just to enjoy the sweetness?

# *Chapter Seventeen*

George Lanyon's funeral was a simple affair. The cemetery sat on a hill with an awe-inspiring vista of the mountains towering to the west and the sweep of prairie to the east, but the breeze blowing over the exposed hilltop was mournful and sharp with the warning that winter, real winter, was moving in at last.

There weren't many mourners. Just Mrs. Lanyon and the children, Mrs. Scoggins, dressed in the same grim brown bombazine dress she'd worn on the train, Mrs. Fisk, Hetty and Michael, and Mr. Harrison from the depot, all gathered to one side of the grave and the plain brown coffin, all dutifully attentive to the minister's words of comfort, each of them lost in his or her private thoughts.

Hetty stood silent through it all, uncomfortably

aware of Michael in his somber black beside her. Except for handing her in and out of the buggy, he hadn't touched her since she'd brushed against him in the hall that morning, and had scarcely spoken beyond the absolute minimum necessity decreed.

It was as if he'd gone away from her, Hetty thought, withdrawn into someplace deep inside himself she could never hope to reach. Even when the wind batted at her heavy skirts, blowing them against his legs with impertinent intimacy, Michael seemed not to notice—or not to care.

Hetty bent and grabbed at her skirts just as the fretful wind tugged them out of her hands. She made another grab, and this time she inadvertently touched his thigh. Her body jerked at the shock of it.

Michael gave no sign that he noticed. He just stood there staring at nothing while she gathered her skirts decently about her and tried to pretend she was listening to the minister and not to Michael's cold and distant silence.

The service didn't last long. Mr. Harrison paid his respects to the widow with quiet dignity, then went stumping back to his carriage and the work awaiting him. Jessica Lanyon, her face as pinched and pale as a death mask, avoided meeting Michael's eyes as he offered his condolences and seemed relieved when he excused himself to return to his rounds.

Hetty rode beside Jessica Lanyon in the back seat of the carriage, David on her lap, a huddled, withdrawn little Sarah on Jessica's. Neither of them said a word during the short journey from the cemetery to Mrs. Scoggins's house, nor later in the wide hall of the house while they took off hats and shawls and straightened wind-blown hair. Not until after Mrs. Fisk had slipped away and Mrs. Scoggins had taken the children off to the kitchen for milk and a bite to eat and to check on the food Betty had been preparing for their return did Jessica really acknowledge Hetty's presence.

"I . . . I never had the chance to . . . to thank you," Jessica said hesitantly, holding out her hand. The lines of strain and exhaustion in her face cut deep, but she stood erect, a strong, enduring figure in black.

"There's no need, you know," Hetty said, taking the woman's black-gloved hand in hers and giving it a comforting squeeze. She felt helpless and clumsy, knowing there was nothing she could say or do that would ease Jessica Lanyon's loss. "I lost my mother after a long illness. I know how hard it is. If there's anything I can do . . ."

"Mrs. Scoggins, Mrs. Fisk . . . they've been so kind." Jessica's words caught on her unshed tears, and her voice dropped to a whisper. "So kind."

"Yes," said Hetty helplessly.

Jessica pulled her hand free of Hetty's, blinking hard. "I'd best go see about David and Sarah," she said a little unsteadily, withdrawing into the solace of her responsibilities. "If you'll excuse me?"

Hetty joined Mrs. Fisk in the sitting room, but even that loquacious lady was subdued, flipping through a lady's magazine she'd picked out of a stand without really looking at anything on the pages in front of her. Waiting for tea, no doubt, Hetty thought, suddenly remembering that she hadn't had any breakfast herself.

The thought of breakfast brought back other, more uncomfortable memories, which Hetty hastily pushed to the side. She wouldn't think about Michael right now. She couldn't.

Instead, knowing it was rude but unable to find anything else to distract her, she wandered about the room, checking out the garden view from the side window, running her fingers over a Chinese vase in a corner, poking into what was none of her business because she couldn't stand to think about what was.

She was standing in front of the Scoggins family photograph, studying it, when Mrs. Scoggins came in a few minutes later bearing a loaded tea tray.

Embarrassed and not wanting to be thought prying, Hetty quickly moved away, but Mrs. Scoggins crossed to the photograph and picked it up.

"This horrible disease has taken so many good people," she said sadly, staring down at the faces of the good people she had loved and lost. She gently touched the glass above her son, a small, sad smile on her thin face. "This morning, there in the cemetery, my little Lester seemed closer to me somehow. I looked at David and Sarah, but I saw his face."

She shook her head and gently set the photograph back down on the table. "I don't know why, because he and his father are buried out at the other house in a little plot under a pine tree, looking toward the Peak. They liked it so much out there, you know. I thought it would be where they'd want to stay."

"Come have some tea, Lettitia," Mrs. Fisk said with calm practicality as she settled into a chair in front of the tea tray. "I imagine you need it as much as Mrs. Lanyon, if not more. Having so many people in your house all of a sudden has to be a bit unsettling."

Hetty started and felt her cheeks grow hot, but neither of the women even glanced at her. Mrs. Scoggins took a chair across from her friend, but she didn't touch anything on the tray. Her gaze was on something far beyond the confines of the room around them. Despite the stiff, somber dress she wore, she seemed softer somehow, more fragile than Hetty had ever seen her.

"You know, Clarabelle," she said thoughtfully, "I've actually enjoyed having people around. Especially the children. Not that it's been very cheerful, of course," she added, but without the usual sharp tone of disapproval in her voice. "But . . . I don't know. How can I say it? The house doesn't seem so empty now."

"That might be because it's not," Mrs. Fisk said matter-of-factly. Ignoring etiquette, she picked up the heavy silver tea pot and started to pour. "Miss Malone? Would you mind serving the sandwiches and shortbread, please?" She nodded at the small platter of neat finger sandwiches and buttery cookies as she added, "So, what does she plan to do now? Jessica, I mean. Go back home? Stay here? Two sugars, slice of lemon—right, Lettitia? It's going to be hard for a young widow with two small children, I'm afraid. She can't be a day over twenty-five, though her troubles make her look a good deal older, I think. I'll take two of those shortbreads, if you please, Miss Malone."

Hetty couldn't help smiling at Clarabelle Fisk's ability to worry about food without missing a scrap of gossip. Dutifully, she searched for the largest piece of shortbread she could find and added it to the heaping plate.

Mrs. Scoggins waved away the plate Hetty offered her, but took a cautious sip of tea before answering. "Mrs. Lanyon hasn't said anything about her plans. The poor thing really hasn't had much chance to think about it. I don't imagine she has much money. They sold everything they had to come West for her husband's sake, and now . . ."

As Hetty listened, she thought of Mr. Rheiner, anxious, ashamed, and exhausted, trying to explain to Michael why he didn't have money to pay. Michael, equally embarrassed, had angrily brushed aside any concern for immediate payment, but not everyone would—or could—be so understanding. If Mr. Rheiner—a man with all a man's chances for obtaining decent-paying jobs—was struggling, how much more difficult would life be for a woman with two small children and few, if any, skills?

A comment by Mrs. Scoggins brought Hetty's

attention back to the conversation with a snap.

"To tell the truth, Clarabelle," she was saying, "I'd like to offer Mrs. Lanyon a job as my housekeeper, if she'll take it. There's the carriage house out back. They could have it all to themselves and the yard for the children to play in. It would be better for them than most work she'd find."

Mrs. Fisk's eyebrows shot upward. "What about Betty?"

"Betty's eager to find a real job." Mrs. Scoggins's mouth twisted in a wry smile. "And I've just about given up trying to get her to walk up the stairs. I've tried to teach her how to behave like a lady, but there's only so much I can do, after all. It's time she got on with it."

"Mmmm," Mrs. Fisk agreed around a mouthful of sandwich. She swallowed, and delicately wiped a crumb off her lower lip. "Then all you'd have to worry about would be finding a caretaker for the other house. I know you're thinking about that Thomas Durnam, but he's never held any job for longer than a month or two. You'd be better off with a decent family man this time, Lettitia, instead of a drunkard like that last one or—"

"A family man!" Hetty sat up in her chair with a start, then blushed as her two friends turned to stare at her in surprise.

She carefully set her tea cup down, fighting to control her rising excitement. "And there's a house, isn't there? Mrs. Scoggins, tell me, do you pay your caretaker? Is your property *very* far from town? Would you—?"

She stopped abruptly, desperately trying to get

her thoughts in order. Her friends were staring at her as if she'd suddenly lost her mind. Hetty stared back. Then she started to smile.

"I just had the most wonderful idea," she said.

He'd looked at the document a hundred times over the course of the afternoon, but Michael pulled it out again and spread it flat on the desk in his office. The heavy, cream-colored paper looked impressive there against the scarred oak, its surface printed with all the official scroll work and fancy lettering deemed appropriate to the occasion.

His marriage license. His and Hetty's.

If he'd been superstitious, he would have ascribed magical qualities to it. This afternoon his patients had all seemed better than he would have expected. The boy who had been run over by a wagon was fussing over lunch, not his leg, where the incisions were already beginning to heal. The serving girl who had suffered her first hemorrhage was smiling, still blushingly excited by a visit from a young man she'd thought had forgotten her. Even in his own happiness, Michael had felt a wry regret that smiles from her swain had more power to help the girl than did any of his pills and potions.

Only old Mr. Meissner had been difficult, tired out from having spent too many hours translating some absurd recipes for Samuel—at Hetty's request. The old man had waved away Michael's concerns and handed the translations to Michael to deliver for him. He'd enjoyed the job, he said;

it made him feel useful, and next time Hetty came visiting she was to bring the boy with her. He'd poked Michael in the ribs, teasing him about his competition, but his laugh had disintegrated in a wheezing cough that had taken several minutes to pass.

When Michael scolded him, the old man retorted that his doctor was becoming a bigger fussbudget than his housekeeper and he should go away and leave an old man in peace. So Michael had gone away, and tried hard not to be angry at Hetty's interference. The consoling crackle of the license in his inner coat pocket had helped.

When he'd finished his rounds, he'd stopped at Mrs. Scoggins's, but Hetty had been out. Betty was too flustered to remember where she'd gone or when she was expected back, and Mrs. Scoggins had had a visitor, so Michael hadn't intruded. He'd come home, instead, half hoping he'd find Hetty waiting for him.

He'd been doomed to disappointment. She hadn't been there, either. Without her presence, the house seemed smaller, emptier, and grimmer than he ever remembered it.

They'd have to be married soon. He couldn't endure another night like last night, lying awake in a fever of wanting, knowing Hetty was so close . . . and that he wouldn't be able to face himself if he gave in.

It had taken every scrap of will power he possessed to resist her this morning. In his imagination, he saw the impertinent angle of her head as she'd stood in the bedroom doorway, the tangled fall of gold-brown hair and the green of her eyes, dark with sleep and desire.

She'd meant him to suffer for his restraint. Well, he'd suffered, all right—and he'd resented every minute of it. He didn't intend to suffer much longer.

Michael pressed the license flat against the desk top, carefully smoothing his hand over the sharp creases he'd made in the paper. For a long while he simply stared at it; then he carefully set it aside and rose to his feet.

There was no telling when Hetty would appear. In the meantime, he had work waiting for him. He would always have work waiting for him. Not even a marriage license could change that.

Hetty found Michael right where she'd expected to find him, in his lab. This time he was bent over a complicated contraption of jars and pipes and hoses and so intent on whatever he was doing that he hadn't even heard her come in. Whatever the contraption was, it didn't seem to be cooperating because he was muttering to himself and scowling, clearly frustrated with some connection that was refusing to connect.

Hetty couldn't help smiling. He'd been so engrossed in his work, he hadn't even noticed that the afternoon sun was fading fast.

Softly, so as not to startle him, she said, "Wouldn't it be easier to turn on the lights, so you could see what you're doing?"

Michael sat up with a jerk, dropping the fitting

he'd been holding. "Damn it, Hetty! Now look what you made me do! And where the devil have you been, anyway? Do you have any idea how long I've been waiting?"

"Well! And I've missed you too," Hetty retorted, trying hard to swallow her laughter. "Did you notice that you dropped that thingamabob you were holding?"

"I noticed!" He scowled at her for an instant, then ducked under the table to retrieve his lost property.

Hetty settled onto a chair near Michael. "Whatever is that thing you're working on?"

Michael reappeared from under the table, his face flushed. His scowl deepened.

"This," he said, glaring at the monstrosity, "is the Universal Multi-Nebular Vaporizer."

"I see," said Hetty cautiously. She studied the thing. "I don't mean to be rude," she added after a moment, "but what is it?"

Michael tossed whatever it was he'd retrieved onto the table and picked up a printed flyer. "It is," he said, reading from the flyer "the most successful treatment that has ever been employed in respiratory and aural affections. It should, therefore, be in the hands of every physician who gives any attention to diseases of the respiratory organs and middle ear."

"Oh," said Hetty.

"It is also the one of the biggest, most expensive pieces of junk I have ever seen in my life," Michael added, tossing the flyer after the fitting.

"And what's that?" Hetty asked, pointing to a

pile of rough, drab cloth that had been shoved to the back of the table.

"Those are spruce-bark bedclothes, guaranteed," he recited, "to help sufferers of consumption, asthma, and other related affections of the lungs."

"Really?" Hetty studied the coarse linens dubiously. "They don't look like they'd be very comfortable."

"They probably aren't, and I don't imagine they're of any more use than the vaporizer. A colleague sent them to me," Michael added, before she could open her mouth to ask. "He thought I might be interested."

"But you aren't."

He scowled at her instead of at the vaporizer, but Hetty could tell his ill humor was fast disappearing. "It gave me something to do while I waited for you."

It was the only opening Hetty needed. She gave an eager little bounce, unable to sit still a moment longer.

"Michael, the most wonderful thing! Mrs. Scoggins has hired Robert—Mr. Rheiner!—to be the caretaker for her property outside of town!"

Michael frowned. "What? I know he's been looking for work, but—"

"Not just that! They'll have a house, with a bedroom with *lots* of windows for Ruth so she doesn't have to sleep out in that awful shelter, and there's a well, a good one, which means they don't have to use muddy river water. It's even closer to town than where they are now, Robert says. He rode out there to see the place before he agreed. And he'll be paid. A regular salary every month. Not a lot, but since they won't have to pay for the right to live there . . . And he'll be close for Ruth if she needs him, and oh! it's so . . ."

She laughed, then, a real laugh that felt good right down to her toes. The morning had started so black, but something good had come of it and she meant to savor it.

"It's so *wonderful,* Michael! Isn't it?"

She didn't give him a chance to respond, just rushed into a recital of the conversation over the sandwiches.

"The minute Mrs. Scoggins said she'd be willing to talk to Robert, I rented a buggy and drove right out," she added breathlessly. "I stayed with Ruth while he came in. Michael, it was so *hard,* waiting and wondering. And Ruth could hardly talk, she was so excited at the thought that she might have a house again instead of a tent, only she was worried, too, in case it didn't work out and she'd gotten her hopes up for nothing. But she didn't! They're going to move tomorrow! That is, if you think it's all right for Anna. Mrs. Scoggins said they could! And I'm going to go out and help them because it would be easier for Ruth and Anna to go in a buggy, you know, and—"

"Hetty, Hetty! Hold on!" Michael exclaimed at last, throwing his hands up to stop her. The expression on his face was as forbidding as the one he'd given the vaporizer.

Hetty took a deep breath and felt some of the light go out of the room. All the way back from the clearing she'd been picturing how it would be, how she would tell him the good news and he'd start to laugh and then he'd swing her up in his arms and kiss her until she was breathless and then they'd dance around the room and—

But that wasn't the way it was, after all, because Michael wasn't even smiling, let alone laughing, and rather than sweeping her up in his arms, he was sitting in front of her, stiff as a paperboard box and just as enthusiastic.

The last of Hetty's enthusiasm drained away into a sudden, discomforting doubt.

"I know you're trying to help, Hetty," Michael said sternly, "that you think this is all in their best interests, but—"

"Of course it is, Michael!" she exclaimed, dismayed. "You should have seen Ruth. She was smiling and laughing and her eyes just glowed, she was so glad!"

"But think about how hard the move will be on her! And what about Anna?"

"We talked about that, Michael! What do you think? That we'd just throw her in the back of the wagon with the goat?"

"I hadn't gotten that far in my worrying!"

"Mr. Greble at the stable said he has a buggy that's closed in and very smooth riding. We'd go slowly and wrap Anna up so she'd be as warm as if she were in front of the stove. We've already worked it out."

Hetty stretched out her hand and placed it on Michael's, anxious to convince him. "It will *work,* Michael. Really it will!"

At her touch, Michael surged to his feet, throwing her off balance. For a moment he simply stood there glaring at her; then he jerked around and stalked off. Halfway across the room he stopped, dragged his hand through his hair like a man struggling against a strong urge to do violence, then turned and stalked back to stand in front of her.

"Yesterday Ruth Rheiner suffered her first hemorrhage. That came on top of a difficult, premature birth. And now you want to move her? Do you have any idea what you're suggesting, Hetty?"

"Yes, I do!" Hetty shot back. "Ruth told me they've been in that camp for almost six months, ever since they had to leave that farm when it was sold. They haven't been able to find anyplace else because nobody wants to rent to them, not with her being sick and Robert not having any steady work."

Hetty could feel her control slipping, but she charged on, her voice growing louder and sharper with every word. "Do you have any idea how hard it's been for her, being out there all alone like that? Do you?"

"Of course I do!"

"Well, then, help them move to someplace better! If you're there, you can make sure they're all right, can't you?"

Michael opened his mouth, then clamped it shut and carefully sat back down.

"No, I can't," he said, his face grim. "There's not

a damn thing I can do to protect them . . . either one of them."

His flat admission deflated Hetty's anger like a pin popping a bubble. "Oh," she said, and stared at him, wondering what to say next.

"Look, Hetty," he said, "*I* know they need a better place to live, but this isn't a good time to move them. Why can't they just wait a few weeks?"

"Mrs. Scoggins can't leave her property unattended that long, and she has someone else who wants the job if Robert doesn't."

She leaned forward, suddenly anxious. "Would it *really* be that bad to try to move them, Michael? Really?"

He glared at her, dragged his fingers through his hair until it looked like a wild bush sticking up every which way; then he heaved a long sigh and said, "Hell, Hetty, I don't know. It won't be good. They're both too frail and Anna . . . But I don't like that camp any more than they do and if this is the only chance they'll have to get into a house before winter really hits . . ."

He shook his head angrily. "I just don't know. I wish they wouldn't, but I can't tell them what to do. They didn't listen when I told them they shouldn't try to have a baby, and look where it landed them."

Hetty smiled suddenly, relieved. Michael was over-protective, cautious because he had to be cautious, but he wasn't saying the Rheiners couldn't move.

"It will be all right, Michael. You'll see," she said.

Michael's jaw hardened. "One of these days, Hetty, you're going to find out that things don't always work out for the best."

The corner of Hetty's mouth twitched. She couldn't help it. "Seems to me we've had this conversation before."

He glared at her.

Hetty folded her hands in her lap and smiled innocently back.

Michael refused to rise to the bait. Instead, he looked away, his face set in the rigid lines of a man trying to keep hold of his temper.

Hetty watched him silently, waiting. Once she could have teased him back into good humor, but not now. She'd tried teasing him this morning—admittedly, a bit more wantonly—and it hadn't accomplished anything except to make him angrier and more determined than ever to do what he thought best.

This morning, he'd been trying to protect her reputation. Now he was trying to protect his patients. As much as she might disagree with his viewpoint, she couldn't fault him for having it. He certainly wasn't getting anything out of it except grief. From her, especially.

The thought wasn't pleasant.

"Michael?" Hetty ventured at last, when she could stand the silence no longer.

He picked up a rubber hose with an awkward-looking face mask that Hetty supposed must belong to the vaporizer and slowly began turning it over in his hands, staring at it as if he found it incredibly fascinating.

"I'm sorry, Hetty," he said at last, his voice hard, his attention still fixed on the mask he held. "You're right. We have had this argument before."

Abruptly, he dropped the hose and rose to his feet. "I think I'd best escort you back to Mrs. Scoggins's, before it gets dark."

Hetty stiffened indignantly. "Just like that?"

"Just like what?" he snapped.

"Like there's nothing else to say?" Hetty glared up at him, all her guilty feelings of a moment earlier gone in a flash.

"What do you expect me to say? That I approve of this move? I don't. But you didn't ask me, did you?"

This time Michael made no effort to control his temper. His anger rolled over Hetty like a breaking wave, shocking her with its force and throwing her off balance.

He suddenly reached into his coat pocket and dragged out a sheaf of papers covered in crabbed, wavery handwriting.

"You didn't ask me if Mr. Meissner was up to translating all those damned recipes you gave him, either. Did you know he was up until all hours last night, working on these damned things, Hetty?" Michael flung the papers on the table in front of her. "He looked like hell warmed over this afternoon, and he sounded worse. And that was thanks to you!"

Hetty snatched up the papers and jumped to her feet in one swift, furious move. "I never asked him to work that hard on them! He was glad to do it! And glad that someone realized he's not a useless invalid just because he's old!"

"I don't think he's a useless invalid!" Michael roared.

"Well, you treat him like one! He was right, you know. You worry so much about your patients dying on you that you forget they still have their lives to live, in spite of everything!"

His head snapped up as if she'd punched him, but Hetty didn't give him a chance to recover.

"The Rheiners are moving tomorrow, Michael. Because *they* want to, not because I'm pushing them into it. No matter what you think!"

Hetty spun on her heel and marched toward the door, Mr. Meissner's papers firmly clutched in her hand. Halfway there she stopped and swung back to face Michael.

"And I won't need you to walk me back to Mrs. Scoggins's. I can manage perfectly well on my own, thank you very much."

This time it was her turn to slam the door behind her.

It was only long after she'd left that Michael remembered the marriage license on his desk.

# *Chapter Eighteen*

Ruth cried when she saw the small frame house, great, silent tears that coursed down her gaunt cheeks. "A home," she said, her voice little more than a whisper. "A real home."

Robert had already arrived with the heavy wagon and the first of their possessions, including Ruth's bed. He would go back to the clearing to dismantle the tent and cook stove, but had come earlier with the things his wife and daughter would need first. Already smoke trailed out of the cook stove pipe at the side of the house, mixing with the snow the darkened sky was beginning to spit at them.

He was striding toward them now, a wide smile on his face, heedless of the cold or the threatening storm. He looked ten years younger, Hetty thought. The prospect of having decent shelter for his family, a steady job, and some security had lifted a burden from his shoulders that had become almost too much to bear.

At Ruth's insistence, he took Anna in first, still securely bundled in her drawer under layers of blankets and shawls. The infant had endured the journey with only small complaints. A bottle of milk, kept warm under the blankets with her, had easily silenced most of the protests and the lulling rumble of the carriage had dealt with the rest.

While they waited for Robert to return, Hetty and Ruth studied the caretaker's house that was to be the Rheiners' new home. It was set back from the main house, out of sight behind a ridge of rock and a small grove of twisted pine and juniper, with a small barn farther on. At some time, someone had made a home of it, for there were traces of a small flower garden at one side, with the scraggly remains of a vegetable garden beyond. To the west of the house they would see a jaw-dropping sweep of mountain once the storm clouds lifted, while behind the house rose a rocky, grass- and pine-covered hill that would be enticing on a bright summer's day.

"It's so beautiful," Ruth said happily, as if the world around her weren't cold and gray and grim. "I can get well here. I *know* I can."

Impulsively, she turned to Hetty and took her hand. "I can't ever thank you enough for this. I'd been so . . . so frightened, so worried. And Robert . . . But now . . ." Her words trailed off as her lower lip trembled. She blinked, fighting against the tears that filled her eyes. Her thin hands tightened around Hetty's. "Now we can be happy again, I think."

Hetty settled for a smile in response; her own voice was too shaky to be trusted. If only Michael were here to see the difference that hope made! But he wasn't, and there was no sense wasting time wondering when he'd show up—or if he would come at all.

Robert came out then to fetch his wife, and while he carried Ruth in, Hetty clambered down to stable the horse. She'd stay with Ruth and the baby and Samuel while Robert returned to the clearing to pick up the last of their possessions. Since he didn't expect to be back until dark—if he was lucky and the snow didn't get any worse—Hetty had brought a few things so she could stay overnight.

Samuel appeared just as she finished, bounding across to the barn as eager as a puppy let free to play.

"Da says, he has coffee on, if you'd like some," he said, grinning. "Him and Zach gotta get back 'count of the snow and 'cause Zach's da said he could help out for the move, but he's gotta be home for evening milking. So Da, my da, says they're gonna go right back, now Ma and Anna are here. So could you come?"

Hetty smiled and gave the top of his head a rub. Samuel laughed and yelped in protest, then dodged out of reach.

"Of course I'll come," she said, falling into step beside Samuel. "And once your father's gone, you and I are going to make one of those recipes out of your grandmother's recipe book. Special for your mother. How does that sound?"

"You mean it? You really got 'em?"

"You bet. I even brought all the fixings for the recipe for chocolate cake," she added, swinging the lidded basket she carried.

"Yipee!" Samuel cried, leaping into the air. "I gotta go tell Ma!" And away he raced, leaving Hetty to trail happily after.

The kitchen, which occupied the entire east end of the house, was a big, echoing space with a substantial wood-burning stove, a sink with a hand pump, a table with six mismatched chairs, and a large square of green linoleum covering the center of the floor. Despite the room's size, the massive stove had heated it to an almost sweltering level.

Hetty immediately shed her coat and gloves and crossed to the vast black monster to warm her hands. Samuel was made of hardier stuff. He crept across to his mother's unheated room at the opposite end of the house, where his father was still getting everything settled.

Anna was safe in her drawer on the camp table in the corner behind the stove, where drafts from open doors were least likely to reach. Hetty only needed one sniff to know that a fresh pad and some clean blankets were required. Anna was beginning to make it clear that more milk wouldn't come amiss, either.

Ignoring the tempting pot of coffee on the back of the stove, Hetty set some milk to heat, then dragged a couple of chairs closer to the stove so she could hang blankets and clean cloths to warm. By the time Samuel and his father reappeared, she had Anna clean and changed and soundly asleep after only a few good pulls at the bottle.

"I'll be off, then, Miss Hetty," Robert said, pulling on his coat. "You'll be all right, just you and Samuel?"

"Yes, we'll be fine." Hetty gave him an encouraging smile.

He frowned, clearly troubled. "I'd stay and wait to move the rest later, but I promised Zach's Pa I'd get him home and—"

"Don't worry. Besides, Michael's bound to be coming soon. He knew you were moving today." Bold words, but even as she spoke Hetty was conscious of a little twinge of worry. They'd worked everything out, but they hadn't counted on the storm. She could hear the wind whining about the chimney even over the comfortable crackle of the fire.

With stern determination, she pushed those unpleasant thoughts aside. If she indulged in them, she'd soon become as bad as Michael, fretting about troubles that might never happen.

"We'll be fine. Really," she said. "And Samuel's here, after all. He can take my horse and go for help if necessary."

"True." Robert's frown deepened as he glanced down at his son, who was watching him anxiously. His expression softened as he gently brushed a finger across Samuel's cheek. "That's something to be grateful for, isn't it?"

Samuel let out the breath he'd been holding and straightened proudly. All his earlier doubts about his father's role in Anna's birth and his mother's illness seemed to have disappeared with the move, as though he'd left them behind in the tall, dead grass of that clearing.

"Well, tend to what Miss Hetty tells you, then. I'll be back as soon as I can." Robert glanced at the frosted window, then shook his head doubtfully. "If it weren't for Zach . . ."

Hetty made a shooing motion. "Just go, and don't worry about us."

Once Robert was gone, she set Samuel to digging out his mother's mixing bowls and cooking pans and went to check on Ruth.

After the warmth of the kitchen, the little bedroom at the opposite side of the house seemed like ice. None of the three windows was covered with curtains, and one had been opened just a crack to let in the fresh air Michael had insisted Ruth needed. The sound of the wind-driven snow splatting against the glass was almost comforting, a testament to the house's comfortable solidity.

In the little time he'd had, Robert had obviously worked to make the room as welcoming as possible. A tall bureau with a missing drawer had been shoved against one wall. It stood canted a little to one side from the unevenness of the plank floor, with a rather florid china vase claiming pride of place on top. An old daguerreotype of a stern-looking woman had been hung from a nail on the wall beside the bed. The battered stand beside the bed held a book, a half-empty glass of water, and a lighted oil lamp, wick turned low.

Despite the cold, Ruth had readily fallen asleep beneath her mountain of blankets. Her mouth curved upward in a faint smile that softened the thin, drawn lines of her face, even in sleep; her cheeks seemed to have drawn color from the thick red wool cap she wore.

Hetty's mouth curved in an answering smile. It was going to be all right. Everything, she thought, was going to be all right.

Her confidence lasted just long enough for her and Samuel to get the cake baked, cooled, and frosted.

Anna was contentedly asleep in her corner near the kitchen stove, but Ruth, exhausted by the move, had awakened and was coughing up blood.

"I'm just tired, that's all," she told Hetty weakly as she tried to swallow the heavy syrup Michael had given her. "I'll be fine . . . once I get . . . rested."

Instead, fever engulfed her, quickly drenching her in sweat that soaked through her gown in minutes.

With Robert gone and Michael who knew where, Hetty had to rely on a frightened Samuel for guidance.

"Da uses ice, sometimes, if he can get it," he told her, manfully fighting against the tears that threatened him. "And cold, wet towels, like you got. Dr. Ryan, he said there wasn't much else to do. But Miss Hetty," he added plaintively, "she don't usually get the sweats 'cept at night. Does that mean she's worse 'cause of the move?"

"Ice," Hetty muttered, listening to Ruth's fevered tossings in the other room. The snow had long ago settled thickly on the ground, but, unlike the snow she was accustomed to back East, it was dry and didn't pack well. "Samuel? Can you drive a buggy?"

When the boy nodded nervously, she grabbed her bag and dug out a few coins. "Take this and my buggy and go back to that grocery we passed on the way out. You remember? They might have some they can sell us, or they can tell you where to get it. You can go by Dr. Ryan's house first and see if he's there, or leave the note I'll write him. Can you do that?"

Samuel nodded again, but he looked none too confident after they'd hitched the horse back to the buggy and he'd awkwardly scrambled into the seat, hampered by the heavy layers of clothing he'd donned.

"Don't rush," Hetty warned him. "It's more important you get back here safe than that you go fast. And if Dr. Ryan isn't at home, don't spend time looking for him. You just come straight back. Understand?"

Even though the wind and falling snow muffled sound, Hetty could tell when he hit the public road because the big tin washtub they'd thrown in to hold the ice rattled and clanged as Samuel forced the horse into a fast trot on the graded surface. He hadn't even waited until he was out of earshot before ignoring her warning, but there was nothing she could do about that now. Ruth needed her, and Anna had awakened and was beginning to fuss in the kitchen. They were both here because of her interference, her refusal to listen to Michael's concerns, and she hadn't the slightest idea of what to do to help.

With a nervous prayer that Michael would come soon, Hetty turned back to the house.

Snow had already covered the roof and small front stoop an inch deep and was mournfully swirling around the corners of the caretaker's house when Michael drove up. Except for the smoke drifting out of the stove pipe, the place looked deserted. He'd spent last night worrying about the move, but most of the day berating himself for having treated Hetty so badly because of it. The stillness about the place now brought all his worries back with a vengeance.

He tied his horse up under a huge old pine, threw the horse blanket over the beast, then grabbed his medical bag from beneath the seat and hurried across to the front door, head bent against the blowing snow.

"Oh, Michael!" she exclaimed, throwing herself into his arms before he could cross the threshold. "Thank God you've come!"

The muscles in Michael's gut tightened painfully, and his shoulders tensed.

"What is it? Anna?" he demanded roughly, putting Hetty from him.

"Ruth. She's coughing and feverish and I . . ."

Hetty's voice caught. "I don't know what to do. Samuel's gone for ice, but . . ."

"Where? Through here?" Michael waited only long enough for Hetty's confirming nod.

Ruth was propped up in the bed, pillows behind her back and buried to the neck under a pile of blankets. Her face was drawn and white, dewed with sweat and circled by damp strands of hair that clung to her skin like wet waterweed. At the sound of his steps on the bare plank floor, her eyes opened. It took a moment for them to focus.

"Dr. Ryan," she said weakly with a pitiful attempt at a smile. "Hetty shouldn't have . . . bothered you. I'm . . . just tired."

"Hetty didn't bother me," Michael said sharply, setting his bag on the floor by her bed. "I came to see how you were doing after the move."

"So silly. Be better . . . tomorrow. Now I'm here," she indicated the room with her chin, "I know . . . I'll get better."

Michael glanced at the room around him. It was a plain, unpretentious room, but infinitely more comfortable than a tent or a crude shelter in the open air—and just as healthy.

Ruth followed his inspection of the room. "Going to have to move . . . that bureau, though. It's crooked."

"Yes, but you can worry about that later," Michael said, turning his attention back to her.

She made no protest when he took her wrist between his fingers, just shut her eyes and leaned back on the pillows, exhausted by the effort at speech.

His brief exam told Michael all he needed to know. Ruth Rheiner was suffering from the results of exhaustion and over-exertion and, much as he hated to admit it, there was nothing he could do for her that Hetty hadn't already done.

He told Hetty so a few minutes later when they'd withdrawn to the kitchen and left Ruth to rest.

"But don't think I'm glad of the move," he added as warning, "because I'm not. Not so soon."

"At least Anna hasn't taken any hurt," Hetty said, calmer now, but still shaken. Her voice held none of the defiance of the night before. "And isn't this kitchen better for her than that awful old tent?"

Michael didn't answer. He washed his hands at the sink, then squeezed into the corner to check on Anna. The infant was sound asleep, content in her cocoon of blankets and oblivious of his gentle touch.

He folded the blankets back over her and turned to find Hetty watching him anxiously. She'd poured two cups of coffee from the blue enameled pot set at the back of the stove and retreated to a chair at the far side of the table.

"She's all right?" she asked, her eyebrows rising in an anxious query. Her hand closed around her mug, but not before Michael caught the betraying tremble.

Michael nodded reluctantly. "She's fine. Which leaves just her mother to worry about, since there's nothing else we can do for her." The acknowledgment of his limitations and the limitations of the science in which he'd put so much faith galled him. He hesitated, then added, "Believe me, Hetty. She's had night sweats before. The move has worn her out badly, but that's all."

Ignoring the chair in front of him, he picked up the steaming cup of coffee and started to take a careful sip when his gaze fell on the chocolate cake sitting on the far end of the table.

"Samuel and I baked it," Hetty explained defensively. "I thought—" She blinked, as if fighting against tears. "I thought Ruth would like it, and he wanted to do something. For her, you know."

Michael nodded and took a swig of coffee. It burned his throat as it slid down and made his eyes water, but he turned away so Hetty couldn't see.

He knew. He knew all about a boy's desperate need to do something—*anything*—that might make his mother happy and help her get well.

He knew, but knowing hadn't been enough to help another small boy. Samuel had flung the horehound drops away, yet Michael had no doubt he'd been more than eager to help Hetty bake a chocolate cake.

Michael stared, unseeing, at the far wall, achingly conscious of the cake sitting on the table just a couple of feet away and of a pain that had suddenly lodged in his chest, just below his breastbone.

Becoming a doctor had given him explanations and a few skills, a few scraps of knowledge, but it hadn't helped him understand.

The sound of a horse and buggy coming up the

road abruptly broke the quiet of the kitchen. Hetty was up from her chair and out the door before Michael could put his cup down on the table.

"I got the ice, Miss Hetty!" Samuel shouted as he drew the tired horse to a halt beside Michael's. He fastened the reins, then leaped to the ground and hurried around to the back of the buggy, where Hetty was already peering over the tailgate.

A tin washtub sat on the floor of the buggy, covered with snow and filled to overflowing with a big block of ice and the damp newspapers laid over it as insulation. Hetty and Michael each grabbed a handle on the tub and lifted it out, then carried it into the barn while Samuel trailed beside them, chattering anxiously.

"How's Ma? She okay now? Is her fever worse? I was careful, honest I was, but I hurried as fast as I could."

As soon as she put the tub down, Hetty knelt before Samuel. "Your mother's fever is down a bit, and she's trying to sleep right now," she said, "but maybe, if you're real quiet, you can just sit in the corner of the room and keep an eye on her. Would you like that?"

Michael started to protest, then bit the words back.

Samuel nodded eagerly. "Yes, please. I'd be *real* quiet. Honest."

Hetty smiled. "I know you would. Go in and wash up, then. And be careful not to bother her."

Samuel scooted off, obviously relieved.

Michael watched him go, but in his mind he was seeing the dull brown gleam of candy drops scattered in the grass.

With Anna still sound asleep and Samuel quietly ensconced in a chair in the farthest corner of the room from his mother's bed, Hetty helped Michael stable the two horses in the barn.

Michael had withdrawn into an icy silence, as alone with his thoughts as if she were back in Boston. His withdrawal worried her, but Hetty was too full of self-blame for Ruth's attack to blame him for it. He'd warned her, but she'd refused to listen, and the fact that he now said Ruth would recover and agreed that the situation would be best for her in the long run did nothing to ease Hetty's guilt.

She *had* charged in, blithely unaware of the real risks involved and so determined to help that she'd refused to listen to Michael's legitimate concerns.

Well, now she knew better.

George Lanyon's death had touched her with the tragedy of a life cut short too soon and a family left alone in an uncaring world, but this was different . . . and far more difficult to deal with. Over these past few days she'd come to know the Rheiners and to care for them. Their sufferings were now personal.

They were also far more frightening. She'd had time to adapt to her mother's illness. Ruth's collapse, on the other hand, was devastatingly brutal and abrupt.

Michael had gone through this, she silently reminded herself, over and over again. First as a boy, and now as a man who had dedicated himself to helping others, then found himself almost as helpless as the people he was trying to help. Yet for the past few days she'd arrogantly lectured him about understanding and looking on the bright side and all the other little things that now seemed like so many trivial idiocies when weighed against the heavy burden of reality.

Hetty watched as Michael washed his hands at the pump set near the barn door. He looked tired and all too grimly intent on the simple task, but there was something solid and comfortingly secure in his angular strength and lean, unconscious grace. Despite his frustrations and his own self-doubts, despite the daily burden of others' pain and suffering and desperate hopes that he had assumed by becoming a doctor, he was unconquered, his belief in his calling as deep and as passionate as it had been all those years ago when he could only dream of his future . . . and hers.

The tears Hetty had fought against for the past two hours stung her eyes. A tight pain gripped her chest, like inner tears burning to be let loose, and her hands knotted into the folds of her skirt. She moved toward Michael, her hand out, but before she'd gone two steps, a crash sounded from the house, followed by a scream that shattered the icy air around them.

Michael jerked upright, body tensed as he strained to hear. He glanced at her, then turned and raced for the house.

# Chapter Nineteen

Hetty was right on Michael's heels as he burst through the front door and dashed into Ruth's bedroom.

Samuel lay on the floor, limp as a half-empty sack of flour tossed aside and forgotten, his eyes closed and his skin gone white with shock. An ugly scrape on his forehead oozed blood and the opposite side of his face was scraped raw.

Ruth was kneeling helplessly on the floor beside him, sobbing, her hands clasped at her chest as if she were afraid to touch him and afraid not to, all at the same time.

Behind her, the tall bureau, the one that had stood at an awkward angle on the uneven floor, now lay tipped on its side, its drawers open and their contents spilling across the floor.

"It fell on him," Ruth gasped, choking on her wild sobs. "The bureau. I moved it off, but . . . Oh, God! Samuel!" She buried her head in her hands as her frail body shook in a paroxysm of fear and grief.

Michael immediately knelt beside Samuel while Hetty wrapped her arms around his mother, vainly trying to quiet her and pull her away. At Michael's probing, Samuel stirred; then his eyes fluttered open. He groaned and tried to roll away.

"Hold still," Michael snapped, grabbing hold of him.

"I didn't mean to," Samuel whimpered. "Honest."

"I'm sure you didn't, but don't move."

While Samuel lay blinking up at him, his face crumpled into a red, wrinkled ball as he fought against tears of fear and pain, Michael checked his pupils, then ran his hands over the boy's body, looking for broken bones or signs of internal injuries. Ruth watched, her sobs dwindled now to anxious hiccups and choked gasps for air.

"Well," he said a little more mildly a couple of minutes later, "I don't think you've broken anything, but you're going to be awfully sore for a few days. What happened?"

Samuel ignored the question and struggled to sit up. This time Michael helped him, careful of the scrapes and the bruises that were already starting to show.

"My fault," Ruth cried. "All my fault."

"No, Ma!" Samuel protested as the tears he couldn't stop suddenly streamed down his face. "I'm sorry."

Michael glanced at Hetty, but she looked as bewildered as he felt.

"You tried to move the bureau, is that it?" Michael said, fighting for calm.

Samuel nodded violently, digging the heels of his hands into his eyes to wipe away the tears. "Ma woke up and we was talking, you know, about how nice this place is, and . . . and . . ."

"I just said . . . too bad the bureau . . . was crooked." Ruth stretched out her trembling hand and gently touched her son's battered cheek, heedless of the tears streaming down her own. If he hadn't ruthlessly drummed in the importance of not letting Samuel get too close to her, Michael knew she would have gathered him into her arms and hugged him tightly against her breast.

Samuel stared doubtfully at the toppled bureau. "I tried to shove it over, but . . . but it caught, an' then I tried to grab it, but . . ."

Michael glanced at the bureau, then back at Samuel, and something Ruth had said when they came in suddenly registered. "*You* moved that thing off him?" he demanded, staring at her.

She nodded, the memory of her fear for her son clearly written in her eyes.

The thought of so fragile a woman's trying to lift so heavy an object chilled him, and the fear made his words sharper than he'd intended. "Are *you* all right? Do you feel any pain? Does your chest hurt? Your stomach?"

At each question, Ruth shook her head, her attention still fixed on her son. "No, no, I'm fine," she insisted weakly. "Fine."

She sniffed, then shoved her fist against her mouth to stop the sobs that clearly threatened. "I shouldn't . . . have said anything. About the . . . bureau. I didn't mean . . ."

Michael edged around Samuel and took Ruth's wrist. Her pulse raced feebly beneath his fingers. With one easy scoop, he picked her up, then stood and carried her to the bed. Her face was so pale and bloodless, she almost disappeared against the sheets.

"Hetty, take care of Mrs. Rheiner," he said, his worried gaze on Ruth. She might be all right, despite her extraordinary exertion. "I'll take Samuel and tend to his scrapes, then I'll be back to check on her. All right?"

Hetty nodded, clearly shaken. While she gathered up the covers Ruth had flung aside in her panic, Michael dragged Samuel off to the kitchen. Five minutes later, he had the various scrapes cleaned and, against Samuel's wincing objections, was dousing them with tincture of iodine when Hetty suddenly appeared in the doorway.

He glanced up at the sound of her footsteps, then started to his feet, shocked by the sudden, sick pallor of her face.

"Michael, please," she said, her voice shaking. "You have to come. *Now*."

Michael slammed the bottle of iodine down on the table and, after a stern order to Samuel not to move from his chair, rushed after Hetty.

"She's bleeding, Michael," Hetty quavered. "I— It's—"

A glance was all the diagnosis he needed. Severe postpartum hemorrhage.

Ruth stared at him, too terrified to speak. The front of her gown was drenched with red that was rapidly spreading down her legs and across the sheets. The effort of lifting the heavy bureau off her son had made her start bleeding internally. As debilitated as she already was, if he couldn't get it stopped, she'd bleed to death in as little as a quarter of an hour.

With an oath, Michael ripped the covers off the bed and out of the way and immediately began massaging her belly, digging into her flesh with almost vicious force, trying to induce her uterus to contract and close off the bleeding vessels inside.

"My bag," he snapped at Hetty without taking his eyes off his task. "In the kitchen. Send Samuel out to chop up ice for me, lots of it. And find some clean linen we can tear into strips. *Now*!"

A frightened Hetty was back with his bag two minutes later, a wad of white cloth scraps in her hands. "What do I—?"

"There's a bottle of tincture of marigold in the rack at the top of the bag," he commanded. "Put three or four drops of it *under* her tongue."

Hetty quickly found the small, dark brown bottle and its glass dropper, but at the sight of Ruth, who was fast slipping into unconsciousness, she hesitated.

Michael snapped instructions. "Be sure it's *under* her tongue," he added as Hetty bent over the bed.

After a moment's fumbling, Hetty managed to do as he'd ordered. Her hands were shaking badly as she closed the bottle and set it on the bedside stand.

"Good. Now, pour the calendula lotion over those cloths. See, there? That square glass bottle. You have to really soak the cloth, but don't waste it. It's all I have with me."

The slack muscles beneath his hands seemed to have turned to dough, but Michael didn't stop as he watched Hetty pour the oily liquid over the rags.

Though she was wavering on the verge of shock herself, she carefully followed his directions for packing the lotion-drenched strips of cloth internally, where they could absorb the blood even as the lotion acted to shut off its flow.

Michael's hands were growing cramped by the time Samuel returned with the ice, but he kept kneading Ruth's flesh, willing her body to respond and stop bleeding her life away. Hetty, after one quick, questioning glance, wiped her blood-stained hands on a corner of the sheet and went to collect the basin of ice Samuel had left on the parlor floor while he darted back outside to chip more ice.

Only when Hetty had finished wrapping the chipped ice in torn pieces of toweling, then covering Ruth's belly from just below her ribs to midway down her thighs, did Michael pull back, slowly working his fingers to ease the cramps while his mind raced.

He picked up the bottle of calendula lotion, but there was little left, not even enough for one more full dressing. He frowned at his bag, considering its contents. Nothing that would help. Not for this. Then his gaze fell on the bottle with the tincture of marigold.

"Hetty," he snapped, grabbing up the bottle. "Tell Samuel to milk the goat. Every drop. The kid will have to go hungry for a while."

"Michael?" Hetty was staring at him as if he'd gone mad.

"Boil the milk, then mix half the contents of this bottle in it. I'll try to make the lotion last as long as possible, but we haven't got much time."

Hetty gulped. "You want to mix that tincture in the goat's milk?"

"Unless you can find some marigold petals at this time of year, it's all I have. No? Then *hurry*."

She was halfway out the door when he added, "And bring me more ice. *Now*!"

The struggle for Ruth Rheiner's life became a mad, mindless routine. Changing the ice packs, soaking strips of linen torn from clean sheets in the milk and marigold broth, wringing them out and putting them in place of the blood-soaked ones. And then changing the ice packs again.

Every now and then Michael took Ruth's pulse and checked the inside of her lower eyelid to see if color was returning. It was so hard to tell. A hemorrhage like this was dangerous even to a strong and healthy woman. Ruth Rheiner was weak, worn down by illness, her blood already thinned because of fever and the coughing. At best, she would keep bleeding for some time even after the worst of it had stopped. At worst . . .

Michael refused to think of the worst. As he worked, he talked to the unconscious Ruth, exhorting her, cajoling her, ordering her to respond and talking to her about any trivial, cheerful thing that occurred to him. He had no idea if she could hear him, but if sheer force of will would save her, Ruth Rheiner would live. He would make sure of it.

At his insistence, Hetty kept Samuel busy chipping ice, well away from his mother's room so he couldn't see her pale, seemingly lifeless face or the dark red stains that seemed to cover everything.

Hetty herself flitted in and out of the bedroom, taking care of Anna when she fussed once, bringing him the ice, the linens, a basin of water and soap to wash his hands. Her face was still drawn and unnaturally pale, but she was calmer now, and the gentle, encouraging smiles she gave him brought an odd sort of comfort.

Like chocolate cake, Michael thought, turning back to his task. The comfort she offered had no logic. It came from the heart, and that was what gave it its strength.

The night had closed in, almost imperceptible in the storm, when Ruth Rheiner finally regained consciousness. She floated back to an awareness of her surroundings slowly, so slowly that Michael almost stopped breathing while he waited for her eyes to open.

She blinked, once, twice.

"Samuel?" she said, so faintly that Michael wouldn't have heard it if he hadn't been so close.

"Samuel's in the kitchen with Hetty and Anna," he said gently, suddenly conscious of an immense sense of relief . . . and of his own exhaustion. He wrapped his hand around hers where it lay on the coverlet. "I'll go get him, shall I? But you can only see him for a minute."

She nodded and shut her eyes. Her fingers closed around his briefly in a slight, almost imperceptible gesture of thanks.

Michael pulled on his jacket as he quietly crept out of the room. Once he'd been sure the hemorrhaging had stopped, he and Hetty had cleaned Ruth up and changed the sheets and covers, then Hetty had bundled everything up and carried it off to soak. There was nothing here to frighten Samuel except his mother's paleness and the memory of the long and frightening hour just past.

The moment he appeared in the kitchen doorway, Samuel and Hetty abandoned their chairs and came rushing up.

Michael smiled down at them tiredly. "You can go in, Samuel, but only for a minute. All right? Your mother needs to rest."

Hetty went in with Samuel, but when the boy emerged a few minutes later, he was alone. For a moment he stood in the kitchen doorway, looking blindly about him as if he were dazed and trying to get his bearings. Then his gaze fastened on Michael.

Michael, slumped in the chair at the end of the table, watched him cross the room and fought down the panic rising inside him. Somehow he'd known this would happen, that Samuel would come to him for an explanation, for some comfort against the horror of almost having lost his mother.

If only the right words came as easily to him as they did to Hetty! They didn't. They probably never would. But Hetty couldn't tell Samuel what the boy needed to know.

Samuel stopped just out of reach, nervously studying Michael.

Michael felt his fingers dig into his thigh, just as they had when he'd faced Samuel in the clearing. This time he forced them to relax, and then he waited. Better, he thought, to let Samuel lead the conversation than blunder in himself and risk making a mess of things before he'd scarcely begun.

"Ma's gonna be all right?" Samuel said at last.

Michael cleared his throat, then nodded. "Yes, she's going to be fine. She'll be tired and very weak for a while, but she's going to be all right."

Samuel's lips thinned. He started to speak, then stopped and carefully edged closer to Michael. He ran his finger along the edge of the worn table, working up the courage to ask his next question.

"Ma almost died, didn't she?" He didn't look at Michael as he spoke.

Michael had thought a lot about the answer he should give to that question. "Yes," he said. "But she didn't."

He reached out and gently pulled Samuel onto his lap. For an instant the boy stiffened. But only for an instant. Then he sniffed and suddenly collapsed, burying his head on Michael's shoulder.

Michael drew the boy closer against him, as much for his own sake as Samuel's. The warm, wiry little body was a comforting anchor to hold on to, and he needed that anchor right now.

"Your mother didn't die, Samuel, because *you* were here to help," he said fiercely. "Do you know how important that was? If you hadn't been here to help by chipping all that ice and milking the goat—" His voice caught, but he plunged on. "Well, we don't have to think about that, because you *were* here and your mother will be all right. Do you hear me, Samuel? Your mother is going to be all right."

"If I hadn'ta tipped the bureau over—"

"You didn't tip that bureau, Samuel! Do you hear me? You didn't tip it, it just happened. Do you understand that? *It just happened!*"

The words spilled out unbidden, but in their wake came a startling awareness of their full import. Samuel hadn't done it. It happened, that was all. Just as sometimes his patients died, despite everything he could do to save them. Just as his mother's illness happened. It didn't have a reason and no one was responsible. *It just happened.*

So simple, now that he saw it. Hetty had been

right. Things didn't have to have a reason, they just . . . happened. And when they did, the only thing you could do was go on, make the best of it, keep on living instead of fighting against what couldn't be changed, no matter how hard you tried.

"But—" Samuel started to protest

"Sometimes—" Michael stopped, fighting against the sudden hot sting of tears. He was a grown-up. A doctor. He was supposed to comfort his patients, not cry with them.

"Sometimes things happen that we don't want," he said, forcing the words past the lump in his throat. "Terrible things or sad things. Things we don't like. But just because they happen doesn't mean we're responsible for them, Samuel."

The tears slipped past his restraint to trace hot tracks of wetness down his cheeks and into his mouth, and suddenly, Michael didn't care.

"I was so scared," Samuel whispered into his shoulder. "I was afraid she'd die and leave me because . . . because I couldn't move that bureau and—" Samuel never finished, because his sniffles turned to hard, wrenching sobs that came from deep within him.

Michael felt the thin little arms tighten around his neck and at that moment, for the first time since forever, he was absolutely sure of the right words to say, the words that *had* to be said.

"It's okay to cry, Samuel," Michael said, pressing his cheek against the tousled yellow head on his shoulder, heedless of the tears that coursed down his own face. "It's okay to cry, because everything's going to be all right. You'll see."

Robert Rheiner came rattling up the road shortly before midnight, almost two hours after the snow had stopped falling.

Hetty was in Ruth's room. At her insistence, they'd taken turns watching over the sleeping woman, then warming up in the kitchen. Michael had wanted to argue, had wanted to talk to her about what he'd learned in these past few hours, but she'd carefully avoided him. In the end, he'd had no choice but to agree with her arrangements.

Michael was in the kitchen playing Old Maid with Samuel. Hetty had laid Samuel's pallet on the floor near the kitchen stove, but despite his evident exhaustion, the boy had refused to go to bed until his father returned. Michael suspected he'd proposed the card game as a way to keep awake as much as to help pass the hours while they waited.

Samuel heard his father first. Without hesitation, he threw down his cards and jumped to his feet.

Michael grabbed him before he could dart out the back door of the kitchen. "I'll go help your father. You tell Hetty he's here, all right? I think it's better if I tell him about your mother."

After a moment's hesitation, Samuel obeyed. Michael grabbed his coat and gloves and slipped out through the back door. The night air was biting cold, but most of the clouds had blown away so that the full moon shone through, illuminating the snow-covered hillsides and revealing the dark lines of the wagon's tracks like ropes of black velvet on the wind-scoured road. Like magic, Michael thought, stunned by the cold, moon-silvered beauty of the scene. The storm had come and gone, and left magic and an incredible beauty in its wake.

In the barn, Robert was working quickly to settle the horses. He'd left the wagon outside, securely covered.

"Had to wait 'til the storm stopped," he said, grinning tiredly in the lantern light, "but it's all done. Every bit of it. We can forget about that damned clearing, settle in and live decent now. Ruth's all right?" he added anxiously. "And the baby?"

Choosing his words carefully, and without going into too much detail about his wife's accident, Michael told Robert what had happened. "But they're fine now," he added hurriedly. "Anna's happy as a mouse in her corner, and Ruth's sleeping comfortably."

Robert listened, white-faced and still, through Michael's explanation. The minute Michael finished, he cursed and raced toward the house, abandoning the tired horses before he'd even finished unharnessing them. For a moment, Michael debated following him, then wearily decided that Hetty would be better at soothing his worries, and there were the horses still to tend to, after all.

When he walked back into the kitchen fifteen

minutes later, Hetty was in the corner by the stove bent over Anna, her back turned toward him. She didn't even look up as he hesitated beside the door.

"Robert's . . . all right?" Michael asked, suddenly uncertain what to do next. Hetty mumbled something indistinguishable and waved him away.

Reluctantly, Michael obeyed. He found Robert seated in the chair beside Ruth's bed, his gaze fixed on his sleeping wife's face and Samuel curled on his lap, already sound asleep.

"She's going to be all right," Michael said at last, softly. He'd said the same thing to Samuel, but he found the words came more readily with repetition—and they carried more conviction.

Robert merely stared at him silently, then gently drew his son more securely to him and turned his gaze back to the pale face on the pillow.

After a moment, Michael quietly crept away, leaving them there in the golden lamplight while the moon shone silver-cold outside the windows, too far away to touch them any longer.

Hetty was standing at the kitchen sink staring out the small window into that same moon-drenched night, her back turned toward him, her shoulders hunched. Michael hesitated, then slowly crossed the room to her.

He needed to touch her, talk to her. Whatever breach he'd created between them could be healed if only she'd give him another chance, if only she'd forgive him for his pig-headed insistence on caution when what was needed—what had always been needed—was love and her ardent belief in tomorrow.

As the linoleum creaked beneath him, Hetty whirled to confront him. To his astonishment, it wasn't anger Michael saw on her face, but tears.

"Oh, Michael," Hetty sobbed, opening her arms in mute appeal. "Hold me. Please."

"For God's sake—*Hetty*!"

In an instant he had eliminated the distance between them, folding her against his breast with a sudden, fierce protectiveness that only made the tears flow hotter and faster.

"It's all right, Hetty," he tried to soothe her, stroking her hair and holding her pressed so tightly against him that her tears soaked his vest. "Really it is! It's all *right.*"

"I'm so *sorry,*" she sobbed. "If only I'd listened, if I'd—"

"Stop that!"

His hand trembled as he brushed a stray lock back from her temple. Hetty's tears spilled even faster.

"You did the right thing, Hetty," he said, his voice low and comforting, if a little unsteady. "In spite of me and my carping worries, you did the right thing. Do you hear me?"

"But Ruth—"

"Ruth isn't going to die. Not from this. Believe me."

"But she—she was shaking and sweating and coughing up blood and nothing I did helped, Michael. Nothing! And if she hadn't moved, then the dresser—"

"If she hadn't moved, she might still be coughing and feverish. And who knows what other accident might have happened. It could have been far worse. *Trust* me, Hetty. You were right all along. What you did will help. Just as you said it would."

"You told me, you said I didn't know what I was doing, and you were right," Hetty got out between her tears, too wrapped up in her own misery and self-blame to heed his words. "I thought if we were just careful enough, if we went slowly enough . . . And the house is so nice and she hated that tent, and the shelter even more, and—"

"And now she has a decent house, and her husband has a job so he doesn't need to worry about how to feed his family, and Anna is safe and cozy in that corner by the stove, and you were right, Hetty. You *were.*"

He held her to him as his words came tumbling out, rolling over her tears and her protests like an avalanche. "They wouldn't have had any of that if they hadn't taken a chance, if they hadn't looked for the hope instead of worried about the risk. All last night I worried, Hetty, thinking of all the things that could go wrong, all the disasters that could strike. But all my worrying would never have prevented an accident. It wouldn't even have prevented that fever she went through. *Believe* me, Hetty."

"But you seemed so angry, so—"

He laughed, then, a quavery, mocking laugh

that cut through Hetty's tears as all his comforting words had not.

"Of course I was. But I was angry with *me*, not with you."

"With—!" Hetty shoved away from his chest, tilting her head so she could look up at him out of eyes swollen with crying. "But why?"

His mouth lifted in an uncertain smile. "Because I've been thinking about that cake you and Samuel baked—"

He broke off suddenly to pull her back against him, tight and fierce as if she'd threatened to escape from him.

"A cake! My God!" he said, and the sound echoed in his chest. "A chocolate cake! You helped them to a home and the kind of hope that can think of chocolate cakes, and all because you thought about *them*, Hetty, while I—" His fingers dug into her shoulder, anchoring him to her.

"Do you know why Samuel threw those horehound drops away?" he demanded suddenly.

She shook her head. "No. I wondered, but . . . No."

"Because I tried to offer him a neat, rational, scientific explanation for his troubles. It was all I had. I couldn't think of anything else, but—" He drew a deep breath.

"It wasn't enough. It was all words and no heart, and when Samuel threw the drops away, he was throwing my words away with them. But you gave him your heart, Hetty, and that," he said softly, bending his head to meet her questioning gaze, "that made all the difference."

Hetty gave a small, tear-choked laugh and melted back into his arms. Michael gathered her close against him while the fire in the stove crackled and roared with its comforting warmth.

Why had he ever thought he could keep his life divided, with his work on one side and Hetty, carefully sheltered from reality, on the other? Why had he ever wanted to?

What had she told him, there in the clearing? That it was love that bound the Rheiners together, that offered hope in the face of the troubles that beset them and gave them the courage to go on, in spite of everything?

Something like that. The words themselves didn't matter, because Michael was just beginning to understand what she'd meant.

Love wasn't a divisible part of living, to be shut away and hidden from the dark side of existence. It was at the center of it all, the foundation on which everything else was constructed. And if it couldn't always offer an explanation for the evil that life sometimes seemed to throw at people, at least it offered the meaning that made that life worth living.

He'd forgotten that. Or maybe he'd never understood, too caught up in his own loss and his own dreams to grasp what Hetty had instinctively known all along.

But he could learn. With Hetty by his side, Michael knew he could learn.

"Let's go home, Hetty," he said. "Let's go home."

# *Epilogue*

*Colorado Springs—May, 1899*

"What do you think? Should we have six, or try for a full dozen?" Michael blinked lazily up at the sun-haloed face of his wife. He lay with his head comfortably cradled in her lap, his hands crossed over his stomach and his long legs stretched out in the tall grass on the hill above the house, every muscle heavy with the lassitude that sunshine and utter contentment brought.

The corner of his wife's adorable mouth twitched. "Are we talking poultry or pastries, Dr. Ryan?"

"We're talking progeny, Mrs. Ryan. Children. Babies. Offspring. You know. Little Ryans." Michael let out a slow sigh of contentment, shut his eyes, and nestled his head deeper into the warmth of her. "I think I'd like a dozen."

"Really? Even after Anna piddled all over your shirt yesterday?"

Michael grimaced, then opened one eye and squinted up at her. "Well, we could keep diapers on them, couldn't we?"

"I don't know. Ruth swears she tries, but Anna just crawls right out of them. Even Samuel can't keep up with her, and you know he follows her around like a sheepdog just to keep her out of trouble. Whenever he's not messing up his mother's kitchen fixing those crazy recipes he and Mr. Meissner are always dreaming up, that is."

Michael groaned at the memory of Samuel and Mr. Meissner's most recent culinary adventure, yet he couldn't help smiling at the same time. Those two, with almost eighty years dividing them, were perfect examples of what he had refused to see until Hetty had taught him to open his eyes—that life couldn't be lived through logic and reason, but only through love and an appreciation of the joys it brought. He still tended to forget that lesson sometimes, but he was luckier than most, because Hetty was always there to remind him.

He smiled up at her now. "Well, I still say we should have twelve of our own. Properly diapered. If you don't mind, that is," he added, almost as an afterthought.

"Oh, so I'm to have a say in the matter, am I?"

Her laughter spilled over him, making his heart skip a beat and the very air catch somewhere in the middle of his chest.

"Well, I thank you, sir. And where," she demanded, playfully poking him in the ribs, "are we to find these remarkable progeny of ours? Do they stock them at the local grocer's, or should I order them from Sears and Roebuck? With a discount for quantity, of course!"

Michael heaved himself up, grabbed Hetty by the waist, and bore her backward into the grass, pinning her with the weight of his body.

"Trying to take the easy way out, are you?" he growled, exquisitely conscious of her beneath him, of the sweet scent of crushed grass and lavender water and woman that enveloped them both. Her breasts, primly confined beneath the multitudinous layers of jacket, shirtwaist, shift, and vest, pressed against his chest, tantalizing in their imprisoned roundness.

Hetty squirmed beneath him. "The easy way! Do you have any idea how upset our mailman gets if I receive more than two boxes in a week?"

Michael curled his lips in the best imitation of a satyr's leer he could manage. "Actually, I had another approach in mind."

"Indeed?" She stopped wriggling. "And what would that approach be, if I might ask?"

"You can always ask, but it would be far more effective if I showed you. Don't you agree?"

He lowered his head, already anticipating the sweet taste of his lips on hers. Instead, his treacherous wife slipped in under his defenses, hitting the ticklish spots on his sides with fiendish accuracy. Michael gave a grunt of choked laughter and barely managed not to roll away.

The skirmish was brief. With a muffled cry of victory, Michael captured her wrists and pressed her back into the grass.

"Cheat!" Hetty protested, sticking her tongue out at him as she dug in her heels and arched upwards in a vain attempt to throw him off.

"Vixen!"

"Bully!"

"I'm a prudent man, Mrs. Ryan. Didn't you know? I believe in protecting myself against those who fight dirty." Panting slightly, Michael propped his elbows on either side of her, twined his fingers through hers, and claimed the spoils of victory.

Her kisses were sweet and infinitely tempting, but Hetty displayed a dangerous tendency toward subversion. The instant he released her hands, she wrapped her arms around his neck and drew him closer, and this time her squirming beneath him could not, by any stretch of the imagination, be interpreted as an attempt at escape.

Michael managed—though only barely—to break free before it became impossible. He didn't care to make a scandal of them both by taking her right here on the hillside. They were well out of sight of the dozen patients and their attendants who were the first residents of the Lester and Thadeaus Scoggins Memorial Sanatorium, but there was no telling when one of the laborers working on the new canvas-roofed cabins that were going up in the meadow beyond the house might suddenly decide to go for a stroll.

"Coward," Hetty murmured, refusing to release her hold around his neck. Her voice was thicker and slightly lower, heavy with desire.

"That too," Michael agreed. He kissed her chin lightly and tried to ignore the unsettling urgings of his body. "Imagine what the members of the Ladies Medical Auxiliary would say if they were to catch me with my pants down in public."

Hetty chuckled wickedly. "I suspect they'd be pea-green with envy."

"They *want* their husbands to go parading around half naked in public?"

"Not that, silly. This!"

Hetty had managed to slide her hand between them and her light touch on a portion of his anatomy that was peculiarly sensitive at the moment—even under the protective layers of his clothes—sent a hot, electric shock tingling through his body. Michael choked.

"Don't do that! Do you want me to embarrass us both, right here in front of God and the world?"

Hetty laughed. "I suspect God already knows about it, and as for the world . . ." She raised her head and planted a kiss on the tip of his nose. "If I have *you*, Michael David Ryan, who cares about them?"

"Well, I do, for one," Michael said, trying to sound severe. "And what's this about the Ladies' Auxiliary, anyway? Surely you don't talk about . . ." He hesitated, searching for words that would be proper for a man to use with his wife.

"About husbands? Of course we do. All the time."

"Not about husbands. About their . . . our . . . er . . ."

"Of course we do. Oh, not in so many words!" Hetty hastily added when his face started to go red. "But it *is* an interesting topic of conversation, after all. And from something I once overheard Mrs. Grimes say to Mrs. Lewellen, I suspect that Dr. Grimes—"

"Hetty!" Michael tried to push himself up into a position more appropriate for a display of masculine indignation, but Hetty held him fast.

Michael broke free of her grip and rolled to his side, intent on climbing to his feet. Hetty was quicker. She rolled with him, and this time he was the one who found himself pinned to the ground with her breasts pressed against his chest, her hips against his. He tried to get his feet under him, but his legs were inextricably tangled in the mass of her skirts and petticoats.

Hetty grinned. "You're blushing. Do you know, you're extremely handsome when you're blushing."

"I am *not* blushing!"

"Oh, yes, you are."

"This is outrageous and—Hetty, stop that!"

"Stop what?" Hetty inquired innocently.

Michael grabbed her hips and held her hard against him in an effort to stop the tormenting motion that was undermining his already shaky self-control.

As a protective strategy, it failed utterly. The

firm pressure of her belly against him only made matters worse. Or more enticing, depending on how you looked at it.

"Used to be you worried about what people might say if you didn't dust," Michael said, despertately grasping at straws. "How can you possibly—"

"That was dusting. Of *course* I worry about what people would say! Do you think I want them telling everyone that I don't take care of you properly?"

"But—!"

"We're a quarter mile from anyone, Michael, and you know it. Besides," Hetty added, dimpling enchantingly, "nobody's going to find us. If you'd quit shouting, that is."

"I'm not shouting!"

He was choking, if the truth be admitted. Hetty had started a distinctly unnerving movement with her hips that was distracting him from his quite reasonable arguments against the shocking impropriety of her behavior. Worse, she had somehow managed to work her skirt and petticoats up so they spilled over his chest and legs and the grass around them, leaving her free to straddle his hips and still work at the buttons of his trousers.

"You know," Michael gasped, suddenly breathless in the face of a new and even more startling revelation, "I always thought . . . the openings . . . in ladies' drawers . . . were . . . for sanitary purposes."

"Silly man," Hetty said. "And not very observant, either."

"Observant?" It wasn't easy getting the word out. He had other, more pressing distractions.

"I'm not wearing a corset," Hetty said, pausing in her abuse for an agonizing moment. "Didn't you notice?"

"Not wearing a—? What does that have to do with anything?" Michael demanded. If she didn't start moving again, and soon, he might well forget his good intentions and all his concerns about the wandering workmen.

"I thought I'd give my tummy a little room since I suspect—only suspect, mind you!—that I'm going to be getting a good deal too fat to wear one pretty soon."

"Too fat?" His distracted mind turned sluggishly, trying to grab hold of her words. There was a meaning behind this ridiculous conversation if only he could think what it was. The trouble was, with Hetty on top of him, he was finding it almost impossible to think at all.

"Much too fat." Hetty nodded, complacently

A thought began to form. Rather a startling thought. "Hetty?"

"Very, very fat," Hetty cooed in his ear.

"Hetty! You're not—?" Michael jerked upward, but she easily shoved him back down.

"And you a doctor!" Hetty chided, beginning to move again.

"Really?"

"Silly, silly man," she said, an instant before she made sure rational speech became impossible . . . for both of them.

# *A Note to the Reader*

Tuberculosis has a long and tragic history. Archeologists have found evidence of its afflicting mankind as far back as early Egypt. In the 19th century, pulmonary tuberculosis was the number-one killer, a "white plague" that was responsible for as many as a quarter of the recorded deaths in some areas of the country. (Various forms of tuberculosis can strike parts of the body other than the lungs, but they tend to be less deadly than the pulmonary variety.)

Notables such as the theologian John Calvin and the authors Robert Louis Stevenson and Henry David Thoreau died of pulmonary tuberculosis, while Sir Walter Scott managed to recover from it as a young man. Other sufferers such as Helen Hunt Jackson, the 19th-century activist and author of *A Century of Dishonor* and the influential novel, *Ramona*, relocated to what they hoped would be a healthier clime. In Mrs. Jackson's case, Colorado Springs, Colorado, offered the cure which her own mother, who died of tuberculosis, had not found by remaining in the East.

Until the German physician and bacteriologist Robert Koch finally identified the tubercle bacillus in 1882, tuberculosis—or consumption, as it was known then—was generally thought to be a hereditary disease. Since the disease often took years to run its deadly course and tended to leave its sufferers as wan and wasted as the doomed, romantic heroes and heroines in 18th-century gothic novels, commentators of the time tended to ascribe an almost noble status to the victims. Not that being considered tragically noble and romantic did the victims any good. They ended up dead, regardless.

With no cure available, victims of tuberculosis tried a number of treatments, including moving to different and, they hoped, more healthful surroundings. Despite the rigors of travel, sufferers began coming to Colorado as early as the 1860s in hopes that simple outdoor living and the area's high, dry climate would offer a cure that medical science could not.

At first, communities like Colorado Springs actively sought to attract health seekers under the comfortable belief that the new immigrants would bring their money with them. As germ theory and the communicable nature of TB began to be better understood, however, those same communities began to shun the health seekers they had originally courted with such enthusiasm. Inevitably, stresses developed between established citizens and anxious health seekers. By 1903, writers were noting that consumptives "can scarcely secure accommodations," even though, as in Colorado Springs, many boarding houses had been built specifically to house them twenty years earlier.

At the same time, major eastern cities such as New York, Boston, and Philadelphia were struggling with a growing immigrant population which, forced by poverty into crowded, unhealthful tenements and without access to clean water, good food, and proper sanitation, quickly fell victim to the scourge. Many of our present public health laws and organizations owe their existence to the efforts of pioneer health workers battling to control the spread of tuberculosis at the turn of the century.

Through the 1870s and 1880s, Colorado Springs, which had advertised the benefits of its healthful air and sparkling mineral waters in eastern newspapers, struggled to cope with the influx of cure seekers. It was a major center for TB treatment in the state, although Nordrach Ranch, the first open-air sanatorium operated along the lines established by Dr. Edward Trudeau in 1884 at his path-breaking sanatorium at Lake Saranac, New York, was not established until 1901. By 1896, Colorado as a whole was referred to as "The World's Sanatorium," although Arizona, New Mexico, Utah, and California drew their share of pilgrims, as well.

The sheer number of people involved is staggering. A survey published in 1908 in the *Denver Medical Times* found that almost 33% of all physicians in Colorado had originally come to the state because either they or a member of their family suffered from the disease. In 1925, a report entitled *TB In Denver* estimated that as much as 60% of Colorado's population had migrated to the state, either directly or indirectly, because of TB. They came as patients, family members accompanying patients, health care providers, or merchants and tradesmen who saw a lucrative market for their various services.

As the number of tuberculosis sanatoriums across the United States increased, TB sufferers trying to decide where to go for treatment could consult national directories which described each sanatorium's history, size, facilities, rates, and indicated whether or not it would accept children, "negroes," or patients in the most advanced stages of the disease.

Although the sanatoriums' strict routines stressing rest, diet, and clean air undoubtedly saved many lives, TB continued to claim tens of thousands of victims each year until the discovery of the first antibiotics in the 1940s.

With the introduction of isoniazid in 1948, the first truly effective drug against tuberculosis, TB patients could finally be declared cured and sent home and the hundreds of tuberculosis sanatoriums built up across the country over the preceding 50 years closed or converted to other uses. In Colorado Springs, a campus of the University of Colorado now occupies what was once the city's premiere tuberculosis treatment facility.

Unfortunately, new, more resistant strains of TB have begun to appear in the past few years. These new strains do not respond to traditional treatment and scientists, who are struggling against a growing number of drug-resistant diseases and infections, have not yet found anything to replace the antibiotics we have come to rely upon over the past half century.

Although the characters and events in *The Snow Queen* are entirely my own invention, I have taken the liberty of adopting two actual references to my story's use. The scene in Chapter 4 in which Hetty first glimpses the Turner brothers, who are dying of tuberculosis, is closely based on an incident recorded in Isabella Bird's *A Lady's Life in the Rocky Mountains*, published in 1879.

The mention in Chapter 7 of the young servant girl who has no one to care for her and has been relegated to a hospital is taken from the 1923 "Report of the League of Friendship" of St. Stephen Parish in Colorado Springs. The League was formed by women who dedicated their time and efforts to visiting and reading to TB patients who were alone and, in many cases, destitute. According to the report, the majority of the patients were "young girls, practically all of them suffering from tuberculosis because they are motherless and consequently have overworked . . . and had no proper home care." The League's records record the regular visits, the reading groups, and the efforts to tutor some of the young women in history, philosophy, and, in at least two cases, Latin. The records also carry the sad notation, "passed on," beside the names of a number of the patients the League visited regularly.

For those interested in reading further, a very few of the many fine books available on the subject include *Living in the Shadow of Death, Tuberculosis and the Social Experience of Illness in America* by Sheila M. Rothman; *Bargaining for Life, A Social History of Tuberculosis, 1876–1938,* by Barbara Bates; and *In the Shadow of the White Plague: A Memoir,* by Elizabeth Mooney. For Colorado Springs especially, try *Asylum of the Gilded Pill, The Story of the Cragmor Sanitarium* by Douglas R. McKay, and *The Business of Getting Well,* by Marshall Sprague, a TB sufferer who came to the region to recover from tuberculosis and remained to become one of the state's most noted historians and authors.

I very much enjoy hearing from readers. My address is P.O. Box 62533, Colorado Springs, CO 80962-2533. A self-addressed, stamped envelope would be appreciated.

Sincerely,
Anne Avery